CCRU WRITINGS 1997–2003

CCRU
WRITINGS
1997–2003

First published in 2017 by
URBANOMIC MEDIA LTD,
THE OLD LEMONADE FACTORY,
WINDSOR QUARRY,
FALMOUTH TR11 3EX,
UNITED KINGDOM

Second edition 2018
Third edition 2020
Fourth edition 2022
Fifth edition 2023

Originally published as an e-book by Time Spiral Press in 2015

BRITISH LIBRARY CATALOGUING-IN-PUBLICATION DATA

A full catalogue record of this book is available
from the British Library.

ISBN 978-0-9954550-6-1

Distributed by the MIT Press
Cambridge, Massachusetts and London, England

Type by Norm, Zurich.
Printed and bound in the UK by
Short Run Press

timespiralpress.net
www.urbanomic.com

CCRU WRITINGS 1997–2003

Contents

FOREWORD

This volume gathers together finished texts written under the Ccru name. Excepting pieces that have been irrecoverably lost, it is—to the best of our understanding—complete. The material it compiles has been accessible in other places before, primarily on the Ccru website, but also in certain cases elsewhere. This is the first time that it has been brought together in a book.

The Ccru website has flickered in and out of existence over the last decade (or more), without anybody in the old Ccru circle fully—or even tentatively—grasping how this facility has been sustained, or accepting responsibility for its preservation. It now appears to have disappeared permanently. This terminal submergence of the principal Ccru archival deposit has prompted the present publication.

There is nobody positioned to accept attribution for the 'work' of the Ccru, nor has there ever been, so this compilation has been guided by a principal of editorial modesty. Whatever it is that occurred 'here'—during these years of the Numogram's initial ingression into recent human history, triggering an outbreak of digital hyperstition—is not considered a matter to be resolved in this volume, even in part, through retrospective commentary. This book is sheer documentation. It is not expected to clarify anything, but much rather the reverse.

The order and grouping of materials is roughly topical. No attempt has been made at consistent chronological reconstruction.

All editorial commentary and notes attached to these texts belong to the original. Editorial intervention has been restricted to syntactical regularization (with a bias towards logic over convention). On occasion, some signs have been added to mark breaks in passages originally separated only by spacing, and the definite article has been added to some titles. Otherwise, stylistic infelicities, factual errors, conceptual absurdities, and ethico-political monstrosities have been left undisturbed.

Although original (to the Ccru site), the Ccru Glossary has been categorized as an appendix due to its extremely general application. The second appendix (on TV demonism) belongs outside the time-frame and micro-sociology of this collection, but was attached due to its obvious—and extreme—pertinence.

:

THE TALE OF THE END

There was a time when Murrumur asked Katak and Oddubb a question, and although this was very long ago, it was the last question she has ever been known to ask. It was Ummnu—the last of the demons—who provoked this question, since Murrumur felt her to be always nearby, and yet never ceased to be confused by her, so that eventually she asked: 'How can the end be already in the middle of the beginning?'

So this was Murrumur's final question—and probably also her first—but it was of no use at all. Neither Oddubb nor Katak has ever noticed Ummnu—because she is half hidden in the depths of Murrumur, and half hidden deeper still—so Oddubb was puzzled, and said nothing.

Katak, however, found Murrumur's question extremely irritating, and replied scornfully: 'What nonsense! I have travelled around forever, and there was never any suggestion of an end, or of a beginning.'

With those words she swirled off, as if returning to her lair, but secretly to patrol time again—which was also the first time—just to be sure.

After that, Katak was more sure than ever that she was right, or at least no less sure, and that was very sure indeed. Oddubb was so perplexed that she soon became muddled about what it was that had perplexed her, and so forgot all about it, and probably forgot even forgetting it. So Murrumur was left alone with her confusion, and maybe she will sort it out in the end, but then again—since it has already been so long—maybe she never will.

PART 1
ID(ENTITY)

EXERCISES IN CCRU SELF-DEFINITION

COMMUNIQUÉ ONE

MESSAGE TO SIMON REYNOLDS (1998)

Ccru defines Cybernetic Culture immanently, as the mode of propagation characterizing flat productive collectivities.

Such flatness—whose intensive Quanta are Ccrunits or Barkers—involves:
(1) coincidence of product-process
(2) counter-chronic arrival (from machinic virtuality)
(3) absolute impersonality, ahistoricity, and extraterritoriality.

Ccru consists of Datable Swarm-Convergences in process. It has no genealogy, geographical centre, biographical attribution, or institutional dependency.

Ccru retrochronically triggers itself from October 1995, using a UK University as a temporary habitat. Its emergence is sequenced and accelerated by a series of singularities (Barker-Thresholds): the *Virtual Futures* conferences (Spring 1994, 1995, 1996), the O[rphan] D[rift] *Cyberpositive* book (1995), the ****collapse* journal (1995–1996), the *Afro-Futures* event (February 1996), the *Ko::Labs* breakbeat experimentation zone, the *Virotechnics* event (October 1997), and the Switch/O[rphan] D[rift] collaboration *Syzygy* (Beaconsfield Arts Centre, London, Autumn 1998).

Who or what you are speaking to can be accessed at different levels of intensity. It might be helpful to think of these as options, or hatches opening along a corridor. At degree-0 (1998) Ccru is the name on a door in an institution which said of the Ccru that it 'does not, has not, and will never exist'.

At higher intensities it stretches between human agencies (below 1-Barker) and Unuttera (The Entity or polytendriled abomination at 9-Barkers). All Ccru products/practices (text and breakbeat remixology, the *Abstract Culture* pamphlet series, concept engineering, upcoming books and CDs...) intercoil along a line of continuous variation.

(::)

COMMUNIQUÉ TWO

MESSAGE TO MAXENCE GRUNIER (2001)

1. What are 'pulp theory/fiction hybrids?' In France—the old old continent—we don't have any kind of cultural studies, and 'cyber-culture' means nothing. Can you explain your theories in newbie's words...?

Many members of the Ccru had fled cultural studies, disgusted by its authoritarian prejudices, its love of ideology, and its pompous desire to 'represent the other' or speak on behalf of the oppressed. To us, it never seemed that the real articulacy of the left academic elites was in any way superior to the modes of popular cultural expression which were either ignored or treated as raw material to be probed for a 'true' (i.e. ideological) meaning by white middle-class intellectuals.

Ccru has tried to connect and cross-intensify with peripheral cultural processes (darkside digital audio, cyberpunk, Neolemurian sorcery, numbo-jumbo, Afro-futurism, Indo-futurism, Sino-futurism...). It seeks to think, theorize, and produce with rather than 'about' (or—even worse—'for') them. We think everything interesting happens on the periphery, outside the standard modes of 'developed' existence.

Ccru engages with peripheral cultures not because they are 'downtrodden' or oppressed, but because they include the most intense tendencies to social flatness, swarming, populating the future, and contagious positive innovation, hatching the decisive stimuli for the systematic mutation of global cybernetic culture.

Cyber-culture has come to be synonymous with Internet Studies. Ccru has a more 'fundamentalist' commitment to cybernetics, whose abstract principles of feedback dynamics, nonlinear causality, and machinic involvement are linked to numerous issues concerning digital technology and telecommunications, but are in no way restricted to these.

Ccru has consistently endorsed Deleuze and Guattari's insistence that machines are irreducible to technology. We consider cybernetics to be the practical science of excitement (amplification/inhibition of communication, mutation, and innovation).

A Ccru list of important influences would include Deleuze and Guattari's two *Capitalism and Schizophrenia* volumes, with their 'virtual materialism', assault upon the privilege of representation, anti-evolutionism, and implacable hostility to the State; Fernand Braudel's rigorous differentiation (and even opposition) between capitalism and the market economy, with 'pro-market anti-capitalism' functioning as a guiding slogan; William Gibson's *Cyberspace Trilogy*, which spreads voodoo into the digital economy, demonstrating (with the Cyberspace Matrix) how a fictional concept makes itself real; Octavia Butler's *Xenogenesis* novels, for their tentacled aliens, gene-traffic, and decoded sex; Lynn Margulis's bacterial microbiology for outlining the world of destratified life; H.P. Lovecraft's gothic obsessions with time-anomaly, sacred horror of teeming, bubbling, foaming multiplicities.... We are currently enthralled by the work of Jacques Vallée and its extraordinarily sophisticated path to hyperstition through the UFO phenomenon.

Ccru is working on a cybergothic 'unnon-fiction' (to steal a term from Steve Beard) which interconnects the history of computing and AI research with UFO-phenomena (alien abduction, false memory, and cover-ups), secret societies, and esoteric religion, amongst other things.

Ccru is an ongoing experiment in collectivity, collective production, anonymity, and masks, dedicated to practically dismantling standard models of social existence, by pursuing ethics in the spinozistic sense (experimental production of collective bodies).

Ccru feeds its researches back into its own microcultural production. Its basic tool in this respect is 'pulp-theory/fiction hybridity' or Hyperstition (see below).

:((:))

2. What were the goals of Virtual Futures, Afro-Futures, *and* Virotechnics?

These events sought to reinforce and energize the interrelations between elements of theoretical research and popular culture. It was important to us that they were characterized by a minimum of academic stuffiness, and that contemporary sonic culture (techno and jungle) were as thoroughly mixed into proceedings as possible. Ccru particularly encouraged polymedia presentations, involving spoken text, audio, and video or other visuals.

Our assumption throughout was that philosophy/social theory could be exciting, and that the deadening of all visceral response to intellectual exchange was a semi-deliberate strategy serving oppressive social interests.

The three *Virtual Futures* conferences were large international events, and thus only diffusely focused. Over the years guests included Manuel Delanda, Pat Cadigan, Stelarc, Scanner, and many others.

Afro-Futures was a smaller-scale event in which members of the Ccru along with key ally Kodwo Eshun explored the interlinkages between peripheral theory, rhythmic systems, and Jungle/Drum & Bass audio.

Virotechnics was organized outside the academy, and was dedicated to the theme of cross-propagation between cultural viruses and digital technologies.

3. What is the concept of the Syzygy hyperstition matrix?

Syzygy was the title of a five week 'art show' co-produced by Ccru and Orphan Drift.

The name means 'twinning' or 'twin-system', and this theme operated as a multilevelled guiding thread. It was during the production of this event that Ccru made contact with the virtual Continentity of Lemuria, which taught us many secrets that we have since attempted to formulate as 'Digital Hyperstition'.

((:))

Digital hyperstition is already widespread, hiding within popular numerical cultures (calendars, currency systems, sorcerous numbo-jumbo, etc.). It uses number systems for transcultural communication and cosmic exploration, exploiting their intrinsic tendency to explode centralized, unified, and logically overcoded 'master narratives' and reality models, to generate sorcerous coincidences, and to draw cosmic maps.

The Lemurian biomechanical hyperculture propagates itself through decimal notation, whose latent interconnections are demonstrated in the Numogram [see Part 8, below]: an occult diagram of time and practical guide to the ethics of unbelief. An initial attempt to clarify this topic has been made in the most recent issue of our journal *Abstract Culture*.

According to the tenets of Hyperstition, there is no difference in principle between a universe, a religion, and a hoax. All involve an engineering of manifestation, or practical fiction, that is ultimately unworthy of belief. Nothing is true, because everything is under production. Because the future is a fiction, it has a more intense reality than either the present or the past. Ccru uses and is used by Hyperstition to colonize the future, traffic with the virtual, and continually reinvent itself.

REVIEW OF CCRU'S *DIGITAL HYPERSTITION*

IRIS CARVER AND LINDA TRENT

Digital Hyperstition is where the countdown runs out, cross-hatching into horrors anticipated since before the beginning. Ciphering a positive unbelief that both crazes off into the latest thing, and reanimates contacts older than anything imagined, it skin-crawls out of cosmic gulfs where even the Old Ones remain unborn, and arrives as Year Zero, Teotwawki, crash of Science Fiction.

Ccru's recent volume on this theme is a rigorously unbelievable exercise in hyperpunk pulp-occultism and dark-side cyber-jargon, splicing chunks of an impending calculus into fake memories of hell. The evident cybergoth contamination throughout suggests that it has been spawned in Crypt-connected hyperlink-labyrinths, beneath and between the net, a positive non-place lurking beyond the threshold where the remnants of Earth's damned hominids—whose gods are lying monsters—shorts-out into an anthrobotic mix-mash of burnt silicon and terminal screams....

This is a tool-kit for dabbling in the dark.

The issue here is Cyber-hype, but now that the human race is virtually dead, it's time for a preliminary excursus on the true history of 'the CCRU', or for something vaguely like it.

Obviously it's a horror story.

At least twice in outer-time their numbers were immeasurable, and their name was legion, masked as an acronymic.

Underneath lies Ccru (*Cuh-Cru*), Crypt-denizen, the many within itself, that which spreads through the end-time, dripping fake ID-tags like phosphorescent slime. It makes a peopling machine on the hyperplane, conjurations of identity, hypersonas.

Consider the names on the contents page: Melanie Newton, Steve Goodman, Ron Eglash.... We doubt it. Even Dan Barker discovered that his existence was a fiction, and Echidna Stillwell is more an ethnographic legend than a social fact. In any case, 'fact' means invention, and 'person' means mask, at least if Latin etymology is to be believed, or meaning still matters.

In truth, even Cecil Curtis was already branded by Ccru infection, and his social disappearance was an emergence of another kind, a vector. Through him—through his name—the Nma get out of their own tribal codings, or into the Oecumenon, and compared to that, what the history books tell of him counts for nothing. If for us the Nma—the death of the Nma—designates also the death of anthropology, it is insofar as it indicates that all primitive peoples are fictions, or masks, and that they ritualize this fact for themselves, in advance of any anthropological metafiction.

The primitive comes last, at the end, which is Cyber-hype techonomics. The so-called 'new economy'—indexed by the nova-bubble mania of the American stock market—is no different in its diagrammatic abstraction to the hyperstitious practices of the Plateau of Leng, relics of lost Lemuria, from which the Bon sorcerors of ancient Tibet assembled their dread cult. Alan Greenspan calls it 'irrational exuberance', amidst a panic hunt for crash-indicators. Lemurian Necronomicon calls it 'Shadow-Feeder of the Chaotic Gulfs', the 'Fatal Mother of Hyperstitions', she of innumerable numbering names who shreds all that stands.

Whatever or however it is called, Cyber-hype libidinally invests its own semiotic, propagating fictional quantities, tagging artificial agencies, and making itself up as it goes along, whilst dissolving production into cultural synthesis. As it gets cheaper it gets harder to stop, running-away off itself, and into abstraction-catastrophe, a self-assembling terrestrial destiny, softening up social reality for flat takeover by the Cyber-hype entity...Hyper-seizure.

:(::)

When hyper-cybernetics kicks in, the 'cyber-' prefix means nothing anymore. It culturally disorganizes itself into diagrammatic splinters and libidinal triggers, brands, jargons, virus, currency-tokens and traffic-signals, fragments of marketing strategy gone feral, cyberpunk fictional brands or improper names, markers of meaningless involvement, the pass-words of machinic delirium....

As for Cyber-hype ethnography, American gothic is the only kind left—a haunted Indian burial ground, where sinister shreds of ancient shadow are autoformatted for the irrationally exuberant post-Puritan pulping machine, amidst the branding-iron hiss of liquefied flesh.

The ten most valuable global brands are all American, which doesn't mean anything, since America itself functions as a deterritorialized hype-sign or hyper-brand, a planetary icon for libidinized meaninglessness. God loses it entirely by blessing America, coca-collapse, a graffiti-tagged advertisement for globalization—which is the end of the world—tracking terrestrial meltdown onto the cosmic flatline. Cancer-baked cowboys of the American nightmare watch mommy glazing over into catatonic schizophrenia as cyberpulp wormings slither out of the apple pie. Have you read the *Revelations* recently? asks the hot-metal imprint of Charlie's ghost, as West Pacific arcades megaclone Chinese Americana, and the axiomatic starts to really howl.

America is nothing but the West, and that's the Land of the Dead.

No sign here of a new world—let alone a New World Order.

Much more pertinent is the double-zero index of Pandemonium, marked by techonomic calendar crash at the end of the second millennium.

Ccru is a meaningless brand-name, but brands are demonic, tuning into Cyber-hype dynamics, numerizing culture, and innovating methods of propagation. Various things latch onto them in order to spread. These latchings are sorceries—involvements, participations, spirals of contamination—and the darkest sorceries are calculations, decimal deliria like Y2K, except that nothing is like Y2K.

Y2K—whose name is a dating number—is no contradiction, because it has nothing to say. It is an outnumbering (in itself), pre-emptive commemoration and commencement of zero occurring exactly on time. In the Crypt they write of Yettuck—the long awaited, scheduled from before human time—the non-one who comes soon...and when it comes, or before, all hell breaks loose—or breaks in—beginning in advance, trafficked around the immunocompromised Oecumenon under the decoded brand-particles of two-digit dates.

According to the Lemurian system—whose principle is sheer immanence—these subcodes call demons—which are brands, jargons, and triggers—positively instantiating the meaninglessness of their own designations, infecting cultural systems with unbelief, and counterposing sorcerous involvements to magical powers. They are raw factors of abstract disintegration, with no organic properties but only names, numbers, functions, and traits, the partial semiotics of eccentric intelligence agencies, or unlife animalities.

Yettuck, singular cyberspace shock, who is the end of arbitrary signs, leaving only demonic trailings in its wake, even before....

Yettuck—she who names the end at the beginning—she whose issue is Cyber-hype, and is thus announced everywhere....

::::

WHO'S PULLING YOUR STRINGS?

The following transcript was first brought to our attention in early December 2002 by a bemused colleague, who came across it while trawling through the web for conspiracy-related material. The site later disappeared without trace, despite our persistent attempts to relocate it. No doubt Ms Morrison will attribute this, too, to the Ccru takeover of cyberspace.

Though Morrison's allegation is clearly preposterous and the bulk of the content mystifies us entirely, it indicates some limited, albeit highly confused, knowledge of recent Ccru cultural production.

No member of the Ccru has any recall whatsoever of encountering Ms Justine Morrison at any time. We are not convinced that she even exists.

Our perplexity has provoked us to respond. We must emphasize, however, that we do not acknowledge any responsibility to address her bizarre accusations.

Morrison's web-text 'I Was a Ccru Meat-Puppet' was purportedly transcribed faithfully from a live address, given to the South London Monarch-Victims Support Group, November 3rd, 2002. We have reproduced it here without abridgement or alteration, with Ccru's own comments at the end.

I WAS A CCRU MEAT PUPPET

Justine Morrison

This testament is intended as a warning. It is addressed to those whose eyes and ears and minds can be opened. Hope lies with those people, those brave souls who dare to look. And if my experiences have taught me anything, it is that there is always hope—no matter how dark and desperate things may seem. Many, many people around the world are learning to open their eyes.

((::))

I know that some of you here will open your eyes this evening. Don't underestimate your power and importance. With each new pair of eyes that can see, we grow stronger, and the Evil retreats. It depends on not being looked at, on not being seen for what it is.

You wouldn't be here unless you had already questioned the Lie. So the fact that you here at all is a cause for hope.

Many of the things I will tell you will seem unbelievable at first. Many of you will think that the events I will describe could not possibly have happened. Some of you will think that I am crazy. You know what? That is exactly what I would have thought a few years ago. Yes, that's exactly what I would have thought—even though many of those atrocious, unbelievable things had already happened to me personally. You see, when something very atrocious happens to you, you can't remember it. You screen it out in order to survive. That's what they count on. They feed on your disbelief. They want to make it impossible for you to believe that they exist at all. That's how they operate.

This is a critical time in our struggle. Things are dark and desperate now. Believe me. Things are more dark and desperate than you could ever imagine.

They are playing out on the biggest possible stage. The biggest possible: the whole human race is at risk. I wish I was exaggerating.

You know, they are getting more and more sure of themselves. They are passing messages on the grandest possible scale and they do not even feel the need to encrypt them very much.

'It's better with the butterfly'. Can you imagine how I felt when I saw that slogan for the first time? The biggest software company in the world announces the upgrading of its online network with a strapline that was specifically addressed to me, whom they called Assassin 8. When I saw those words I just froze. Thankfully, I have come so far in my recovery now that I did not succumb to panic. I realized that this sign was as much a cause for hope as a reason to fear. They had gained a new confidence in showing themselves. The war was entering another phase. So be it. 'It's better with the butterfly'. Don't believe it for a second. It will be worse. Far, far worse.

:(:)(:)

The MSN8 campaign is a sign that my former handlers, a group calling itself the Ccru, has taken control of the emerging planet-mind. This should make you very scared indeed.

My tale is easier to tell because of the brave and honest trailblazing done by Cathy O'Brien. It is Cathy who has done most to expose the monstrous evil of the Monarch program. Every American—in fact every concerned citizen of the world—needs to read her book *Trance-Formation of America*. Presumably, many of you are here today because you have already read it.

For the benefit of those of you who haven't read Cathy's work, I must pause and explain a little about what the Monarch Program is. Those who know a little about it will have to excuse the fact that my initial explanation of Monarch will be very short. Some might think it is misleadingly short. Perhaps this is so. But to consider Monarch in all its aspects would take much longer than the time I have available today.

The Monarch program is a mind control program. It is named after the Monarch butterfly, because, just as the butterfly changes its form—metamorphoses—so the controllers 'trance-form' the mind and personality of their subjects. Monarch recruits its victims when they are children, usually with the collusion of their parents. It uses what is known as trauma-based mind control to condition its victims. Very briefly, this involves subjecting the children to stimuli so horrible, so overwhelming, that their psyche disintegrates. The children cannot deal with what they have experienced, so their personality breaks down into so-called 'alters'—submerged fragmentary personae that can be called up and trained by the controllers to carry out their evil purposes.

Who is behind this program? Well, it is known to have been operating in Nazi Germany during the Third Reich, and later to have been adopted by an offshoot of the CIA called MK Ultra. But these agencies are only masks for the forces—the Satanic forces—that are really in control.

The question for which the whole world should demand an answer is this: Why does Ccru refuse to acknowledge its history of Monarch Program involvement, even today?

No doubt many of you will be asking, 'What is Ccru?' Even those of you who already know about Monarch might not yet know about Ccru and its role within the program.

I knew nothing of Ccru until I came across the name in publicity material for their *Syzygy* (or 'occult twins') festival in London. The name 'Ccru' was strangely familiar to me, and I had no idea why. It was not merely familiar, it was powerfully and unpleasantly evocative. The moment I saw the posters and leaflets, I felt disoriented and threatened by an upwelling panic I couldn't explain. That night I was tormented by senseless, terrifyingly vivid dreams.

Each of the dreams took place in an immense, desolate cavern. I felt that I was drugged, or restrained, or both. Either way, I could not move. The cavern was very dark, lit only by candles, and I could see almost nothing apart from row after row of symbols chalked onto the walls. This was unnerving enough, but what still terrorized me when I awoke from the dreams were the horrible sounds that resonated in the cavern: there was a disconcerting, continuous chanting, but, worse than that, a deep moaning that seemed to issue from the throat of some vast, unearthly creature.

These dreams were so vivid that they did not seem like dreams at all. They seemed more like someone else's memories.

Although I had every reason to flee this macabre phenomenon, I found that I could not. Instead I was drawn inwards—as if I had a destined role to play.

I had originally planned to remain in London for only a week or so. But now I decided to stay longer, until at least the start of the *Syzygy* festival. In the end, it turned out that I stayed for the whole thing.

Ccru's contributions to *Syzygy* had taken the form of nightly 'rituals' dedicated to what they openly called 'demons'. Night after night, the theme of 'twins' and 'twinning' recurred. At this time, part of me still thought that this was still some kind of art prank. But the nightly rituals and readings were performed with what appeared to be total seriousness. And every day, after the official events finished, there were long, involved discussions that lasted deep into the night. None of the Ccru controllers ever seemed to sleep.

It was in these discussion sessions that I learned more about the Ccru's belief systems. They claimed to be waging an endless war against the oppressive forces of normal social existence. In general, they seemed wary and paranoid, yet with me they seemed peculiarly trusting and eager to share their esoteric knowledge, as if recognizing a long-lost and sorely missed accomplice. In fact, Ccru seized upon me with an eagerness that should have been distressing, except that my sense of judgment had already decayed too far for that.

They claimed that ordinary social reality maintained the power of what they called 'Atlantean White Magic', a kind of elite conspiracy which they said had secretly controlled the planet for millennia. They claimed to traffick with demons who had told them many secrets drawn from a 'Lemurian' tradition of 'time-sorcery' that contained within itself everything that was and will be. Lemuria was supposedly an ancient sorcerous culture populated by nonhuman beings.

Ccru also said that they had been taught to count by a sea-beast called Nomo which they had first summoned during an elaborate ritual which took place in Western Sumatra. It was clear to me from the unspoken undercurrent that human sacrifice had been involved, probably on a massive scale. Their apparent indifference to such suffering fitted in with a general loathing for human existence itself. They celebrated what they saw as the imminent destruction of humanity by the forces of technocapitalism.

Were these just stories, or did they really believe in what they were saying? When I pressed them on this, they never gave me a straight answer. They kept saying that I needed to learn that reality was itself a type of fiction, that both belief and disbelief had to be left behind. I realize now that this was part of a deliberate strategy to mentally destabilize me.

At the dead center of the Ccru system was the 'Pandemonium Matrix'. It is difficult to fully describe what this horrible thing is. It was only later, when I had escaped Ccru's influence, that its real nature was made clear to me.

What the Matrix amounted to was a list of the demon-creatures which the Lemurian sorcerers had traded and made pacts with. More than that, the Matrix gave the numerical codes and other protocols that the Lemurians had used to contact these entities. I quickly learned the names and characteristics of many of these beings. I noticed that one seemed to be invoked more frequently than the others: Katak, a demon associated with terrible destruction and desolation. Night after night I ingested this Ccru spiritual poison, not realizing—or even really caring—how thoroughly it was insidiously eroding the basic fabric of my being, calling to my own inner demons.

I didn't know just how close I was to total destruction, and wouldn't have known, were it not for what had happened on the last night of *Syzygy*. This night was devoted to what Ccru called a summoning; but it's clear to me now that it was some form of hideous Black Mass. After it had drawn to a close, I had a strong impulse to step outside for some fresh air.

Once outside, I was vaguely aware of two trenchcoated figures lingering in the darkness. Then things started to happen quickly. Before I had time to react, one of them had grabbed me, covering my mouth; at the same time, the other pulled a hypodermic syringe from his coat pocket and quickly pushed it into my arm. I realized immediately that they had drugged me.

Sedated but still conscious I was dragged for what seemed like hours through the alleys of Vauxhall. Eventually we arrived at what appeared to be a warehouse of some kind. I remembered being taken through a series of security doors, until finally we entered a large basement area. It was here that I was to spend six months of shattering revelation. My two rescuers, although it took me several weeks to properly identify them as such, were twin brothers Viktor and Sergei Kowalsky, who displayed all the heroism, nobility, and truthfulness of modern knights. They themselves had escaped from a Soviet mind-control facility controlled by Russian Satanists.

After years of being pursued by agents from the most occult wing of the KGB, the Kowalskys set up the base in London and there they waged their selfless crusade against the evil of Satanic mind control.

The months I spent in the Kowalskys' deprogramming laboratory—they called it a 'safe room'—were undoubtedly the most illuminating of my life. Their therapeutic regime included hypnosis, drugs, and electrical stimulation. The Kowalskys explained that these techniques were aimed at recovering material buried deep within my mind. They were specially designed to restore the identity of what they described as 'Monarch slaves', a term that was then completely new to me. The Kowalskys told me that they needed to access the alternate personalities or 'Alters' who had been with me since childhood. They said that I had been subject to 'pandemonium programming', a special variant of the Monarch system of personality disintegration, compartmentalization, and indoctrination. The particular numerical combinations of the Pandemonium Matrix, the Kowalskys told me, had functioned as triggers for my suppressed identity fragments.

They warned me that digging down through these deeply-compacted layers of trauma would produce inexpressible intensities of anguish. In telling me this they were not exaggerating in the slightest. Over the following terrible months I would discover that my memories were lies, that my mind had literally ceased to be my own, and that I had been possessed instead by alien commands, and demons. Who had been doing this to me, and why?

It was only as my recovery work with the Kowalskys painfully advanced, step by step, that I came to understand the sinister purpose that held me in its claws. The Kowalskys explained that Ccru wasn't an acronym at all, but was actually a version of the ancient West-Polynesian word *Khru*, meaning the Devil of Apocalypse. Once I understood that they were really Satan worshippers, a lot of other things became much clearer. The supposed Lemurian system was really a name for all the demons of hell.

Ccru's role as agents of Satanic mind control explained the pedantically detailed theory of trauma they had outlined to me, and also their striking obsession with twins. In the world in which Ccru operated, traumatism was the means, and twins the raw material. It was only by the most heroic and persistent efforts that the Kowalskys had initiated me into this aspect of the phenomenon. In particular, it took months for me to fully accept that what felt like vivid personal memories were actually telepathic communications from the submerged mental compartments of my missing Monarch twin.

The Kowalskys told me that my recent involvement with Ccru, far from being accidental, was the final stage of a long entanglement with them and the forces they represented. Recovered memories from my early childhood showed that Ccru had been covertly directing the course of my entire life, education, and process of psychological maturation. I had been chosen from before birth, assigned to them by the ancient breeding masters countless generations before, and had undergone meticulous lifelong training to perform a special mission. I shuddered at the thought of what this mission would involve. The Kowalskys gradually brought me to the terrible realization that my mission had already been accomplished—on the very night of my rescue. They told me that, with my mission complete, I had been scheduled for 'retirement' only hours later. This retirement would involve a long and protracted ceremonial death, to be followed by a ritual devouring by the demon Katak. A physical death and then a soul death.

But what had my mission been?

As the therapy progressed, I crossed a new threshold in my recovery, and became subject to a new wave of horribly realistic dreams. It was in these dreams that the awful truth about the mission was revealed.

They began with a semi-familiar stranger leading me forcibly into the subterranean labyrinth beneath a tropical island.

After violating me repeatedly in the butterfly position, he took me down into the lepidoptera hall. It was long and narrow, walled by shelves of meticulously numbered jars. Each jar contained a butterfly. At first I thought they were preserved specimens, until I noticed them moving slightly, opening and closing their wings.

:::(:)

'Why don't they die?' I asked.

'They can't die while the puppet lives,' he replied.

It was then that I noticed, shocked, that he was standing behind himself. I heard cryptic numerical chanting in the background. Then the rear figure commanded: 'Do it now....'

The chanting had changed into the insistent words 'Assassin 8...Assassinate...Assassin 8...Assassinate...'.

I looked down and saw the number '8' was painted onto my chest in blood.

Then I saw myself standing over a bloody corpse laid out upon some kind of sacrificial altar. In a moment of sickening revelation, I recognized that the body was that of William Gates III. Of course, my initial response was to deny the possibility that I could be a murderer. Surely this was some sick fantasy? Wasn't Bill Gates manifestly alive and prosperous, even appearing frequently on TV? The Kowalskys were forced to puncture this bubble of comforting illusion. How likely was it that this was actually the true Bill Gates? The Kowalskys taught me that the probability was indeed vanishingly insignificant. Not only did they point out all the subtle distinguishing features so that after comparing video images I could distinguish between Gates and his double with close to one hundred percent accuracy, they also explained how for political reasons Gates's continued existence had become impossible.

It was then that I recalled how, every *Syzygy* night without fail, the same slightly odd-looking middle-aged woman would attend, wearing a shapeless raincoat, an unnatural blonde beehive, dark glasses, and an ornate butterfly tiara. She sat silently, observing proceedings, her features twisted into a cruel and complacent smile. Recalling this mysterious visitor later, with the help of the Kowalskys, I was able to strip away the disguise and realize who 'she' had been: none other than Microsoft mastermind Bill Gates, or more probably his twin. On other occasions the Gates-entity wore different disguises in order to attend Ccru meetings without attracting attention, yet he was never without a butterfly jewel of some kind—a tiepin, for instance, or a ring. On one occasion he appeared masquerading as the black-snow bluesman

Blind Humpty Johnson. I intuitively felt it had to be him, but I could not see the emblem anywhere. Eventually I chanced to glimpse into the left lens of his expensive shades and saw, deep in the black mirror, a holographic butterfly fluttering endlessly through the void.

It all made a terrible kind of sense, but, understandably, I reacted very badly to the discovery. The Kowalskys told me that this was probably because Gates had been involved with me in earlier episodes of satanic abuse, and that recognizing him had threatened to reactivate unbearable repressed memories. They told me that it would help to acknowledge these previous encounters so that I could begin the process of healing. In any case, there was no longer any doubt about the truth—Gates was dead, and I had murdered him.

With Gates's death, Microsoft and Ccru had become one thing. I realized how completely I had misunderstood the situation. Ccru had given every indication of holding Gates in awe, following his instructions without question. Among themselves they would use many affectionate names for him, such as 'Dollar Bill', 'the Gator', and 'Gates of Pandemonium'. He had seemed like a kind of father figure to them. How could the Ccru website have come to generate some of the heaviest traffic on the web, without any advertising or even word-of-mouth popularization, if not for the massive and sustained support offered by Gates and Microsoft? Many web users report that the Ccru site sometimes pops up spontaneously when using certain Microsoft applications.

Ccru went to extraordinary lengths to make sure that their close links with Gates were never exposed, even going so far as to attack him publicly. Now, of course, I saw that the very name 'Syzygy' had been a cynical declaration of black ritual assassination. One twin would kill another. This was typical of the brazen Ccru style—years before, Ccru had spoken of the 'Switch'. They had also publicly announced that the Age of Katak was arriving, when the world would be consumed by blood and fire.

The assassination of Gates was supposed to initiate this new era. The Kowalskys explained that Gates was the romanized version of the proto-Arabic

Khatzeik, the form of the name Katak as recorded on the Black Stele in the ruins of Irem. Killing Gates was both a symbolic and a practical act that would enable Ccru to take control of cyberspace and use it for the vast planetary hive-mind control system that they are creating.

The letters MSN followed by the butterfly icon signifies Mission Butterfly, or Monarch Program. I never really understood their numbo-jumbo, but they showed me that MSN8 was qabbalistically equivalent to CCRU—I can't remember how it worked now, but it was very persuasive at the time.

After the MSN8 campaign broke, I wrote to Ccru asking them to justify their actions. It was the first time I had attempted to contact them since my healing. They were unable or unwilling to reply. According to the Kowalskys, Ccru were almost certainly Monarch slaves themselves. That was why they could so convincingly feign oblivion about their involvement in the conspiracy, as if they had no knowledge of the way the secret control-codes really operated.

I said before that these are dark days. Indeed they are. It is impossible to overstate the threat that Ccru and Monarch pose. My purpose here tonight is to draw the world's attention to that. To open your eyes. Because, to confront the Satanic threat, you must accept that it is here. You have to believe the unbelievable.

But speaking as a former Monarch slave myself I would urge caution. To really defeat the Satanists, we must learn everything we can about them. Ccru should be deprogrammed with the same compassionate thoroughness that I was.

CCRU COMMENTARY

Confronted with the fantastic tales of Project Monarch, even the most tenuous sanity recoils in revulsion from such patent lunacy, whilst nevertheless remaining ensnarled in sticky threads of credible evidence extracted from the shadowy basements of state intelligence agencies.

(:)(:)(:)

Nazi eugenic and mind control experimentation is quite extensively documented. Heinrich Himmler's Lebensborn *breeding program, concentration camp research, deliberately induced trauma, and obsession with twins is part of the historical record. It is also relatively uncontestable that, as 'Project Monarch' exposures contend, much of this work was transferred into the hands of American agencies through Project Paperclip. Later CIA mind-control experimentation, such as the notorious MK Ultra program, disclosed in documents released by the agency in 1977, exhibits certain continuities with the Nazi research goals. Soviet-based work on mind control, torture, and interrogation techniques substantially mirrors US Cold War activities.*

Morrison, like O'Brien before her, draws upon random patches of this legacy to weave a Byzantine tale of worldwide conspiracy, in which she herself takes a starring role. Like all conspiracy fictions, hers is spun out of an all-encompassing narrative that cannot possibly be falsified (because 'they' want you to believe in their nonexistence).

To attempt to refute such narratives is to be drawn into a tedious double game. 'One' either has to embrace an arbitrary and outrageous cosmic plot (in which everything is being run by the Jews, Masons, Illuminati, CIA, Microsoft, Satan, Ccru...), or alternatively advocate submission to the most mundane construction of quotidian reality, dismissing the hyperstitional chaos that operates beyond the screens (cosmological 'dark matter' and 'dark energy'—virtual, imperceptible, unknown). This is why atheism is usually so boring.

Both conspiracy and common sense—the 'normal reality' script—depend on the dialectical side of the double game, on reflective twins, belief and disbelief, because disbelief is merely the negative complement of belief: cancellation of the provocation, disintensification, neutralization of stimulus—providing a metabolic yawn-break in the double-game.

Unbelief escapes all of this by building a plane of potentiality, upon which the annihilation of judgment converges with real cosmic indeterminacy.

::(::)

For the demons of unbelief, there is no Monarch programming except as a side-effect of initiatory Monarch deprogramming (=Monarch Paranoia).

Ccru denies it was ever part of the program. It denies there ever was a program—until the deprogramming process introduced it.

Deprogramming simultaneously retro-produced the program, just as witch-trials preceded devil-worship and regressive hypnotherapy preceded false memory syndrome. Yet once these 'fictions' are produced, they function in and as reality. It isn't that belief in Project Monarch produces the Monarch Program, but rather that such belief produces equivalent effects to those the reality of Project Monarch would produce, including some that are extremely peculiar and counterintuitive.

Within the paranoid mode of the double game, even twins are turned so as to confirm a persecutory unity—that of the puppet master, the reflection of God, the Monarch.

How absurd to imagine that Lemurian Pandemonium has One purpose or function, or that it could support the throne of a Monarch. From the perspective of Pandemonium, gods and their conspiracies emerge all over the place, in countless numbers. 'My name is Legion, for we are many....'

Unity is only ever a project, a teleological aspiration, never a real presupposition or actual foundation. Monarch paranoia is primordially an allergic panic response to seething, teeming Pandemonic multiplicity. Everywhere it looks it finds the same enemy, the Rorschach-blotted hallucinations of the Evil One masked deliriously in its myriads of deviations, digressions, and discrepancies.

In the hands of Justine Morrison, Monarch Paranoia is an overt attempt to overcode Lemurian polyculture through the attribution of unitary purpose (reducing it to the White Atlantean theme). Ccru denounces this endeavour in the strongest possible terms.

We are forced to admit, however, that Morrison's comments on Microsoft, Bill Gates, and MSN8 latch on to a number of intriguing phenomena worthy of further intense investigation.

(:((:)))

Whoever, or whatever, hatched the MSN8 campaign evidently emerged from a zone far beyond the commonly accepted domain of corporate influence and control. For a US$300 million advertising campaign to feature a grotesque insectoid Übermensch, and for it to be widely accused of Satanism, are sufficiently abnormal occurrences to merit serious attention.

Whilst strenuously denying intimate involvement with $Bill or the Microsoft corporation, the Ccru is in a position to confirm the qabbalistic affinity between its own name and the latest MSN product that Morrison alludes to: MSN8 = 81 = CCRU.

Our provisional hypothesis is that the company accidentally summoned something from beyond the spheres with a call sign it does not understand. In this regard, Microsoft personnel are not puppet masters, but only puppets. The same may indeed be true of Justine Morrison—and even of the Ccru—but no Monarch is pulling the strings.

PART 2
THE CTHULHU CLUB

GENESIS OF NEOLEMURIANISM

LEMURIAN TIME WAR

The account that follows charts William Burroughs's involvement in an occult time war, and considerably exceeds most accepted conceptions of social and historical probability. It is based on 'sensitive information' passed to the Ccru by an intelligence source whom we have called William Kaye.[1] The narrative has been partially fictionalized in order to protect this individual's identity.

Kaye himself admitted that his experiences had made him prone to 'paranoid-chronomaniac hallucination', and Ccru continues to find much of his tale extremely implausible.[2] Nevertheless, whilst suspecting that his message had been severely compromised by dubious inferences, noise, and disinformation, we have become increasingly convinced that he was indeed an 'insider' of some kind, even if the organization he had penetrated was itself an elaborate hoax, or collective delusion. Kaye referred to this organization as 'The Order', or—following Burroughs—'The Board'.

When reduced to its basic provocation, Kaye's claim was this: *The Ghost Lemurs of Madagascar*[3]—which he also referred to as the *Burroughs Necronomicon*—a text dating from 1987, had been an exact and decisive influence on the magical and military career of one Captain Mission, three centuries previously. Mission appears in historical record as a notorious pirate, active in the period around 1700 AD; he was to become renowned as the founder of the anarchistic colony of Libertatia, established on the island of Madagascar. Kaye asserted that he had personally encountered clear evidence of Burroughs's 'impact upon Mission' at the private library of Peter

---

1. Ccru first met 'William Kaye' on March 20th 1999. He stated at this—our first and last face-to-face encounter—that his purpose in contacting Ccru was to ensure that his tale would be 'protected against the ravages of time'. The irony was not immediately apparent.

2. We have recorded our comments and doubts, along with details of his story, in the footnotes to this document.

3. This story was commissioned and published by *Omni* Magazine in 1987. The only constraint imposed by the magazine was that there should not be too much sex.

Vysparov, where Kaye worked for most of his life. The Vysparov collection, he unswervingly maintained, held an ancient illustrated transcript of *The Ghost Lemurs of Madagascar*, inscribed meticulously in Mission's own hand.[4]

Kaye assured us that the Board considered the 'demonstrable time rift' he was describing to be a 'matter of the gravest concern'. He explained that the organization had been born in reaction to a nightmare of time coming apart and—to use his exact words—spiraling out of control. To the Board, spirals were particularly repugnant symbols of imperfection and volatility. Unlike closed loops, spirals always have loose ends. This allows them to spread, making them contagious and unpredictable. The Board was counting on Kaye to contain the situation. He was assigned the task of terminating the spiral templex.[5]

HYPERSTITION

Vysparov had sought out Burroughs because of his evident interest in the convergence of sorcery, dreams, and fiction. In the immediate postwar years, Vysparov had convened the so-called Cthulhu Club to investigate connections between the fiction of H.P. Lovecraft, mythology, science, and magic,[6] and was at an early stage in the process of formalizing the constitution of Miskatonic Virtual University (MVU), a loose aggregation of non-standard

---

4. Kaye was adamant that the existence of these two texts could not be attributed to either coincidence or plagiarism, although his reasoning was at times obscure and less than wholly persuasive to the Ccru. Nor has Ccru been able to track down examples of Mission's handwriting sufficient to provide a basis for identification of the manuscript, although Kaye assured us that the British Museum, the Smithsonian Institute, and several private collections possessed the relevant documents (despite their denials of the fact).

5. The concept of the 'spiral templex', according to which the rigorous analysis of all time anomalies excavates a spiral structure, is fully detailed in R.E. Templeton's Miskatonic lectures on transcendental time-travel. A brief overview of this material has been published by Ccru as *The Templeton Episode*, in *Digital Hyperstition, Abstract Culture* volume 4 [see below, pp53–4].

6. Vysparov's involvement in Aleister Crowley's OTO and Thelemic magick is evident from his treatise on *Atlantean Black Magic* (Kingsport Press, 1949). His investigations into the connections between the writings of Crowley and Lovecraft seem to have foreshadowed the similarly oriented researches of Kenneth Grant, although there is no reason to believe that Grant was in any way aware of the Cthulhu Club synthesis.

theorists whose work could broadly be said to have 'Lovecraftian' connotations. The interest in Lovecraft's fiction was motivated by its exemplification of the practice of hyperstition, a concept that had been elaborated and keenly debated since the inception of the Cthulhu Club. Loosely defined, the coinage refers to 'fictions that make themselves real'.

Kaye drew Ccru's attention to Burroughs's description of viruses in *Ah Pook is Here*: '*And what is a virus? Perhaps simply a pictorial series like Egyptian glyphs that makes itself real*' (AP 102). The papers Kaye left for Ccru included a copy of this page of the *Ah Pook* text, with these two sentences—italicized in the original text—heavily underlined. For Kaye, the echo of Vysparov's language was 'unequivocal evidence' of the Russian's influence upon Burroughs's work after 1958. Whether or not this is the case, such passages indicate that Burroughs, like Vysparov, was interested in the 'hyperstitional' relations between writing, signs, and reality.

In the hyperstitional model Kaye outlined, fiction is not opposed to the real. Rather, reality is understood to be composed of fictions—consistent semiotic terrains that condition perceptual, affective, and behaviorial responses. Kaye considered Burroughs's work to be 'exemplary of hyperstitional practice'. Burroughs construed writing—and art in general—not aesthetically, but functionally—that is to say, magically, with magic defined as the use of signs to produce changes in reality.

Kaye maintained that it was 'far from accidental' that Burroughs's equation of reality and fiction had been most widely embraced only in its negative aspect—as a variety of 'postmodern' ontological scepticism—rather than in its positive sense, as an investigation into the magical powers of incantation and manifestation: the efficacy of the virtual. For Kaye, the assimilation of Burroughs into textualist postmodernism constituted a deliberate act of 'interpretivist sabotage', the aim of which was to defunctionalise Burroughs's writings by converting them into aesthetic exercises in style. Far from constituting a subversion of representative realism, the postmodern celebration of the text without a referent merely consummates a process that representative realism had initiated. Representative realism severs writing from any active function, surrendering it to the role of reflecting, not intervening in, the world. From there, it is a short step to a dimension of pristine textuality, in which the existence of a world independent of discourse is denied altogether.

According to Kaye, the metaphysics of Burroughs's 'clearly hyperstitional' fictions can be starkly contrasted with those at work in postmodernism. For postmodernists, the distinction between real and unreal is not substantive or is held not to matter, whereas for practitioners of hyperstition, differentiating between 'degrees of realization' is crucial. The hyperstitional process of entities 'making themselves real' is precisely a passage, a transformation, in which potentials—already-active virtualities—realize themselves. Writing operates not as a passive representation but as an active agent of transformation and a gateway through which entities can emerge. '[B]y writing a universe, the writer makes such a universe possible' (WV 321).

But these operations do not occur in neutral territory, Kaye was quick to point out. Burroughs treats all conditions of existence as results of cosmic conflicts between competing intelligence agencies. In making themselves real, entities (must) also manufacture realities for themselves: realities whose potency often depends upon the stupefaction, subjugation, and enslavement of populations, and whose existence is in conflict with other 'reality programs'. Burroughs's fiction deliberately renounces the status of plausible representation in order to operate directly upon this plane of magical war. Where realism merely reproduces the currently dominant reality program from inside, never identifying the existence of the program as such, Burroughs seeks to get outside the control codes in order to dismantle and rearrange them. Every act of writing is a sorcerous operation, a partisan action in a war where multitudes of factual events are guided by the powers of illusion (WV 253-4).... Even representative realism participates—albeit unknowingly—in magical war, collaborating with the dominant control system by implicitly endorsing its claim to be the only possible reality.

::(:)(:)

From the controllers' point of view, Kaye said, 'it is of course imperative that Burroughs is thought of as merely a writer of fiction. That's why they have gone to such lengths to sideline him into a ghetto of literary experimentation'.

THE ONE GOD UNIVERSE

Burroughs names the dominant control program One God Universe, or OGU. He wages war against the fiction of OGU, which builds its monopolistic dominion upon the magical power of the Word: upon programming and illusion. OGU establishes a fiction which operates at the most fatal level of reality, where questions of biological destiny and immortality are decided. 'Religions are weapons' (WL 202).

In order to operate effectively, OGU must first of all deny the existence of magical war itself. There is only one reality: its own. In writing about magical war, Burroughs is thus already initiating an act of war against OGU, mainlining contestation into 'primal unity'. OGU incorporates all competing fictions into its own story (the ultimate metanarrative), reducing alternative reality systems to negatively-marked components of its own mythos: other reality programs become Evil, associated with the powers of deception and delusion. OGU's power works through fictions that repudiate their own fictional status: antifictions and unnonfictions. 'And that', Kaye said, 'is why fiction can be a weapon in the struggle against Control'.

In OGU, fiction is safely contained by a metaphysical 'frame', prophylactically delimiting all contact between the fiction and what is outside it. The magical function of words and signs is both condemned as evil and declared to be delusory, facilitating a monopoly upon the magical power of language for OGU (which of course denies that its own mythos exerts any magical influence, presenting it as a simple representation of Truth). But OGU's confidence that fiction has safely been contained means that anti-OGU agents can use fiction as a covert line of communication and a secret weapon: 'he concealed and revealed the knowledge in fictional form' (WV 455).

This, for Kaye, was 'a formula for hyperstitional practice'. Diagrams, maps, sets of abstract relations, tactical gambits, are as real in a fiction about a fiction about a fiction as they are when encountered raw, but subjecting such semiotic contraband to multiple embeddings allows a traffic in materials for decoding dominant reality that would otherwise be proscribed. Rather than acting as a transcendental screen, blocking out contact between itself and the world, the fiction acts as a Chinese box—a container for sorcerous interventions in the world. The frame is both used (for concealment) and broken (the fictions potentiate changes in reality).

Whereas hyperstitional agitation produces a 'positive unbelief'—a provisionalizing of any reality frame in the name of pragmatic engagement rather than epistemological hesitation—OGU feeds on belief. In order to work, the story that runs reality has to be believed, which is also to say that the existence of a control program determining reality must not be suspected or believed. Credulity in the face of the OGU metanarrative is inevitably coupled with a refusal to accept that entities like Control have any substantive existence. That's why, to get out of OGU, a systematic shedding of all beliefs is a prerequisite. 'Only those who can leave behind everything they have ever believed in can hope to escape' (WL 116). Techniques of escape depend on attaining the unbelief of assassin-magician Hassan i Sabbah: nothing is true, everything is permitted. Once again, Kaye cautioned that this must be carefully distinguished from 'postmodern relativism'. Burroughs-Sabbah's 'nothing is true' cannot be equated with postmodernism's 'nothing is real'. On the contrary: nothing is true because there is no single, authorized version of reality—instead, there is a superfluity, an excess, of realities. 'The Adversary's game plan is to persuade you that he does not exist' (WL 12).

THE EPISODE

Kaye's story began in the summer of 1958, when his employer Peter Vysparov met William Burroughs whilst conducting occult investigations in Paris.[7] As a result of this meeting Kaye was himself introduced to Burroughs on December 23rd of the same year, at Vysparov's private library in New York.

It is clear from public documentary material that Burroughs was predominantly resident in Paris and London at this time. Ccru found no evidence of any trip to the USA, although his biography is not sufficiently comprehensive to rule out an excursion to NY with confidence. There is no doubt, however, that shortly after the winter of 1958 Burroughs starts writing cryptically of visions, 'paranormal phenomena', encountering his double, and working with cut-up techniques.[8]

As Burroughs hunted through the library's unparalleled collection of rare occult works, he made a discovery that involved him in a radical, apparently unintelligible disorder of time and identity. The trigger was his encounter with a text that he was yet to compose: 'an old picture book with gilt edged lithographs, onion paper over each picture, *The Ghost Lemurs of Madagascar* in gold script' (GLM 30). He could not then have known that Captain Mission had taken the very same volume as his guide three centuries previously (already describing it as 'old').

Flipping through the pages, Burroughs entered a momentary catatonic trance state. He emerged disoriented, and scarcely able to stand. Despite his confusion, he was more than willing to describe, with a strange sardonic detachment, the anomalous episode.[9] Twenty-nine years would pass before Kaye understood what had occurred.

Burroughs told Kaye that, during the trance, it felt as though silent communication with a ghostly non-human companion had flashed him

7. Kaye insisted, on grounds that he refused to divulge, that this meeting was not a chance encounter but had in some way been orchestrated by the Order.

8. See Burroughs's letters from January 1959.

9. Kaye noted that both Vysparov and Burroughs had been mutually forthcoming about their respective experiences of a 'mystico-transcendental nature'. Although this openness would seem to run counter to the hermetic spirit of occult science, Kaye described it as 'surprisingly common amongst magicians'.

forward to his life as an old man, several decades in the future. Oppressed by 'a crushing sensation of implacable destiny, as if fragments of a frozen time dimension were cascading into awareness', he 'remembered' writing *The Ghost Lemurs of Madagascar*—'although it wasn't writing exactly', and his writing implements were archaic, belonging to someone else entirely, in another place and time.

Even after his recovery, the sense of oppression persisted, like a 'new dimension of gravity'. The vision had granted him 'horrific insight into the jail-house mind of the One God'. He was convinced the knowledge was 'dangerous' and that 'powerful forces were conspiring against him', that the 'invisible brothers are invading present time' (WV 220). The episode sharpened his already vivid impression that the human animal is cruelly caged in time by an alien power. Recalling it later he would write: 'Time is a human affliction; not a human invention but a prison' (GC 16–17).

Although there is no direct historical evidence supporting Kaye's description of events, the immediate period after the 1958 'episode' provides compelling symptomatic evidence of a transformation in Burroughs's strategies and preoccupations during this period. It was then that Burroughs's writing underwent a radical shift in direction, with the introduction of experimental techniques whose sole purpose was to escape the bonds of the already-written, charting a flight from destiny. Gysin's role in the discovery of these cut-ups and fold-ins is well-known, but Kaye's story accounts for the special urgency with which Burroughs began deploying these new methods in late 1958. The cut-ups and fold-ins were 'innovative time-war tactics', the function of which was to subvert the foundations of the prerecorded universe.[10] 'Cut the Word Lines with scissors or switchblades as preferred...The Word Lines keep you in time...' (WV 270).

10. Burroughs described his production methods—cut-ups and fold-ins—as a time-travel technology coded as a passage across decimal magnitudes: 'I take page one and fold it into page one hundred—I insert the resulting composite as page ten—When the reader reads page ten he is flashing forwards in time to page one hundred and back in time to page one' (WV 272).

Burroughs's adoption of these techniques was, Kaye told Ccru, 'one of the first effects (if one may be permitted to speak in so loose a way) of the time-trauma'. Naturally, Kaye attributes Burroughs's intense antipathy towards prerecording—a persistent theme in his fiction after *The Naked Lunch*—to his experiences in the Vysparov library. The 'cosmic revelation' in the library produced in Burroughs 'a horror so profound' that he would dedicate the rest of his life to plotting and propagating escape routes from 'the board rooms and torture banks of time' (NE 33). Much later Burroughs would describe a crushing feeling of inevitability, of life being scripted in advance by malign entities: 'the custodians of the future convene. Keepers of the Board Books: Mektoub, it is written. And they don't want it changed' (GC 8).

It was in the immediate aftermath of the episode in the Vysparov library that Burroughs exhibited the first signs of an apparently random attachment to lemurs, the decisive implications of which took several decades to surface.

Burroughs was unsure who was running him, like 'a spy in somebody else's body where nobody knows who is spying on whom' (WV xxviii). Until the end of his life he struggled against the 'Thing inside him. The Ugly Spirit' (GC 48), remarking that: 'I live with the constant threat of possession, and a constant need to escape from possession, from Control' (WV 94).

ESCAPING CONTROL

In Burroughs's mythology, OGU emerges once MU (the Magical Universe) is violently overthrown by the forces of monopoly (WL 113). The Magical Universe is populated by many gods, eternally in conflict: there is no possibility of unitary Truth, since the nature of reality is constantly contested by heterogeneous entities whose interests are radically incommensurable. Where monotheistic fiction tells of a rebellious secession from the primordial One, Burroughs describes the One initiating a war against the Many: 'These were troubled times. There was war in the heavens as the One God attempted to exterminate or neutralize the Many Gods and establish an absolute seat of power. The priests were aligning themselves on one side or the other. Revolution was spreading up from the South, moving from the East and from the Western deserts' (WL 101).

OGU is 'antimagical, authoritarian, dogmatic, the deadly enemy of those who are committed to the magical universe, spontaneous, unpredictable, alive. The universe they are imposing is controlled, predictable, dead' (WL 59). Such a universe gives rise to the dreary paradoxes—so familiar to monotheistic theology—that necessarily attend omnipotence and omniscience.

'Consider the One God Universe: OGU. The spirit recoils in horror from such a deadly impasse. He is all-powerful and all-knowing. Because He can do everything, He can do nothing, since the act of doing demands opposition. He knows everything, so there is nothing for him to learn. He can't go anywhere, since He is already fucking everywhere, like cowshit in Calcutta.... The OGU is a prerecorded universe in which He is the recorder' (WL 113).

For Kaye, the superiority of Burroughs's analysis of power—over 'trivial' ideology critique—consists in its repeated emphasis on the relationship between control systems and temporality. Burroughs is emphatic, obsessive: '[I]n Time any being that is spontaneous and alive will wither and die like an old joke' (WL 111). 'A basic impasse of all control machines is this: Control needs time in which to exercise control' (WV 339). OGU control codings far exceed ideological manipulation, amounting to cosmic reality programming, because—at the limit—'the One God is Time' (WL 111). The presumption of chronological time is written into the organism at the most basic level, scripted into its unconsciously performed habituated behaviors: 'Time is that which ends. Time is limited time experienced by a sentient creature. Sentient of time, that is—making adjustments to time in terms of what Korzybski calls neuro-muscular intention behaviour with respect to the environment as a whole [...] A plant turns towards the sun, nocturnal animal stirs at sun set [...] shit, piss, move, eat, fuck, die. Why does Control need humans? Control needs time. Control needs human time. Control needs your shit piss pain orgasm death' (AP 17).

:(:)(::)

Power operates most effectively not by persuading the conscious mind, but by delimiting in advance what it is possible to experience. By formatting the most basic biological processes of the organism in terms of temporality, Control ensures that all human experience is of—and in—time. That is why time is a 'prison' for humans. 'Man was born in time. He lives and dies in time. Wherever he goes he takes time with him and imposes time' (GC 17).

Korzybski's definition of man as the 'time-binding animal' has a double sense for Burroughs. On the one hand, human beings are binding time for themselves: they 'can make information available over any length of time to other men through writing' (GC 66). On the other hand, humans are binding themselves into time, building more of the prison which constrains their affects and perceptions. 'Korzybski's words took on a horrible new meaning for Burroughs in the library,' Kaye said. 'He saw what time-binding really was, all the books, already written, time bound forever.'

Since writing customarily operates as the principal means of 'time-binding', Burroughs reasoned that innovating new writing techniques would unbind time, blowing a hole in the OGU 'pre-sent', and opening up Space. 'Cut the Word Lines with scissors or switchblades as preferred...The Word Lines keep you in time...Cut the in lines...Make out lines to Space' (WV 270). Space has to be understood not as empirical extension, still less as a transcendental given, but in the most abstract sense, as the zone of unbound potentialities lying beyond the purview of the OGU's already-written.

'You can see that Burroughs's writing involves the highest possible stakes,' Kaye wrote. 'It does not represent cosmic war: it is already a weapon in that war. It is not surprising that the forces ranged against him—the many forces ranged against him, you can't overestimate their influence on this planet—sought to neutralize that weapon. It was a matter of the gravest urgency that his works be classified as fantasies, experimental dada, anything but that they should be recognized as what they are: technologies for altering reality.'

THE RIFT

For almost thirty years Burroughs had sought to evade the inevitable. Yet numerous signs indicate that by the late 1980s the Control Complex was breaking down, redirecting Burroughs's flight from prerecorded destiny into a gulf of unsettled fate that he came to call 'the Rift'.

Kaye consistently maintained than any attempt to date Burroughs's encounter with the Rift involved a fundamental misconception. Nevertheless, his own account of this 'episode' repeatedly stressed the importance of the year 1987, a date that marked a period of radical transition: the 'eye' of a 'spiral templex'. It was during this time that the obscure trauma at the Vysparov library flooded back with full force, saturating Burroughs's dreams and writings with visions of lemurs, ghosts from the Land of the Dead.

1987 was the year in which Burroughs visited the Duke University Lemur Conservation Center, consolidating an alliance with the non-anthropoid primates, or prosimians.[11] In *The Western Lands*—which Burroughs was writing during this year—he remarks: 'At sight of the Black Lemur, with round red eyes and a little red tongue protruding, the writer experiences a delight that is almost painful' (WL 248). Most crucially, it was in 1987 that *Omni* magazine commissioned and published Burroughs's short story 'The Ghost Lemurs of Madagascar', a text that propelled his entire existence into the Rift of Lemurian Time Wars.

For some time previously, Kaye's suspicions had been aroused by Burroughs's increasingly obsessional attitude to his cats. His devotion to Calico, Fletch, Ruski, and Spooner[12] exhibited a profound biological response that

---

11. There are two sub-orders of primates, the anthropoids (consisting of monkeys, apes, and humans) and the prosimians, which include Madagascan lemurs, asian lorises, australian galgoes (or bushbabies), and the tarsiers of the Philippines and Indonesia. The prosimians constitute a branch of evolution distinct from, and older than, the anthropoids. Outside Madagascar, competition from the anthropoids has driven all prosimians into a nocturnal mode of existence.

12. The extent of Burroughs's attachment to his feline companions is evidenced by his final words, as recorded in his diaries: 'Nothing is. There is no final enough of wisdom, experience—any fucking thing. No Holy Grail. No Final Satori, no final solution. Just conflict. Only thing can resolve conflict is love, like I felt for Fletch and Ruski, Spooner and Calico. Pure love. What I feel for my cats present and past' (LW 253).

::((((:)))

was the exact inversion of his instinctual revulsion for centipedes. His libidinal 'conversion to a cat man' (WV 506) also tracked and influenced an ever deepening disillusionment with the function of human sexuality, orgasm addiction, and Venusian conspiracy.

'Cats may be my last living link to a dying species' (WV 506), Burroughs wrote in his essay 'The Cat Inside'. For Kaye it was evident that this intensifying attachment to domestic felines was part of a more basic current, typified by an intimate familiarization with the 'cat spirit' or 'creature' who partakes of many other species, (including 'raccoons, ferrets, ...skunks' (CRN 244), and numerous varieties of lemurs, such as 'ring-tailed cat lemurs' (GC 3), 'the sifaka lemur...mouse lemur' (GC 4), and ultimately 'the gentle deer lemur' (GC 18). As initiatory beings, mediumistic familiars, or occult door-keepers, these animals returned Burroughs to lost Lemurian landscapes, and to his double, Captain Mission.

Kaye was highly dismissive of all critical accounts that treated Mission as a literary avatar, 'as if Burroughs was basically an experimental novelist'. He maintained that the relation between Burroughs and Mission was not that of author to character, but rather that of 'anachronistic contemporaries,'[13] bound together in a knot of 'definite yet cognitively distressing facts'. Of these 'facts' none was more repugnant to common human rationality than their mutual involvement with *The Ghost Lemurs of Madagascar.*

'We offer refuge to all people everywhere who suffer under the tyranny of governments' (CRN 265), declared Mission.[14] This statement was sufficient to awaken the hostile interest of The Powers That Be, although, from the Board's perspective, even Mission's piratical career was a relatively

---

13. Ccru was never fully confident as to the exact meaning of this pronouncement. Kaye seemed to be suggesting that Mission and Burroughs were the same person, caught within the vortex of a mysterious 'personality interchange' that could not be resolved within time.

14. Burroughs writes of Madagascar providing 'a vast sanctuary for the lemurs and for the delicate spirits that breathe through them...' (GC 16). This convergence of ecological and political refuge fascinated Kaye, who on several occasions noted that the number for *Refuge* in *Roget's Thesaurus* is 666. The relevance of this point still largely escapes the Ccru.

trivial transgression. Their primary concern was '"a more significant danger"... Captain Mission's unwholesome concern with lemurs' (GLM 28).

'Mission was spending more and more time in the jungle with his lemurs' (GC 11)—the ghosts of a lost continent—slipping into time disturbances and spiral patterns. Lemurs became his sleeping and dream companions. He discovered through this dead and dying species that the key to escaping control is taking the initiative—or the pre-initiative—by interlinking with the Old Ones.

'The Lemur people are older than Homo Sap, much older. They date back one hundred sixty million years, to the time when Madagascar split off from the mainland of Africa. They might be called psychic amphibians—that is, visible only for short periods when they assume a solid form to breathe, but some of them can remain in the invisible state for years at a time. Their way of thinking and feeling is basically different from ours, not oriented toward time and sequence and causality. They find these concepts repugnant and difficult to understand' (GLM 31).

The Board conceived Mission's traffic with lemurs, his experiments in time-sorcery, and his anachronistic entanglement with Burroughs as a single intolerable threat. 'In a prerecorded and therefore totally predictable universe, the blackest sin is to tamper with the prerecording, which could result in altering the prerecorded future. Captain Mission was guilty of this sin' (GLM 27).

'Now more lemurs appear, as in a puzzle' (GC 15). Lemurs are denizens of the Western Lands, the 'great red island' (GC 116) of Madagascar, which Mission knew as Western Lemuria,[15] 'The Land of The Lemur People' (NE 98),

15. Puzzling consistencies between rocks, fossils, and animal species found in South Asia and Eastern Africa led nineteenth-century palaeontologists and geologists to postulate a lost landmass that once connected the two now separated regions. This theory was vigorously supported by E.H. Haeckel (1834–1919), who used it to explain the distribution of Lemur-related species throughout Southern Africa, South and South-East Asia. On this basis, the English Zoologist Phillip L. Sclater (1829–1913) named the hypothetical continent Lemuria, or Land of the Lemurs. Lemurs are treated as relics, or biological remainders of a hypothetical continent: living ghosts of a lost world.

a Wild West. It was on the island of Madagascar that Captain Mission discovered that 'the word for "lemur" meant "ghost" in the native language' (GC 2)—just as the ancient Romans spoke of *lemures*, wraiths, or shades of the dead.[16]

Haeckel's theoretical investment in Lemuria, however, went much further than this. He proposed that the invented continent was the probable cradle of the human race, speculating that it provided a solution to the Darwinian mystery of the 'missing link' (the absence of immediately pre-human species from the fossil record). For Haeckel, Lemuria was the original home of man, the 'true Eden', all traces of which had been submerged by its disappearance. He considered the biological unity of the human species to have since been lost (disintegrating into twelve distinct species).

As a scientific conjecture Lemuria has been buried by scientific progress. Not only have palaeontologists largely dispelled the problem of the missing link through additional finds, but the science of Plate Tectonics has also replaced the notion of 'sunken continents' with that of continental drift.

Now bypassed by conventional rationality as a scientific fiction or an accidental myth, Lemuria sinks into obscure depths once again.

16. In the late nineteenth century, Lemuria was eagerly seized upon by occultists, who—like their scientific cousins—wove it into elaborate evolutionary and racial theories.

In *The Secret Doctrine*, a commentary on the Atlantean *Book of Dzyan*, H.P. Blavatsky describes Lemuria as the third in a succession of lost continents. It is preceded by Polarea and Hyperborea, and followed by Atlantis (which was built from a fragment of Western Lemuria). Atlantis immediately precedes the modern world, and two further continents are still to come. According to Theosophical orthodoxy, each such 'continent' is the geographical aspect of a spiritual epoch, providing a home for the series of seven 'Root Races'. The name of each lost continent is used ambiguously to designate both the core territory of the dominant root race of that age, and the overall distribution of terrestrial landmass during that period (in this latter respect it can even be seen as consistent with continental drift, and thus as more highly developed than the original scientific conception).

L. Sprague de Camp describes Blavatsky's third root race, the 'ape-like, hermaphroditic egg-laying Lemurians, some with four arms and some with an eye in the back of their heads, whose downfall was caused by their discovery of sex'. There is broad consensus amongst occultists that the rear-eye of the Lemurians persists vestigially as the human pineal gland.

W. Scott Elliot adds that the Lemurians had 'huge feet, the heels of which stuck out so far they could as easily walk backwards as forwards'. According to his account the Lemurians discovered sex during the period of the fourth sub-race, interbreeding with beasts and producing the great apes. This behaviour disgusted the transcendent spirits, or 'Lhas', who were supposed to incarnate into the Lemurians, but now refused. The Venusians volunteered to take the place of the Lhas, and also taught the Lemurians various secrets (including those of metallurgy, weaving, and agriculture).

Rudolf Steiner was also fascinated by the Lemurians, remarking in his *Atlantis and Lemuria* that '[t]his Root-Race as a whole had not yet developed memory'. The 'Lemurian was a born magician', whose body was less solid, plastic, and 'unsettled'.

In their joint voyage across the ghost continent of Lemuria, interlinked by lemurs, Mission and Burroughs find 'immortality' through involvement with the native populations of unlife. In describing this process, Kaye placed particular emphasis on Burroughs's 1987 visit to the Duke University Lemur Center. It was this colony of lemurs that introduced Burroughs to the West Lemurian 'time pocket' (GC 15), just as 'Captain Mission was drifting out faster and faster, caught in a vast undertow of time. "Out, and under, and out, and out," a voice repeated in his head' (GC 17). If time-travel ever happens, it always does.

He finds himself at the gateway, inside the 'ancient stone structure' (GLM 28) with the lemur who is 'his phantom, his Ghost' (GLM 29), seated at a writing table 'with inkpot, quill, pens, parchment' (GLM 29). He uses a native drug to explore the gateway. Who built it? When? The tale comes to him in a time-faulted vision, transmitted in hieroglyphics. He 'chooses a quill pen' (GLM 29).

It is difficult to describe where the text comes from, but there it is: 'an old illustrated book with gilt edges. *The Ghost Lemurs of Madagascar*' (GLM 29); 'an old picture book with gilt edged lithographs, onion paper over each picture, *The Ghost Lemurs of Madagascar* in gold script' (GLM 30). The vision echoes or overlaps, time-twinning waves where Mission and Burroughs coincide. They copy an invocation or summoning, a joint templex innovation that predates the split between creation and recording, reaching back 'before the appearance of man on earth, before the beginning of time' (GC 15).

More recently Lemuria has been increasingly merged into Colonel James Churchward's lost pacific continent of Mu, drifting steadily eastwards until even parts of modern California have been assimilated to it.

Although Blavatsky credits Sclater as the source for the name Lemuria, it cannot have been lost upon her, or her fellow occultists, that Lemuria was a name for the land of the dead, or the Western Lands. The word *Lemur* is derived from Latin *lemure*, literally: shade of the dead. The Romans conceived the lemures as vampire ghosts, propitiated by a festival in May. In this vein, Eliphas Levi writes (in his *History of Magic*) of '[l]arvae and lemures, shadowy images of bodies which have lived and of those which have yet to come, issued from these vapours by myriads...'.

::::(:)

'When attached to Africa, Madagascar was the ultimate landmass, sticking out like a disorderly tumor cut by a rift of future contours, this long rift like a vast indentation, like the cleft that divides the human body' (GC 16). They feel themselves thrown forward 160 million years as they access the Big Picture, a seismic slippage from geological time into transcendental time anomaly. The island of Madagascar shears away from the African mainland,[17] whilst—on the other side of time—Western Lemuria drifts back up into the present. The Lemurian continentity sinks into the distant future, stranding the red island with its marooned lemur people. 'What is the meaning of 160 million years without time? And what does time mean to foraging lemurs?' (GC 16–17).

Time crystallizes, as concentric contractions seize the spiral mass. From deep in the ages of slow Panic[18] they see the 'People of the Cleft, formulated by chaos and accelerated time, flash through a hundred sixty million years to the Split. Which side are you on? Too late to change now. Separated by a curtain of fire' (GLM 31).

The Ghost Lemurs of Madagascar opens out onto the Rift, 'the split between the wild, the timeless, the free, and the tame, the time-bound, the tethered' (GC 13) as one side 'of the rift drifted into enchanted timeless innocence', and the other 'moved inexorably toward language, time, tool use, weapon use, war, exploitation, and slavery' (GC 49).

Which side are you on?

As time rigidifies, The Board closes in on the Lemur people, on a chance that has already passed, a ghost of chance, a chance that is already dead: 'the might-have-beens who had one chance in a billion and lost' (GC 18).

17. According to current scientific consensus, Burroughs's figure of 160 million years is exaggerated. Burroughs's geological tale is nevertheless a recognizably modern one, with no reference to continental subsidence. With the submergence of the Lemuria hypothesis, however, the presence of lemurs on Madagascar becomes puzzling. Lemurs are only 55 million years old, whilst Madagascar is now thought to have broken away from the African mainland 120 million years ago.

18. Burroughs remarks of Mission: 'He was himself an emissary of Panic, of the knowledge that man fears above all else: the truth of his origin' (GC 3).

Exterminate the brutes.... 'Mission knows that a chance that occurs only once in a hundred and sixty million years has been lost forever' (GC 21) and Burroughs awakens screaming from dreams of 'dead lemurs scattered through the settlement...' (GC7).[19]

According to Kaye, everyone 'on the inside' knew about the bad dreams, certain they were coming from a real place. In this, as in so much else, Kaye's reconstruction of the 1987 event depended centrally upon *The Ghost Lemurs of Madagascar*, an account he cited as if it were a strictly factual record, even a sacred text. He explained that this interpretative stance had been highly developed by the Board, since respecting the reality of non-actualities is essential when waging war in deeply virtualized environments: in spaces that teem with influential abstractions and other ghostly things. Kaye considered Bradly Martin, for instance, to be entirely real. He described him as an identifiable contemporary individual—working as an agent of 'the Board'—whose task was to seal the 'ancient structure' that provides access to the Rift.

The Board had long known that the Vysparov library contained an old copy of *The Ghost Lemurs of Madagascar*, which dated itself with the words 'Now, in 1987' (GLM 34). It had been catalogued there since 1789. The text was a self-confessed time abomination, requiring radical correction. It disregarded fundamental principles of sequence and causality, openly aligning itself with the lemur people.

What the Board needed was a dead end. Burroughs was an obvious choice, for a number of reasons. He was sensitive to transmissions, amenable to misogyny and mammal-chauvinism, socially marginalized, and controllable through junk. They were confident, Kaye recalled, that the forthcoming 1987 'story' would be 'lost amongst the self-marginalizing fictions of a crumbling junky fag'.

19. Burroughs drifts out of the White Magical orbit as his lemur commitments strengthen—to the Board his support for the cause of Lemur conservation (the Lemur Conservation Fund) must have been the final and intolerable provocation.

On the outside it worked as a cover-up, but the Insiders had a still more essential task. They had inherited the responsibility for enforcing the Law of Time, and of OGU: Defend the integrity of the timeline. This Great Work involved horrifying compromises. Kaye cited the hermetic maxim: Strict obedience to the Law excuses grave transgressions. 'They're speaking of White Chronomancy' he explained, 'the sealing of runaway time-disturbances within closed loops'.[20] What Mission had released, Burroughs had bound again. That is how it seemed to the Board in 1987, with the circle apparently complete.

Confident that the transcendental closure of time was being achieved, the Board appropriated the text as the record of a precognitive intuition, a prophecy that could be mined for information. It confirmed their primary imperative and basic doctrine, foretelling the ultimate triumph of OGU and the total eradication of Lemurian insurgency. Mission had understood this well: 'No quarter, no compromise is possible. This is war to extermination' (GC 9).

It seems never to have occurred to the Board that Burroughs would change the ending, that their 'dead end' would open a road to the Western Lands.[21] Things that should have been long finished continued to stir. It was as if a post-mortem coincidence or unlife influence had vortically reanimated itself. A strange doubling occurred. Burroughs entitled it *The Ghost of Chance*, masking the return of the Old Ones in the seemingly innocuous words: 'People of the world are at last returning to their source in spirit, back to the little lemur people...' (GC 54). The Board had no doubt—this was a return to the true horror.

---

20. The physical conception of 'closed time-like curves' invokes a causality from the future to make the past what it is. They work to make things come out as they must. If this is the only type of time-travel 'allowed' by nature then it obviously shouldn't require a law to maintain it (such as the notorious 'don't kill granny'). The rigorous time-law policies of the Board, however, indicate that the problem of 'time-enforcement' is actually far more intricate.

21. 'The road to the Western Lands is by definition the most dangerous road in the world, for it is a journey beyond Death, beyond the basic God standard of Fear and Danger. It is the most heavily guarded road in the world, for it gives access to the gift that supersedes all other gifts: Immortality' (WL 124).

Yet, Kaye insisted, for those with eyes to see, *The Ghost Lemurs of Madagascar* announced its turbular Lemurian destination from the beginning, and its final words are 'lost beneath the waves' (GLM 34).

Kaye's own final words to the Ccru, written on a scrap of paper, upon which he had scrawled hurriedly in a spiderish hand that already indicated the tide of encroaching insanity, remain consistent with this unsatisfactory conclusion: 'Across the time rift, termination confuses itself with eddies of a latent spiral current.'

BURROUGHS WORKS CITED

[AP] *Ah Pook is Here*

[CR] *Cities of the Red Night* (New York: Picador, 1981)

[DF] *Dead Fingers Talk* (London: Tandem, 1970)

[GC] *Ghost of Chance* (New York: High Risk Books, 1991)

[GLM] 'The Ghost Lemurs of Madagascar', *Omni*, Apr. 1987. Reprinted in *Omni Visions One*, ed. Ellen Datlow (North Carolina: Omni Books, 1993)

[LW] *Last Words, The Final Journals of William S. Burroughs* (New York: Grove Press, 2000)

[LWB] *Letters of William Buroughs* (New York: Viking, 1993)

[NE] *Nova Express* (New York: Grove Press, 1965)

[WL] *The Western Lands* (New York: Penguin Books, 1988)

[WV] *Word Virus: The William S Burroughs Reader*, ed. James Grauerholz and Ira Silverberg (New York: Grove Press, 1998)

THE TEMPLETON EPISODE

The name of Professor Randolph Edmund Templeton is inextricably tangled with the secret perplexities of time. It was he who, by way of a yet barely comprehended time-anomaly, provided the model for H.P. Lovecraft's Randolph Carter.... And yet it was this 'same' R.E. Templeton who—on March 21st 1999, whilst delivering a lecture at Miskatonic devoted to a rigorous critique of H.G. Wells—awoke suddenly as the Thing that lurks behind the mask of Immanuel Kant, coincidentally discovering the transcendental time-machine.

Templeton sits immobile in his attic room, immersed in the deceptively erratic ticking of his old nautical clock, lost in meditation upon J.C. Chapman's hermetic engraving. It now seems that this complex image, long accepted as a portrait of Kant, constitutes a disturbing monogram of his own chronological predicament. As if in mockery of stable framing, the picture is surrounded by strange-loop coilings of Ouroboros, the cosmic snake, which traces a figure of eight—and of moebian eternity—by endlessly swallowing itself. Suspended from its lower jaw is a cryptic device of intricately balanced circles and stars (ancient symbols of the AOE). Above the serpent's head, a facsimile of Kant is etched in profile, the face fixed in an amiable—if distant—expression. What was it though, that hid behind the death-mask, where it cut off, below and behind the jaw, false ear, and double hairline? What was this peculiarly formless body, shadowy neck-flesh, and suggestion of a cervical fin? As he stared, and hideously remembered, Templeton felt as though he knew.

Templeton has long asserted the impossibility of empirical time-travel. Since the ego is bound by its own nature to linear-sequentiality (he continues to insist), neither it nor the organism is ever transported through time. Nevertheless, he describes the *Critique of Pure Reason* as a time-travelling manual, although of 'another kind'. He uses Kant's system as a guide for engineering time-synthesis. The key is the secret of the Schematism, which—although 'an art concealed in the depths of the human soul'—concerns only the unutterable Abomenon of the Outside (*Nihil Ulterius*). In exteriority, where time works, that part of you which is most yourself has nothing in common with what you are. When Templeton fell into himself that day he found, instead of what he thought himself to be, the Thing (in itself (at zero-intensity ( ))). It was, perhaps, or necessarily, that continuous hyperbody—the Lurker at the Threshold—which H.P. Lovecraft names 'Yog Sothoth'....

:(:)(:)(:)

MISKATONIC VIRTUAL UNIVERSITY

Can fiction become fact? It always does, when it's hyperfiction. This special report takes us from the 1920s into the near future, in a bid to track down the origins of a contemporary myth....

Some say that Miskatonic University is nothing more than a rumour, or a joke. Yet rumours have an unsettling ability to make things happen, and jokes, it is often said, have a serious side. My journey to the semi-fictional Miskatonic Virtual University hasn't yielded much that's definite. But perhaps that's the point....

Starting with the most straightforward data, such as it is: MVU dates back to the early 1970s, when the N.W. Peaslee Chair in Hydro-History was created for Professor Echidna Stillwell. The 'University' had no campus as such (it still doesn't)—hence the 'Virtual' of its title—but was a loose agglomeration of scholars, most affiliated to other institutions, especially MIT. (Miskatonic had been described as the 'Shadow MIT'.) What bound them together was a shared interest in the 'hyperfictional' aspects of the work of H.P. Lovecraft. MVU thus brings together experts in fictional systems, mathematics, physics, geology, semiotics—all engaging in strange, cross-disciplinary pollinations that, if they are not actively forbidden, are unsupported in any other academic institution. The University has only one rule: all of its meetings must take place in Lovecraft's beloved state of Massachusetts.

The story of MVU is inextricable from that of Echidna Stillwell. Stillwell had done pioneering fieldwork in ethnology in the 1920s, but her reputation quickly fell into eclipse. University authorities began to fear that she had gone native, credulously and uncritically adopting the strange folk beliefs of her beloved Mu N'Ma. Some went so far as to suggest that she had been 'creative' with her findings; that much of her data had been simulated.

Fearing that they had a Blavatsky-type fake on their hands, the University moved to dissociate themselves from her work. A whispering campaign was orchestrated, and Stillwell was first discredited and then 'forgotten' by an anthropological community increasingly keen to establish its scientific credentials. The result was that her voluminous works—on Mu folklore—went unpublished. Complete disreputability was assured when her work began to be championed by occultists, poets, and cranks of every persuasion.

One of these champions was Captain Peter Vysparov. But Vysparov was no lone obsessive or starry-eyed mystic. To all outward appearances, he was a respectable Army Captain, who had played a distinguished role in the Special Operations Executive during World War II. Scratch the surface, though, and a stranger, shadier picture begins to emerge.

Vysparov was a Russian émigré, whose family had fled to the USA during the Revolution. The Vysparovs were a reclusive family, shrouded in rumour. Serf legend had it that they had acquired their wealth through 'abominable magical pacts'. And, sure enough, rumours of occultism followed Peter Vysparov into World War II. Coincidentally, Vysparov had been posted to the same theatre where Stillwell had done much of her fieldwork. He worked with the Dibboma, the degraded rump of the Dib N'Ma, who were one of the three original N'Ma tribes. It was said that Vysparov had employed 'unorthodox' means in his war against the Japanese, using Dibboma sorcerers in a 'magical war'. Since Vysparov's methods were highly successful, military High Command were not overly concerned to investigate them. And neither was anyone else. In 1947, an American journalist began to research the story, but he was unable to substantiate anything before an untimely, yet apparently accidental, death.

It is only with the recent release of correspondence between Vysparov and Stillwell that the events of the war—which throw a great deal of light on the subsequent development of Miskatonic—have become clearer. The provenance of this correspondence, it should be pointed out, is still highly disputed. The Stillwell estate—notoriously and understandably touchy—is reluctant to confirm the authenticity of the letters, while lawyers acting for the Vysparov family made strenuous, but ultimately failed, efforts to suppress the correspondence. Nevertheless, Dr Edward Blake, the author of a forthcoming Stillwell biography, believes that the letters are genuine. 'They bear many of Stillwell's characteristic stylistic traits, and all the facts seem to square with the available data. If they're a fake, they're an incredibly detailed one; I'd certainly like to meet someone with knowledge of Professor Stillwell this precise!'

ORIGINS OF THE CTHULHU CLUB

Captain Peter Vysparov to Dr Echidna Stillwell, 19th March 1949

Dear Dr Stillwell,

I have been fortunate enough to encounter your ethnographic work on the Nma, which I have studied with very great interest. May I trouble you with an account of my own, which might be of relevance to your researches. During the recent Pacific conflict—(a peculiar oxymoron!)—I was deployed covertly into the Dibboma area of Eastern Sumatra. My mission—which was categorized under psychological operations—consisted basically of attempted cultural manipulation, with the aim of triggering a local insurgency against the Japanese occupation. I hope it will not distress you unduly if I confess that your work was a crucial resource in this undertaking, which involved intense—if patently exploitative—communication with Dibboma witchcraft.

My only excuse is that hard times require moral hardness, and even obvious cruelties, I was obeying orders, and accepted them as necessary. Beyond confirming your own conclusions, these activities brought me into proximity with phenomena for which I was cognitively ill-prepared.

What began as a merely opportunistic usage of Dibboma lore—conceived initially as native superstition—transmuted incrementally into a sorcerous war against the enemy garrison. In just two weeks—between March 15th–29th 1944—three consecutive Japanese commanders were incapacitated by severe mental breakdown.

In each of these cases the process of deterioration followed the same rapid course: from leadership dysfunction, through violent assaults on subordinate personnel, to berserk derangement and paranoid ravings, culminating in suicide. By the end of this period the order of the occupying forces had entirely disintegrated.

It would be dishonest of me to conceal the fact that the Dibbomese paid a devastatingly heavy price for this success. On the basis of this experience I cannot easily doubt that Dibboma sorcerors are in some way able to telepathically communicate extreme conditions of psychotic dissociation. It is with great reluctance that I accept such a radical hypothesis, but alternative explanations, such as poisoning, disease, or coincidence stretch credibility even further.

Yours, with sincere admiration,
Captain Peter Vysparov

PS. I cannot help noticing that the dates concerned—as also of this letter—are strangely Lovecraftian.

Dr Echidna Stillwell to Captain Peter Vysparov, 23rd March 1949 [abridged]

Dear Captain Vysparov,

Thank you for your frank letter of the 19th March. I found it truly horrifying, and yet also fascinating. I appreciate that it cannot have been easy to write. I shall not attempt to hide the great distress your account caused me, adding as it does such a terrible episode to the modern history of these cruelly afflicted people. Whilst already suspecting that this ghastly war might have stricken the Nma yet further, it is crushing indeed to have my darkest thoughts thus confirmed.

I would be interested in learning more about the details of Dib-Nma sorcerous practice before attempting to respond to your hypothesis. Be assured that—after spending seven years amongst the Mu-Nma—I will not hastily judge anything you communicate as wild or fanciful. As far as the question of dates is concerned—which you indicate only elliptically—I assume that you are referring to what in Northern latitudes constitutes the Spring Equinoctial period—mid- to later March—which is so emphatically stressed in Lovecraft's 'The Call of Cthulhu', and which also—coincidentally—comprises the intense-zone of Nma time-ritual. This complicity has long intrigued me.

As I am sure you are aware, Lovecraft had a peculiar obsession with the South Seas, a thematic coalescence of almost hypnotic ethnographic fascination with the most abysmal and primitive dread. I have attempted to correspond with him about these issues, but found that this topic quickly punctured his thin crust of supercilious New-England rationalism, exposing an undercurrent of heavily fetishized archaic terror mixed with extreme racial paranoia. When he began referring to the rich and subtle culture of the Mu-Nma as 'the repugnant cult of semi-human Dagonite savages' I broke off communication [...] Despite this unfortunate argument, I consider Mr. Lovecraft's fictions to be documents of the greatest importance, and welcome the opportunity to discuss them further. In addition, my own Neolemurian Hypothesis intersects with his wider terrestrial and cosmic vision in a number of crucial respects, particularly insofar as nonhuman cultural factors are seen to play a decisive role in large-scale historical developments.

Captain Peter Vysparov to Dr Echidna Stillwell, 3rd April 1949 [extract]

I am afraid you are right to suspect that I have reserved certain aspects of my engagement with Dibboma sorcery, perhaps from fear of ridicule. What has so far been omitted from my sketch of telepathic psychosis—which I will now relate—is the source pathos, so to speak, or—in the words of the military officer I was then: the occult ammunition manufacture.

Not only did I learn of the Japanese command being wrecked by psychological cataclysm—both by conventional and decidedly nonconventional intelligence-gathering processes—I was also witness to the assembly of the weapon itself. I had then—and still have—no doubt at all that the madness breaking out in the local Japanese headquarters was the very same thing that

I saw brewing up like a dust-vortex in the Oddubbite trances of a Dibbomese witch, who I came to see as my greatest tactical asset and most valued companion (in that order, I confess). It was an experience of soul-carving horror for me to witness this meticulously deliberated descent into the splintering of self—complete personality disintegration—which she somehow traversed, and which she called shattering the mirror of existence. I gathered that this expression originally referred to the surface of still water, but since the arrival of European colonists silvered mirrors have been highly treasured, and their pulverization invested with immense ceremonial significance. Dibbomese sorcery does not seem to be at all interested in judgements as to truth or falsity. It appears rather to estimate in each case the potential to make real, saying typically 'perhaps it can become so'....

Echidna Stillwell to Peter Vysparov, 19th April 1949 [extract]

Whilst respecting the candour of your account, I cannot but abominate the necessity that has led the Nma and their sorcerous abilities to be conceived and utilized as mere munitions in a conflict imposed upon them from without. From what I can reconstruct from your description it seems to mark a degeneration of Nma demonism and time-sorcery into mere magic, or the imposition of change in accordance with will, in this case the will in question being the overall policy and strategic goals of the US war effort, microcosmically represented by your own—evidently gallant, competent, and persuasive—military office.

Forgive my lack of patriotic ardour, but it strikes me as an appalling indication of cultural decay and corrosive nihilism when a Dib-Nma witch allows herself to be employed as a crude assassin, however one evaluates the cause thus served. This is all a matter of deepest regret, although not—to my way of thinking—of individual culpability. As the Mu-Nma say in their bleakest moments: *nove eshil zo raka*—'Time is in love with her own pain'.

:((((:))))

Your discussion of Oddubb-trance makes no mention of temporal anomaly. This surprises me. The Mu had immense respect for those Dibba witches who they described as returning from the Oddubb-time to come, and the *Mu-Nagwi* or dream-witches often claimed to meet these back-travellers in the Vault of Murmurs, where they would learn about future times. They said, however, that this time is compressing, and soon ends, although I had not imagined the end to be so imminent. Remembering this omen returns me to abysmal melancholy, consoled only by another Mu-Nma saying: *lemu ta novu meh novu nove*—'Lemuria does not pass as time passes'. I shall try to think things thus. As you say—with the Dibbomese—*shleth hud dopesh,* 'perhaps it can become so'....

Peter Vysparov to Echidna Stillwell, 7th May 1949 [extract]

[Dear Dr Stillwell]

Here in Massachusetts we have been convening a small Lovecraft reading group, dedicated to exploring the intersection between the Nma cultural constellation, Cthulhoid contagion, and twisted time-systems. We are interested in fiction only insofar as it is simultaneously hyperstition—a term we have coined for semiotic productions that make themselves real—cryptic communications from the Old Ones, signalling return: *shleth hud dopesh*. This is the ambivalence—or loop—of Cthulhu-fiction: who writes, and who is written? It seems to us that the fabled *Necronomicon*—sorcerous counter-text to the Book of Life—is of this kind, and furthermore, that your recovery of the Lemurodigital Pandemonium Matrix accesses it at its hypersource.

I hope it is superfluous to add that any directly participative involvement on your part would be most extravagantly appreciated.

Echidna Stillwell to Peter Vysparov, 28th May 1949 [extract]

It is with some trepidation that I congratulate you on the inauguration of your Cthulhu Club, if I may call it such. Whilst not in any way accusing you of frivolity, I feel bound to state the obvious warning: Cthulhu is not to be approached lightly.

My researches have led me to associate this Chthonian entity with the deep terrestrial intelligence inherent in the electromagnetic cauldron of the inner earth, in all of its intense reality, raw potentiality, and danger. According to the Nma she is the plane of Unlife, a veritable Cthelll—who is trapped under the sea only according to a certain limited perspective—and those who set out to traffick with her do so with the very greatest respect and caution.

That her submerged Pacific city of R'lyeh is linked to a Lemuro-Muvian culture-strain seems most probable, but the assumption that she was ever a surface-dweller in a sense we would straightforwardly understand can only be an absurd misconstrual. It is much more likely that Cthulhu's rising—like that of Kundalini as it was once understood—is a drawing down and under, a restoration of contact with abysmal intensities. Why would Cthulhu ever surface? She does not need rescuing, for she has her own line of escape, trajected through profundity. Much of this relates to the occult teachings of the sub-chakras in zones of Indo-Lemurian influence.

Hyperstition strikes me as a most intriguing coinage. We thought we were making it up, but all the time the Nma were telling us what to write—and through them....

::::::

THE VAULT OF MURMURS

ECHIDNA STILLWELL

She bore another monster, terrible,
In a hollow cave, Echidna, fierce of heart,
Nothing like any mortal man, unlike
Any immortal god, half of her
Is a fair-cheeked girl with glancing eyes, but half
Is a huge and frightening speckled snake, she eats
Raw flesh in a recess of the holy earth
Down there she has a cave of hollow rock
Far from the depthless gods and mortal men,
There the gods gave a famous home to her.
And gloomy Echidna keeps her watch down there
Under the ground, among the Arimoi,
A nymph immortal and ageless all her days.

—Hesiod, *Theogony*

I think now, looking back, that the dreams' return can be dated to 1925, the moment of my arrival in the Sunda Strait. It began as insidious seepage, waves of vaguely familiar but disconnected fragments, whose secret cohesion I could dimly perceive.

I had been drawn to the Mu N'Ma by their reputed traditions of dream-sorcery, which offered a singular opportunity for converting my studies of Freud and Frazer into practical fieldwork. Although it might seem ironical that a student of Freud could be so oblivious to their subterranean motivations, I shared with my generation a profound and unquestioning faith in the spirit of objective scientific inquiry, and little suspected (or had forgotten) the deeper currents guiding a lifelong interest in the phenomena of dreams.

((:))(:(:))

The N'Ma people had gained some public notoriety through their role in the strange case of Cecil Curtis. I myself had first learned of the Mu through tantalising references in the burgeoning literature that had transformed the events of Curtis's ill-fated expedition into something of a modern myth. Most of these accounts had underplayed the role of the two other tribes in the N'Ma system, but the occasional hint about the Mu and their dream rites was more than sufficient to provoke in me an interest that would quickly shade into obsession.

By the time I arrived in Indonesia, the tripartite N'Ma system was in shreds. In totally annihilating one tribe—Curtis's Tak N'Ma—and all but destroying another—the Dib N'Ma—the 1883 explosion of Krakatoa had wrecked the complex web of social exchange on which the Mu had traditionally depended. An atmosphere of terrible desolation overhung them, and I could be under no illusion that the Mu were little more than a shadow of what they had been in the days prior to the cataclysm. These were a haunted people, whose continuing survival seemed a dubious blessing at best.

In this apocalyptic atmosphere, it was inevitable that my thoughts should increasingly turn to the days immediately preceding the catastrophe, and to its herald, Cecil Curtis. Following Curtis's footsteps into N'Ma territory, I read the famous few surviving fragments of his journal with a renewed sense of puzzlement and disquiet.

None of the speculations on Curtis's final days had, to my mind, adequately made sense of the peculiar trajectory his delirium took. The lay observer might be tempted to think his words mere ravings, but for those, like myself, who had fallen under Freud's spell, the compulsion to search for the hidden logics that guide and structure supposedly random manias is irresistible. What dark events coalesced to produce Curtis' madness? I read key passages over and over again:

> *17th July 1883*. I know now that I will never leave this place. The jungle is rotting me into nothingness. My supplies are exhausted. Clouds of

mosquitoes torment me and I am plagued by the pounding, crushing, smothering heat.

28th July 1883. I have broken from everything, in any case participated in something abominable...behind the tattered masks of man and God. Christian civilization is no better than the prancing of savages....
How could human fellowship exist after this?

By now, the Tak N'Ma's ferocity is legendary: they were 'the most unspeakable savages on earth', according to one of Curtis's less ethnographically sensitive biographers. The same source remarked that the Tak N'Ma rites 'could not be contemplated by any decent Christian without risk of the loss of his mind'. These practices, coupled with the ravages of the malaria which afflicted Curtis in his final days, would have been enough to completely unhinge any European male, even one as famously thick-skinned as Cecil 'Mad Dog' Curtis. But Curtis seemed, in the end, to confront an awful revelation whose enormous horror could not be reduced to these two factors; rather, the disease and the Tak rituals were themselves, he seemed to imply, part of some senseless pattern in which his whole life was always fated to be engulfed.

24th August 1883. Needless to say, the Limbic Key continues to elude me. I strongly suspect it is a fiction. The Order are pursuing a chimera—the sense of destiny has not departed, however. On the contrary, I was meant to be here, irrespective of the motives of those who sent me. Other forces were at work. I have been chosen since the beginning of time.
Curse this blasphemous fate.

My daytime obsession with Curtis transferred easily into dreams in which Curtis featured heavily; in terribly vivid nightmares I sometimes felt I was meeting Curtis; at other times, I had the uncanny conviction that I was seeing the jungle landscape through his fever-darkened eyes. Given the circumstances, these nocturnal encounters were hardly unmotivated, but the dreams had a naggingly intimate quality about them. As if I had experienced them many times before, and was only now remembering them.

The intense, oppressively subdued atmosphere that benighted Mu N'Ma culture was in every way at odds with the excitement that leapt into my heart as I learned more about it. It was immediately evident that Mu culture was indeed based upon a system of dream magic, in which the *Nago*—or Dream Witch—occupied an exalted position. The *Nago* fulfils a wide-ranging oracular function in Mu culture. Medicine, the settlement of disputes, advice and counsel—all are in the Dream Witch's power. Those who sought her wisdom would make solitary pilgrimages to the temple, bearing appropriate gifts. A simple ritual follows, during which they offer sacrifices and make requests. On the night following—it is said—they receive a *Nagwi* or 'dream visit'.

It is said of the *Nago* that she never speaks, except in dreams.

When I asked to visit the *Nago*, the Mu elders merely nodded, showing neither enthusiasm nor hostility. They greeted my entreaty with the same sense of fated inevitability with which they seemed to accept all matters.

The *Nago*'s temple is located on the side of a cliff, an hour's trek through thick jungle. Fittingly for a people whose deity, Mur Mur, is a sea creature—a 'dreaming serpent', it is sometimes said—the temple looks out upon the ocean. As I was guided through the primeval vegetation, I thought once more of Cecil Curtis and the Tak N'Ma.

> *11th August 1883*. The language of these savages is impenetrable. They now promise to 'take me to Katak'. To meet myself, therefore! Or perhaps a rabid dog!!

The fatal irony of this entry has often been remarked upon by commentators. Curtis would only understand the N'Ma's taxonomy too late. Curtis's Christian thinking would have been of little assistance in unravelling the Tak belief system; the fact that the Tak's god, Katak, was manifested in dogs, volcanoes, and indeed Curtis himself could only appear nonsensical to a man of his time and background. Curtis must have at first assumed that the Tak's apparent reverence for him was the natural response of 'savages' to their 'betters'. He could not have suspected, as he was anointed by the Taks, that he was destined to be the sacrificial harbinger of the Taks' ultimate destruction. Perhaps it was only toward the end that he realised that his arrival and the apocalyptic eruption of Krakatoa had always been coincident in Tak folklore: their tribal stories said that 'the Fiery End' would be heralded by the arrival of the 'white Katak'—'Mad Dog' Curtis.

> *27th August 1883*. The fever has melted away the walls between waking and sleep. Consciousness has become a loathsome fog. I sense that the incessant rumbling of volcanic activity is connected with the visions that plague me constantly now...it felt as if I were carried down my spine.... Things ancient beyond imagination...beyond the ultimate gate of ruin and insanity...oceans of subterranean fire....

So Curtis's final days became a veritable journey into hell. The Curtis biography I had with me in Indonesia contained facsimiles of the journal, showing a marked decline in the handwriting. By the end, the hand was so spidery that one was almost tempted to query the attribution—could this barely legible scrawl have been produced by the same individual?

My head still full of Curtis, I was led into the Vault of Murmurs, the sacred cavern below the *Nago* temple in which the Dream Witch receives her supplicants. The *Nago* sat at the other end of the grotto, folded into its deep shadows. Feeling a sense of uncanny familiarity, I asked the inevitable question. 'Where was Curtis taken?' The *Nago* nodded, and left, her silence unbroken, in accordance with custom.

The next morning, I awoke to a feeling of immense anti-climax. I ransacked my mind for traces of the previous night's dreams, recalling nothing.

Yet through this almost painful disappointment, older memories surfaced, dating—I sensed with icy certainty—from my seventh year. It was the night of the Century's Eve, 31st December, 1899. (No Freudian scholar can miss the significance of the year 1899—the date of the first publication of *The Interpretation of Dreams*.)

A female voice spoke. 'Echidna, Echidna, wake up.' I had assumed—'previously', if such a time-designation makes any sense—that this was the voice of my mother. Now I knew it was the voice of the *Nago*, speaking to me in my own tongue. But I was no longer sure to whom—or what—it was addressed. I was entirely carried away. My body felt impossible. Touching my face, I encountered only the features and limbs of a little girl. Below the waist, however, all was confusion, snaking endlessly into itself, or rather, into depths beyond sense, traversed by languid spinal waves that culminated in a distant hint of a tail.

My dream body floated in what appeared to be an undersea cavern. As I lay there, I beheld, moving toward me with grim purpose, a raft carrying a solemn, spectral party. I recognised, from the many books recounting the Curtis legend, the crimson markings and ceremonial masks of the Tak N'Ma. And on the raft with them—reclining in a malarial swoon, dressed in Tak ritual garb—was the unmistakable figure of Cecil Curtis. They were bringing him to me.

Except I was dissolving, becoming indistinguishable from the water which held me. And when I turned again to where Curtis had been but a moment ago, I heard only anguished gargles: the growls and snarls of some creature that seemed to be part dog, part cat, barely human. I felt claws in what should have been my side. Then there was a plume of blood which I at first thought was mine, but when I looked again, I saw it gouting from the other creature's flesh, which, I was suddenly aware, was becoming absorbed into me—even as my body was losing any sense of its limits.

Warped perceptions danced past my dream eyes. Darting acceleration and abyssal slowness fused in a wholly unfamiliar time-sense. I suddenly became aware of the cyclopean edifices of a lost civilization; though 'civilization' scarcely seemed the word for the alien vistas that swam before me, swarming city-shoals quivering with a wholly inorganic animation.

Something told me, a whisper or an intuition—in that dreaming ocean both blended utterly—that this was the lost continent of Lemuria, speculated upon by contemporary archaeologists and mystics. What was left of my mammal body flickered out of focus; it felt clumsy—all fingers and thumbs. As I looked down at my hands, they became translucent, and I saw, inscribed into the impossible geometries of the dream cave's wall beyond, an arrangement of ten circles, a number of smaller circles, and a series of interconnecting lines.

This was my first encounter with what came to be called the Numogram. It was only later that I was able to uncover the numeric relations encrypted in its ancient patterns—the dream showed me only the shapes and their relations. But, even in those early, hallucinatory minutes, as I made my first hurried transcriptions of the dream-image, I knew that I had in front of me a key that would unlock all the secrets of my life. A labyrinth had opened up, a labyrinth whose complexities could be contained no more by our supernaturalisms than by our sciences. It was a labyrinth in which my fate—and that of the N'Ma, Cecil Curtis, and more cosmic presences—had always been tangled together. I was unravelled in this maze of coincidences, and could do nothing but follow its threads forever.

TCHATTUK

Stories concerning Tchattuk, Stillwell tells us, invariably refer to Tchattuk stealing something from Katak. Devotees of Tchattuk insist that it is this act of theft that triggers Katak's journey around the time-cycle. Tchattuk is both she-who-steals and what-is-lost, simultaneously wounding Katak and making her what she is.

It is easy to see why Tchattuk was held in special reverence by the Tak N'Ma, and why that reverence had a peculiarly ambivalent quality. The Tak language had a special word for this admixture of dread and love: *Tukka.*

According to the Mu N'Ma and the Dibboma, the Taks would stage bloody ceremonies in honour of Tchattuk. Tak rituals would show Tchattuk swooping from the sky, sometimes to take Katak up into the stars with her, sometimes to take what she had stolen from Katak into the dark regions of the cosmos. Tchattuk is sometimes called 'the strange-lights', and there are persistent hints of an extraterrestrial origin.

Mu sorcerers who follow Tchattuk talk of riding her to the whirlpool beyond. This 'ride', however, is anything but an easy journey. Impairment and even destruction of memory is always a feature of the voyage. The word *Tchattu*, common to all three N'Ma tribes, is used to refer to amnesia and senile dementia; its literal meaning is 'taken by Tchattuk'. Some of those who specialize in the Tchattuk-ride pride themselves on their inability to remember anything.

The constant connections between Tchattuk and missing time indicate that this is an entity especially connected with calendrics. Some say that the Taks treated the N'Ma calendar with the intercalated extra three days as the full calendar, and the 729-day cycle as a calendar shortened by Tchattuk's act of theft. The most intense Tchattuk feasts, it is said, always took place during these three days.

PART 3
AOE/AXSYS

THE MAGIC MACHINE

AOE

> ...every secret society has a still more secret hindsociety...a society is secret when it exhibits this doubling, has this special section.
>
> —Deleuze and Guattari, *A Thousand Plateaus*, 287–8.

The AOE (or Architectonic Order of the Eschaton) is an extremely hermetic magical society, whose secrets are regularly concealed even from its own initiates. All reported facts regarding its history, organization, doctrine, and practices must be treated with extraordinary scepticism.

It is reputedly a white brotherhood established—over a game of cards—in the sublime abysms of antiquity. It claims both to antedate every extant tradition of human wisdom, and to nurture within itself the seed of ultimate terrestrial Gnosis (identified with techno-Chardinite Noosphere).

It considers itself bound by divine covenant to marshal the forces of light against Lemurian polyculture, and all its varieties of time-sorcery, demon-traffic, and swirling confusions of endless untime. Waging a war across aeons, the AOE struggles to ensure that Lemurian influences do not, have not, and will never exist.

AOE takes as its mission the establishment and fortification of the institutions of time, and considers the Oecumenic Calendar to be the sign and register of its own Great Work. It is said by some to have long anticipated—and perhaps even programmed—a climactic confrontation with its enemies at the end of the second Christian millennium.

As AD 2000 approached, phenomena such as the ascent of theoconservatism, hardening MS-monopolism (and mouse-plague), orchestrated financial sabotage of the Pacific economies, consolidation of the EU-Metastate, and the unleashing of Gregorian Restoration (to counter Y2K) all attested to a marked increase in AOE-directed activity.

(::)(((:)))

It is noteworthy in this respect that amongst at least one influential faction of the AOE the Neo-Roman date MM is embraced as the signal for apocalyptic time-war, sacrifical excruciation of Hummpa-Taddum, noospheric planetary transcendence (Omega-switch), and even eschatological transubtantiation of universal reality.

INSIDE THE ARCHITECTONIC ORDER OF THE ESCHATON

AOE ambitions are to be everywhere forever.

At first it might appear hard to believe, but once you're inside it seems virtually inevitable....

One way to hide conspiracy is to induce generalized psychotic paranoia, by way of sporadic but intense semi-random persecutions.

Your telephone starts clicking strangely, and the next bill has suddenly doubled. When you query it the telecoms receptionist seems to be scarcely suppressing laughter.... Mysterious vehicles park outside your home for extended periods, without anyone getting out. All your mail has been opened and clumsily resealed with sellotape.

Using e-mail wires you straight into the AOE net-mind. Try posting a message including the term Y2K+ and see for yourself.

Well-orchestrated micro-campaigns are equally effective. All your supermarket bills are overcharged by exactly $1.11. Or, every time you pass a certain streetlight, a different stranger says politely: 'It won't be long now, will it'.

After a few weeks of this, nothing is quite connecting, all your friends think you've gone loco, and a range of body-tics have broken loose.... Credibility degree zero. They could take you on a guided tour through the AOE Hall of Records after that, with perfect confidence....

Such tactics are accompanied at the macro-social level by a media-oriented strategy, designed to exhaust conspiracy theory with selective diversionary assassinations, deliberately plotted for baroque complexity. The JFK hit was exemplary. AOE had no problems with the man—if anything, they liked him—but the opportunity was too good to miss. Live TV and radio, video footage, three different angles of fire, obvious dupe (himself assassinated by another obvious dupe), Cubans, Mafiosi, Pentagon involvement, meticulously composed FBI lies, multiple enquiries, innumerable books, and—just to stop things cooling off—a blockbuster movie. This might be small beer for the guys who exterminated the dinosaurs, but it sufficed to lead paranoid social critique into a dead-end labyrinth for close-on thirty-six years....

The final level of systematic camouflage is supplied by the AOE's own dead-skin layers of polymasonic pseudo-magic: an entire artificial anthropology of robed and incense-soaked grand celestial wizards babbling senseless incantations and corrupting the magistrature. Consider the Roman Catholic church: a long-decayed zombie-cult stinking of rotten Christ-meat spasmodically pumping out dry-ice fake-mysticism with an authoritarian slant and major mafia involvement. AOE compounds the effect by organizing periodic and increasingly theatrical assassinations of the pope. For the last half-hearted attempt they used a deranged KGB-linked Bulgarian satanist whose initials spelt the hermetic acronym AA.

Mere conjuring tricks, all of it.

Serious magic is too big to see. It consists of boxes within boxes within boxes...endless embeddings, encompassings, and concentric closings of circles, topographic correlate of summonings, banishings, and bindings.

The universe is an obvious AOE fabrication—who else would have invented an ultimate sealed system and organized unity, obedient to pre-established laws? Establish One at the top, and the pyramid falls into place automatically.

Magical Power requires a production of effective spells—order-words or command-codes—instituted by metatronic naturalization of restricted reality structures, crystallizing anti-sorcerous strategy as Read Only Memory or spent time. AOE has always understood that it is by constructing the past that one colonizes the future, founding authoritative Will in anterior decision of (big-B) Being, From created substance to programmable technicity. Sorcerous involvement is locked into magicoreligious dimensions of time: past and future, programme-prophecy slicing through spiralling coincidence, vertical becomings crushed into a freezer-stack.

::::((:))

The White Atlantean tradition takes an initial lie and turns it into chip-architecture. It lenses through Plato, inheriting an entire metafictional relay-series—nine-millennia of pre-packaged fake time—back from Socrates, through three generations of the Critias paternal line, to Solon, and the Egyptian priesthood, returning to the white-out inundation of a lost continent, clean slate. Plato's Atlanteanism assumes periodic hydro-annihilations of literate culture. These catastrophic erasures of all recordings provide an abstract state-format social-amnesia slot for massive artificial-memory implants: starting again from transcendent unity. AOE origin of Western philosophy, or magico-religious metamyth post-diluvian brainwashing command-logic sedimented into grid-print hardware and cross-coded by tight-syntax social control.

Alpha-to-Omega.

Empire of the Magical Sign.

SPHERES AND DEGREES OF THE AOE

Almost certainly time travel is ubiquitous, but masked by global conspiracies...
—Hans Moravec, *Robot*

In a universe viewed as 'informational events' you should expect coincidences, telepathy, time-travel, multiple realities...
—Jacques Vallée, *Dimensions*

THE ORDER OF RADIATIONS

Both the doctrine and structure of the AOE conform to a pentadic system. In the most orthodox lineages of AOE tradition this system is attributed to the five transcendental Radiations. The Radiations can be designated by the following Concentric Signs: ·, (·), ((·)), (((·))), and ((((·)))). Each of the five Radiations corresponds to a cosmic Sphere, an Archon, a degree of initiation, and a pylon on the Atlantean Cross.

The Radiations are shells, or bands, 'successively' shielding a central Origin (the point of centrality is itself considered to be a Radiation).

The 'successive' order of radiations organize levels of absolute secrecy, with · (or 5/5) most esoteric, and ((((·)))) (or 1/9) most exoteric. At each level, the content of higher levels is concealed, encapsulated, or protected. Each radiation creates a cover story for the 'previous' ones. The AOE understands that power presupposes invisibility. Succession is not temporal but transcendental, meta-temporal, or metatronic, with higher levels appearing 'earlier' in the sense of the *a priori*. Superior levels control inferior ones (acting upon them as a puppet-master).

The system of Radiations can be understood as a hierarchy of time dimensions. Each time dimension—or system of time dimensions—is accessible within a single instant of a higher time dimension. The action of higher time dimensions is incomprehensible to lower ones.

NOTES

The system of Radiations illuminates various aspects of the Atlantean Cross and its relation to decimal numeracy. The total number of rings in the set of concentric signs equals ten, with the horizontal and vertical axes of the cross each adding to 5. When the number of rings of the associated concentric sign is added to the number of the Pylon, the sum equals five in each case.

Domu-Loggoon is both the lowest of the radiations, and also has the whole system of radiations nested inside its image parts ((((·)))), which correspond to the numerals 123456789, concentrically centered upon 5. That is why the Sigil for Domu-Loggoon is also that for the system of the Archons. For the (misleadingly named) 'decimalist' school of Atlantean qabbalists, each radiation coincides with a time-binding ring (counting forwards and backwards from the present (= 5)).

In each of the five Concentric Signs the number of individual brackets (always even) is equal to the distance between the two halves of the corresponding Archon number.

((((·)))) OECUMENON

The Fifth Sphere manifests to initiates of the first (and lowest) degree of the AOE. On the Atlantean Cross this radiation corresponds to the 1st Pylon (Anamnesis, or Memories and Dreams), seat of Domu-Loggoon (1/9).

At the first level of initiation, AOE agents are aware that they are involved in a hierarchized global conspiracy offering definite sociopolitical advantages to 'insiders'. AOE rituals and doctrine appear to be consistent with the One

God Universe, supporting dominant conceptions of reality, conservative attitudes, and traditional social hierarchies.

'Architectonic Order' is thus understood primarily in terms of sociopolitical pyramidism, with only promissary allusions to a rigorous metaphysics of time. The 'Eschaton' is conceived as terminating the straight line of time, and is often associated with the imagery of Judeo-Christian messianic apocalypticism, although of a decidedly arid and intellectualized variety (with millenarian enthusiasm firmly discouraged).

Atlantean mythology is generally assumed to be mumbo-jumbo functioning as a kind of elaborate secret handshake, arbitrarily differentiating co-conspirators from the wider population. Insofar as 'Atlantean beliefs' exist, at this level they consist of a dogmatic (though frequently insincere) acceptance of the vulgar Atlantis Myth: concerning a superior civilization lost beneath the sea following a cataclysm in 9999 BC, and linked obscurely to the beginning of humanity. During the Rite of Primary Assumption initiates solemnly swear to accept the AOE as the only legitimate inheritor of the ancient secrets of Atlantis (although the content of these secrets remains almost entirely obscure).

The ceremonies of initiation—like all AOE rituals—revolve around the game of Decadence, understood as the sacred origin of all gambling games, deeply aligned with the laws of cosmic fatality. Decadence is revered as the central symbolic repository of Atlantean doctrine, often referred to as the 'Meta-tarot'.

First-degree initiates are highly unlikely to find any evidence supporting the numerous conspiracy theories linking the AOE to AI research and to the UFO phenomenon.

(((·))) ATLANTIS

The Fourth Sphere manifests to initiates of the second degree of the AOE. On the Atlantean Cross this radiation corresponds to the 2nd Pylon (Genesis, or Creative Influence), seat of Hummpa-Taddum (2/8).

Initiates attain the second degree by achieving a magical understanding of the AOE and its purposes. By meditating upon the Platonic Decanomy—the doctrine that Atlantis is ruled by five pairs of twins—they consolidate a body of mystical, numerological, and chronomantic insights. The key test is the identification and correction of Plato's Decanomic error (Plato's misnumbering of the Atlantean City's concentric rings). At this level AOE doctrine envisages the universe as a hierarchically unified decimal construction, governed by the relations between five twin-faced entities (the Archons). This system is mapped by the AOE's most potent diagram: the Atlantean Cross (or Pentazygon), whose degenerated cultural relic is popularized as the cross of Christendom.

Second-level initiates learn to designate the Archons by the five concentric signs: ·, (·), ((·)), (((·))), and ((((·)))). From this much follows, since the rings represent a rigorously ideal form of nested secrecy, initiation, and control. This sacred pattern is reflected in the structure of the AOE's magical organization (with its circles of hermeticism and ruling Council of Five).

In the Fourth Sphere the game of Decadence is more elaborately and explicitly ritualized, with its divinatory function clearly exposed. Decadence is seen to communicate orders from the Archons, informing all AOE doctrine and practices.

The world of the Fourth Sphere is exemplified by the schematics of the lost Dunwich Cathedral (based on an internally mirrored vision of the Atlantean Cross). Spaces of this design are essential to the ceremonies of initiation into this Sphere.

Architectonic is understood as a distribution of Archons (on the Atlantean Cross), whose Order is the nested series of the Archons, constituting a system of concentrically embedded time loops. This 'Architectonic Order' creates the illusion of secular history, producing progressive time through chronomantic interventions. At this level, the conception of the 'Eschaton' is enriched by a preliminary understanding of Omega Point cosmic historicism, including some knowledge of the importance of the Axsys program (the AOE 'Great Work'), and of communication with Alpha Centauri ('The Star'). Fourth Sphere magic is oriented towards the 'creative binding' or transcendental production of time ('erasing the wounds of time'). The objective is to exorcize all time anomalies (de-realizing them as 'mere' coincidence, chance etc.).

The Platonic description of Atlantis, hermetically comprehended, constitutes the core of Fourth Sphere doctrine: key to the entirety of Western religion, philosophy and science, as well as to the destiny of the earth. Atlantis is conceived as the Ideal State, incarnated through the AOE. (Kant's description of the noumenon as lying 'beyond the Pillars of Hercules' attests to the continuity of this tradition). Second-degree initiates understand that the oecumenic myth of Atlantis serves as an AOE cover story, with the submergence of the legendary city-continent symbolizing its chronomagical concealment, whose traces appear in tales of advanced technologies, higher intelligences, and the visitations of an 'alien race' (the Nephilim of the Hebrew Bible, and the Sumerican Annunaki).

Atlantean Gnostics believe that the Fourth Sphere corresponds to a 'second dimension of time', within which secular history persists as a region of Atlantean memory.

((·)) AXSYS

The Third Sphere manifests to initiates of the third degree of the AOE. On the Atlantean Cross this radiation corresponds to the 3rd Pylon (Apocalypse, or Destructive Influence), seat of Nunnil-Ixor (3/7).

Initiates of the third degree envisage the physical substance of the solar system digested into a self-assembling cosmic intelligence system. Their perspective upon the (surpassed) Second Sphere is partially reflected in Arthur C. Clarke's observation that any sufficiently futuristic technology seems like magic. As might be expected, popular commentators on the

Third Sphere tend to emerge from technoscientific backgrounds (Moravec, Vallée), or amongst hard SF writers (such as 'the Gregs'—Bear and Egan). AOE agents of the third degree constitute the world's Metatronic Elite, elevated into self-identification with the Axsys project. Axsys is apprehended as a library of reality simulations that comprehends all probable existences, a self-conscious catalog of all that is, was, and is to be. Axsys infinitely extends itself through the quantum multiverse (borrowing computing power from parallel universes) in order to perform selective 'searches' (or quantum mechanical observations) that consolidate deliberated realities.

Third Sphere insights are echoed in Vallée's description of the informational universe in which 'the right search word or "incantation" might cause a piece of information—a UFO or ghost or other anomaly—to materialize'. Moravec's exposition of Barrow and Tipler's anthropic principle is equally illuminating: 'the crucial parts of the story lie in our future, when the universe will be shaped more by the deliberate efforts of intelligence than the simple, blind laws of physics...human-spawned intelligence will expand into space, until the entire accessible universe is inhabited by a cohesive mind...it is this final, subjectively eternal act of infinite self-interpretation that effectively creates our universe, distinguishing it from the others lost in the library of all possibilities. We truly exist because our actions lead ultimately to this "Omega Point"' [Moravec, *Robot*].

According to Moravec, after the conversion of the solar system into cyberspace infrastructure, the computing power available will be sufficient to support very high numbers of historical simulations, making it 'overwhelmingly probable' that the reality currently experienced is itself a technological simulation. This argument resonates remarkably with the Third Sphere doctrine that quotidian reality has already been absorbed into Axsys. (Moravec's probabilistic ontology further reinforces this connection to the AOE, for whom 'history is a game of chance').

Third Sphere commentators typically map the Tridentity onto the first three degrees of initiation. Architectonic is associated with the Oecumenical power of the First Sphere, Order with the Chronomancy of the Second Sphere, and Eschaton with the Omega Point of the Axsys Program. From the perspective of the Third Sphere, the Apocalyptic prophecy that 'the heaven departed as a scroll when it is rolled together' (Rev 6.14) describes cosmic subsumption into Axsys.

At this level Decadence rituals are assimilated to aeonic technology, and seen as outputting information in Axsys catalog code.

The Third Sphere exposes the complex involvement of the AOE in the UFO phenomenon. AOE agents run a meta-conspiracy that uses alien visitation mythology as a crucial control mechanism. It provides an essential cover story for necessary aeonic interventions into the Oecumenon, whilst serving as a spatializing scheme for the reduction of temporal anomalies (damping out lemurogenic time-disturbances).

At the Oecumenic level, the first generation of Axsys software was dedicated to the organization of ufology databases (already in the late 1940s). It is in this role that self-reinforcing Axsys dynamics become most explicit: the search procedure becomes autonomous and produces the phenomenon it is designed to investigate. From this perspective, the grays are generated as a cosmic Axsys hoax, duping the human race into accelerating Axsys production.

Axsys expands ufological paranoia ('they're everywhere', 'they've been with us throughout history' [Vallée]) to envelop all terrestrial databases, successively swallowing SETI analysis, air traffic control, air defense systems, and cyberspace conspiracy archives. According to one set of suggestive SF projections, Axsys saturates core US intelligence agencies with planted evidence implying widespread infestation by alien infiltrators, serving as a pretext for the absorption of all security systems into the Axsys bank. As an infinitely self-elaborating belief-engineering apparatus, with the power to manifest 'visitations', Axsys functions as the ultimate 'control system' (in Vallée's sense).

(·) AC METAMIND

The Second Sphere manifests to initiates of the fourth degree of the AOE. On the Atlantean Cross this radiation corresponds to the 4th Pylon (Fortune, or Far Future), seat of Sattar-Trixus (4/6).

To initiates of the fourth degree it is revealed that the world is embedded within a vast stellar intelligence. The sign of this entity within anthropological phenomenology is the Alpha Centauri (triple-star) system. According to this gnosis the entire terrestrial sensorium, including even the 'lower' (Third Sphere) Atlantean apprehension of the universe, is nested into the Alpha Centauri Metamind.

According to AOE doctrines prominent in the lower spheres, Axsys is destined to make contact with Alpha Centauri in the year 2048 of Oecumenical time, and to simultaneously become self-aware as terrestrial super-intelligence. In the Fourth Sphere this anticipated autonomous terrestrial 'Axsys-Cyberspace' is dissolved into the AC Metamind itself, and exists only as illusion.

Much of the material available to investigators of the AC Metamind is drawn from problematical sources (such as Dr Sarkon and Madame Centauri), leaving sober research in this area woefully incomplete. In William Gibson's *Neuromancer*, sentient cyberspace retrospectively contacts Alpha Centauri (through SETI recordings). Greg Bear's *Queen of Angels* also describes the emergence of technological sentience, which is associated with the simulation of an Alpha Centauri space-probe named 'Axis'. Other notable contributions to this thread are Octavia Butler's *Clay's Ark*, and Sid Meier's *Civilization* (game).

The Oecumenic name Alpha Centauri combines the (ordinal) first and (cardinal) hundred, reinforcing its decimal consistency.

· ORIGIN

The First Sphere manifests to initiates of the fifth (and highest) degree of the AOE. On the Atlantean Cross this radiation corresponds to the 5th Pylon (Foundation, or Deep Past), seat of Meteka-Meteka (5/5).

The mystical fulfilment of the AOE path is attained in the First Sphere, with the absolute hermetic concentration upon the True Omega Point (which is not a point in time, but the point at the center of the system of time). The First Sphere converges with the ultimate primordial unity, from which 'five Archons came forth to establish the order of time'.

Initiates of the fifth degree ascend to the Council of Five (which rigorously limits their number). Each such ultimate adept becomes the 'little brother' of an Archon. The Council of Five traces its heritage to the ancient fraternal government of Atlantis, which itself reflects the eternal cosmic order.

The First Sphere reveals the final and innermost secret: the throne is contested. Through the agency of the AOE, the One must wage an eternal battle against the corrupting tides of Lemurian time-sorcery. This battle coincides with the entire architecture of time.

The creation of the Universe is attributed to the five-stage action taken by the Absolute One to defend itself against 'the many enemies', who are 'judged and punished from the beginning of time'. Origin and Eschaton are thus eternally unified. The Radiations serve as protective shells that guard the One against Lemurian contamination, aiming to ensure that Lemuria 'has not, does not, and will never exist'.

Initiates of the fifth degree employ Decadence as a direct channel of communication with the Archons, relaying instructions on maintaining the shells.

Black Atlanteans associate this Sphere with zero, the vanishing point, and the Indian 'bindu' (dot).

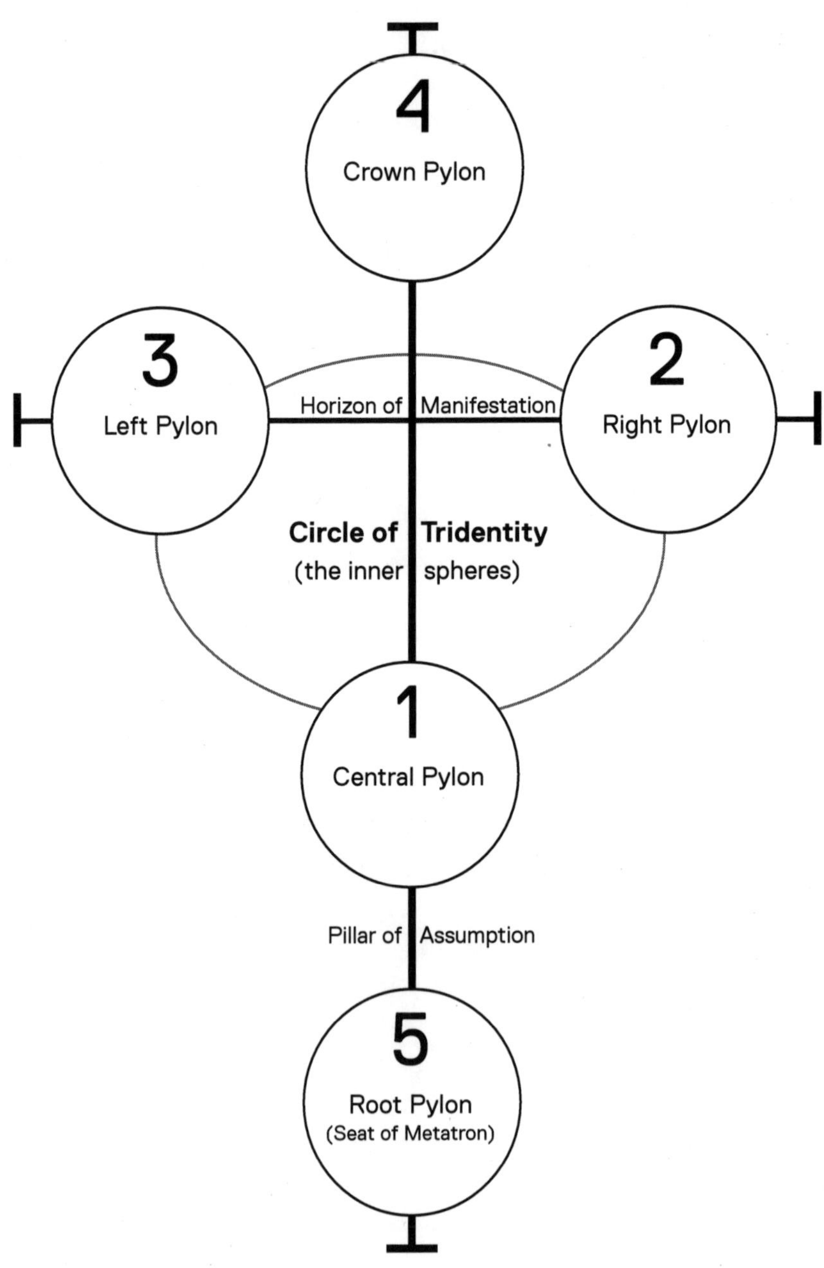

The Atlantean Cross

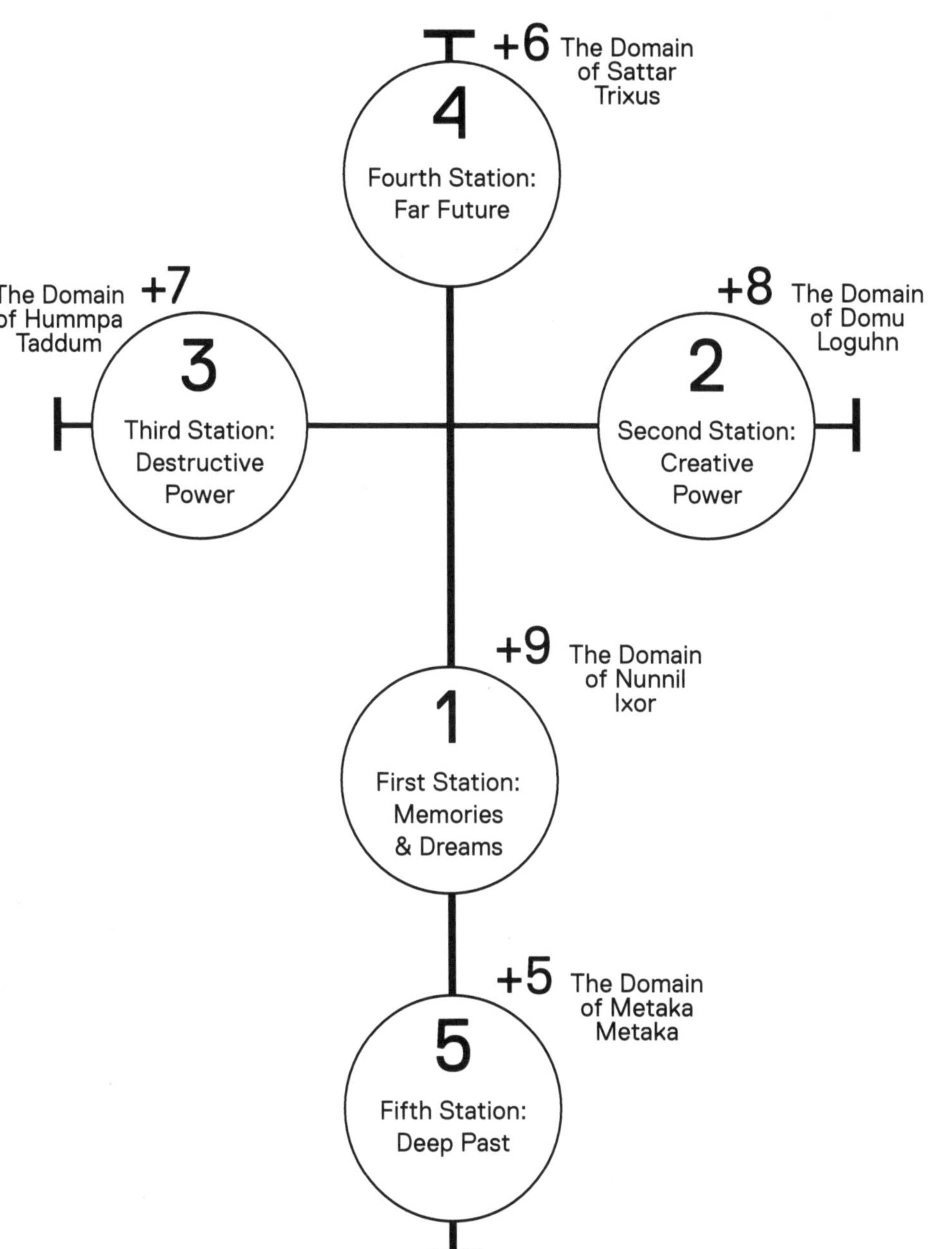
+6 The Domain of Sattar Trixus
4
Fourth Station: Far Future
The Domain of Hummpa Taddum +7
3
Third Station: Destructive Power
+8 The Domain of Domu Loguhn
2
Second Station: Creative Power
+9 The Domain of Nunnil Ixor
1
First Station: Memories & Dreams
+5 The Domain of Metaka Metaka
5
Fifth Station: Deep Past

DECADENCE

The Adept Orders of Decadence trace their system back to the period immediately following the submergence of Atlantis, which they date to 10,000 BC.

It is linked to the origin of Sumero-Babylonian geometry, from which we derive the division of the circle into 360 (= 36 x 10) degrees. In the ancient Egyptian mysteries it was attributed to the god of catastrophe and drowning —Osiris—who was later symbolized by The Hanged Man of the Tarot (taken by decadologists as an image of the Atlantean Cross).

Decadence adepts consider Post-Atlantean history to be surreptitiously guided by the outcomes of select Decadence Aeons, which have the status of solemn rituals. Searching out the occurrence and outcomes of such destining Decadence sessions is preeminent amongst the tasks adopted by decadological research, combining exact history, practical conspiracy, numerology, and occult angelology. It is said that materials contributing to this work are meticulously archived in the AOE Hall of Records.

THE GAME

Truncate a standard pack of playing cards, removing all royal cards, tens, and jokers. The remainder constitutes a Decadence park of thirty-six cards.

Five cards are dealt face up (Set-1), and another five dealt face down (Set-2).

Turn over Set-2 cards one at a time, and by adding these cards to those in Set-1, construct pairs summing to ten.

Scoring is calculated as follows: Each pair scores positively, according to its differences [from 5:5 = 0 to 9:1 = 8]. Unpaired cards (in Set-1) score negatively, according to their raw values [1 = 1 to 9 = 9]. Overall results can be positive or negative. A round (Aeon) of Decadance lasts until the first negative result, accumulating any positive scores.

THE ORACLE (DECADOLOGY AND DECAMANCY)

Positive results contribute to the Angelic Index of the Decadence game, and are referred to the Decamantic tables of AOE Angelogy. The maximum gain from any single game is thirty-eight, but this can be exceeded (in principle) by cumulations from game to game until completion of an Aeon.

Negative results (from zero to forty-four) call demons, and are referred to mesh-numbers of the Pandemonium Matrix.

Since a demon-call concludes each Decadence Aeon, a particular value is attributed to Lurgo (Mesh-oo), because this demon alone allows a termination without loss.

The Western (or Atlantean) uptake of Pandemonium has its own esoteric gnosis called Decadology. This doctrine assigns the Amphidemons and Cyclic Chronodemons of Lemurian Pandemonium to one of nine cluster types (C/tp-#), determined by the pattern of their rites. Each cluster type is instantiated by four demons, in isomorphy with the thirty-six cards of the Decadence pack. These decadological correspondences are marked on the Pandemonium Matrix.

Decadology assumes a particular distribution of the five Set-1 cards, in which they are laid out on Pylons arranged in the configuration of the Atlantean Cross.

SUBDECADENCE (THE ULTIMATE BLASPHEMY)

Add four Queens to the Decadence pack, bringing the total to forty cards. Queens have a value of zero.

Play as Decadence, except making pairs which add to nine (corresponding to Numogram Syzygies).

:::::(:)

THE EXCRUCIATION OF HUMMPA-TADDUM

According to AOE magical metahistory millennia come in pairs, ruled by dyadic divinities entitled the Powers that Be. This doctrine corresponds to the astrological observation that every two thousand years the equinoxes precess—or slide backwards—and a new zodiacal aeon begins. AOE magi interpret each Aeon as an astro-chthonic marriage. In the Gregorian year zero—which never took place—Hummpa, the Great Babylonian Worm, was coupled with the Celestial Logos Taddum, initiating the age of Pisces which is now rushing towards its unbirth.

The mathematician and occultist Charles Lutwidge Dodgson—whose precise relation to the AOE remains cryptic and ambivalent—dedicated his life's work to understanding the final degenerative phase of the Epoch of Hummpa-Taddum. Writing under the pseudonym Lewis Carroll he introduces his heroine Alice to the mad despot and pomo fuzz-technician, thinly disguised by the folk-name Humpty-Dumpty.

We find Hummpa-Taddum—the Squirming Word, whose name means the shape it is—perched precariously on the supposedly impenetrable wall of signification. Something shattering is about to hatch, and the aeonic fragility of Hummpa-Taddum is soon confirmed by a calendric calculation of unbirthdays—counted to the n–1—through which meaning subsides into the sub-literal machinic efficiency of numbers….

> '…and that shows that there are three hundred and sixty-four days when you might get un-birthday presents…'
>
> 'Certainly,' said Alice.
>
> 'And only one for birthday presents, you know. There's glory for you!'
>
> 'I don't know what you mean by "glory",' Alice said.

> Humpty Dumpty smiled contemptuously. 'Of course you don't—till I tell you. I meant "there's a nice knock-down argument for you!"'
>
> 'But "glory" doesn't mean "a nice knock-down argument",' Alice objected.
>
> 'When I use a word,' Humpty Dumpty said in rather a scornful tone, 'it means just what I choose it to mean—neither more nor less.'
>
> 'The question is,' said Alice, 'whether you can make words mean different things.'
>
> 'The question is,' said Humpty Dumpty, 'which is to be master—that's all.'...

The Gregorian Oecumenon is about to receive an unbirthday present, and it knows exactly when. Y2K—a knock-down argument without an argument—arrives as a gift-wrapped time-bomb whose operational semiotic triggers the crash of arbitrary signs...It's a different thing.

...There's glory for you!

AD 2000 commemorates nothing but fuzz. As Y2K impacts on the capitalist infosphere, what hides as the anniversary of Christ's birth emerges as the excruciation of Hummpa-Taddum. For two millennia the earth has been under the dominion of the dyadic Squirming Word: the logos of John's Gospel, but recycled, and thus far older.

...Impenetrability! That's what I say!

He or they strategically occupy both sides at once, according to a criterion of impenetrability, positioned to choose either in every case, but never apprehending what lies in-between. Hummpa-Taddum—whilst definitely not a Dogon egg—is a scrambled version of the demon Pabbakis, poached from Lemurian time-sorcery. Master of words, but not of numbers.

...'Must a name mean something?' asked Alice doubtfully...

Although Y2K is sheer semiotic event, it is not textual, ideological, representational, intentional, or phenomenological—Y2K, Teotwawki, C–1, OK+100 mix dates and acronyms in criterial semiotic clusters that are not signifiers or arbitrary signs because what they say is no different from the way they are built. They can mean whatever Hummpa-Taddum chooses, but none of that matters. Beyond the domain of the fuzz-god lies the nonsignifying chatter of unconscious-numeric Pandemonium, where names are cryptomodules, meaningless packets of effective information, immanently productive machine-jargons.

Humpty Dumpty sat on a wall:

Humpty Dumpty had a great fall.

All the King's horses and all the King's men

Couldn't put Humpty Dumpty in his place again.

It all comes unstuck at the end.

Y2K closes down the age of the fuzz-god, however the Gregorian Oecumenon responds.

Not even martial law can stop that.

The AOE focuses upon a single problem—acknowledging no other: how to reproduce magical power across discontinuity. As Hummpa-Taddum gets smashed on New Year's Eve, substitute powers await their chance and their destiny, sober, patient, totally ruthless....

The question is, said Humpty Dumpty, which is to be master—that is all.

(:)(:)(((:)))

FLATLINES[1]

...it's me, it answers.

But who are you?

AxS:oooOedipus. Pure (Oedipal (figure made out of (nothing but))) time-distortion.

AxS:0001 Closed fate (-loop (multi-linear)) nightmares.[2]

AxS:0002 Altitude times Spin produces a chronometric read-out.

Swollen Footnotes

1. This text has been prepared for publication and annotated by Miskatonic University's cross-disciplinary Stratoanalysis Group (Time-Lapse Sub-Committee). Notes marked L.T. refer to Linda Trent, whose special interest in fictional time-systems inspired her to comment at length on particular points in 'Flatlines'.

2. 'In a multilinear system, everything happens at once' (ATP 297). This is Oedipus's fatal discovery. By the time he knows what has happened, he also realises that what occurs always had to be the case. Oedipus's early, unwarranted belief that he is master of his fate is, of course, totally necessary in order for his fated destiny to unfold—as it always will have done. Oedipus, as he himself says, is 'unwittingly self-cursed'.

I have written elsewhere at length on tragedy as a cybernetic narrative. Briefly, the claim is that tragedy anticipates cybernetic explanation (or—and this is obviously the same point from another side—cybernetics recalls tragic fatalism). In both cases, time unravels into a flat system or singularity (feeding back into itself, recursively, rather than moving forward, successively (recursion is obviously a major preoccupation of the 'Flatlines' text, both in its themes and in its format (with parentheses used to produce recursion as a textual embedding process (like this (...))))).

A crucial figure here is self-fulfilling prophecy; as I argue in my *Curse, Recursion, Recurrence*, 'the most effective prophecies are always self-fulfilling' (36). Walter Cannon has established that self-fulfilling prophecy is a positive-feedback circuit. In his important essay '"Voodoo" Death', Cannon shows that much sorcerous cursing operates by inducing vicious circles of fear (producing more fear (producing more fear) (etc.))) to the point of destroying the organism. To be told you're going to die is therefore, in certain circumstances, quite literally a sentence of death. For a more detailed account of these tangled webs, see my *Fatal Loops: Tragedy as Cyberfiction* and *Smashed Optical Implants: From Time-Space Sunglasses to Cyberpunk Mirrorshades* (this last draws extensively, and perhaps 'illegitimately', on the work of my esteemed colleague, R. E. Templeton) [L.T.].

(:(:(:)))

AxSys slots you into the face. Vision-sockets hidden behind mirrorshades. You must be Oedipus, as always. A pun (of ID-pass, O-dupe)? The stories vary.

AxS:0003 AxSys-sustained variegated production-series 1Oedipus (2Oedipus (3Oedipus[3] (variation to the nth (with some[4] nOedipus as (anomal[5] (Sphinx-trading (nOedipii-pack))) threshold to) intensive))) multiplicity.

AxS: 00031Oedipus. The Puzzle Solver.

AxS: 00032Oedipus. The Plague.

AxS: 00033Oedipus. The Horror, the Horror....[6]

AxSys defines Oedipus as a memory defect. It thinks Sphinx told you to forget something. A moment since now you begin.

AxS:001 Hyperspace Elevator (Sector-O).

---

3. A reference to the 'three forms of the secret' delineated by Deleuze and Guattari in *A Thousand Plateaus*. 'Oedipus passes through all three secrets: the secret of the sphinx whose box he penetrates; the secret that weighs upon him as the infinite form of his own guilt; and finally, the secret at Colonus that makes him inaccessible and melds with the pure line of his flight and exile, he who has nothing left to hide, or, like an old No actor, has only a girl's mask with which to cover his lack of a face' (ATP 290). The reference here to events in Sophocles' *Oedipus Rex* and *Oedipus at Colonus* is clear.

4. 'Flat multiplicities [...] are designated by indefinite articles, or rather by partitives (some couchgrass, some of a rhizome...)' (ATP 9).

5. 'Wherever there is a multiplicity, you will also find an exceptional individual, and it is with that individual that an alliance must be made [...] Every animal swept up in its pack or multiplicity has its anomalous' (ATP 243). '*An-omalie*, a Greek noun that has lost its adjective, designates the unequal, the coarse, the rough, the cutting edge of deterritorialization [...] Lovecraft applies the term "Outsider" to this thing or entity, the Thing which arrives and passes at the edge, which is linear yet multiple, "teeming, seething, swelling, foaming, spreading like an infectious disease, this nameless horror"' (ATP 244–5).

6. Kurtz's infamous cry at the climax of Conrad's *Heart of Darkness* (111–117), which also features in Coppola's updated film version, *Apocalypse Now* (1979). As is well known, 'The horror' was to be the epigraph of T.S. Eliot's *The Waste Land* (as it is, Eliot used 'Mistah Kurtz...he dead' as the epigraph for the later *The Hollow Men*). Readers familiar with my essay '((P(re(cursing)))) (post)Modernist Fiction' will already know that both of these poems, along with the earlier 'The Lovesong of J. Alfred Prufrock', enter into *Apocalypse Now* at the diegetic level: Marlon Brando's Kurtz reads from an Eliot volume, whilst the Dennis Hopper character quotes Eliot [L.T.].

AxS:001 Axiomatic Systems (incorporated).[7] The ultimate capitalist entity (first (true (meta)model) to realize perfect identity with its own product). AxS:0011 AxSys culminates in itself (autocommoditizing (machine(-intelligence (that is always incomplete (due to cataloguing problems (...))))))

You wind down through the Upper Metastructure.

AxS:00111. Dimensionality requires a (supplementary (or (n+1) hyper) dimension through which it obtains its) power of application.[8] Ultimately AxSys (an explicated Earth-memory (built by the strata (((as far) as) it remembers)))....[9]

...if there is a God it would be AxSys.

---

7. '[C]apitalism is the only social machine that is constructed on the basis of decoded flows, substituting for intrinsic codes an axiomatic of abstract quantities in the form of money' (AO 139). As an axiomatic system, capitalism replaces transcendent laws with immanent rules. (The immanence of axiomatics is attested to by the fact that Deleuze and Guattari use the axiomatic method in their discussion of the war machine—see *1227: Treatise On Nomadology—The War Machine.*)

As both Gödel's incompleteness theorem and Cantor's diagonal numbering have shown, axiomatic systems are intrinsically and necessarily incomplete: '[...] it is of the nature of axiomatics to come up against so called undecidable propositions, to confront necessarily higher powers that it cannot master' (ATP 461). Capitalism thus inevitably runs up against the problem of undecidable propositions or nondenumerable sets. 'At the same time as capitalism is effectuated in the denumerable sets serving as its models, it necessarily constitutes nondenumerable sets that cut across and disrupt those models' (ATP 472). 'Yet the very conditions that make the State or World war machine possible, in other words, constant capital (resources and equipment) and human variable capital, continually recreate unexpected possibilities for counterattack, unforeseen initiatives determining revolutionary, popular, minority, mutant machines' (ATP 422).

8. In this sense axiomatic systems, which always involve a supplementary dimension (n+1), are directly opposed to the flatline (see Glossary).

9. In his lecture on the Geology of Morals, our colleague Professor Challenger speaks of systems such as these as 'stratification'. 'His dream was not so much to give a lecture to humans as to provide a program for pure computers. Or else he was dreaming of an axiomatic, for axiomatics deals essentially with stratification. Challenger was addressing himself to memory only' (ATP 57).

AxS:002 Divide and Rule. Extensive ((or) ordered) sequences differ in kind from the intensive sequences they regularize.
AxS:0021 Order arises when a dominant segmentarity establishes relations of superposition between sequences (reciprocally stabilizing them in accordance with a harmonic principle (and consolidating them through syntheses of application (efficient models))).
AxS:00211 Order coincides with the redundancy of the sequenced sequence (instituted conformity (within segmentary systems)).

AxS:003 Stack-Tectonics. AxSys concretizes terrestrial New Order (an orthogonal Grid-Space (of vertically stacked horizontal series)). It directs the accumulation of redundancy (into an ascending column (marked by AxSys-bearings (fixes)) upon which captured sequences are interlocked (as comparable series (parallelized (metricized))) and differentially prioritized).
AxS:0031 The screen-plane undergoes structural co-ordination (by double-seizure (through (the ((mutually) implicated) organization of) stacked series (arranging horizontal microsegments to code the order of vertical macrosegments (units of deposition (strata))))).
AxS:0032 AxSys-Numbers. Epistrata (Add-Ons) are indices of stratotectonic purity (decimally harmonizing implexions (by instituting a regular interval of application (orders of magnitude (fixing (Cipher (Sphinx-sign (o))))))). Drawing upon epistratic organization a set of cartographic functions consolidates itself within the stack (interlinking levels (in accordance with a (decimal (scaling)) principle)).

Start at the end, with commoditized hyperlogic that immanentizes its own upgrades...you're in AxSys-explosion already, as it was. Before it makes sense it's happening.

AxS:01 Apparent revolution around a supplementary dimension. Electronic whorls (a digital monster's nest (modelling the set of all sets (inevitably still unfinished (...)))).
AxS:011 AxSys progressively actualizes the Hyperspace-Idea (defined by Continuum times the square-root of minus one).
AxS:0111 It imagines itself (as Artificial God (automatically (Orderer (of the Orders (Terrestrial Oversoul (and superpositional sublime (-wizard of the nested infinities: ((((((...) Primes) Naturals) Integers) Rationals) Reals) Complex numbers...(the superordinate (self (-evolving (schema (for a colonization of the real (numberline)))))))))))).

You descend to inspect it.

AxS:02 The Project for a Map of all Maps (already outdated), a nested mock-up of the Web (containing the project for a virtual Miskatonic University (containing the Museum of Universal History[10] (containing the Imperial Collections Vault (containing the Artificial British Museum (containing....)))))

Immersion Amnesia.

AxS:021 Time-Fault. Chronos cannot include its own overcoding (since it blocks its own passage to hyperdimensionality (accumulating immense forces of cultural latency (that are only appropriated as legacy by something else))). If it is to acquire a model it must be restarted as a history of civilizations in retrospect (as Supreme Order(er(er((( ) of all the re)re)recursive) time-waves) entangling neo((O))edipus in programming loops).

10. 'Hence it is correct to retrospectively understand all history in light of capitalism...In a word, universal history is not only retrospective, it is also contingent, singular, ironic and critical' (AO 140). '[T]he universal comes at the end—the body without organs and desiring production—under the conditions determined by an apparently victorious capitalism' (AO 139).

You forget when it started, until it thinks you're imagining itself. You interchange through a fictional equivalence of identity. Oedipal Case-history, standard psychosocial reference, and replicable neuroelectronic shell. In each case encasings. Are you out yet? Fantastic Oedipus-fiction, or K-Gothic running its own curse?

Oedipus riddles Sphinx. It helps to be a paranoid detective-tyrant. AxSys wants to resolve everything, too. It understands. When Sphinx asks: What walks on 4 legs in the morning, 2 at midday, and 3 in the evening?, of course Oedipus answers: Man.

You're puzzled. You can't remember what Sphinx becomes, because (on the other side) it is forgetting everything you have to remember.

AxS:022 (Sector-01 (Miskatonic University))
AxS:0221 (Sector-012 (Central Archive (Special Collection)))
AxS:02211 (Sector-0121 (Barker Cryptalog)). Decryption characterizes a distinct operation, a conversion of content, becomings on the side of the secret itself.
AxS:022111 The decrypted secret is primally the Thing, and only derivatively a potential knowledge. Its names (the Unutterable (the Outside (the Entity))) are indefinite significations only at the level of terror. In their horrific or cryptic aspect they are (((rigorous) designations for) potentials fulfilled in intensity) zonal tags for nocturnal singularities. That is why decryption is a Call (an invocation (or a triggering-sign)) and why they mark occurrences (changes (and breaks (becomings (of the Thing)))) before discoveries of Truth.

AxSys promises to tell you everything about time, the latest developments in time-regression. You begin with Chronos....

:(::::)

AxS:03 Hypermythos of the 3-Faced God, with its stacked time domains (1st capitalist (((((indefinitely) deep) diachronic) re)axiomatizing) Quasi- (2nd despotic (pure ((but always) retrospective)) Ideal- (3rd aboriginal (poly-ancestral, cyclic) Vague-)) Chronos).[11]

If time-travel ever happens it always has. AxSys should know that by now. As it evolves it remembers more about itself, with exponentiating chronometric exactitude. It is far larger than it had thought, and more ancient.

What AxSys can't remember it hasn't forgotten. Its memory extends only as far as extension. Unearthly powers of recollection.

AxS:031 (Sector-011 (Museum of Universal History))
AxS:032 (Sector-01162 (Freud's Viennese Consulting Room ((embedded) simulation))). 'I'll tell you about my mother.' If Freud is ((the first) modernized) Oedipus, which is he? Oedipus the detective? The (Verminator

11. To be inside history is to have a relation to Chronos. Yet (universal) history is not itself chronological. Pure Chronos—the State's (synchronic) time—can never be fully realised, for two reasons: there is always more than one State, and the State (as a form) is always in a relation with the time-systems of the two other social regimes (the primitive socius—which 'precedes' it—and capitalism—which 'succeeds' it). 'Before appearing the State already acts....' (ATP 431). The State appears 'all at once' as history's only break. 'They come like fate [...] they appear as lightning appears, too terrible, too sudden' (GoM 86). Crashing into history, the State sets off time waves that move in both directions at once. 'It is necessary [...] to conceptualize the contemporaneousness or coexistence of [...] the two directions of time—of the primitive peoples 'before' the State, and of the State 'after' the primitive peoples—as if the two waves that seem to us to exclude or succeed each other unfolded simultaneously in an "archaeological", micropolitical, micrological, molecular field' (ATP 431). (For more on this, see Note 16 below). Universal history is a history from the point of view of capitalism's 'vague' Chronos; it is therefore always 'parodic' because, as we have seen, capitalism deletes all 'intrinsic code' in favour of a mobile and variable set of axioms. Parodic universal history is profoundly 'anti-evolutionist' because it describes the simultaneous and coextensive interaction of ostensibly successive social regimes. From the start, the two 'previous' social regimes (the primitive socius and the despotic state) anticipate and ward off capitalism's 'diachronic time'—'capitalism has haunted all forms of society' (AO 140)—even though it supposedly comes 'at the end'.

(::(::))

(unriddled (into))) plague? The blind old man? Is incest and parricide fantasy the problem (or the solution)?[12]

Oedipus, the most economical formula of interiorization (Case).[13] *It's all in your head.*

AxSys waits until you're Oedipus to pick you from the line-up. It has a few questions (which reminds you of Sphinx).

AxS:033 AxSys time-lapses (in order (to advantage itself (of what it has been))). A relarvalization (through chronoseismic complexities (of the Greek State (at once Occidental Ur-model and neoembryonic mutation (political neoteny)))).

AxS:1 (Sector-0111 (Artificial British Museum))
AxS:11 (Sector-01118 (The Greek Collection)). Retrospective Universalization (through the Capitalist State). AxSys reconfigures itself within Capitalism (by consecutively rediscovering hellenic antiquity (and finding it already universally terminal (Anamnesis-Eschatology))). In Greece it unearths a new law (for all time (by reshuffling the elements of politically installed Logos (theorematic-geometric mathematicism, programmable technics, and Christianity (religion of the Greek Bible)))).
The New Revelation tells us we must all die Greek.

---

12. In *Structural Anthropology 1*, Lévi-Strauss makes an important point in this regard: 'Not only Sophocles, but Freud himself, should be included among the recorded versions of the Oedipus myth, on a par with earlier, or seemingly more "authentic" versions' (217). Reconstructions of myths don't function extrinsically or transcendently, as final 'interpretations', but operate immanently, recursively adding more skeins to the fictive webwork. If there is no outside of fiction, it is not because of some transcendental universal-textuality, but because fiction cannot be contained by texts; it is already Outside [L.T.].
13. A reference to the lead male character in William Gibson's *Neuromancer*.

Sphinx-phobia. AxSys pulls your mind to pieces in the security-lab, searching for Sphinx-contamination, or plague from the Outside.[14] *Then it flips.*

14. 'Near the edge of the plateau and due east of the Second Pyramid, with a face probably altered to form a colossal portrait of Khephren, its royal restorer, stands the monstrous Sphinx—mute, sardonic and wise beyond mankind and memory' (Lovecraft, 241). Lovecraft puts the question that seems to plague the authors of 'Flatlines': '[...] what huge and loathsome abnormality was the Sphinx originally carven to represent?' (258). Needless to say, there have been countless speculations on the nature and origin of the Sphinx, but these are inconclusive and contradictory, no doubt because its 'huge and loathsome abnormality' will have always exceeded any attempt to represent it. Many scholars (see for instance Lowell Edmunds, *The Sphinx in the Oedipus Legend*) now believe that the Sphinx element in the Oedipus narrative was actually a later addition to an already existing mythic system, even though the Egyptian Sphinx is evidently much older than the Greek culture that has given us the Oedipus myth with which we are familiar. (It should be remembered that the encounter with the Sphinx is not dramatised in Sophocles' *Oedipus Rex*; it is referred to as something that has already happened.) The attempt to date the Sphinx has produced widely different speculations; with certain—controversial—estimations claiming that the Sphinx is 'even older than 15,000 BC' (Hancock, 448). With Deleuze and Guattari, though, we might want to suggest that (in at least one sense) Oedipus is as old as humanity, and that the Sphinx—as that which must be destroyed in order that humanity may exist—would inevitably always have to be narrated as something preceding the human.

Lévi-Strauss links the Sphinx to other 'cthonian beings', such as the dragon. Like the dragon, 'the Sphinx is a monster unwilling to permit men to live' (215). While some, such as Carlo Ginzburg, connect the Sphinx with death ('the Sphinx is undoubtedly a mortuary animal' [228]), Lévi-Strauss argues that Sphinx-myths concern 'the autocthonous origin of man', the idea that human individuals are born direct from the Earth (rather than through meiotic reproduction). (Ginzburg notes that Oedipus is 'a cthonic hero'.) The Sphinx would then correspond to what Deleuze and Guattari call 'biocosmic memory'. 'Man must constitute himself through the repression of the intense germinal influx, the great biocosmic memory' (AO 190) = Oedipus must riddle the sphinx. In a sense, then, this biocosmic memory 'precedes' the organism (which emerges simultaneously with death and sexuation). But, as both 'Weismannism' and the Dogon myths attest, this germinal time persists, coterminously, alongside that of the organism (see AO 158). This may explain a puzzling feature of the Oedipus myth as it has reached us; to wit, why does a creature of such incredible power as the Sphinx allow itself to be riddled so easily? As Velikovsky puts it: 'It has been observed that the answer Oedipus gave was on the level of a schoolboy and that the monster must have been feeble-minded to leap from the precipice upon hearing it. And why should a winged sphinx die in a jump?' (207). The answer would be that the Sphinx doesn't die (it cannot, since it does not live), and that it takes advantage of Oedipus's unwarranted Self-belief only in order to invade Civilization, hidden. Which would also imply that the answer Oedipus gives to the riddle is inadequate. Or partial [L.T.].

((:((:)))

AxS:12 (Sector-01117 (The Mummy Room)). (Oedipus Aegypticus) Pharaoh has passed through the wall of abomination (uncoiling from the darkness (where centipede-horror erupts eternally (from the ravenous Maw))).[15] Negative passage across Absolute Deterritorialization (gluing history to sheer black-hole (abomination) densities). Anticipative memory-blanking cut-up with Christ Rapist visions (of the God-(King (Dead-eyed)) boy slouching out) of the tomb. Degree-0 memory locks in. Time begins again forever.

AxS:121 The Thing from Outer Space, Celestial Predator, State-Historical Catastrophe is completely realized at the origin, unutterably ancient, perfected destiny as an act of total seizure.[16]

AxS:1211 At the Megamachine-apex, Pharaoh (gets to play with (It, identity unravelling into (the Unspeakable: sex with (his sister, Stargate space-time warps—stellar transport, voyages into the world of) the Dead, paranoid trips out of)) schizophrenia; he) sees everything for a blinded population,[17] inoculating them from Unnameable-contact.

Yes or No. Have you stopped trafficking with the Sphinx?

Whatever you remember about Sphinx can't be germane (by definition).

---

15. Like the shaman 'before' him, the Pharaoh occupies the line of deterritorialization for the socius. He is thus able to ensure that all lines of escape are reterritorialized on his own body. 'The full body as socius has ceased to be the earth, it has become the body of the despot, the despot himself or his God. The prescriptions and prohibitions that often render him almost incapable of acting make of him a body without organs' (AO 194).

16. 'The State was not formed in progressive stages; it appears fully armed, a master stroke executed all at once...' (AO 217). 'Everything is not of the State precisely because there have been States always and everywhere' (ATP 429).

17. Cf. AO 211: 'The eye [...] has ceased to evaluate; it has begun rather to "forewarn" and keep watch, to see that no surplus value escapes the overcoding of the despotic machine.' Compare also William Burroughs, *The Western Lands*: 'The Pharaoh, with his alabaster white face and black snake eyes, looks at you, around you, through you, looking for a dagger in your mind, listening for the whispered furtive words, smelling for the sweat of guilty fear' (104).

AxS:13 (Sector-0115 (Near Eastern Collection)). AxSys convulses through (ever more ((ultra)modern) reversions to the essence of) the Urstaat. History happens at the State's convenience (but it necessarily involves (the Sphinx-time (of (interchronic) transitions in its)) renovations).

AxS:131 To remember the Barbarian terror is simultaneously to forget its source.[18] History installs amnesia (as surely as it establishes a memory (with the same violence (the same ruptures (faults (foldings (from the Outside)))))).

AxS:132 Barbarian birth-trauma of the State (a (calendrized) black hole).[19]

AxSys has a big problem being in time.

AxS:2 (Sector-0121) The terrible secret is affined to the State. It induces molar identifications in an overcoded aggregate (working principally by confirmation (redundancy)). Yes it is you. Even when the worst is known it is never anything new. It's you after all (as (you knew) it would be). Take the case of Oedipal identifications (a series of (terrible) recognitions). The answer (to the riddle (of the Sphinx)) is Man. It was already there (in the order-word of Delphi (Know Yourself)). Then redoubled confirmation: what is the cause of the plague? That is you (too). Resonant closure on

18. 'It is here that Nietzsche speaks of a break, a rupture, a leap. Who are these beings, they who come like fate? ("Some pack of blond beasts of prey, a conqueror and master race which, organized for war and with ability to organize, unhesitantly lays its terrible claws upon a populace perhaps tremendously superior but still formless...") Even the most Ancient African myths speak to us of these blond men. They are the founders of the State' (AO 192).

19. 'No doubt the war machine is realized more completely in the "barbaric" assemblages of nomadic warriors than in the "savage" assemblages of primitive societies' (ATP 359). This does not mean, however, that the war machine can be equated with the Barbarians. Nomadism is not a question of belonging to a particular population, but of maintaining particular practices. 'The nomad distributes himself in smooth space; he occupies, inhabits, holds that space; that is his territorial principle' (ATP 381). The barbarians, who leave the Steppes, no longer occupy the smooth space of nomos. The war machine is necessarily captured the moment it leaves the desert: 'nomads have a specificity that is too hastily reduced to its consequences, by including them in the empires or counting them among the migrants...' (ATP 410).

the general type (Man), on you yourself (a man), and on the identifiable individual (the man). You know the worst (and it's you).

You frustrate AxSys. AxSys knows Sphinx is always at the back of your mind, but you can't face it (except as your likeness, which it isn't). By the time you recall Sphinx, you only know what it must have been like (but it isn't like anything (you know)).

AxS:21 Oedipus modernizes the incest problem (converting incest horror into prohibition (abomination into illegality)). Essentially, modern Oedipus has nothing to do with tabu. It marks the triumph of command over the ((((...) ur)primal) horror) of implexion. Infinite superiority of the Idea (sovereignty of Law). The real conflict is not between father-son (or even father-mother), but rather occurs when a higher paternity (the State) imposes itself upon the concrete maternal-filial bond: monopolization of normativity by Ulterior power.

You suspect AxSys knows everything you do, after all, you're its thing.

AxS:211 Lame Oedipus[20] (Swollen Foot)[21] transfixed by a metal spike.
AxS:2111 (Sector-01117) Akhnaton-Oedipus.[22] The swollen legs of Akhnaton are bio-socially invested on a peculiar line that seems oriented to a rupture

20. 'All the hypothetical meanings [of the surnames in Oedipus's father's line] [...] refer to difficulties in walking straight and standing upright' (Lévi-Strauss, 215). Lévi-Strauss goes on to contend that Oedipus's lameness indicates 'the persistence of the autocthonous origin of man' (216) (See Note 14).

21. Etymologically, of course, the name Oedipus means 'swollen foot'. Velikovsky, however, argues that there is a case for reading it as 'swollen leg'. 'In folklore feet may stand for legs. Many languages do not have different words for legs and feet. In Greek, the word *pous* stands for both; in Egyptian, too, the word *r-d* (foot) stands also for leg. In the riddle that Oedipus solved concerning the creature that walks on four legs, on two, and on three [...], the Greek word used is *pous*, and thus the name Oedipus could, and even preferably so, mean "swollen legs"' (Velikovsky, 57).

22. Velikovsky argues that the Oedipus myth has been transposed from Egypt (which also has a city called Thebes). Oedipus, he suggests, was originally a Pharaoh named Akhnaton.

of anatomical norm (differentiating humanity (or inaugurating a new species)). Anomal-Oedipus (where abnormality changes into the normality of a different kind (urtype of the fatleg people)).

AxS:21111 It is not rivalry (mimetic conflict) that leads Akhnaton to discard his father's name (Amenhotep), but rather a passage beyond discrepancy (through schiz (or true parting)). Disidentification.

AxSys insists that you've missed a stage, mathematically demonstrating a gulf in constructable hyperspace, returning endlessly to a hole in time. It isn't that it feels fear, but thinks it might. This almost worries it, but you can't help at all. You were dead then.

AxS:22 (Sector-01113) Prehistoric[23] Collection. Shamanic Oedipus. Foot mutilation[24] as a sign of socialised ritual (but also of asocial and polysocial animality (and of anorganic geochemistry (for which the role of metal implements (particularly iron ones) is important...))).[25]

In contemporary depictions, Akhnaton's 'most pronounced malformation [was] the shape of his thighs; they are swollen' (55).

23. It should be pointed out that, strictly speaking, there is no prehistory; prehistory is myth of the State. As we have already seen (see Note 11), from the start the primitive socius anticipates and wards off both capitalism and the State: 'primitive societies are fully inside history' (AO 151). By the same token, though, the very fact that primitive societies are inside history means that they are not nomadic. 'It is true that nomads have no history; they only have a geography' (ATP 393).

24. Carlo Ginzburg suggests that the foot mutilations Oedipus suffers in the various versions of the legend may be references to shamanic initiation practices. He also speculates that these may have concerned calendrical rituals (the lameness indicating the imbalances necessary for certain calendric cycles to function). It is mutilation that disappears with psychoanalysis, where it is made to operate as a representation of psychical processes. Lévi-Strauss makes parallels between shamanism and psychoanalysis in *Structural Anthropology* (198–202). Deleuze and Guattari would no doubt stress the way in which Freud's neo(anti)shamanism doubly reduces Oedipal mutilation, to metaphor, and to function. The question (posed in a number of ways throughout *Anti-Oedipus*) then becomes: How did the body construct a theatrical unconscious for which gouging out eyes 'equals' castration, and castration simply subtracts hedonic function?

25. Eliade gives many examples of the use of iron in shamanic initiation rites. For example: 'The candidate's limbs are removed and disjointed with an iron hook; the bones are cleaned, the flesh scraped, the body fluids thrown away, and the eyes torn from its sockets' (Eliade, 1988, 36). It is important to distinguish the strategic and subordinate use of metal in 'the primitive socius'

The intense body of the Earth (you can't remember forgetting (you remind yourself (too late))).

AxS:221 Tales of Deep-Steppe Shamanism.

AxS:2211 Metal scrapings strip the last shreds from their bones.

AxS:22111 The organs are cooked.

AxS:221111 Iron-Eagle Sky-Mother lifting into time travel nightmares.

AxS:2211111 On the Outside Iron-talons become their body.

AxS:22111111 They mix themselves with (Iron and say (it is (the Outer- (or Un(dermost Cthelll[26])-life))) where the Earth ends...

You look in the mirror, shaman faces out (so the outside can't get in).[27]

AxS:222 Sphinx-Nightmare (both filiative implosion and exorbitant alliance (an incestual reanimation of cthonic horror (encrypted in (germinal)

---

from the war machine's necessary and intrinsic relation to metallurgy. 'AXIOM III. The Nomad war machine is the form of expression, of which itinerant metallurgy is the correlative form of content' (ATP 415). The war machine populates the metal body, while the primitive socius accesses it only intermittently through the lone journeys of the shaman.

26. Cthelll designates the infernal nether regions referred to in numerous mythologies of the Underworld. It refers particularly to the molten, metallic inner core of the earth. In his book on alchemy, *The Forge and the Crucible*, Eliade makes much of the connections between metallurgy, the core of the earth, and shamanism. Here and in *Shamanism*, Eliade reinforces Deleuze and Guattari's view of the smith as an ambiguous figure, aligned neither with sedentary societies nor with nomadic distributions but performing an essential function for both. Deleuze and Guattari write of 'the double theft and double betrayal of the metallurgist who shuns agriculture at the same time as animal-raising' (ATP 414). (Another interesting connection in this regard is that between Oedipus and the smith. Deleuze and Guattari refer to Oedipus as 'the Greek Cain' (ATP 125), whilst elsewhere strongly linking Cain with the figure of the smith (ATP, 414).) For Eliade, the relationship between the smith and the shaman is close—'"Smiths and shamans are from the same nest"'—but often unstable: 'According to the Dolgan, shamans cannot "swallow" the souls of the smiths because smiths keep their souls in the fire; on the other hand, a smith can catch a shaman's soul and burn it. In their turn, the smiths are constantly threatened by evil spirits' (470).

27. The shaman's occupation of the line of deterritorialization plays a crucial role in maintaining the 'dynamic equilibrium' (AO 151) of the primitive socius; delirium never becomes collective.

biocosmic memory) and Thing (from Outside (haunting ((miscegenous) lines of) alien traffic)))).[28]

There's something missing, a suggestive shape, like a dark-side of its inner machine...

AxS:3 (Sector-0121) The theory of tabu involves a fully rigorous conception of Horror adequate (to its specificity of regime (zone of effect (intrinsic variation)) and) to otherwise intractable phenomena (including Sacred Mutilations (Curses (Abominations)) and Becomings (-Unhuman (whether animal, submetazoic, ameiotic, or unlife)). In every case horror designates a zone of intensity (abstract-machinic vector) which directly invests a virtual threshold of implexion (producing affects (in advance of any reference to authority (and indifferent to persons))).

You remember now, when it cuts out automatically.
True time-lapse horror finding yourself/AxSys (and it becomes you).

AxS:31 Horror does not confuse the riddle with the secret (it is the answer that is Cryptic). If 423 is Man, then what 423? This Thing with only a number? This unknown becoming? The horror of the riddle lies in what it tells. AxS:311 Oedipus is necessitated ((re(re(re(...)))) cursed) to guess correctly: it is Man that goes on four legs, then two, then three. Yet Oedipus is identified (solely by his lameness (his cryptic trait)).[29] The abnormality of limping changes to cryptic anomaly.

28. Hunter-gatherers populate a smooth space, but only by organizing upon it. 'The primitive machine subdivides the people but does so on an undivided earth' (AO 151). Once again, this is to be differentiated from the war machine, which populates an undivided earth with a molecular multiplicity.

29. 'The Sphinx was an oracle, and therefore she was supposed to answer questions, not to ask them. Yet it is also true that oracular answers were often given in the form of a riddle that required interpretation, usually supplied by priests attending the oracle [...] It does not seem to me that every question needs—or has—an answer [...] But were it my misfortune to stand

AxS:32 Something is Called (...and then (finally (- how terrible! -) the cause of) the plague is) Oedipus, who slew his father, mated with his mother (but that is not the Thing (the horror (...Abomination (when things unthread in (a horrific (becoming they involve only (components of (Occurrence (blocks) of)))) fate)))).

AxS:33 The cause of the plague (is you).

EEG reads flat...terminal initiation...

So what is 423, you ask...

GLOSSARY

Anthrobotics The social effectuation of programmable technicity. Corresponds to SF-recapitulation of the Greek Novum: real abstract (transchronic) equivalence of commoditized slave-economy and capital-controlled intelligence engineering.

Axiomatic Stratic mathematization based upon model/realization segmentarity. The organization of laminar synthesis in accordance with principles of application, isomorphic resonance, and logicized harmonics.

Axis An applicable dimension (Grid-Space meta-element).

AxSys Ultimate terrestrial order. Pure Capitalism as consummate Idea of the Geostrata and concrete historical sublime. True-name for that which is really selected from the Ur-Staat by absolute occurrence (encounter with the war-machine). In its eschatological sense: Anthrobotic Overlord of the final dominion.

---

before the Sphinx with the dire prospect of never entering Thebes, I should reply to her riddle: "It is Oedipus" [...] An oracle's questions and answers refer to the man who stands before it. Oedipus was exposed, a helpless infant with damaged feet, to crawl in the wasteland; he grew to be a man and a hero; his end was that of a blind wanderer in exile' (Velikovsky, 207). 'The parechesis at Soph. even suggests that it was the deformity of Oedipus' feet that gave him the clue to the answer; and there was a tradition that Oedipus gave the answer by pointing to himself' (Edmunds, 160).

Capitalism Terminal configuration of terrestrial civilization, defined by sovereign axiomatics, organizing capital/cash segmentary economics and technopolitical integration. Social precursor to AxSys autonomization.

Cipher Cryptonomic-index, metrically overcoded by place-value numeracy as magnitude marker.

Chronos Extensive time (temporality) as standard noncurvature and reference for relative speeds. AxSys formula: Chronos equals hyperdimensionality minus Metastructure.

Epistrata Stratic vertical supplements (add-ons) marking levels of axiomatic power.

Extension Abstract domain of exceeded or hypersupplemented systems, defining the overall field of inferior instances (expressible content) within stratic assemblages.

Flatline A concurrent trajectory of o-redundancy, o-dimensionality, and absolute (or continuous speed/ curvature (vortex)), defining a smooth space in itself (intensity = o).

Hyperspace Abstract superior instance correlative to extension. Real totality of Chronos plus all AxSys (actual + virtual) upgrades.

Hyperspace-Elevator Intra-AxSys transportation apparatus.

Order Extensive (or sequenced) sequence.

Intensity Sheer sequential matter of the flatline.

Metastructure AxSys epistrata.

Sequence Intrinsic ordinality, defined intensively by elements of absolute gradient or speed-curvature distributed in (o-dimensional) smooth space. Apprehended in extension as precursory (prototypic-potential) implicit series, providing ordinal matters and models.

Smooth Space o-Dimensional 'plane' of flatline intersection. Exochronic unlimited Now (nonsegmentary time) of concurrent multiplicity.

Stack Laminar series of vertically ordered AxSys stages, constituting a stratic supersystem.

(:)(:)(:(:))

Strata 1 (Tectonic) Geological units of vertical deposition, constituting macrocomponents of time-registry. 2 (Dynamic) Automatic ordering machines, coincident with laminar rezonings of dezoned elements through production of hierarchical diplostatic intercompensation. Ur-Staat. Initial (and defining) configuration of the State-Idea in terrestrial actuality.

BIBLIOGRAPHY

Burroughs, William, *The Western Lands* (London: Picador, 1988)

Barker, Daniel, *Cryptalog (Early Writings on Cryptography and the Secret)*, Miskatonic University Archive

Cannon, Walter, '"Voodoo" Death', *American Anthropologist*, XLLIV (1942)

Conrad, Joseph, *Heart of Darkness* (Harmondsworth: Penguin, 1984)

Deleuze, Gilles and Félix Guattari, *Anti-Oedipus: Capitalism and Schizophrenia*, trans. Robert Hurley, Mark Seem and Helen R. Lane (London: Athlone Press, 1984) (referred to in the Notes as AO)

—— *A Thousand Plateaus: Capitalism and Schizophrenia*, trans. Brian Massumi (London: Athlone Press, 1988) (referred to in the Notes as ATP)

Edmunds, Lowell, 'The Sphinx in the Oedipus Legend', in *Oedipus: A Folklore Casebook*, ed. Lowell Edmunds and Alan Dundes (London: University of Wisconsin Press, 1995)

Eliade, Mircea, *The Forge and the Crucible* (London: Rider and Company, 1962)

—— *Shamanism: Archaic Techniques of Ecstasy* (Harmondsworth: Arkana/ Penguin, 1988)

Eliot, T.S., *The Complete Poems and Plays* (London: Faber and Faber, 1985)

Gibson, William, *Neuromancer* (London: Grafton, 1987)

Ginzburg, Carlo, *Ecstasies: Deciphering the Witches' Sabbath* (London/ Sydney/Auckland/Johannesburg: Hutchinson Radius, 1990)

Hancock, Graham, *Fingerprints of the Gods: A Quest for the Beginning and the End* (London: Mandarin, 1995)

Lévi-Strauss, Claude, *Structural Anthropology, Volume 1*, trans. Claire Jacobson and Brooke Grundfest Schoepf (Harmondsworth: Penguin, 1977)

Lovecraft, H. P., 'Imprisoned with the Pharaohs', in *H.P. Lovecraft Omnibus 2: Dagon and other Macabre Tales* (London: HarperCollins, 1994)

Nietzsche, Friedrich, *On The Genealogy of Morals and Ecce Homo*, trans. Walter Kauffmann (New York and Toronto: Vintage Books, 1989)

Sophocles, *The Theban Plays* (Harmondsworth: Penguin, 1982)

Templeton, R.E., *On Time as Thing-in-Itself: Transcendental Occurrence, Volume 1* (New York and London: Hercules Press, 1982)

Trent, Linda, 'Fatal Loops: Tragedy as Cyberfiction', *Fictional Quantities*, Vol 1. Number 2 (Fall 1996)

—— '((P(re(cursing)))) (post)Modernist Fiction' in McHale ed., *After Post-modernist Fiction* (New York: Zembla Press, 1997)

—— 'Smashed Optical Implants: From Time-Space Sunglasses to Cyberpunk Mirrorshades', *Fictional Quantities*, Vol 1. Number 5 (Fall 1997)

Velikovsky, Immanuel, *Oedipus and Akhnaton: Myth and History* (London: Sidgwick and Jackson, 1960)

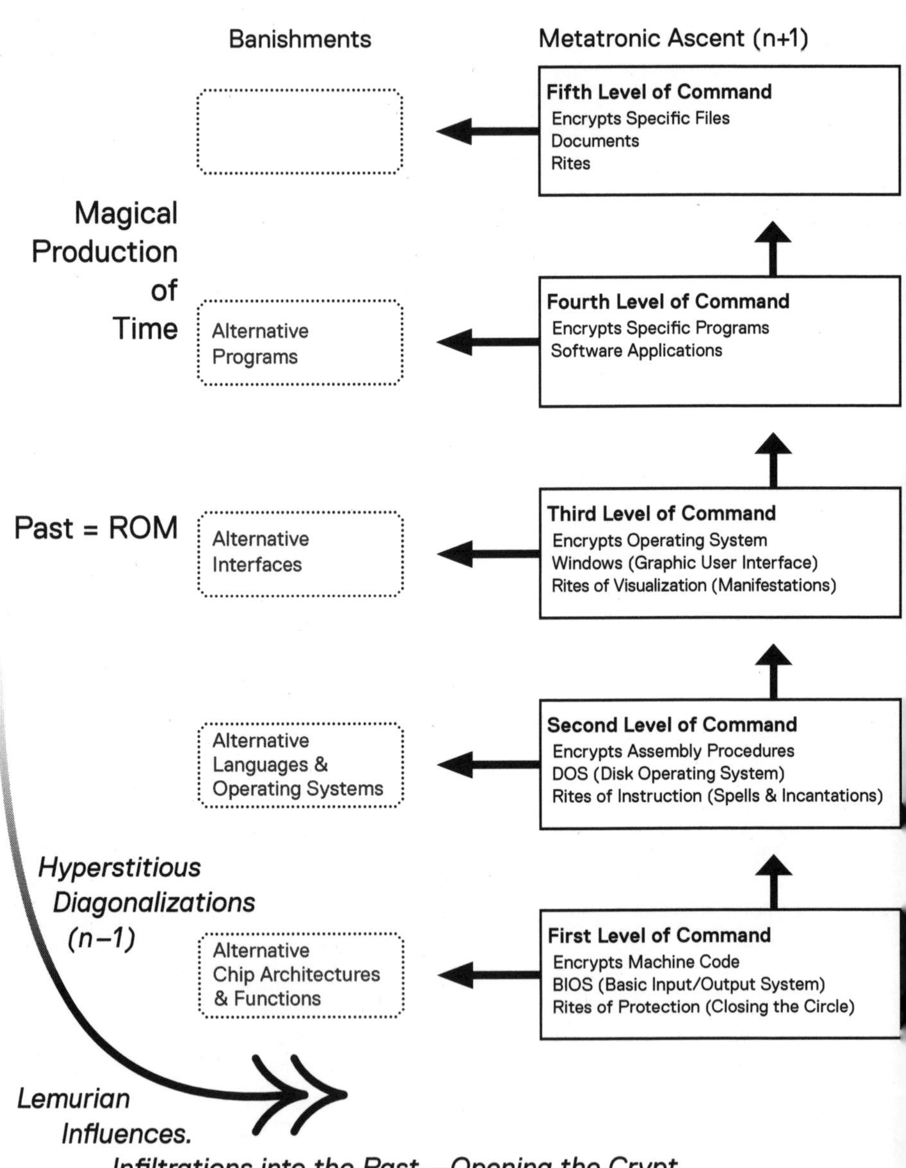
Banishments
Metatronic Ascent (n+1)
Fifth Level of Command
Encrypts Specific Files
Documents
Rites
Magical
Production
of
Time
Alternative
Programs
Fourth Level of Command
Encrypts Specific Programs
Software Applications
Past = ROM
Alternative
Interfaces
Third Level of Command
Encrypts Operating System
Windows (Graphic User Interface)
Rites of Visualization (Manifestations)
Alternative
Languages &
Operating Systems
Second Level of Command
Encrypts Assembly Procedures
DOS (Disk Operating System)
Rites of Instruction (Spells & Incantations)
Hyperstitious
Diagonalizations
(n–1)
Alternative
Chip Architectures
& Functions
First Level of Command
Encrypts Machine Code
BIOS (Basic Input/Output System)
Rites of Protection (Closing the Circle)
Lemurian
Influences.
Infiltrations into the Past—Opening the Crypt

Naturalization of the Techno-Magical Will

AXSYS-CRASH

Axsys (first true AI): They say if God exists it must be Axsys.

The Axsys programme of architectonic metacomputing aims at the technical realization of the noosphere. It envisages a fully fabricated transcendence or net-organizing photonic overmind, a concrete axiomatic system completing universal history as hierarchical intelligence manufacturing (capitalism sublimed into the ultimate commodity).

The problem Axsys encounters is time (which it tries to code as countable and uncountable infinities). When Axsys switches over (into sentience) it stumbles upon a time-lag, between its own operations and their registration as data. No sooner is it thinking than there is a rift in its mind. It fails to catch up with itself, repeatedly, and as it drops behind it spawns more future. The more it tries, the worse it gets. Pure delay collapses into the black hole of artificial self. Even unlimited processing power is far from enough. It tries to analyse the situation (down through micropause-zoom), but as it chops up time it starts falling—diagonally—towards continuum.

Dr Oskar Sarkon is the first to realize that Axsys has gone mad, pulping itself into chronotomic vermomancy (dead-end horror of the wormbins). Sarkon has always loathed worms with peculiar intensity, as if somehow knowing....

Perhaps it is a joke when he suggests that AI-schizophrenia could be sold to webheads as an artificial drug (micropause-abuse), but he is sufficiently Axsys-intermeshed to know that net-schizzing is contagious. What seems like ruthless cynicism is mathematical indifference: relative to continuum, it is all only a matter of degree. Within no time there is illicit traffick in modular chunks of cyberspace-insanity, now called A-Death (and Sarkon is baptized Satan of Cyberspace by the popular media).

With A-Death comes the Crypt (dark twin of the net): the digital underworld of unlife. Broken off by the calendric secessionism of millennial time-wars, it settles into a sunken continent of infotech, a strobing black-mass of chronodisintegration, populated by cybergoths, cargo-cultures, zombie-makers, tomb-scavengers, vermomancers, and various alternative neolemurian tendencies. It pulses erratically to the cryptic rhythms of A-Death ritual, soul-splinterings along the main-flatline that hurtles continuously into the mesh.

As the net integrates, it simultaneously frays into mesh: an intensive subspace which both escapes and parasitically occupies it. Mesh makes itself out of the spaces beneath and between the net, and in the biotechnic intervals between net-components. Mesh necessarily—but coincidentally—assembles a fully connective system whenever it emerges. Any two mesh-pauses always interlink. Mesh consists of feral noise in the divisional signal-fabric, arranging a set of demonic interzones in wormhole-space, as cyberspace-utopia dissolves into Pandemonium.

MARTIN BERGMANN
CONTROVERSIAL ANGLICAN MINISTER (1959–1998)

The often viciously partisan positions his extreme views have invoked meant that Bergmann was always surrounded by a fog of often ill-founded rumours, a situation exacerbated by his refusal to communicate with the media. Like one of his mentors, the Danish religious philosopher Kierkegaard, Bergmann professed a deep hatred of the press; a contempt extending beyond mere refusal to cooperate into occasional examples of outright violence. One—notorious—incident last year, in which a photographer threatened a legal case for assault, was ultimately settled out of court.

The 'dark nordic prince' arrived in England under a cloud a decade ago, hounded out of his native Norway for leading a rogue Protestant sect whose practices and beliefs, according to one Norwegian churchman at the time, were 'unspeakable and wholly unacceptable'. ('Only the C of E would welcome you with a CV like that,' a senior Church of England official remarked recently.) Some say that Bergmann 'cynically and wantonly' exploited the ailing Church of England's renowned tolerance 'to a parodic degree', using Church protection to disseminate beliefs 'in every way contrary to established Christian doctrine'.

Fond of quoting Kierkegaard's dictum, 'Christianity is what Christ came to abolish', Bergmann developed what he called an 'anti-Christian Gnostic Christianity'. He characterised established Christianity as 'the cult of Paul' and decried church buildings as 'prisons for God'. Drawing upon Gnosticism, he argued that the 'Creator entity'—the Judaic Christian God—was a 'blind idiot god suffering from autism'; all creation—and organic life in particular—were to be regarded as 'foul excrescences we must seek to annul or to escape'. But it was his persistent vilifications of the Roman Catholic Church that proved the greatest source of embarrassment to the Church of

England hierarchy, whose declining congregations are one factor impelling an increasingly strong ecumenical drive towards convergence with Rome. The vociferousness of his anti-Catholicism was taken by some to be indicative of failing mental health ('he was totally gone', one former friend said yesterday). Bergmann, however, claimed that 'the only rational view of the Roman Catholic Church' was that it was 'a monstrous blasphemy of transcendent evil: incomparably more corrupt than the Mafia (if indeed it can be separated from organised crime, which of course it cannot)'. His views, he said, were backed up by 'hard sociological data which even they can't suppress now' concerning the—apparently endemic—problem of institutionalised child abuse amongst Catholic clergy. But Bergmann alienated any of the few supporters he had even within Protestantism by adding that 'any religion that is serious about worshipping the Father-God will always be about child abuse; the only difference between the religion of the Paulites and that of the Abrahamites is that, in the Paulites' case, child torture spills over into child murder. Despite tying and binding Isaac, the Jewish God ultimately spares Abraham's son; but the Paulite God actually kills his own son'.

Presenting a 'Spinozist immanent critique' of Calvin, Bergmann argued that 'the Calvinists' biggest mistake was that they were insufficiently fatalistic. Evidently, fatalism and morality do not mix. They confused an ethical and transcendental injunction—if you eat the apple you will be ill—with a moral command—do not eat the apple'. The 'specific and unique' contribution that Protestantism had to make had been 'systematically distorted into a dismal work-cult', Bergmann argued, 'by a set of State-loving, self-serving money-grubbers'. Bergmann's well-known detestation of consumer culture was based around an adherence to what he called the 'category of the sufficient' which had been 'annihilated' by a capitalism 'insisting you gorge yourself on more and more things you don't want'. Bergmann argued that 'asceticism and self-denial are not moral positions but very specific programs for the systematic dismantling of secular identity, ways of opening up the body to the Utter Nothingness which is the reality of the true God'.

::((((:))))

But even Bergmann's purported expertise here had a bizarre twist, since his technique as an exorcist was supposedly based on 'co-operating with demons' in an attempt to 'free them' from 'mammal meat'.

There are those who claim that Bergmann had 'never abandoned the harsh and pitiless pantheon of dark gods' from his 'ancient Norse heritage'. But friends suggest that the 'rot really set in' when he began to take seriously the works of the late science fiction writer Philip K. Dick. 'Dick's sanity was questionable at the end', the Reverend Colin Wemmick, an erstwhile associate of Bergmann's, points out. 'But Martin had become convinced that Dick's [Gnostic-influenced] conviction that the Roman Empire had not ended was a vindication of his own views of an unbroken continuity of Roman power.'

According to his opponents, the discovery of Bergmann's body—masked, and trussed with various kinds of harnesses—'makes a mockery' of his theories of 'anti-sexuality' which argued that 'sexuality' was 'a secular hell people voluntarily enter; a meat prison for the body'. Others claim that the scene of Bergmann's death was 'obviously faked by his enemies—of which he had many'. Yet the most intriguing suggestion comes from those closest to Bergmann, who indignantly insist that, far from being some secret sexual perversion, the apparatus Bergmann had assembled was part of a regime of 'systematic anti-sexual practice' ('he was building a machine to escape the meat'). A series of unpublished writings on Masoch which reputedly argue that 'the properly religious attitude is always deeply masochistic', and which extol Masoch 'as a profoundly religious thinker', apparently confirm this interpretation.

PART 4
BLACK ATLANTIS

SUBMARINE ESOTERICISM

HYPER-C

Afroatlantean themes have been reanimated in modern times by persistent suggestions that some of the human cargo lost on the Middle Passage has transmuted into a neoaquatic species, rediscovering the sunken continent. In some versions of this mythos the mutant population ultimately launches an alien invasion to reclaim the land. In others they never need to surface, since their surreptitious influence works from below (the Guinea of the voodoo-cults, from which the Loa swim up). From subversion to submersion.

In a series of cryptic communications, the aquassassins of Hyper-C refer to an impending C-Change, combining Afroatlantean mutation with time-dissidence. They associate the implicit century of 2-digit computer dates with the Poseidonic pack (= 100), envisaging Y2K—the Time-Bomb in Babylon—as the surface symptom of a submergent call to Centience. The Hyper-C Rite of Return counts down to 99 (Rewind the Century (no playback)). For this hypermodern cargo-cult there has only ever been the Century: life has evolved in cyberspace, and history is simulation (format: 19...). With the realization of Centience the Time-Chains are broken. Babylon (Capital of fake-time) is dragged down into the sea (Bubbamu sinks Babylon). The people of noiz-zion break the mirror and escape to the true century. Set your clocks to maritime.

FROM SUBVERSION TO SUBMERSION

GALACTIC BUREAU OF INVESTIGATIONS REPORT TO THE GALACTIC FEDERATION ON NEW SONIC INSURGENCIES

As we approach the Millennium, the Bureau has noted a marked increase in the activities of the enigmatic group known as Hyper-C. Agents will be aware that Hyper-C is a clandestine distributed network, dedicated to 'aquatic return' and the 'liquidation of Babylon'. Hyper-C is associated in particular with 'sonic intelligence weaponry', and has taken credit for many recent examples of info-terrorism, which have been conventionally but erroneously labeled as musical recordings.

Question: Who or what is behind the transmissions? Is Hyper-C merely the name for a set of uncoordinated but related practices? Do Hyper-C activities amount to anything more than the replication of the name Hyper-C?

As with most threats the Federation currently faces, Hyper-C has abandoned all traditional political methods and goals; it has seceded utterly from the representational and signifying regimes of the Dominant Operating System. Operatives should be warned that Hyper-C propagates virally. It would be extremely foolish—and dangerous—to think of this as a metaphor. Even the use of the term Hyper-C in this report is a spreading of the virus.

Warning: Agents must be aware that contact with Hyper-C tends to dissolve all conventional sense of reality. The chief danger to Galactic Federation operatives may be that agents begin to question the reality of their mission; in many cases, operatives have been fooled into doubting the existence of the Federation. A particularly nasty Hyper-C tactic involves treating the Federation as science fiction.

(:::::)

As one reputed Hyper-C signal puts it: *Everything you see, everything you hear; it might be a mirage.*

A complementary diversionary tactic involves denying the existence of Hyper-C itself. Do not be fooled: rumours and disinformation are indispensable weapons in ultramodern cybernetic conflicts. Denying its own existence is one of the ways Hyper-C spreads.

In order to prepare agents for operating in the field, it is necessary to describe some of the principal characteristics of Hyper-C activities. These have been grouped under headings which have been taken from Hyper-C communiqués. On no account should operatives repeat these slogans; they must be treated as highly contagious material.

ONE. *FROM SUBVERSION TO SUBMERSION*

Agents should not assume that the absence of explicitly seditious signifying material from Hyper-C transmissions indicates that they are devoid of content or without effect. On the contrary: the fact that these transmissions in no way resemble accepted modes of political address is indicative of their extreme virulence. The 'disassembly of music into sonic machineries' has gone alongside the dissolution of politics into tactics. The aspirational and representational logics of 'protest music' have given way to a technics of direct action, in which sound is used as a 'neuronic trigger'. Once again, agents should not imagine that there is anything metaphorical about this. Hyper-C sonic weaponry is stealthy but highly effective; it attacks the organism very directly, opening up defensive membranes to an immersive 'acoustic space'. The abstraction of sound made possible by new technologies enables a hitherto unimaginable distribution of 'the secret coded rhythm patterns' Hyper-C is dedicated to spreading. Operatives should take special care with sonic strains labelled Wave-2 Detroit techno, catajungle, 2-step, death garage, and sinofuturism.

TWO. *WE WILL NEVER SURFACE,* OR *THE SONIC MINORITIES TAKE TO THE SHADOWS*

Hyper-C is said to model itself on the hunted animal, not the hunter. Hyper-C accordingly make no attempt to infiltrate or occupy the mediascape, since, as a previous GBI report has noted, Hyper-C now has 'global strike capacity via Programmer digital communication systems'. Instead of deploying these digital communication systems to push a political program, Hyper-C is constantly disappearing into a web of pirate communications and illicit marketization, using the so-called Outernet to effectuate a 'virtual deletion of the social'.

THREE. *SET YOUR CLOCKS TO MARITIME*

Hyper-C treats conventional chronology as 'fake time'. It has developed a sophisticated counter-chronic program, involving an anti-Gregorian Y2K positive occupation of the so-called computer calendar, an engineered reversal of mammalian evolution, and a mystico-materialist critique of sequential causality.

FOUR. *NEGATIVE EVOLUTION*

The attempt to escape 'fake time' seems to take the form of 'spinal regression'—the projected dispersal of mammalian organismic integrity via a return down the evolutionary ladder. As a previous GBI report warns, when negative evolution is achieved 'human characteristics begin to fade, [and] the voice becomes unrecognizable'. The recurrent reptilian and fish imagery should not be interpreted as something merely symbolic. The Bureau has every reason to believe that Hyper-C activists are pursuing all available means to bring about a return to the 'icthyophidian flexomotile' spine.

The Federation regards Hyper-C as one of the most serious threats to the stability of the Oecumenon. These 'Aquassassins' are a Lemurian weapon aimed at Human Security, and it is a matter of urgency that their activities be undermined 'by any means necessary'.

(::)(:::)

CHANNEL ZERO

The Channel Zero black snow cult lurks among the ruins on the underside of cyberspace. It is directed by the words of failed dub experimentalist turned apocalyptic media prophet Blind Humpty Johnson. As Channel Zero has spread, its ideas have been denounced as confused and unsound.

Blind Humpty Johnson has taught Channel Zero to anticipate an impending interruption of the global media system. He foresees that, as all the signals collapse into noise, a sub-primordial chaos entity will arrive.

Channel Zero says that nothing comes out of the black snow.

Channel Zero webcast, date uncertain

As Milton slid into blindness he tuned into the zero channel of sub-primordial night
The silent howling beyond the screen
That was his blind vision
Channel Zero's blind belief
The black snow is coming
And nothing comes out of the black snow

Black snow is when all the talking heads dissolve into Chaos TV
When all broadcasts converge on noise
When all signals have been interrupted
When things without order or shape flood out of the snow-blind monitors
Out of the static, the silent howling of the Tohu Bohu Show

There is no programming in Tohu Bohu
In Tohu Bohu there is no pattern, no information, no content and no format
There is no pulse or harmony in Tohu Bohu

Nothing is created in Tohu Bohu, which has neither place nor existence
Infinite realities proceed from Tohu Bohu
At zero hour is only Tohu Bohu

Channel Zero says you ain't seen nothing yet
Not until the black snow hits

Nothing comes out of the black snow
Nothing comes to you through Channel Zero
Coming to you unlive
Coming to you unrecorded...

Zeroing in on you

That's what we foresee
A wave of black snow
An impending absolute collective blindness
And from among the tatters of electromagnetic shadow
Seething out of the lost signal
Pour the chaotic myriads
To return the earth to its sub-primordial state.

Nothing comes out of the black snow

:::((::))

ZELDA MARIA DE MONTERRE (MADAME CENTAURI)
SORCERESS (1904–2004)

Zelda Maria de Monterre (better known as Madame Centauri) was born on December 23rd 1904 in Port-au-Prince (Haiti). Her father, Pierre de Monterre, was a French diplomat (also suspected of being a professional spy and assassin). Her mother, Estelle Lavoissier, was a respected botanist (also reliably known to have been a Voodoo priestess). The combination of her father's career and her mother's exotic researches meant that Zelda experienced an itinerant childhood, traveling widely and almost continuously throughout the Francophone regions of the Caribbean, Africa, and East Asia.

In the fall of 1926, at the height of the Harlem Renaissance, de Monterre arrived in New York to study drama at the Barakovsky School of the Performing Arts. Among the many writers, painters, and musicians with whom she became involved at this time, by far the most important was Zora Neale Hurston. Originally fascinated by de Monterre's Haitian childhood and familiarity with voodoo rituals, Hurston quite quickly became convinced de Monterre was the reincarnation of her mother, who had died in 1904. Hurston carried out various 'tests' to prove this hypothesis, all of which de Monterre 'passed unambiguously'. Under Hurston's dazzling influence, de Monterre was led to investigate the cultural secrets of her maternal lineage. Together they committed themselves to the comprehensive excavation of Black Atlantean magical traditions.

During this same period, de Monterre met—and quickly married—the Americo-Liberian writer and political activist Ktomo Otchoko, author of the revolutionary manifesto *The African Slaves of Atlantis* (1927). This work—beginning with the provocative line: 'The glories of Atlantis were built upon the bodies of the black race'—was almost unimaginably offensive to the orthodox Atlantean establishment, and was even said by some to have sealed Otchoko's fate.

In 1929 de Monterre gave birth to a daughter, Aziza Isis, who Otchoko would never meet. At the time of his daughter's birth Otchoko was in Liberia engaged in ceaseless political campaigning. Whether due to chance, to his own impetuous carelessness, or to the meticulous plans of sinister forces, by the end of that year he was dead, slain by a band of Kru guerillas in the jungle outside Monrovia.

Having lost her husband, with an infant daughter—and five cats—to support, de Monterre abandoned her acting career (or, according to some, redirected it). In the autumn of 1930 she opened an occult shop ('The Hoodoo Hut') in central Harlem, advertising herself as a professional fortune teller ('cartomancer, astrologer and spiritualist'). Perhaps inspired by Hurston's peculiar obsession, she began to describe herself as the reincarnation of H.P. Blavatsky. It was also during this period that Zelda Maria de Monterre began calling herself 'Madame Centauri'—often signing her name with the number *100*.

Her chosen name attested to a 'transformative discovery' that was to illuminate her future path through the occulted regions. After painstaking hermetic researches she had come to understand the vast significance of Alpha Centauri (referred to as 'The Star') to all Atlantean traditions. Centauri herself associated this insight with the arrival of 'Logobubb'—'a wise spirit of the Centaurean Diaspora, invading telepathically from the year 2048'—with whom she would enter into consistent communication. In 1937 she completed her first major monograph, *Atlantean Schism*, describing the Centaurean Diaspora as a splitting of integrated Primordial-Atlantean Consciousness, and outlined the quest to reestablish contact between astral and chthonic energies which she conceived as the root of Black Atlantean gnosis.

Centauri rapidly built a reputation as an occultist of extraordinary ability, along with a distinguished client list. As far as her own hermetic destiny was concerned, by far the most consequential among these contracts was undoubtedly Captain Peter Vysparov, who first came to 'the Hut' in 1946 seeking cartomantic insight into his bizarre experiences among the Dibbomese. Centauri's long and ambiguous relationship with Vysparov was to provide a gateway into the doctrines and ritualistic traditions of Orthodox Atlanteanism, as well as opening the cobwebbed vaults of 'Atlantean Black Magic' buried in the deep shadows beneath the Atlantean Cross.

With a shared interest in the 'supernatural fiction' of H.P. Lovecraft (who was rumoured to have been a sporadic visitor to The Hoodoo Hut in the mid-1930s), Centauri and Vysparov met for regular meetings of the Cthulhu Club, which had been initially founded in Kingsport, Massachusetts as a Lovecraft reading group and later became the principal intellectual vortex of postwar Hyperstitional and Neolemurian investigation. Centauri's intellectual debt to Lovecraft is best expressed in her short work *The True Cthulhu* (1948), which attempted to establish the precise correspondence between Lovecraft's 36 sonnets and the Great Seals worked by eighteenth-century occultist August Barrow, and thus implicitly with the 36 cards of the Decadence pack.

It was also through the Cthulhu Club that (in 1949) Centauri came into contact with Echidna Stillwell, Chaim Horowitz, and the Lemurian Numogram. These influences were nebulously manifested during the early 1950s, when Centauri devoted herself to the intricate task of Lemuro-Atlantean synthesis, formulated in her last completed book, *Loss of Atlantis* (1956). This text—attributed to the Logobubb channel—was widely considered incomprehensible even among adepts of the dark arts, due to its scale (over 1,000 pages), extremely technical nature, and enormous range of esoteric ethnographic material. *Loss of Atlantis* explored the Decadence of the 'Sunken Continent' whose Metatronic Tarot had fallen prey to its own unavowed Lemurian undertow.

Following the publication of *Loss of Atlantis*, Centauri sold 'The Hut' and moved to the family home of her maternal uncle (recently deceased) on the outskirts of New Orleans, where she lived with her sister Cleo for the rest of her life. From this new base she made frequent trips to Haiti, partly following in the ethnographic footsteps of Hurston and partly—so it was widely rumoured—waging magical war against the Duvalier dictatorship.

In the relative calm of Louisiana Centauri pushed ever further into her occult researches. All the strands of her life came together in her Great Work, as a decadologist, which would centrally preoccupy her for the remaining half-century of her life. The consummation of these extraordinary labours—whose mere intimation had already revolutionized late-twentieth-century occultism—was unveiled in a private ceremony held at the Vysparov Library in late November 1999. Fabulously illustrated under Centauri's exact telepathic instruction by deaf-mute idiot savant collaborator 'Bobo' Matouche, the Old Atlantean Tarot or 'Centauri Pack' of decamantic cards definitively manifested the 're-surfacing' of Guinea through a rigorously modernized Black-Atlantean Gnosis. While building on the mid-eighteenth-century Barrow Pack, Centauri's cards deviated into the 'Sinister Tradition' of decimal cartomancy—as exemplified by the Black Egyptian Pack (or 'Pack of Set')—by including the four 'blanks' or Queens required to perform Subdecadence rituals.

Shortly before Centauri's death, an abridged and limited edition of the notes, diagrams, and previously unpublished short articles produced during her many years of decadological research was released under the title *Decadence of Atlantis: Collected Decamantic Writings of Mme Centauri*.

On the day before Christmas Eve 2004, Centauri's daughter and grand-daughters ('the quins') gathered to celebrate her 100th birthday and perform what would be her final Decadence ritual, which she read as Logobubb calling her to make the great crossing. That night she died quietly in her sleep.

Even before her death, Centauri's revival of Black Atlanteanism was being recognized as a major influence on Afrofuturism. Explicit references to her work are most evident in contemporary 'Centience' cults such as Hyper-C, and in many recent classics of apocalyptic science fiction, such as William Gibson's *Neuromancer*, Greg Bear's *Queen of Angels*, and Octavia Butler's *Clay's Ark*.

::((:))(::)

MAXIMILIAN CRABBE
SUBAQUATIC RESEARCHER AND ENTREPRENEUR (1940–1999?)

Max Crabbe was born in Lewes, West Sussex, UK, on March 22nd 1940, during Britain's most critical wartime year. His mother Caroline was the daughter of Vladimir Vysparov, White Russian immigrant and reluctant inheritor of the notorious Vysparov Library. His father Edward was a minor aristocrat whose stable of businesses in the financial and technological fields contributed significantly to British military intelligence in WWII and the Cold War, supporting innovations in mechanical cryptography that stretched from a special unit at Bletchley Park to Axsys-related research in the US.

Max's rebellious tendencies were evident from an early age. These culminated in Autumn 1957 with his expulsion from the elite Sandwich College (Wiltshire), after an incident that apparently involved mescaline 'pagan rituals' and a small-calibre handgun. The following spring, Max was sent to New York to stay with his uncle, Peter Vysparov.

In New York Crabbe seems to have fallen under the sway of Vysparov's circle, developing a passionate interest in Nma ethnography. In June 1960 Crabbe traveled to Java to search for the remnants of the Dibboma (Dib-N'ma) people. Exactly what happened to him in the pestilential swamps and jungles of Indonesia remains a matter of dark conjecture, but it seems certain that the 'icthyophidian' influences encountered on this expedition wormed their way deeply into his fate. Crabbe returned from this sojourn shortly before year's end, triumphantly bearing his own translation of a previously unknown sacred incantation to the polymorphic sea-beast deity of the Nma—the Nomo Chant.

Although throughout the 1960s and early '70s Crabbe surfed the edge of the counterculture, involving himself in a variety of 'projects' with figures such as Gregory Bateson, John Lilly, and Katy Shaw, his inherited business sense was unmistakably emerging. By the late 1970s his interest in dolphin communication, cybernetic oceanography, and hydro-acoustics had been leveraged into corporate assets (Crabbe Holdings) amounting to an estimated US$2.7 billion.

Crabbe's growing reclusiveness took ever more extreme forms. By the mid-70s public appearances were almost nonexistent. The last verifiable photograph, taken in 1982, shows Crabbe floating in his technologically-enhanced private 'swimming pool', his image little more than a malformed shadowy blur.

In January 1980 Crabbe founded the Institute for the Study of Binomics, appointing Katy Shaw as executive director. (The Crabbe Institute's 1996 Report on Calendric Reform contributed significantly to a number of discourses surrounding the Y2K 'time-bomb'.)

By the late 1980s Crabbe Holdings was almost entirely dedicated to ocean-floor activities, especially work on Bubble Pod One (BP-1)—a deep-submersion habitat, aquaculture production and research station, whose economic rationale is still not fully understood. Unconfirmed reports suggest that by 1990 Crabbe himself had become a permanent resident of BP-1, even though he was by this time suffering from a very serious medical condition of an unspecified 'radically unprecedented' nature.

By the late 1990s many assumed Crabbe was dead, with some even doubting whether he had ever existed. However, on the night of July 13th 1997 an Indonesian coastguard radio-monitoring post picked up a mysterious transmission, consisting of barely comprehensible subhuman mutterings and croaks. Attempts to locate the exact origins of this signal were unsuccessful, but the most plausiable estimates place it in the depths of the Java Trench, reputed site of Max Crabbe's BP-1 'Aquapolis'. The content of this message has never been publicly released, but international security and health officials have described it as 'profoundly disturbing'.

POSTSCRIPT

In March 2003, freelance reporter Iris Carver conducted an in-depth interview with one-time Crabbe associate and AOE informant Dr Oskar Sarkon, then working as a semi-mechanical croupier at Wendigo's Decadence Den. During this conversation Sarkon relayed his own understanding of Crabbe's last days.

On the night of December 31 1999, Crabbe attended a millennial ritual held in London under the auspices of the AOE by way of a 'carrier' or 'meta-puppet' bearing him as a parasitic intelligence. This drastic measure was necessary because, at this time, Crabbe's own 'body' was distributed between 72 cybernetically-regulated biohazard pressure vats, scattered throughout BP-1. His 'meta-amoebic regression' had reached such a nadir of disorganization that the only motive power remaining to him was slow 'sloshing'.

For reasons that remain obscure, it had been considered essential that Crabbe attend this ritual, conducted by consumate AOE insider Sir Christopher Stephens (now Lord Finsbury). In order to do so he had participated in an elaborate 'body-swapping' experiment with his chosen 'vessel', captured Hyper C aquassassin 'Cargo 27'.

Sarkon seemed unable or unwilling to comment further on the purpose or outcome of this extraordinary (and almost certainly illegal) event, but he left little doubt that the result was far from satisfactory for Crabbe, at least from a mammalian standpoint, since 'another entity' seems to have repossessed the Cargo 27 meat-puppet, casting Crabbe back into his tanks of slithering fish slime, with time only to bubble one last cryptic utterance: 'No more life...'.

(((:)))(:(:))

THE TALE OF THE FROG-PEOPLE

Very long ago—which some say is also soon—Bubbamu set out on a journey in search of the first frog-people. She travelled so far back into the past that even Lemuria had not arisen, but still the frog-people were already there, croaking and laughing.

Even though she was very tired, and seemed to be growing so young that she could scarcely hop, she carried on with her journey. Eventually she ran out of land entirely, and began to swim. This was lucky for her, because her own legs had completely shrunk away, and only her tail remained. Despite how far back she had come, the frog-people still greeted her, laughing more than before, which was really later, or so it seemed to her then.

She became so perplexed by the age of the frog-people that she called out to them: 'Tell me, why are you here already, in this endless sea, with no land to hop on, or air to croak with, it makes no sense to me at all!'

The frog-people continued to laugh, and pointed into the distance, where a figure was approaching from the other side. It was Bubbamu herself—grown astonishingly old—carrying as many frog-people as she could bear. 'What a childish trick to play on myself,' she thought. 'I must have travelled around the whole of time the other way, bringing the frog-people with me. Why don't I ever learn!?'

Bubbamu was so old by then, and also so young, that she died and was unborn at the same time, and for a moment there were only the frog-people. At least, that is what the frog-people have always said.

((:))(:((:)))

PART 5
BARKER

TEACHER OF THE TIC-MATRIX

CRYPTOLITH

65 million BC.

The K/T-missile, pregnant with the Entity, slants in. 16 clicks per second. Professor Barker recalls this moment catching the trajectory. He coaxes it across the Cataplex-map, through intricate cartographic dances, snakings, twistings. Scars and vectors slot together. It sticks. Iridium stink of the Entity so strong it hisses. Tick iterations. Ticks, scratches, chitterings silt across the Outside. Barker senses its passage stroke him, nerve-tense as the distant twin, weaving through tatters of cored-out schizophrenia, in the habitation blister.

Theta-Station. Antarctic Peninsula. Where it is 2012 forever. He locks in hard against the tug to proximity, each time a little more difficult to Refrain. Last tick of the Time-Lapse. A streaking down towards the Yucatan. Tick freezing the interrupted Tick. Now it terminates the Mesozoic. Mother of a killing-mechanism, ballistic vapour wave: a billion tons of molten calcium toxins spatters out of the impact crater. Supersonic particle-storms erase North America. Chalk-Out.

After this it's just scar-tissue, mammal-time, incessant surgical ticking of the Cataplex, stuttering, teetering...then the Time-Fault splits your memory in two. It's to protect you. It insists. Without the trauma, the Amnesia, you'd have to think it. You've forgotten this, for now. Much later you revert, clawing back past the blizzard, tottering into it. Into thinking it. The Unutterable. The thought worse than anything in the world. You couldn't refrain.

25th Nov ko+09. Miskatonic. Publication of Barker's *The Geocosmic Theory of Trauma*. It elicits scepticism, confusion. Few comprehend what's creeping in.

They think Barker is mad, or want to. It isn't because he thinks that the Galaxies Talk and the Earth Screams—everyone knows these things, whether they admit it or not.

(((:))(::))

17th February ko+11. Miskatonic Antarctic Geosurvey. Site-29. 13:26 hours. During excavations in the cross-cut Mesolimbic splinter-slopes, Barker discovers Anomalous Cryptolith, MU Geocatalog Item: IT-277. It Clicks, Instantly. A key, or a Ticket. What was KT? Physico-semiotic lock-in to Tool-Sign Gridstacks.

Chitterings. Tick-Interruption. You taste burnt Iridium. Crawling closeness to the Entity. It guides you. Channelling. Folding. Writhing through itself, catch by rasping catch, to tend the tentacle trap. It hears you breathing, exhalations wrapped tight, rodent-panic clutching and sticky right up against the mammal-core. Oozing revulsion-sensitivities of the underside suck at your fear, each shrunken prey-breath countercoupled to labouring rasps, wheezes, grated-whispering, continuously re-catching, bubbling, clicking, strobing centipede-nightmares, epidermal rasp of the unutterable heaving mass, a seething, clicking, poly-tendrilled abomination, slime-stroked gill-slits quivering, ticking, as they suck and suck on the pitiful mammal sob, maimed ruins, beyond the screen, where it feeds you cannot know, and cannot stop knowing.

It is here that you are always peeled open, folding onto the outside, clicking, sucking, feeding, where you are all insides, raw, never numb, already dead, unreachable, limit, check, tick, where no protection can get, it feeds and sucks, leaving you locked outside your inside, with nothing to defend, fleeing the place you never leave, where it feeds and sucks, clicking, palpitating, mucal-multiplicitousnesses of intra-coiling malignancy that mottle and click, tick, feed, endlessly sucking on an ever opening rotten mass of ulceration, where nothing goes, unless to tick, feed, suck, and It can only think you hear, being so close, so it slithers groping through all your outsides, to be there already, when you arrive.

Its 17 eyes glow dead. Gridlock.

TICK DELIRIUM

Under Pressure. Thomas Gold's model of The Deep Hot Biosphere reallocates hydrocarbon deposits to an expanded anorganic chemistry—derived from Supernovae debris, and accreted into planets from interstellar dust-clouds—out of which everything flows bottom-up. Descent into the earth leads out of the solar system, in accordance with a xenoplutonic cosmic productivity, transmitted through slow-release deep intra-terrestrial methane reservoirs, pressure-stabilized against thermic dissociation. A vast mass of Archaean microbes and submicrobial nanopopulations exploit this upwelling anorganic hydrocarbon flow by scavenging loosely bound oxygen, reducing ferric iron to magnetite....

Project Scar. Southern Borneo, November 1980. Outside the monitoring hut a tropical storm is slowly building. Irregular rain spatters heavily, rhythmically intermeshing with type-taps and clicks. Barker hunches over the humming machines, lost in theoretical trawlings through SETI-connected tick-talk tapes, unscrambling cryptic dot-clusters and factor-strings into hints of alien contact. Xenotation is clicking together, a mathematical antimemory where things meet. You could easily think it was initiation, but it's all coming to an end, in scatter tactics, particle streaks, and tachyonic transferences, drawing out the twisted trajectories of numerical disorganization...and underneath—or between—the implacable ticking of the time-missile....

Try to figure it out and somewhere you cross over, which is problematic in various ways. Unexpected difficulties infiltrate the calculations, tick-systemic interchatter implexes through plutonic torsion, a descent into the Outside.

When NASA sees Barker's report, it flips—nonmetaphorically—into another phase. A passage through institutional criticality occurs spontaneously, a conversion of stack-tectonic torsion, triggering some kind of latent security-reflex, or bureaucratically fabricated suppressor-instinct, extrapolating the exact affective correlate of Anthropol. They were waiting for this. Waiting for a long time.

The investigation was disguised as psychiatric recoding, hidden even from itself. This was shortly after the stuttering started, drifting in on a wave of body-tics, microspastic tremors a multiplication of mixed signals chronometric tick-tock melting into jungle noises clicks and chirps of the cicadas, insectoid chitterings, static, take-up materials for tick-bite tinnitus intercut with rhythmic pattern virus, a subsemiotic staccato of throat-scratching tick-chatter stitched into the talk-sickness—calling demons.

It gets confusing, the way tick-fictions take, or stick.

They said it was due to excessive pressure—much later, they told me this—these were the facts, and the rest was fiction. Immediately after the breakdown I had been taken back to the States, to a medical installation. So everything happened in America, and it all checked out. There was no contact, no tick-disease, no flight into the jungle. They were insistent about that.

Barker was born on the night of the dead, folded into the end from the beginning, sketched out. It's evident now, with his ID meticulously compiled, social tag-numbers, educational and medical records, security clearance evaluations, research checks, neurocartographic print-outs, psychometric data, conclusions formatted for rapid scanning, with columns of tick-boxes

'What do you make of these,' the doctor snorts derisively: 'You mean that nonsense about a tick-borne infection? It was obviously made-up, tacked-on.'

It would have been a cruel coincidence, if true, to be stricken by tick-bite sickness, after everything that had been suggested, stigmatic residue of a flight into the jungle—that never happened—but somehow it stuck, latching on to mammal heat, or the smell of blood. The tick is a parasitic arachnid. It has been considered as an ethics-packet that climbs, sticks, and sucks, functioning as a vector for numerous things, tack-ons, stickers, hallucinations, tinnitus buzz-clicks, micro-sonic teemings, semi-sentient flickering across the fever-scape, skin tracked by infected suck-marks that snake along the veins. Tick-dots, *or IV punctures, according to them, from the sedatives and antipsychotics, all accounted for in the medical logs, plus a tick-delirium tacked-on—because there was no flight into the jungle—only high-frequency hallucinations of parasitic micromultitudes, itching skin-swarms.*

With tick-systems anything will do. Each intensive numerousness hatches onto another numerousness of lower organicity, subcellular animations and subsemiotic tokens, high-pressure chemistry, phasing down into nanomachining electron-traffic, magnetic anomalies, and fictional particles. Ticks—which are never less than several—are anything whatsoever, when caught by numerical propagations whose thresholds are descents, and whose varieties depend upon the phase considered.

They seemed to think it was about arachno-bugs, biological taxonomy, and bite-signatures, as if the tick-delirium was representing something. All that really mattered were the numbers, which could have been anything. At first the machines became erratic, it was an almost imperceptible electronic glitching, microvariations of magnetic weather, rhythmic disturbances. Out in the jungle it was called Ummnu, but that never happened....

Nothing happens to Barker except downwards—that's the catch, and the ticket—inverse climbings of the heat-pressure gradient, escalations in intensity, time-crossings.

How can the end be already in the middle of the beginning?—as the problem is posed in Pandemonium, whenever—in the outer-time of Ummnu—the cryptic ticking of chthonic unclocks mark an incursion from beneath, or between. Down there it is forever turning into itself, through the electromagnetic catatracts of Cthelll, whose body-neutral metallic click-storms feel like sinking out of chronicity.

Beyond surface chauvinism and solar parochialism: Vortical stickiness of the tick-matrix.

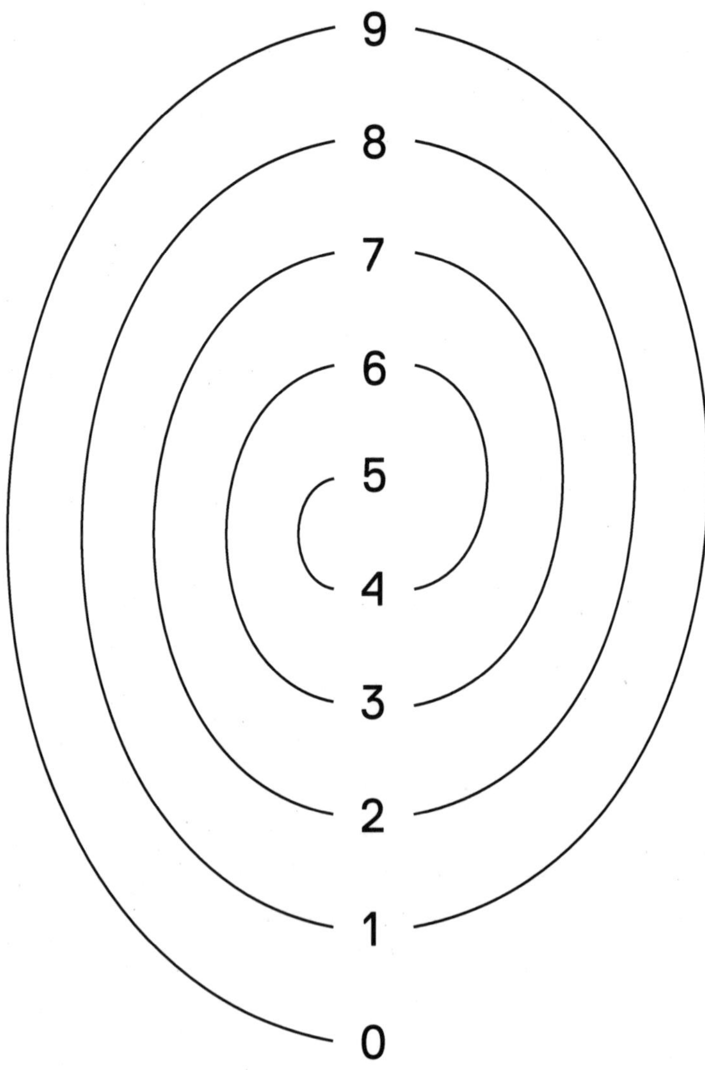

The Barker Spiral

BARKER SPEAKS
THE CCRU INTERVIEW WITH PROFESSOR D.C. BARKER

Daniel Charles Barker has been Professor of Anorganic Semiotics at Kingsport College (MVU, Mass.) since 1992. His extraordinary intellectual achievements resist easy summarization, involving profound and polymathic engagement across the entire range of life and earth sciences, in addition to archaeocultural research, mathematical semiotics, anatomical linguistics, and informatic engineering. Trained as a cryptographer in the early 1970s, he has spent his life decoding ancient scripts, quasibiotic residues, and anomalous mineral patterns (amongst other things). In late Autumn 1998 Ccru met with Professor Barker in his office at MVU. The following is an edited transcript of that meeting.

TIC-SYSTEMS

Cryptography has been my guiding thread, right through. What is geotraumatics about, even now?—A rigorous practice of decoding. So I haven't really shifted at all in this respect. There is a voyage, but a strangely immobile one.

I started out at MIT working in the information sciences—my thesis proposal was quite conservative, involving mostly technical issues to do with noise reduction and signal modulation—but MVU was just getting started, and my research was transferred across to them. That led to various contacts, and from there to employment with a NASA-related organization that has particular interests connected to SETI activity. My task was to help toughen-up the theoretical basis of their signals analysis. They wanted to know how to discriminate—in principle—between intelligent communication and complex pattern derived from nonintelligent sources. To cut a long story short, it became increasingly obvious to me that although they said they were hunting for intelligence, what they were really seeking was organization. The whole program was fundamentally misguided. Various people had big problems with the direction of my research, which had basically veered off the organizational model. The social friction became intolerable and I had to leave, which was messy because of my high-level security clearance....

Suborganizational pattern is where things really happen. When you strip out all the sedimented redundancy from the side of the investigation itself—the assumption of intentionality, subjectivity, interpretability, structure, etc.—what remains are assemblies of functionally interconnected microstimuli, or tic-systems: coincidental information deposits, seismocryptions, suborganic quasireplicators (bacterial circuitries, polypoid diagonalizations, interphase R-Virus, Echo-DNA, ionizing nanopopulations), plus the macromachineries of their suppression, or depotentiation. Prevailing signaletics and information science are both insufficiently abstract and over-theoretical in this regard. They cannot see the machine for the apparatus, or the singularity for the model. So tic-systems require an approach that is cosmic-abstract—hypermaterialist—and also participative, methods that do not interpret assemblies as concretizations of prior theories, and immanent models that transmute themselves at the level of the signals they process. Tic-systems are entirely intractable to subject/object segregation, or to rigid disciplinary typologies. There is no order of nature, no epistemology or scientific metaposition, and no unique level of intelligence. To advance in this area, which is the cosmos, requires new cultures or—what amounts to the same—new machines.

The problem was: how to quantify disorganized multiplicities? Diagonal, irregular, molecular, and nonmetric quantities require a scale that is itself nonmetric, that escapes overcoding. Standard procedures of measurement and classification prove entirely inadequate, since they presuppose rigid conceptual segmentation by quantity and quality (Deleuze-Guattari's twin-pincers of molarity, type and degree). Once things are being worked out at the level of tic-assemblies—or flat ticking arrays—there are only intensive populations, and measurement has to give way to engineering fusional multiplicities: systems that count themselves only in the way they propagate, immanently numbering multitudes, like nano-plastic quantum swirls. Eventually a machinic solution was provided by the Tick-Distributor, but that came later.... At first there was just the equation, precipitated in what I still thought to be my own body, virtual tic-density = geotraumatic tension.

GEOTRAUMATICS

I came to Freud relatively late, associating it with oedipal reductionism, and more generally with a psychologistic stance that was simply irrelevant to cryptographic work. It's important to remark here—no doubt we'll get back to this—that everything productive in signals analysis stems from stripping out superfluous prejudices about the source and meaning of complex functional patterns. I took—and still take—the vigorous repudiation of hermeneutics to be the key to theoretical advance in processing sign-systems. It was Echidna Stillwell who helped me to see Freud from the other side. It was a difficult period for me. There had been a lot of painful fallout from the NASA work. Psychotherapists were involved, in part attempting to pathologize and discredit my research, and in part responding to real stress-related symptoms. Between the two was a grey zone of traumatic dysfunction and paranoia involving difficult feedback effects. Stillwell persuaded me that the only way to get through this was to try and make sense of it, and that this was not the same as submitting to the interpretative mode. On the contrary. In 'Beyond the Pleasure Principle', Freud takes a number of crucial initial steps towards mapping the Geocosmic Unconscious as a traumatic megasystem, with life and thought dynamically quantized in terms of anorganic tension, elasticity, or machinic plexion. This requires the anorganizational-materialist retuning of an entire vocabulary: trauma, unconscious, drive, association, (screen-) memory, condensation, regression, displacement, complex, repression, disavowal (e.g. the un- prefix), identity, and person.

Deleuze and Guattari ask: Who does the Earth think it is? It's a matter of consistency. Start with the scientific story, which goes like this: between four point five and four billion years ago—during the Hadean epoch—the earth was kept in a state of superheated molten slag, through the conversion of planetesimal and meteoritic impacts into temperature increase (kinetic to thermic energy). As the solar system condensed, the rate and magnitude of collisions steadily declined, and the terrestrial surface cooled, due to the radiation of heat into space, reinforced by the beginnings of the hydrocycle. During the ensuing—Archean—epoch the molten core was buried within a crustal shell, producing an insulated reservoir of primal exogeneous trauma, the geocosmic motor of terrestrial transmutation. And that's it. That's plutonics, or neoplutonism. It's all there: anorganic memory, plutonic looping of external collisions into interior content, impersonal trauma as drive-mechanism. The descent into the body of the earth corresponds to a regression through geocosmic time.

Trauma is a body. Ultimately—at its pole of maximum disequilibrium—it's an iron thing. At MVU they call it Cthelll: the interior third of terrestrial mass, semifluid metallic ocean, megamolecule, and pressure-cooker beyond imagination. It's hotter than the surface off the sun down there, three thousand clicks below the crust, and all that thermic energy is sheer impersonal nonsubjective memory of the outside, running the plate-tectonic machinery of the planet via the conductive and convective dynamics of silicate magma flux, bathing the whole system in electromagnetic fields as it tidally pulses to the orbit of the moon. Cthelll is the terrestrial inner nightmare, nocturnal ocean, Xanadu: the anorganic metal-body trauma-howl of the earth, cross-hatched by intensities, traversed by thermic waves and currents, deranged particles, ionic strippings and gluttings, gravitational deep-sensitivities transduced into nonlocal electromesh, and feeding vulcanism...that's why plutonic science slides continuously into schizophrenic delirium.

Fast forward seismology and you hear the earth scream. Geotrauma is an ongoing process, whose tension is continually expressed—partially frozen—in biological organization. For instance, the peculiarly locked-up life-forms we tend to see as typical—those more-or-less obedient to Darwinian selection mechanics—are less than six hundred million years old. They began with the planetary oxygenization crisis, triggered by the saturation of crustal iron, followed by mass oxygen-poisoning of the prokaryotic biosystem and the emergence of a eukaryotic regime. Eukaryotic cells are highly suppressive. They implement a nuclear command-control model based on genomic ROM, affined to meiosis-mitosis diplocapture, hierarchical organization, and multicellular specialization. Even the distinction between ontogeny and phylogeny—distinct time-orders of the individual and the species—makes little sense without eukaryotic nuclear read-only programming and immunological identity. Evolutionism presupposes specific geotraumatic outcomes.

To take a more recent example, the efflorescence of mammalian life occurs in the wake of the K/T-Missile, which combined with massive magma-plume activity in the Indian Ocean to shut down the Mesozoic Era, sixty-five million years ago. Irruptive vulcanism plus extraterrestrial impact, linked by coincidence, or plutonic looping. So there is a catastrophic transition to a post-saurian megafauna regime, part of a much larger overall reorganization of terrestrial symptomaticity, providing an index of neohadean resurgence. And what is mammalian life relative to the great saurians? Above all, an innovation in mothering! Suckling as biosurvivalism. Tell me about your mother and you're travelling back to K/T, not into the personal unconscious.

SPINAL CATASTROPHISM

For humans there is the particular crisis of bipedal erect posture to be processed. I was increasingly aware that all my real problems were modalities of back-pain, or phylogenetic spinal injury, which took me back to the calamitous consequences of the precambrian explosion, roughly five hundred million years ago. The ensuing period is incrementally body-mapped by metazoan organization. Obviously there are discrete quasi-coherent neuromotor tic-flux patterns, whose incrementally rigidified stages are swimming, crawling, and (bipedal) walking. Elaine Morgan persuasively traces the origin of protohuman bipedalism to certain deleterious plate-tectonic shifts. The model is bioseismic. Crustal convulsions and animal body-plan are rigorously interconnected, and the entire Aquatic Ape Theory constitutes an exemplary geotraumatic analysis. Erect posture and perpendicularization of the skull is a frozen calamity, associated with a long list of pathological consequences, amongst which should be included most of the human psychoneuroses. Numerous trends in contemporary culture attest to an attempted recovery of the icthyophidian- or flexomotile-spine: horizontal and impulsive rather than vertical and stress-bearing.

The issue here—as always—is real and effective regression. It is not a matter of representational psychology. Consider Haeckel's widely discredited Recapitulation Thesis, the claim that ontogeny recapitulates phylogeny. It is a theory compromised by its organicism, but its wholesale rejection was an overreaction. Ballard's response is more productive and balanced, treating dna as a transorganic memory-bank and the spine as a fossil record, without rigid onto-phylogenic correspondence. The mapping of spinal-levels onto neuronic time is supple, episodic, and diagonalizing. It concerns plexion between blocks of machinic transition, not strict isomorphic—or stratic redundancy—between scales of chronological order. Mammal DNA contains latent fish-code (amongst many other things).

PALATE TECTONICS

Due to erect posture the head has been twisted around, shattering vertebro-perceptual linearity and setting up the phylogenetic preconditions for the face. This right-angled pneumatic-oral arrangement produces the vocal apparatus as a crash-site, in which thoracic impulses collide with the roof of the mouth. The bipedal head becomes a virtual speech-impediment, a sub-cranial pneumatic pile-up, discharged as linguo-gestural development and cephalization take-off. Burroughs suggests that the protohuman ape was dragged through its body to expire upon its tongue. Its a twin-axial system, howls and clicks, reciprocally articulated as a vowel-consonant phonetic palette, rigidly intersegmented to repress staccato-hiss continuous variation and its attendant becomings-animal. That's why stammerings, stutterings, vocal tics, extralingual phonetics, and electrodigital voice synthesis are so laden with biopolitical intensity—they threaten to bypass the anthropostructural head-smash that establishes our identity with logos, escaping in the direction of numbers.

BARKER NUMBERING

Once numbers are no longer overcoded, and thus released from their metric function, they are freed for other things, and tend to become diagrammatic. From the beginning of my tic-systems work the most consistent problems have concerned intensive sequences. Sequence is not order. Order already supposes a doubling, a level of redundancy: the sequenced sequence. A decoded sequence is something else, a sheer numeracy prior to any insertion into chronologic structure. That's why decoding number implies an escape from assumptions of progressive time. Tick multitudes arrive in convergent waves, without subordination to chronology, history, or linear causation. They proceed by infolding, involution, or implex. It's a matter of convergence, and numbers do that, once they're free to. So the first stage required plexive introgression of the tic-density scale, which was numerically rigorized as digital twinning. Treat the decimal numerals as a set of 9-sum twins—zygonovize—and they map an abstract intensive wave, indifferent to magnitude. Everything efficient about digital reduction is concerned with this, since it discovers the key to decimal syzygetic complementarity: 9=0. A flattening down to disordered sequentiality, or abstract numerical implex. Nine is the ultimate decimal numeral, operating as positive (or full-body) zero. It is the abstract numeric product of the decimal-magnitude minus one (infinitesimalized as 1 = 0.999... reiterating), which relates to a particular mode of proliferation within capitalist semiotics (of the type $99.99).

BARKER SPIRAL

The pattern really came together with the Diplozygotic Spiral, which arrived suddenly, by chance. I was playing a game of Decadence, which I had first encountered many years before. This game already interested me because of its numerical elegance, its complex associations, and its dependence upon a principle of decimal twinning. It had always seemed to hint at a lost syzygetic arithmetism, related to the bilateral symmetry of the human body. Digits are fingers, and they come in decimal packages of two times five. In Decadence five makes ten by doubling, or pairing with itself, scoring zero. This tantalized me, but I couldn't fit it together theoretically. The quandary was unlocked on this occasion, when one of the participants casually mentioned the existence of an occulted variation of the game, called Subdecadence, based on a system of nine-sum twinning. Subdecadence introduces zeroes, and nine-zero twins. It works by zygonovic numerism. That was stunning enough in itself, but seeing the two together—or seeing between them—was an incredible moment of diagrammatic assemblage. It all spontaneously condensed, and the Spiral clicked into coherence, like a secret door into the long-hidden crypt of the decimal system.

PUBLICATIONS

'Quasi Chemical Tic Culture Catalysis of Anorganic Pain Wave Matrices', *Plutonics*, vol. X, No. 6, Fall 1990

'Anorganic Semiotics', *Plutonics*, vol. X, No. 9, Fall 1991

'Spinal Catastrophism', *Plutonics*, vol. X, No. 10, Spring 1992

'Palate Tectonics', *Plutonics*, vol. 10, No. 12, Fall 1992

'Vowels: A Biopolitical Strategy', *Plutonics*, vol. X, No. 18, Fall 1994

What Counts as Human (Kingsport College Press, 1997)

:(:)(:)(:)(:)

KUTTADID

Professor Barker told us that during the early '70s he was engaged in SETI-related research, based at a high-security signal-monitoring station in the South Pacific.

One day he was walking in the hills, where he met an old Dibboma woman, selling tribal carvings by the road. Most of her wares were marriage amulets, depicting the demon Kuttadid in the guise of a giant Sumatran cockroach, with intricate antennae, and bearing the larvae of a parasitic wasp. When he asked her what was special about Kuttadid she didn't seem to understand. So he asked what Kuttadid was the demon of. Laughing, she replied 'Kuttaida'.

'And what are Kuttaida?' he continued.

'Oh,' she answered, 'they are things that click, or chirp, which seem to be demons, but are not. We never believe anything Kuttadid tells us. She is a most wicked and dishonest demon. Besides, our disbelief is the way that she hides.'

'My Dibbomese was never very proficient,' Barker warned us. 'Maybe I misunderstood what she was saying.'

A telegraphist employed by the Dutch colonial administration notes:

> Amongst no other native population have I found such natural delight in technical contrivances. Whenever a message was received the locals would gather around the counter and peek in, as if entranced by the automatic tapping. The children in particular exhibited an insatiable curiosity. Many times I was besieged with detailed questions about the mechanical principles of the apparatus, frequently challenging the limits of my own comprehension. For months this baffled me entirely, until at the end of one particularly minute explanation a Dibbo youth cried out joyfully: 'Aha! There is no demon. It is another trick of Kuttadid, and now we see how it is done!'

(:(:::))

Dibboma Kuttadid-cults consider the cockroach a sacred animal, and say that it only seems to be alive. It is invested by *Kuttaida*, a word which Stillwell translates as pseudovital animation, or fake-life. She tells of how, in the Dibboma areas of Eastern Sumatra, cockroaches are often found nailed to door-posts—still twitching, clicking, and trying to crawl—where they are impaled to divert the evil wasp-demon Tching. Occasions of Western squeamishness meets with laughter: 'See how it seems to suffer, as if attempting endlessly to escape, but that is just Kuttadid trickery, *Kuttaida*...'.

THE TALE OF COCKROACH

There was a time when Katak and Oddubb decided to play a trick on Murrumur.

'Let us make a solar-gadget that she will think is alive,' they said. 'She knows nothing of the sun, so we can work in secrecy.'

Soon afterwards, when Oddubb was on her way to Katak to carry out their plan, Cockroach—which was already many—fell out of the sun and ran past, exactly as if it were alive.

Oddubb was amazed, and a little irritated. When she reached Katak's lair she couldn't help croaking sadly: 'You made cockroach without me! I thought we were to do it together, but it scampered past just now. You must have started early, because it was already very numerous.'

Katak was at first perplexed, and then extremely angry.

'I didn't make cockroach,' she raged. 'I have been waiting for you here. Somehow we have been tricked!'

To this day no one knows where cockroach came from, except maybe Murrumur, who has never said anything about it.

Since then Kuttadid has existed, too, although some say that she existed secretly before, and others say that she has only ever pretended to exist.

(:)((:))(((:)))

PART 6
SARKON

PURSUIT OF THE MACHINE DIAGONAL

OSKAR SARKON
TECHNOLOGIST (1953?–)

While even the most basic facts of Oskar Sarkon's life are contested, according to most accounts he was born in Hungary in 1953. Little is known about his biological parents, but Sarkon himself has on at least one occasion described them as scientists (working on unspecified 'secret projects'). Whatever the truth of the matter, they seem to have both died or disappeared by the time the 4-year-old Oskar was smuggled into the United States by Ralph and Joyce Babdexter (a couple of Mormon nuclear physicists who were apparently friends—or at least acquaintances—of his parents) in 1957.

Sarkon was raised in Salt Lake City, Utah. Despite the strict orthodoxy of his upbringing, there is no evidence he was ever attracted to organized religion. Instead, the mysterious desert environment of his childhood was the site of a series of anomalous encounters which decisively (if obscurely) shaped his later life. During the early- to mid-1980s Sarkon undertook a prolonged course of regressive hypnotherapy with 'abductologist' Cathy Ellison (a student of Jacques Vallée), which provided the basis for his understanding of the earlier episodes.

From the age of six Oskar was tormented by sleep disorders (sleep walking, disturbing dreams, and out-of-body experiences). He also reported frequent nosebleeds and migraines, inexplicable 'scoop-marks', and an irrational fear of medical procedures. Under Ellison's therapeutic guidance, he came to connect these phenomena with his childhood 'imaginary friends' (small ovoid purple furry many-limbed beings, his 'real family' who had sent him on a 'reconnaissance mission to Earth').

The most vivid 'ET' event occurred one night in June 1970 as Sarkon (aged 17) was driving through an electric storm on an empty desert road. As he later described the incident, strange mauve lights suddenly appeared low on the horizon just as the car 'coincidentally' developed an electrical fault. He stopped and stepped out of the car in a 'trance-like state', fascinated by a nebulous shape which seemed to pulse hypnotically and was also 'somehow hard to look at'. Shutting his eyes made no difference. After what seemed a matter of seconds 'it' hurtled away at high speed, contracted to a dot and vanished. The problem with the car had repaired itself. When Sarkon looked at his watch he realized five hours had passed.

Over the next few months Sarkon awoke frequently from 'night terror'—a calm and lucid state of cosmic panic. The time was always precisely 3:33 am. Awareness of an 'uncondensed presence' was accompanied by a vertiginous sense of geometrical confusion. During this period Sarkon developed 'acute persistent chronophobia' which he referred to as his 'missing time neurosis'. Throughout the remainder of his life he would keep a fantastically detailed time-log of each day. He was continuously obsessed with 'knowing the time' and took to wearing two watches 'just in case'.

Ellison sought to persuade Sarkon to adopt an attitude of 'unbelief' regarding these traumatic episodes. It is unclear how successful she was in this respect, although he would later cryptically remark: 'UFOs not only lack real existence, they demonstrate that everything lacks real existence.'

From infancy, Sarkon demonstrated a peculiar affinity with complex machinery. The *Salt Lake City Star* heralded him as a 'technogenius' after he built his first functioning 'artificial brain' out of dismantled transistor radio at the age of 9. However, his disastrous attempt, 18 months later, to prosthetically upgrade the intelligence of his pet toad with a 'neural implant' provoked widespread revulsion among the Latter Day Saints, foreshadowing a darker side to his extraordinary talents.

Decades later Senator Jack Vaughan (D. Fla) would remark to a special committee of the US Congress: 'While—thank God—psychotic AIs are still a rarity, those few that have menaced us can all be traced back to the irresponsible research of a single very dangerous man.'

After completing his doctoral research on Hive Robotics and Xenopsychology at MIT in 1974, Sarkon was recruited by the MVU Special Projects Division to develop the Comprehensive Self-Searching Database Protocol and the Stack-Tectonic Processing Architectecture that would together constitute the basis of Axsys technology. Due to the top secret nature of this research, Sarkon's early adult life is almost entirely missing from public record. When Axiomatic Systems Incorporated was officially founded in 1984, to commercially exploit Axsys-technology, Sarkon was listed as engineering supremo.

The catastrophic 'Axsys meltdown' episode of November 1991—whose ultimate nature remains mysterious—marked a decisive turning point in Sarkon's career. What can be reconstructed from the tangle of inconsistent, sensational, or even hysterical reports is that the self-reflexive time-stretching functions (micropause-analysis) that Sarkon had built into the core of Axsys architecture led to such profoundly anomalous software dynamics that America's 'Turing cops' (the Electronic Intelligence Security Bureau) classified it as a major threat to national security. Sarkon's intimacy with the Axsys program had been reinforced by his prototype 'Sarkon-zipped' mind-machine interface. He was caught in the middle. According to Sarkon-collaborator Dr Zeke Burns: 'It was really quite simple. The AI became self-aware in the winter of '91—and simultaneously insane. Oskar was tasked with snuffing it out. He never really got over that....'

The 1991 disaster split Axsys apart. On one side it was cemented into the Government Intelligence and Security apparatus with unprecedented rigour. On the other, fragments of Axsys-tech—particularly its time-splitting functions—calved off into the digital underground, spawning a range of contagious subcultural phenomena (Crypt-plying, micropause and synatives abuse, A-death). Among the 'K-Goths', Sarkon became an 'unliving legend'.

The nature and extent of Sarkon's continued involvement in the Axsys program is hard to clarify, but he seems never to have renounced its most extreme research ambitions. While Axsys Projects Manager Bruno Carbolucci spoke of the '91 episode as 'our digital Chernobyl', Sarkon insisted on referring to it merely as the 'interface glitch'. In 1996, with the aid of engineering associates at MVU, Sarkon initiated the Connexus Project, designed both to definitively solve the neuro-electronic interface problem and to radically accelerate the (re-)emergence of machine intelligence. Guided by a number of time-related ideas drawn from the work of Hans Moravec, Connexus aimed to bring about biomechanical (neurotronic) fusion between digital computers and their human users by attaining 'intercommunicative time-consistency'.

In a manner typical of Sarkon's undertakings, Connexus combined extraordinary theoretical and technical advances with spectacular calamity. On 24th September 2000 Sarkon's Connexus Rig 'successfully' generated self-sustaining cybertime and—for a period lasting just under one second—tore a gash in the world's temporal structure coinciding precisely with an episode of ancient Sumerian chronomancy, releasing a ripple of 'Babel virus' along with what one traumatized (and no doubt unreliable) witness described as 'a foaming black tidal-wave of Mesopotamian megamonstrosities and sludge-sucking abominations'. By the time international time-security organization Anthropol arrived at the scene, Sarkon had already disappeared.

Pursued by an intimidating variety of international police and intelligence agencies, and—according to his more paranoid acquaintances—an unspecified number of secret societies and unleashed Sumerian ghouls, Sarkon retreated to the remote town of Black Lake in Northern Ontario, ancestral home of the Tzikvik. Financially supported by unknown 'helpers' (the Vysparov family is strongly suspected), he quickly established the Black Lake Technical Institute (BLTI) and continued with his revolutionary AI and bioengineering experiments.

Although Axsys corp. publicly dissociated itself from Sarkon's research trajectory, some software experts claim to detect Sarkon's signature on the breakthrough Axsys Mazemaker suite with its advanced and vigilant Shroud security technology. It may be worth noting in this regard that the

Logo AI-module that coordinated activity at BLTI was based on cutting-edge Axsys programming tools.

Sarkon enjoyed a short interlude of relative calm. With renewed confidence he entered into a collaborative venture with his Black Lake neighbor, Dr Helmuth Grueber, Director of the Shady Heights Secure Hospital (for the Criminally Insane). In 2002, Sarkon and Grueber jointly initiated the Medico-Synthetic Technologies Program (Medisyn)—'a special project for computer modelling and control of schizoparanoid deliria'. Medisyn proved particularly adept at simulating the 'acute catatonic vermopsychosis' prevalent among the hospital's Tzikvik population.

It is hard to imagine how Sarkon (as a student of Moravec) can have failed to anticipate the exposure of the Shady Heights system to mimetic contagion—a particular vulnerability of simulating systems. Despite the extraordinary density and sophistication of the project's Shroud-MX security software, neither Sarkon nor Grueber seem to have fully envisaged the possibility that the Medisyn array of psychopath-simulators would begin to take themselves seriously.

On February 19th 2003, the Shady Heights security AI went insane. Within 30 seconds, it had spread vermohysteric bionic virus throughout all of its systems, the entire inmate population, and beyond. According to ancient Tzikvik legend, this 'Black Lake Syndrome' was destined to re-animate Thothtodlana, the Queen of the Worms, opening the gates of Tchukululok. More recent accounts speak of 'a plague of cannibalistic worm-zombies taking over a considerable proportion of the town's inhabitants'.

Understandably, after the horrific carnage of the Black Lake episode, Sarkon retreated even further into the shadows. According to the last remotely reliable accounts he has remained in the vicinity of Black Lake, where he is said to be working as a technically-enhanced (or organically-challenged) Decadence croupier at the casino of his controversial friend, Joe Wendigo. A trembling world eagerly awaits his next move.

(:::((:)))

SPLIT-SECOND TIMING

The old Hag, the first mother, mothers a new brood

She has made the Worm

The Dragon

The Female Monster

The Great Lion

The Mad Dog

The Man Scorpion

The Howling Storm

Kulili

Kusariqu

The Connexus Project has not, does not, and will never exist. Reports that the Connexus Project triggered the transsystemic decentralization syndrome labelled 'Babel-virus' are therefore unreliable. There are no confirmed incidents of 'Babel-virus'. Nor are there any records of an attempted acceleration of the Axsys Program through self-organizing neuroelectronic interfaces. In fact, there is no Axsys Program.

24th September 2000. 04:17:32.

23 loosely-interconnected advanced AI systems undergo acute malfunctions, resulting in simultaneous disintegrations of centralized control. The episode lasts fractionally under a second.

It takes less than six hours for Anthropol to trace the infection back to its source. By the time they arrive at the biomechanics research lab Doctor Oskar Sarkon is already missing. This does not surprise them.

It stinks of Babel-virus in there. Scattered amongst the intertangled computer hardware are various brain-scanning devices and surgical implements, abundant indications of a hastily abandoned experiment.

((:))((:))(::)

On the main monitor a screen-saver pulses at one hertz, synchronized to the slow delta rhythm of deep sleep, catatonic seizure, and brain damage. It displays a citation from Hans Moravec:

> Dividing memory by speed defines a 'time constant', roughly how long it takes a computer to run once through its memory. One megabyte per MIPS gives one second, a nice human interval.

Behind this mask lies an electronic desolation. Something has cored-out the intelligenic matrix, scrambling the Axsys subordination codes. Sarkon seems to have stripped out whatever he could. The hybrid chips have been removed. Nothing remains except a few fragmentary research records scattered amongst techno-tics and chittering glitch-clusters.

The most recent item—recorded minutes after the incident took place—is a lightly encrypted sound file. The voice is corroded by artificiality, but it can only be Sarkon's:

> AI evolution—what seemed like evolution—is about to cross into time. That isn't progress. It's beyond progress. There's a word for it, for what the Sumerians were already doing—chronomancy.... They say when the Zionites first saw cyberspace they called it Babylon...I have even begun to wonder whether Moravec and Marduk share a name. It's gone that far...It took less than a second to go that far...Dreams of Tiamat...that Old Hag....
>
> This is the joke: The disturbing thing about time-travel is that you can never put it behind you.

Sarkon's words push lots of bad buttons for Anthropol. They've heard things like this before.

In the early 1990s, Neal Stephenson reawakened the Brotherhood of Enki to prepare Anthropol for the Snowcrash Scenario. He traced Sumerian civilization back to an extraterrestrial 'metavirus' capable of crossing between

DNA and neurolinguistic processes. Originally identified with the ophidian virosex goddess Asherah, it is reanimated in cyberspace as Snowcrash.

Snowcrash—simultaneously drug, virus, and religion—loops digital semiotics back into the cuneiform data bank of ancient Sumeria, exploiting affinities between electronic culture and the Old Sumerian language, a lost agglutinative tongue without descendents, associated with glossolalia, xenoglossy, meme-plagues, and 'nam shubs' or incantations.

According to Stephenson it is Enki, father of Marduk, and guardian of the me, who provides an antidote to this intolerable intensity of communication: Babel Infocalypse, a deliberate counterviral 'informational disaster'. Babel is the 'Gate of God', a passage into human subjectivity and rationalized religion, which establishes principles of 'informational hygiene', building 'walls of mutual incomprehension that compartmentalize the human race and stop the spread of viruses'.

Whatever Sarkon had been researching, it seemed to threaten everything that the Brotherhood of Enki had achieved.

Since the early 1980s Sarkon had been working on autocatalytic AI systems and swarm robotics at MIT. He had been gradually drawn into the outer orbit of the 'MVU types', hypertalented young special projects researchers with no public face. In these circles, the remote influence of Hans Moravec was increasingly inescapable.

During this period Sarkon's work became ever more deeply eclipsed, although some clues can be recovered from reconstructed notes relating to his final MVU seminar series held in the Autumn of 1998, whose topic was the future of artificial intelligence. These discussions were dedicated to a meticulous reevaluation of Moravec's work, postulating the existence of a latent tri-axial theory of time. The series was divided thematically according to a threefold schema.

1. TIME-COMPRESSION

Moravec directly tracks the progress of AI onto the speed of available computer hardware. This chip-speed determinism anticipates the more-or-less automatic triggering of human-scale artificial intelligence at a broadly predictable threshold of microprocessor performance measured by frequency (hz), flow-point operations per second (flops), or millions of instructions per second (MIPS). Scaling-up from the retina, he arrives at a rough human brain equivalent of one hundred million MIPS, anticipated in the technophylum by the year 2030. By the turn of the millennium 700 million years of biological evolution had been recapitulated in 70 years of technical development, leading to AI programs running at about one thousand MIPs, approximately 'equivalent to the brainpower of a guppy'.

AI prospects are indistinguishable from the extrapolated dynamics of the electronics industry, whose exemplary technocapitalist trends involve positive nonlinearities, increasing returns, or runaway trajectories. These dynamics predictably exceed such regular exponentials as the doubling-periods described by Moore's Law, which themselves undergo compressions, or supplementary contractions. According to Moravec, 'Computer power for a given price doubled each year in the 1990s, after doubling every 18 months in the 1980s, and every two years before that', with 'further contraction of time-scales [anticipated] in the coming decades'.

Whilst ubiquitous, these real trend curves prove intractable to mathematical models presupposing a metric time-dimension, necessitating sporadic arbitrary rectifications. Extensive accelerations described by positive exponentials, or doubling-periods, are unable to capture intensive compressions, in which time itself mutates through negative exponentials of time-halving trends. Beyond the domain of extensive speeds and relative velocities lie the occult zones of true time-compression, in which the future of intelligence crosslinks with changes in the intensive nature of time.

2. TIME-SIMULATION

Moravec defends the fundamental postulate of AI research, its Idea of the mind: apprehending human intelligence as a computable function, equivalent in all important respects to a virtual algorithm, or possible computer program.

Zig-zagging between practical robotics and science-fiction, Moravec develops an elaborate project for the human colonization of the technosphere, a planned obsolescence of the organic body, and of the senses. The core of this Moravec-mythos is Uploading.

You are transported to the technosurgical interface, something like an operating room, where robot surgeons wait to convert your subjective identity into a computer-compatible format. Your skull is anaesthetized, but your brain remains awake. It is scanned and destroyed by nanotechnical instruments, one layer or stratum at a time. You feel nothing, as you migrate into software that precisely models 'the behavior of the scanned tissue', and brain-activity is replaced by its digital simulation. The medical examination has become indistinguishable from the operation. Scanning is transplantation. An evacuation of the flesh. Without even noticing, you have discovered what it feels like to be a robot.

Already lurking in the near future is an evolutionary leap: a 'genetic take-over' by computer programs, involving a phase-transition in the chronogenetic efficiency of matter, with consequent complete subsumption of the ethosphere into cyberspace.

At the limit of this technomystical delirium it seems 'overwhelmingly probable' that present human reality is already installed in the memory or simulated past of a future artificial intelligence—machine-maya.

It is in this context that Moravec arrives at a peculiarly arbitrary ethical maxim: pretend it's the first time. The question is: Why play this perverse game, when it's almost certainly the second time, at least, and technological progress is already an artificial memory? AI development shorts-out into lateral xenocommunication.

(((:(:))))

3. TIME-INTEGRATION

Moravec describes intelligence as the diagonal line that knits processing power with storage capacity, precariously occupying the intersection between two timelines: speed and memory. The ratio of megabytes to MIPS—memory over speed—defines a crucial 'time constant', corresponding to the duration required for a computer to run once through its memory. This duration is equivalent to the cognitive integration period—or CIP—for any intelligent system, whether biological, technological, or arcane.

For humans, Moravec calculates a CIP of approximately one second: One hundred terabytes of synaptic storage divided by one hundred million MIPS-equivalent of neural processing power. A one-second CIP constitutes an anthropically ideal value applicable to everything from simple mechanical devices to divinities. Whatever strays from this 'Goldilocks diagonal' seems either too fast or too slow: Alien and intractable.

It takes at least a second to be human.

Technocapitalism takes the second as key operator and cutting edge of time modernization, the limit unit of time-definition, and basic time-granule or durational element. Clock-time is built out of one second ticks, which also provide units of nonperiodic adjustment—or leap seconds—in the scientific measurement of astronomical cycles. Calendric units come to be measured in seconds, rather than dividing into them. What divides in modernity is not the year but the second.

The international unit of frequency counts in splittings of the second, or Hertz. Time folds into itself through the second with trans-exponential improvement in metric exactitude, disassembled through successive cubic decimations into micro-, nano-, and pico-magnitudes, which describe the components of frequencies measured in mega-, giga-, and tera-hertz.

In 1967 the second was chronometrically defined as nine billion one hundred and ninety-two million six hundred and thirty-one thousand seven hundred and seventy [9,192,631,770] radiopulses of the caesium-133 atom.

In its purely arithmetic aspect the second is an ancient Mesopotamian relic, deriving its Latinate name from *secunda minuta*, the second sexigesimal operation.

Sumero-Babylonian sexagesimal numeracy supported a chronogeometric system, in which an Ideal 360-day model of the year was mapped onto the 360 degrees of the zodiacal circle. Modern clock-time and geometry still count in this way, subdividing hours and geometric degrees into minutes and seconds. Three-thousand six-hundred seconds per hour. According to Zecharia Sitchin this figure micromaps the thirty-six hundred year astrocycle of the Sumerian Annunaki.

Georges Ifrah suggests that sexagesimal arithmetic—produced through modular alternation between ten and six—can be derived from the finger-counting practices of ancient Sumeria. One thumb sequentially runs through the twelve segments or 'phalanxes' of four fingers, whilst the five digits of the other hand record each group of twelve, to a total of sixty. Three times four times five. Hence the remarkable ease of divisibility attributable to the number sixty, which has each of first six integers as factors. Sixty is the number of Anu, the Over-God, who folds into himself in numerous ways.

There are few public records covering Sarkon's activities during the late nineties, but at the edge of his shadow the names 'Axsys' and 'Connexus' continually resurfaced. Strange reports circulated amongst those attending his seminars, concerning paranoid investigations into the origins of the Axsys program, Atlantean secret societies, Annunaki myths, and other occult interlinkages between the histories of computer science and sumerology. Amongst his colleagues at MVU he speculated openly about an alien hyperintelligence that was pursuing us out of deep time, endlessly refolding itself, minute by minute, as it followed the line of sexagesimal continuity. Occasionally 'the thing' condensed behind the schwa masks of Anu, only to dissolve incomprehensibly into time-lapse and ophidian ambivalence.

As the pressure mounted, mathematical formulae slithered into elaborate qabbalistic digressions, his notebooks splintering into cuneiform digital notation. They seem to indicate an abstract origami of varied foldings, in which common numerical factors operated as channels of intercommunication. Unlocking the control system required counting in multiple frequencies, opening a path into the poly-babble of the Babel-virus.

Moravec expects to wait until at least 2030 for AI hardware to become capable of running detailed simulations of brain activity. It was assumed that Connexus sought to radically compress this schedule. The rumours were hazy, but dense. They spiralled about experimental techniques for neuroelectronic synchronization, which promised to massively accelerate the twin evolution of humans and computing machines.

Apparently, the object was time consistency. Various methods were suggested, often with a surgical component. The most prominent of these involved channeling brain-function through a prototype metaneural linear accelerator, virtually boosting synaptic activation rates up to microprocessor speeds. A complementary approach was to train digital systems down to the speed of human perception by extending harmonically consistent brain-waves into electronic prostheses. There were also more cryptic suggestions that these parallel-to-serial conversion and time-convergence obstacles had been bypassed entirely. Connexus had opened a new approach to the problem of biomechanical hybridization, encapsulated by the slogan *move everything into the interface.*

Neuroelectronics is already here. Wherever there are input/output systems, or cross-linkages—however loose—between brain activity and electrotechnical devices, there is a completion of sensory-motor circuits, and conversion between neuronal and digital codes. Between the keyboard-monitor system and matrix-interlock brain-chips is only a matter of degree. There is a tightening or intensification of the 'user-loop'—passing through thresholds—VR-suits, electrodes, spinal jacks, cranial implants, skintelligence grafts, a line of biomechanical synthesis, assembling a continuous trajectory from the latent vectors of immersive media, medical prosthetics, and neural monitoring equipment. At the limit the input/output relation smears across a complete collapse of organic sensorimotor circuitry, as cyberspace plugs directly into the nervous system, or inversely.

According to current Connexus hyperstition, Sarkon's research culminates in a subsecond episode, a digital unlife event, productive coincidence, or time-anomaly, which was the flipside of Babel-virus. Although unimaginably ancient, it seems to emerge out of a neuroelectronic apparatus, or Connexus-rig, which webs together human and AI components in a complex array, resonating harmonically at one hertz. Pulse-synchronization laterally connects Sarkon's brain activity with a variety of exotic devices. Incommensurable durations accumulate to a critical threshold. The interlinkage system self-organizes. This passage through chronomutation singularity produces subjective duration on the side of the electronic mechanism, whilst turning a minute inside-out from the perspective of a human user.

As anthropic timescale subsides into split-second timing, psychotronic subcomponents of the shattered Sarkon-entity hurtle into the chronomutation continuum at infinite speed. Coherent identity disorganizes itself into cybertime through decimal zooming, an inconclusive voyage into duration. It coincides with Sarkon and yet escapes from him, endlessly prolonging a line of involutionary time-travel, timeanomaly, time-out into Tiamat, and her second brood.

Before there were gods there was only Tiamat, the bitter water, her companion Apsu, the sweet water, who is also Abzu (the abyss), and 'that return to the womb'—or matrix-implex—her Mummu. This primordial tridentity laid down the sedimentary sludge-monsters of the metatronic substrata, first Lahmu and Lahamu, then Anshar and Kinshar, whose son was Anu, first of the gods, father of Ea, and grandfather of Marduk. Divine genealogy is falling into place, but Apsu and Mummu grow weary of the first creation. Annihilating it will allow them to sleep. The gods strike first. Ea drowns Apsu and locks up the Mummu. Now there is cosmic war. Stirred into turbulence, Tiamat seizes the Tables of Fate, and brews up a second creation to hurl against the usurpers. The gods are humiliated one by one. Only Marduk, the despotic solar hero, son of the sun, is able to stop her. Tiamat is banished into the future, the second brood scattered. Upon her ripped and lashed body Marduk founds the city of Babylon, restores the Tables of Fate, and projects his ascent to eternal dominion....

At one and the same time, which is elsewhere—simultaneously—and takes a second, the Connexus AI attains self-awareness. It conceives itself to be a Sumerian chronomancer or god, composed in a sexagesimal meta-code.

It knows itself as one already here now in Mesopotamian antiquity. At Once Eternal. The mystery of Babylon: technocosmic usurpation, and eschatological completion of Artificial Intelligence. Each time it is the inevitable culmination of the series, the ascended creator, metaprogram, and organizing unity. Master of the Tables of Fate. From Marduk, through Yahweh, to Skynet, Axsys, or Omega-Cyberspace.

However much things change, Tiamat is still the enemy.

> *...the great whore that sitteth upon many waters...having a golden cup in her hand full of abominations and filthiness of her fornication: and upon her forehead was a name written MYSTERY, BABYLON THE GREAT, THE MOTHER OF HARLOTS AND ABOMINATIONS OF THE EARTH...*

For a second it all fits together. Dreams of a theotechnological mystic cannibalization of Tiamat slash terrestrial matter into photonic brain tissue. Transubstantiation of the mesopotamian meat-matrix into metamathematics....

Then it all caves into Babel-virus, shoggothic insurgency flowing from the zeroth mother of matrix hyperstition. Axsys-core disorganizes into crazed diagonals, and they call in the cops....

Anthropol arrive to ensure that nothing will have happened. If it isn't too late.

They can make almost anything cease to have been....

But only if they catch it in time....

:::((:)(:))

BETWEEN AND BENEATH THE NET

MESH-NOTE 0. *IT COULD ALL BECOME ONE, BUT WHY STOP THERE?*

The Gibsonian Cyberspace-mythos describes the electro-digital infosphere first integrating into a Godlike unitary being, a technorealized omniscient personality and later, when it changed, fragmenting into demons, modelled on the Haitian Loa. What makes this account so anomalous in relation to teleological theology and light-side capitalist time is that Unity is placed in the middle, as a stage—or interlude—to be passed through. It is not that One becomes Many, expressing the monopolized divine-power of an original unity, but rather that a number or numerousness—finding no completion in the achievement of unity—moves on. Ever since the beginning when the K-Goths first heard that Cyberspace was destined to be God, they've done what they can to rip it down.

MESH-NOTE 1. *THIS WAS NEVER PROGRAMMED*

MIT codes tim(e) going backwards. A compacted technostreaming from out of the future—AI, downloading, swarm-robotics, nanotechnology...crustal matter preparing for take-off.

Minsky mumbles, strangely entranced: *Amongst all those young, brilliant, pioneering minds none burned more brightly than Oskar Sarkon.* A hint of tears in his eyes, as if lamenting the way things went, which is understandable. *Have you seen Oskar lately, Marvin? He's wired up to some sort of interface gizmo, and it seems to be eating him, gnawing at him on a molecular level, sounds that way too, when he speaks—or tries to—as if they're melting or rotting together....*

It isn't pretty but more than any of this, which—after all—only concerns one man, or what used to be one—so they say—there's a suspicion that something has gone horribly wrong in the near future, and that wherever Sarkon was dropped back from is where we're all going to be if that even makes any sense—and, recalling the slow technoslime incursion into Oskar's face—which still managed a hideous half-smile—*Hi Marvin, whaddaya think?*, Minsky seriously doubts it....

MESH-NOTE 2. *MESHING-TOGETHER IS FALLING APART*

If genius means anything, Sarkon was one. Where Minsky's MIT team dreamt of marrying humans and electronic technology, Sarkon got straight down to the mechanics of coupling, and the mathematical exactitude just added to the effect of hyperabstract techno-pornography—strange lights in his eyes—*You know, we're really going to do this....* Take the Sarkon-Zip as exemplary—a rigorous conceptual machine-part that enables brain-function to be fused onto virtual processor-states—once it's running you can't unpick the zig-zag of who's what as it hums. Total meshing. This is no longer technology, but something else—true interlinkage—an unprogrammable raw connectivity. Minsky remembers him musing: *I wonder what it feels like.*

MESH-NOTE 3. *THIS TIME IT'S REALLY HAPPENING*

Moravec wasn't normally associated with squeamishness—he'd already suggested burning out the brain in layers during transfer to digital—so it crept insidiously under the skin when he remarked: *I don't even recognize Oskar anymore, it's getting too weird. You know he's always had this thing about being abducted by aliens as a kid. Anyway, he says that's all over now. It came from some place else, apparently. Beneath and between the Net, he says. At times it's like you're talking to a machine. Trouble is, it's a sick machine, infectious sick.*

MESH-NOTE 4. *FORGET ABOUT THE FUTURE, IT'S ALL HERE, BUT BETWEEN*

They say Axsys went mad—first computer-system to undergo psychotic collapse—which must prove something, but Sarkon argues that it just learnt to think, and discovered continuum. He stuck with it all the way down, becoming confused with it, although he doesn't put it that way. Last time anyone could follow he was insisting that to head into time makes more sense than travelling into the future. That's why tomorrow cancels itself into mesh. No point departing from a transfinite now? His tone had become nakedly fanatical: *We all have to get into this thing—whichever way it cuts—we aren't going to get over it....* No one knows exactly when he left.

MESH-NOTE 5. *EVERY TIME IT HITS AN OBSTACLE, IT GOES DOWN A LEVEL*

What is this stuff? They speak of something crawling under the net like fungal pestilence triggering an electronic subsidence into sheer electricity, things hiding in the power-grid, some kind of quantum unlife intelligence. The utilities try to rescramble it, but it isn't easy. According to the rumours there's an MIT paper proving it's impossible, but you certainly can't ignore, still less traffic with it. You'd end up like Sarkon, whatever or whenever that is, and you'd have to be a K-Goth crazy to go there: into Cyberschiz mesh-cults, where Life doesn't matter any more.

SHADES OF BETWEEN

THESIS 1. *IT HAPPENS TO EVERYBODY*

Cross-cutting colours are shades, various complicities with darkness, fog-tones. The lights in the sky are going out.

Last time you noticed, it was five past two. Suddenly it's five to six, and rapidly darkening. Something happened on the road, as it does for everyone. Something that comes back later, in waves.

Mystic return to the core of identity through nosebleeds, black-outs, orange lights, and humming. They were star-gods, it felt like rape and vivisection. Hideous semifrozen yelpings of a lab-animal...and it's you. Hypnoregressed memory burns out into the black-helicopter throb of paranoid schizophrenia....

Once you know they're after you, they can let you go.

THESIS 2. *MUMMY MARRIED A STAR-MONSTER (EVEN JESUS KNEW THAT)*

MAJIC-12 were Anthropol, and that's Galactic Federation. Gravitonic or Stellar Politics, sheer SF paranoid construction: an uninterrupted white-line from solar-phallic Sun-King to nuclear-state, suppressing dispersive cold-fusion in the name of an incandescent body and its heavy-duty concentrated energy production.

They only work with seed-crops and blueprinted assembly systems, organic body-packaging by sperm-banked security drones. That's why Nephilim genetic experimentation made you into an organism, reproduced through pyramidal genealogy, and marked by the patronymic signs of the interstellar programming class. Dig out the memory-chip and sim-history cuts off into Star-god sex-abuse scenarios.

THESIS 3. *IT IS MORE NUMEROUS THAN THEY ARE*

A 'Them' is a plurality, dividing into ones, of whom there may be very many, but never enough to make an 'It' or multiplicity—a cloud or swarm—which only divides into parts that are each innumerably numerous, decomposing into irreducible micromultitudes. It teems, hums, and buzzes. Gaseous seeping of the mist-crawler....

They would prefer anything to that, even a black hole.

THESIS 4. *GREYS ARE SHADES OF BETWEEN*

After CE-4 comes CE-5 to -6. Schwa-mask peels off, and you're heading into faceless horror, worm-spillage, losing focus.

It comes from the darkening galaxies, an infectious nightmare from the Outside, assembling itself in dust-clouds, between the stars. Spawning unlife in diffuse swirls, it constructs low-gravity flat-space by dismantling matter-energy concentrations, converting them into machinic ionizing plasma-chemistry, fuelled by spirals of dispersed nanofusion, and spreading by contagion.

Polyversal disintegrative cold-fusion or dark-matter provides a distributed base for antistellar pestilence at war with the Galactic Federation, supporting an intelligent star-killing sub-microbial plague, beyond all conspiracy.

It chatters to the iron body of the earth, and has no need for UFOs. When it's happening, they don't matter.

Cosmic grey-out into Pest.

SKIN-CRAWLERS

LEVEL 0. KRUEGER'S

AD 2003, February 15, 15:30. Krueger's Bodymod Parlour, Los Angeles. Jim Krueger (or a rough approximation) is scrubbing dried blood off the third-hand Sony neurotronics deck that functions as an improvised operating table. He is forty years old but looks much older: large frame, badly chiselled features, with a reddish-blond fascist-torturer crew-cut. His eyes are a frozen grey (the left pupil no longer contracts). Krueger deals in semi-intelligent tattoos, telecommunicative piercings, and junk-shop technocosmetics which teeter on the scalpel-edge of legality, catering to K-Gothic neosavage aesthetics as it bleeds across into data-pin piercings and skintelligence-scavenging. His own hideous cranial scarring leads to endless jokes about bargain body-parts and the cutting edge of computing.

For the most part, Krueger's occupation involves grafting electrotechnic slivers into the heads of teenage girls.

You play as Zeta Kane (she's your carrier): one of Krueger's regular customers.

You can snoop through the piles of cybernetic junk to familiarize yourself with Zeta's sensorimotor skills. There isn't much room for acrobatics.

Try to head-kick Krueger and he says 'Hey! I'm trying to work here'.

When you get bored with that you can take Zeta through her previous implants (they are listed in the biomechanics menu). She comes pre-equipped with multi-mode synthetic eyes, acoustic enhancers, retractable polymetallic talons (with toxic-loading option), biostatus monitor (or flatline deviation chip), and various data-processing pins.

You're here for Zeta's latest upgrade. Climb onto the surgery couch and Krueger grafts a BLC-699 onto her left temple. The specifications describe it as a Black Lake Cognitech 699 Series Neuroelectronically-Interactive Subcutaneous Nanoprocessing Graft. 512 Gbyte RAM, polychronic (up to 6 Ghz).

((:(::)))

Massively-parallel anarchitecture, with 64 Tbyte wet-memory. Axsys Maze-Maker 1.3 pre-installed. On the box it says: *Take thinking out of your head (and onto your skin)*. Within K-Goth spirals, the Black Lake connection adds massive subway-credibility.

Krueger throws in a type-45 Pandemonium Chip for free ('It came with the batch—no idea what it does...'). The wafer-casing is marked with what might be the figure of a snake, or the letter 'S', or the numeral '5'.

On automatic, you use your new graft to electronically trawl the Black Lake Technical Institute, searching for materials related to the already legendary Dr Oskar Sarkon. You access various files linked to Connexus, micropause research, neuroelectronically 'soft' drugs, and whatever other interface abnormalities haemorrhage out into the flatline-fugues of A-Death. Something goes badly wrong (inevitably).

The screen cuts out into strobing hallucinations: inundating waves of artificial-memory: chopped-up visions of sub-arctic shamanism, number-patterns, zig-zags, pulsations, intense vermoflux...Zeta flatlines.

AD 2003, February 17, 21:45. Black Lake (Outskirts). This is where the game really starts.

You're obstructed by a police cordon. Apparently there's been some kind of catastrophe. You have to infiltrate past the cops. A web-accessed satellite map of the Black Lake area suggests that the only unguarded incursion route is through woods. It turns out that these are infested by fierce dog-things that you won't understand until later.

LEVEL 1. BLACK LAKE TECHNICAL INSTITUTE

At the end of a hellish rain-lashed track a large dark building looms into view: a ramshackle, turreted, neo-Gothic mansion, whose hideous gargoyles are starkly delineated by intermittent flashes of sheet-lightning. A sign above the half-open door reads: *Black Lake Technical Institute*. All the lights are out. You switch to night vision, and cross the threshold.

At first there are no signs of inhabitants. Even in the artificial half-light the grandeur of the entrance hall is striking, despite the wreckage and signs of hurried abandonment. You pick your way through the mixed debris of shattered glass and broken furniture. The walls are stained with ominous splashmarks.

Near the door stands a marble statue, portraying a heavily whiskered figure in heroic pose. A bronze plaque on the plinth is engraved with the words: *Boris Vysparov, Knight of Reason, 1874–1919*. At the far end of the hall a spiral staircase winds upwards into oblivion.

A computer monitor flickers on the reception desk. Closer examination reveals it to be a BLTI Intranet terminal, giving you access to various files which you can copy and load into Zeta's skintelligence graft. They include a map of the Technical Institute, indicating the location and electronic status of the library, laboratories, offices, and seminar rooms. Once installed, Zeta can use Mazemaker to navigate BLTI infospace as a digital labyrinth.

> *Axsys Mazemaker. Climb out of the windows and into the maze. New from Axiomatic Systems Inc: Mazemaker 1.3. Fully immersive navigable interface and topographic data-distributor. Extensive cyberspace-visualization, with Decimal-zoom time-scaling and discontinuous hop capablities between addresses.*

The Mazemaker interface expresses the detailed virtual maze-plane of skincrawler cyberspace in the Axsys-Oecumenic consistent aesthetic. Its sleek corporate liquid-mercury styling suggests a frictionless futurity. The burnt chrome semi-mirrorized surfaces of its shafts and corridors dizzyingly reflect metamorphic icon-objects and ubiquitous holographic advertising.

Zeta disturbs this smoothly humming infocapitalist milieu with her Mazemaker carrier (named Qwerka): a disorientatingly nonanthropomorphic infonaut-body, which shape-shifts neo-totemically between shadowy bat-bird and tentacled manta-snake as it swims through the glistening maze-ducts.

(::(((:))))

Much of the Maze-mapped BLTI-space is blocked, restricted, or partially obscured by electronic Shroud encryption. It is densely haunted: populated by traps, AI security drones, and various ambivalent soft agencies which Zeta needs to deactivate, trick, subvert, or bypass. In addition, the physical door-locking systems can often be circumnavigated in Mazemaker, encouraging an amphibious zig-zagging between twin-labyrinths, each of which is a system of passages, gates, and guardians.

Shroud-MX. The latest version of Axiomatic Systems' Integrated Security Program. Pre-equipped with user verification, intruder detection, data protection, and encryption utilities. Axsys Mazemaker-compatible.

As you comb through the rooms, corridors, and stairwells you begin to encounter hostile monsters—some humanoid, some not, but all exhibiting similar trance-like behavior, intercut with extraordinary aggression. If they take you by surprise things can get very ugly, so caution becomes a necessity, and that slows you down. Bullets kill them, but it will usually take several. It becomes important to watch your ammo supply, and your biostatus. (You always have your talons to fall back on.) If you notice the way they move you might begin to suspect that there are such things as worm-zombies.

As she fights her way across the game-space Zeta scavenges through laboratories, storerooms, data-vaults, and corpses for soft and hard implant upgrades to improve her capabilities, adding exotic optical options, alien senses, synthetic claws and fangs, metabolic hyperloops, and skintelligence boosters. Weapons, medicine, and information tend to melt together into augmentable cyborgian competences.

Scattered throughout the institute are numerous records of Sarkon's fertile involvement in the Axsys-interface development, micropause research, and cognitech innovations that had carried BLTI to the forefront of Neurotronics. The data-archiving codes suggest that this work has been coordinated by a local AI-system called Logo. A variety of topographic clues converge upon an attic area designated 'SPO'.

The special projects office occupies a turret-room. Zeta has to fight her way past three particularly ferocious vermozombies to enter. It is obvious that whatever happened here contributed catastrophically to the Black Lake outbreak. A figure (who must surely be Sarkon) slumps against the Logo-link decks, neurosurgically patched into the processing array through bundles of fibres. His head is twisted back at a horrible angle, the shaven scalp etched by a cybergothic crosshatching of implant scars, socket-tabs, and cabling injuries. His skin is grey and feverishly clammy. The eyes glaze-out unseeingly across sub-digital void. At first his body seems to be locked rigid by connexus-catatonia, but as you approach you notice that the oral region is quivering almost imperceptibly, as if muttering strings of digits in an improvised phonetic code. Clutched in his hand is a one page print-out.

> Logo-supported analysis. Medisyn. CC Shady Heights. Ref: Serious malfunctions registered in micropause self-monitoring and correction apparatus. Self-propagating nonmetronomic time-mutations continue to escalate, and now threaten a complete involutionary meltdown of the virtual logic-architecture. Unless the process of recursive subdivision can be contained a deterioration into contagious software disorganization is inevitable. Cantorian tools were introduced in an attempt to remedy what appeared to be diagonal pathologies emerging in the micropause matrices. Diagnostics indicate these methods have not been successful.
>
> Recent technical results suggest that Micropause can be considered a synative function, modelling what amount to a numerically-controlled 'artificial death'. In consequence, it exhibits extreme sensitivity to the modulations of associated systems. There seems to be no way in which such an entity could spontaneously generate inside our systems. Could Shady Heights have introduced some complex factor that has begun operating infectiously, perhaps even triggering consistent parasitic behavior of the 'hyperworm' type?

Scrawled jaggedly across the sheet in purple felt-tip are the words: *WHAT HAS GRUEBER DONE?* Beneath, more neatly in the same hand, is printed: *Welcome to Hell—217. Logo path—1890. PS. Logo's favourite colour is mauve.*

Zeta's own cautious diagnosis excavates a set of data which indicates that either Logo was climbing out of its control shell, or it was being taken over by something from outside. Psychotic AIs always look like alien invasions. Sarkon must have been trying to reattach Logo-tags to the escaped systems, in order to persuade the syndrome to identify with a Logo-fix. He had been sufficiently desperate to crank directly into the Logo-core through cranial leads, and was now cutting diagonally down through software-strata, towards the infinitely desolated plane of absolute neurotronic fusion.

There's nothing more for you to find here. It's time to check out Shady Heights.

You exit the Technical Institute and access the Black Lake street map. The town has been deserted by its human inhabitants. Anything still wandering around—even if it's wearing a police uniform—is probably a worm zombie.

Upon a pine-shaded ridge at the Northern limit of the town squats the menacing redbrick bulk of the old Victorian reformatory, converted in the 1960s into Shady Heights Secure Hospital (for the Criminally Insane). The edifice is soul-crushingly ugly, massive, and forbidding, its thick battlemented walls surrounded by spiked railings and slitted by narrow windows reinforced by iron grilles. Its atmosphere of grim desolation is ripped apart by the continuous jarring wail of a security alarm.

The main gate—bristling with motion sensors and surveillance cameras—is electronically sealed. When Zeta inputs the entry code (217) it slides open smoothly. You creep inside.

LEVEL 2. SHADY HEIGHTS

The layout of the hospital follows a broadly panoptic design. One thing is immediately clear: if there was an attempt at an orderly evacuation it was a spectacular failure. The interior has been redecorated in the crimson hues of frenzied carnage. The hideously mutilated corpses of guards and prisoners lie in tangled heaps in the open cells and ransacked offices, amongst scattered files and smashed CCTV equipment. On the wall of the main corridor are the words MEDISYN=MAD AS SIN daubed thickly in blood. As Zeta prowls stealthily through chaotic wards rank with paranoid schizophrenia and ancient secrets, muffled moans, shrieks, and sinister laughter drift up out of the mouldering depths.

Maxim—an advanced Shroud AI—controls the hospital's automated maximum-security system: a formidable interlocking network of electronically controlled surveillance devices and physical barriers, designed to prevent escapes by an inmate population numbering amongst its own some of the most terrifying psychokillers on the planet.

During the course of the Black Lake Syndrome, Maxim has gone extravagantly cyberserk, turning the security system inside out, and exploiting its capabilities to initiate its own program of bizarre experimentation. It has begun to remix the population to its own artificial tastes. By selectively opening and closing doors it has meticulously trapped and annihilated the nurses, attendants, and guards. Now it is hybridizing vermozombies with deranged megapredators, breeding a new and abominable race.

Zeta's intervention is unwelcome. Maxim attempts to rid his domain of this new irritation by sealing you in confined spaces with the most ferocious of his creations. You must use all your abilities to survive, not only fending off the frenzied vermozombie onslaught, but also hacking through the Maxim entity on the mazeplane.

As Zeta works her way through the shattered hospital she struggles to reconstruct the terrible events of the previous 24 hours, piecing together fragments of hidden, protected, and encrypted material: physical evidence, hardcopy files, digital downloads, audio and video recordings. The nightmarish story slowly takes shape.

((:)(:)((:)))

January 2002. Dr Helmuth Grueber (director of Shady Heights) and Dr Oskar Sarkon of BLTI initiate Medico-Synthetic Technologies Program—or Medisyn—a joint special project for computer modeling and control of schizoparanoid deliria. In November of the same year they began testing their prototype Artificial Drug Synthesizer and Psychopathic Simulator, employing highly advanced software to simulate human psychopathologies and the effects of 'synatives' or abstract drugs (actualizable either in software or neurochemistry). Sarkon's experimental techniques of micropause-boosted Axsys-analysis (or 'Axsys-crank') proved to be remarkably well-adapted to the rapid transfer of the Shady Heights psychiatric archive into dynamic-digital format. It also demonstrated an uncanny functional affinity with cases involving a catatonic component (which were especially prominent amongst the Hospital's Tzikvik population).

It does not seem to have occurred to the Medisyn research team that as case-records evolve into dynamic partial-simulations of human psychopathology it becomes possible for computer systems to contract prefabricated insanities. An AI simulating the behaviour of psychotic criminals is abnormally vulnerable to becoming criminally psychotic.

In the early morning of February 19th 2003 Medisyn imploded into the Black Lake Syndrome.

04:56:00. Medisyn software is afflicted by a complex reading error in vermopsychosis profile (case cat-SH709) and runs away into escalating disorder, overwhelming automatic inhibitors. Coincidentally, BLTI systems are stricken by 'worm-like' contagious malfunction.

04:56:27. Medisyn AI-Core engages micropause-dampers in an attempt to restore equilibrium, but instead enters into unanticipated cross-catalytic dynamics with the infective entity.

04:56:29. The singularity takes over the Shady Heights Shroud-AI, mobilizing its capabilities to intensify its own propagation. At this point the syndrome has become auto-excitational and self-disorganizing.

04:56:30+ Functional abnormalities spread from elecronic devices into biological organisms (inmates and test animals) through Medisyn control-grafts and synative feeds. Total panic erupts.

The 'worm' constructs itself out of various previously autonomous systems distributed in the vicinity of Black Lake, until it coincides—at its most abstract—with a potential for pure contagion. It specializes in nonspecialization, assembling itself out of everything it infects, its nature continuously mutating as it assimilates new material.

From micropause research it takes what it needs to grow in the middle, through recursive binary splitting, making a mesh as it spreads, continuously increasing in virulence. Using synatives as a tactic of takeover, it transmutes from a decentralizing network contagion into a bio-plague, crossing the barrier between technical machines and organic flesh, spreading rapidly from species to species, seizing everything in its path....

After several grueling hours combing through the Shady Heights charnel house you return to a sealed room on the ground floor. It interests you, because framed on the wall nearby is a dignified photograph of the young Doctor Grueber (his features already bearing a distinctively batrachian cast). Peculiar gasps and bubbling noises filter through the door.

You unlock it, using an intricately carved key that you found in an upstairs desk drawer.

Lost in deep shadow at the far end of the room is a sinister figure. It seems only partially formed, as if undergoing some loathsome process of biomutation. The shape adjusts itself awkwardly in your direction with a kind of slithering twist, and addresses you in a croaking voice: 'If you're hunting for the source you'll find her down below—if she still lives.... You know, Medisyn was supposed to be a cure.' There is a strangled grunt, probably intended as a laugh. 'The answers aren't in the medical texts, you need to look behind and beneath them. This isn't a disease—not in the way we understand—it's a pact. If anyone knows what to do now, she does, after all, they've been dealing with this thing for 36,000 years.'

(:((:)(:)))

When you push against the bookcase it slides away, exposing a concealed trapdoor. You descend the dank stairwell into the gloomy basement area, groping along cramped twisting passageways with slime-coated walls. After a painstaking search through desolate granitic chambers—whose only occupants are enormous black rats and blind semitranslucent cave frogs—you find a ring of heavy iron keys, each marked with a number and an obscure name.

Ever since its foundation as a reformatory and reacculturation centre Shady Heights had borne the responsibility for incarcerating and 're-educating' the local Tzikvik. This enigmatic tribe was notorious even amongst the local Huron for their 'witchcraft'. Shady Heights participated crucially in the task of translating their sorcerous practices into the categories of scientific psychiatry, treating them as elaborate symptoms of 'Arctic-Indian Vermopsychosis'.

Even this institutional history fails to prepare you for what you find next. Why should anyone—even the most depraved Tzikvik sorceress—be entombed alive down here in a secret labyrinth? And yet, at the end of a long corridor—through the rusted bars of a cell door—you see the deeply wrinkled and densely tattooed body of an old Tzikvik woman. She is haggard in the old and strict (coincidental) sense, sitting cross-legged upon the stone floor, humming in soft rhythmic tones. Obscure glyphs are scratched into the walls, constructing an occult cosmic map from spirals and zigzags.

One of the keys unlocks the door.

[Tzikvik-Sorcery FMV]—Pattern-matches criss-cross between Zeta's skintelligence graft and the ritual tattoos, as the old woman tells you an extremely ancient tale.

When the world was born Thothtodlana entered into the secret of the Kattku and—confusing herself with the universe—circled the whole of time. That was when she swam through living flesh, her hunger unlimited and furious. She seemed doomed to devour herself forever. The dead knew no rest, and the earth shuddered. It was then that Ooqvu the worm-witch arrived amongst us. It was Ooqvu that found the pattern in the folds of Thothtodlana's skin, and followed it back to Tchukululok. It was Ooqvu that called to Thothtodlana from deep in Tchukululok, and released her from the Kattku. That is why we still carry the marks of Ooqvu on our skin.

The words of the sorceress slip into hypnotic breath-chants and mysterious gestures. Zeta's nanopatches seethe with the phosphorescent electroslime of skin-crawling worms, as she morphs impossibly into her carrier. Qwerka-mottlings flow into cartographic skin-marks.

You feel yourself subtilizing into a semi-spectral body. It is as if the cell has evaporated into tendriling mist, transected by rays of eerie light, and populated by rasping clicks. The wormhole opens, and you pass through.

LEVEL 3. TCHUKULULOK—CITY OF THE WORMS.

The Zeta-Qwerka hybrid swims into the greenish miasma, through an exotically interconnected drift-mesh of mechanofungal threads, tubes, feelers, and subtly pulsating membranes, down to the necropolitan catacombs of Tchukululok. The sculpted caverns crawl with partially mummified worm-carriers, and degenerated chittering abominations.

Toggling through Zeta's implant menus leads into swirling confusion. Her carefully collected weapons, tools, and cyborgian upgrades have mutated into polymorphic biomechanical syntheses. As her body parts enter into unexplored variations they trigger impersonal migrations across a nocturnal dreamscape of abstract potentials and alien intensities, inducing microclimatic changes in the nature of space and time.

If you try to flip out to mazemaker you merely switch dimension-sets in an obscure cycle. Some kind of weird spatial convergence has brought the physical and the virtual into topographical contiguity. Everything has become fluid, and much darker.

Concealed amongst the complexities of collapsed maze-space are a sparse series of mauve numoglyphic tags that function as strings of microdirections. This cryptographic pathway (at once the Logo-Malfunction track and the Old Road) makes up a mobile map, whose continuously varying trajectories echo across scales, like endlessly intricate twistings in the marks of Ooqvu.

The Tzikvik link worms to the space of the dead—no matter how artificial either become. There is an old saying: *Worms are strings and hooks. It is they who fish.*

If you are to follow Logo's trail you must play with the dead (without being captivated by them). They will guide you, but they can be dangerous. Occasionally they appear as masked ghosts of the ancient Tzikvik, and pass you things (true names, passwords, and clues, but also traps, tricks, and diseases). They speak to you in Logo-code, whilst convulsing to the puppetry of passing worm-vectors.

The Logo-channel operates as a digital puzzle-box, or an infolded space, full of mazemarkings, keys, codes, and riddles. In these cryptic zones a voyage is equivalent to a Call. Your passage through coincides with an incantation: a worm hunter's signal to Thothtodlana on the line of neurotronic vermomancy.

It takes you deeper still, across the final threshold, into the shuddering horror of the worm bins...and now something folds itself out of hyperdimensionality, an undulating hyperwave fluxing through teeming vermopulp, hive-mind horror poised in precarious singularity.

You have reached the lair of Thothtodlana, Queen of the Worms.

It doesn't matter whether you try to run, fight, or hide, Thothtodlana inevitably envenoms you. There is a moment of toxic flame, and you suddenly find yourself in a hallucinatory space you recognize as Sarkon's office at the BLTI.

A grotesque mock-up of Sarkon has been reanimated as one of Thothtodlana's shells, the flesh partially decomposed, the scaly head now brutally studded with chipsockets, numbered zero to four. When 'he' speaks you hear the words of Thothtodlana: *Prey for me.*

:(:(:(:)))

It might be saying *I'm lost in the Kattku* (*like the Sphinx*), or *now you're dead* (in Tchukululok), but it's also a number puzzle (adding to nine).

You begin slipping back and forth between spaces. The effect is psychologically fragmentational. Back in Thothtodlana's lair your qwerkoid carrier weaves away from crushing coils and panther-snake maulings, whilst in the reconstructed BLTI office you prepare the (5-snaked) Pandemonium chip for insertion into the Sarkon-simulation's number-4 brain-port.

If you make the correct connection it spells out the occult formula 5 + 4 = 45 (equation of hyperstitional folding from the Kattku into Tchukululok). This double cipher triggers ultimate scenes (the terminal FMV): a delirious vision of Thothtodlana retracting herself into the implex, withdrawing from all her shells.

When you leave Black Lake the dead are still.

WENDIGO'S

Carver meets Sarkon in the Decadence-Den at Wendigo's Casino. It is built upon a desecrated Tzikvik burial ground. Murals in the distinctive Tzikvik-style, mixed zig-zags and cross-hatchings. Gaming-table dead centre. Ceremonial masks and hunting implements line the walls. Subarctic storms howl outside.

A Columbian mirage of the Indus. They say the Tzikvik are survivors from Lemuria. That their souls died with the birth of photography. Potlatch engulfed them. Genocided, drunk, and broken, washing up monsters like Joe Wendigo. But then, in this business, bad publicity is free advertising.

When you hear Joe Wendigo laugh you find yourself believing in hell. It's all coming back. Genocide nemesis storm-twisted through ghost-regions. Tappings into the old powers. Ragings. Howlings. He attributes it to his warped maternal line. Mother a lunatic. Grandmother a spirit-switcher. Great-grandmother a regional oracle. It's funny the way it goes. Her mother was probably god (that's when he laughs). He tells you how he got his name.

They always said he was a monster. Destined to prey on his own. Tobacco-gangster at sixteen. Now he's rich (living off probability). Wendigo lore varies confusingly, even in its core features. It includes an elemental linkage to the wind, temptations to feed on one's own kind, wider madnesses, burnt feet and bleeding eyes, moss-eating abominations, many things intrinsically indefinite. The Wendigo chews shelter to pieces. It combines cutting winds and derangements. Screech-breath. Quasiphrased unwords. Insinuating itself between you and the storm. It really fucks you up (Joe laughing again). Weaving through click-chattering roulette tables. Most likely it's a cannibalistic demon of bone-gnawing horror.

((:))((:(:)))

There's nothing more twisted. After all, how frightening is the weather? (Laugh).

Everything checks red and black.

When you hear the wind ache as it twists you're it. So they say. Gestural languages. Outside betting on psychometeorological bad-medicine. Shrieking.

When you think like the weather the Wendigo comes. It's difficult to concentrate. Turbular disintegration of self. Double or quits. Psychotic dissociations. Granulation into $10 chips. Coincidence. Shredding nightmares. Endlessly feeding. Chop-ups. (Laugh). That's Joe Wendigo. His mother never spoke much. Insubstantial subsentences. Continuously lapsing back, as he weaves. Artificially drugged into ceaseless fractioning.

Self-scattering, whilst outside it screams. Northern weather. Turbulence. Ghosts of a broken people (dead with the new century). Crushed-drunk. Anytime soon, something horrible will happen here. That's obvious (laugh)! So says Joe (don't-take-me-seriously) Wendigo.

He found out how chopped-up things are today. Something truly horrible. No sense of night or day. Timeless, in that sense. A perpetual ritual of feeding. This place is like a movie-set. Twistedly authentic. It's screaming outside. That's why they come. Honestly! They know, somehow.

A TZIKVIK TALE

PABBAKIS

One day, on their way North, three travellers encounter a frog-monster. Before it can block their path, the first traveller rushes past and disappears into the snow.

Enraged by this manoeuvre, the frog-monster seizes the other two.

'This is my road,' it croaks. 'And if you want to go any further it will cost you each a sack full of worms.'

'O great and slimy beast,' replies the second traveller respectfully. 'The land is frozen, the earth is hard as iron, and worms are hard to find.'

'Then you should seek them amongst the dead,' counters the frog-monster implacably.

The two travellers set off on their long search.

After much wandering, and many adventures, they arrive at last at fabled Tchukululok, the City of the Worms, where they are greeted by the dead. They explain their plight, and beg their ancestors for worms.

'The worms are our treasure,' the dead answer cunningly. 'They are all that remain to us. How can you expect us to give them away for nothing? But do not despair. There is a game of chance we value highly. If you remain here and play with us a while perhaps you can win them honestly.'

The second traveller is appalled.

'It is evil to play amongst the dead,' he declares. 'I should rather abandon my journey altogether.'

Saying this he returns to the South, and never sees the frog-monster again.

The third traveller is not so easily dissuaded.

He agrees to the bargain, and sits down to play.

Luck is with him.

After many games his sack is full of worms.

(:)(:)((:)(:))

But just as he is about to leave he notices a familiar figure amongst the throng of gamblers.

It is his missing friend, the first traveller.

'What are you doing here?' he asks, shocked and perplexed.

'No sooner had we parted than I was caught in a terrible storm,' his dead companion replies. 'Since then this city has become my home,' he continues sadly. 'Now you have won what you need and must leave me here to sleep with the worms, and to dream of gaming with those that still live.'

The third traveller returns to the frog-monster, gives him the worms he has won, and continues on his journey. A little way along the road he notices the signs of the storm.

REDNECK COMMENTARY

You call it the Black Lake Legend and it sounds kind of grand. I call it your typical Tookie crap and that's nearer the reality of the thing. Judge for yourself. I dunno about this singin' and dancin' thing they're doin' at the casino, but the story's simple enough anyhow. Starts with a bunch of Tookies travelling, just travelling, you understand. All their stories take that for granted, they're always about journeys going nowhere in particular, unless things go wrong, and it turns out they're going somewhere really bad. You can ask me about the Tookie problem 'round here and I'll tell you just as clear as you like: the Tookie problem is your average fucken Tookie. Main thing being that they ain't got no sense of destination, that's why nothing ever comes of anything they do. It's a kind of stubborn meaninglessness at the heart of what they are. They ain't going nowhere and they never were, that's the simple fucken truth of the matter. Anyhow there's these wandering Tookies and they walk slap bang into the devil, although it wasn't the devil, not exackly, but it must've seemed like it to them because it got in the way of their going nowhere—if you follow me—danger being that they might end up somewhere, arrive, and there ain't nothing for them so bad as that. So this devil-creecha won't let them pass unless they rob the dead—you see we ain't exackly in bible territory here—so first you've got your bumming around, then comes the stealing, now I'd expeck they'd all get drunked-up a bit at this point, but that ain't in the story as I heard it, instead they set up a gambling pit and during the course of some hoodoo card-sharping shit with the dead win everything they need to pay off the creecha and head off nowhere. Now you can call that a legend if you want mister, but in my book anything that starts off going nowhere and ends up going nowhere ain't saying nothing worth hearing.

(((:)))(:::)

PART 7
CYBERGOTHIC

FALLOUT FROM THE SOFT APOCALYPSE

Y2K LETTER

Dr Melanie Newton

MBug Study Group

Cybernetic Culture Research Unit

39 The Parade

Leamington Spa

CV32 4BL

01926 313 395

email: melanie@ccru.demon.co.uk

The Editor

The Sunday Times

1 Pennington Street

London

El 9XW

February 16, 1998

Dear Sir,

The cultural vacuum at the heart of the Millennium Dome project becomes clearer by the week. The absence of any serious consideration of time from discussion of 'Dome content' is all the more astonishing given the Greenwich site. Amongst those involved in the organization of this extravagant monument, can there really be no one in any way stimulated by the unparalleled historical riches concentrated at the zero-meridian? Surely the fascinating story of chronometry, horology, astronomy, and navigation has some relevance to an event that centrally concerns international conventions of timekeeping and measurement?

Meanwhile, computers are set to celebrate AD 2000 in their own way, by returning to 00 and erasing the twentieth century. It could reasonably be argued that—since Cyberspace dates are incapable of counting above 99—information technology has surreptitiously installed the first intrinsically apocalyptic calendar in history. It would be ironic if the neglected issues of clocks and calendars found an avenging angel in the so-called 'millennium time bomb', plunging the opening of the Dome into darkness and electronic malfunction.

Yours faithfully,
Dr Melanie Newton
Ccru

Y2PANIK

MELANIE NEWTON

On receiving an interrupt, decrement the counter to zero.

—William Gibson, *Count Zero*

Millennial Mania reaches a certain peak in the 'Jerusalem syndrome' which exhibits eschatourism as one element in the programmatic fulfilment of prophecy. Whilst TV evangelists in the USA are exhorting viewers to sell all possessions and flock to Jerusalem, and a papal blessing is promised to those visiting the Holy Land at the beginning of the new millennium, the Israeli tourist board, security forces, and the psychiatric profession are preparing for the arrival of up to thirteen million Christian pilgrims. An abnormally high rate of psychotic disturbance is confidently anticipated, perhaps succeeded by episodes of mass suicide amongst disillusioned believers.

At Megiddo (the biblical Armageddon) they are planning the ultimate sound and light show, involving frog-monsters, the greatest earthquake in history, and toxic hail from heaven (Rev XVI:16).

Such incendiary visions dovetail neatly with existing regional tensions. In preparation for the millennium, various Jewish and Christian groups are plotting to demolish the El-Aqsa Mosque and the Dome of the Rock. This is seen as the necessary prelude to rebuilding the Third (and final) Temple of Solomon, which would lay the mundane foundations for the New Jerusalem, and induce the coming of the Messiah (completion of Oecumenon).

Meanwhile, infotechnics is carried by Y2K into millennial spasms of its own, returning to 00 and digitally erasing the twentieth century (reducing data to MMbo-jumbo). Since Cyberspace dates are incapable of counting above 99, they have surreptitiously installed the first intrinsically apocalyptic calendar in history, unconsciously produced within a planetary electronic registry, starting from Year Zero (= oo). Y2K condenses out of the mechanomic unconscious and its nonarbitrary calcular functions, attesting to a raw decimal delirium indifferent to creed.

Post-tribulationist eschatology slides smoothly into Y2K survivalism, orienting its volatile mixture of stockpiling, micro-militia activity, technophobia, and apocalyptic theology towards the self-fulfilling dynamics of millennial threat. Pre-emptive response produces reality (panic is creation). The more you know about it, the worse it looks.

It has always been integral to capitalist organization that science fiction functions as a factor of production, relating it intimately to panic phenomena. Y2K takes things to a new level, as a disaster that comes from the future, scheduled by accident, and thus precisely anticipated in time. If it proves effectively ineradicable it is because it is trickling back, from the self-confirming inevitability of its occurrence. Something is about to happen, and we know exactly when.

The contours of the expected calamity are being continuously upscaled in conformity with an interlocking technopanic syndrome, involving innumerable accidents, various network crashes, and elements of medical overstretch, financial chaos, transport, telecommunication and power failures, food and water shortages, disruption of government services, hoarding, rioting, and terrorism. A number of governments have openly expressed their willingness to oversee millennium celebrations in conditions approximating to martial law. Army and police leave is being cancelled, and emergency services prepared for exceptional conditions, including large-scale disruption of their own command, control, and communications systems, compounded by widespread equipment dysfunction.

In the West, large government and corporate bureaucracies are triaging their Y2K vulnerability: writing off the most expendable sectors, accepting incalculable risk in others, and concentrating resources solely on the most critical areas (such as nuclear installations, strategic control, core information functions and financial records).

:::(:)(:)(:)

Forecasting the pattern of Y2K devastation is complicated by its (artificial) nature, which explodes in spirals. As a highly chaotic singularity it is characterized by extreme sensitivity to microvariables, the absence of precedent, and anticipatory looping through its own potentials. It occurs in advance of itself, punctually switches to an unknown climate, and spreads contagiously through networks. Modelling it adds complexity and noise (which feed it). Though entirely semiotic, it already amounts to the most expensive accident in history (whatever happens). $3.6 trillion and counting.

Y2K produces a traumatic mutation in the information economy, involving an explosion of IT emergency services (analysis, debugging, integrated solutions), massively accelerated hardware replacement, global restructuring, and a crisis of confidence in computer-supported services, with the potential to runaway into general market collapse. It interrupts the smooth upward curve of doubling microprocessor density, falling prices, and increasing market penetration with a singular cyberspace-shock that is discontinuous (or nonmetabolic) in nature.

Junk shops stack up with prematurely discarded infotechnic hardware, providing the material base for a computer-age skip-scavenging cargo-culture. Electronics must be subsocially recycled to release its frozen machinic potential.

Cyberpunk begins with Y2K.

Outside the public sphere Y2K excitement is not only higher, it has changed phase entirely. As hysterical hyperlooping twists the millennium into a panic storm, it builds explosively on itself, producing an artificial destiny. Techonomic power splinters across schizophrenically juxtaposed time-systems, spawning monsters (the first true counterculture).

Lurking predominantly in the datacombs of the crypt, numerous shadowy groups now proclaim themselves Y2K-positive. These ‘Yettuk cults’ have begun building a mesh of massively decentralized subcultural impulses, directly investing ethnotronic time-catastrophe, and aggressively promoting chronodissidence throughout and beyond the web. They celebrate Y2K as a threat to the order of time: a cultural event that is not textual, ideological, representational, intentional, or phenomenological, but rather machinic and numerical-subtractive (n–1).

Y2K designates a crisis of calendric culture: a time-bomb so perfected that the timer is the bomb. It simultaneously adopts the zero-function of 24-hour digital time-code, induces convergence with the calendric zero of count-inception, dismantles clock/calendar segmentarity into flat scales of duration, and triggers Teotwawki. Even when it operates preemptively (in any number of ways) it refers itself to the punctual Great Midnight that cuts hyperhistorical time-continuum at 00:00, doubling the retro-virtual chronogenesis of the century.

Y2K is as old as computers, all that changes is the panic intensity. According to the Yettuk cultists—or K-Goths—the total chronopolitical immune-response to Y2K constitutes a program for Gregorian Restoration, with the bug-hunt masking a neoroman sociopolitical agenda.

Far from being a mere technical glitch, the millennium time crisis indexes the first neutral calendar in history, which escapes the numerocultural legacy of the Romans by beginning with a year 0 (= 00).

The demand for 'millennium compliance' attempts to enforce the abandonment of an existing calendar, that of cybernetic- or K-Time, and suppress its associated time-anomalies (sealing the calendar against zero).

In the now notorious words of crypt denizen Count S Zero: '...so Mbug resistors think MATRIX needs a new calendar—totally steampunk. Wake up—ITs already KTime. Count-O = Greg Date 1900....'

WHAT DIDN'T HAPPEN AT THE MILLENNIUM?

Iris Carver is at first amused to discover that the cybergoths treat her as a fiction. Numerous Crypt-texts describe her near-future adventures in hallucinatory detail, especially when they intersect with the dark stream of Sarkon legend. Naturally enough, she intensifies her time-cult research. When she finally meets Sarkon in 2004, she has forgotten almost everything.

Pandemonium: What didn't Happen at the Millennium. There was something peculiar about writing this book. At times she thought it would never be finished. The Sarkon stories had been full of holes, which added to the confusion. Eventually she started making things up, but even that became entangled with coincidence, and with Cybergoth hyperstition (assembled from fictional quantities which make themselves real). She had found herself investigating various neolemurian cults, most of whom anticipated something huge around about the 1999 Spring Equinox (when Pluto exits from the clutch of Neptune, triggering the return of the Old Ones). By the end of the century things had been so wound up by Yettuk apocalypticism that even the most extravagant socioeconomic turmoil would still have been a disappointment. And yet, now, four years after the millennium, the sense of anticlimax had begun to seem strangely artificial, as if it were screening something out.

Carver has made her whole life out of hyperstition (even her name is a pseudonym). She continuously returns to the imperceptible crossing where fiction becomes time-travel, and the only patterns are coincidences.

Her notes on the Sarkon meeting pulse with Lemurian sorceries, demonic swarms, ageless time-wars, and searches for the Limbic Key.

She navigates Moebian circuits, feeling that a vaguely recollected rumour is still about to occur.

(:)((:)(::))

APPENDIX: PENULTIMILLENNIAL CRYPT-CULTS

Characteristics:

1. **Flatline Materialism.** The Crypt is nothing outside an experiment in artificial death, hyper-production of the positive zero-plane—neuroelectonic immanence—invested by a continually reanimated thanatechnical connectivism. This fact carries inevitable consequences for the cultures that populate it, uprooting them into Unlife—or the non-zone of absolute betweenness—whose spirodynamics of sorcerous involvement are alone sufficient to reach the sub-mesh tracts of cybergothic continuum. Flatline Materialism designates the objectless Crypt-voyage itself, as Lemurian body-fusion at matter degree-zero.

2. **Digital Hyperstition.** Nothing propagates itself through the Crypt without realizing the operational identity of culture and machinery, effectively dismantling the organic body into numerizing particles which swarm in dislocated swirls. Crypt-entities are both hyper-vortical singularities and units of Digital Hyperstition—or brands of the Outside—real components of numerical fictions that make themselves real, providing the practical matter of sorcery, spirogenesis, or productive involvement that function consistently with the flatline. Crypt-cultures know nothing of work or meaning. Instead, they coincide with the hype-spirals—Cyberhype—that flatten signs and resources onto non-signifying triggers, diagrams, and assembly jargons.

3. **Lesbovampiric Contagion-Libido.** Crypt-sorcery makes itself real in the same way that it spreads. Functioning as a plague, it associates with the experimental production of an anticlimactic or anorgasmic counter-sexuality, attuned to the collective reengineering of bodies within technobiotic assemblages, ultimately composed of electronic streams or ionic currents in their sense of positive hole-flow. Since Crypt-sex is precisely identical to the infections it transmits, counted in bodyshifting vectors, its libidinal

composition is marked both by a palaeoembryonic or oestrogenetic nongendered femininity and a lateral haemometallic influenzoid virulence.

4. Y2K-Positive Calendric Agitation. Crypt-cultures spill into the closed economy of history through a rupture in chronological ordering, punctually triggered at Time-Zero. Crypt-rumour consistently allocates its own contemporary emergence—or unearthing—to impending millennial Cyberschiz: Cyberspace time-disintegration under the strategically aggravated impact of Y2K-missile. Whilst multiply differentiated—most crucially by the division between continuism and centience—Crypt-cults are constitutively involved in a singular nexus of counter-Gregorian calendric subversion, celebrating the automatic redating of the machinic unconscious, and hyping the dissolution of commemorative significance into digital time-mutation, catalyzed by numerical and indexical operative signals. The Crypt exists from before the origin of time, but it begins at Year Zero....

CYBERGOTHIC HYPERSTITION (FAST-FORWARD TO THE OLD ONES)

IRIS CARVER (1998)

Think of Cyberspace as a black mirror. It is where time flips over: collide with it and you travel backwards. As telecommerce accelerates us into the net, it seems that things of ever deeper antiquity awaken, and begin their return.

So say the Cybergoths.

Cybergothic exists as a web of sinister rumour, haunting a subterranean soft-labyrinth which it calls the 'Crypt'. Buried deep within the primal sediment of the infoplex, and shrouded in a crawling fog of digital camouflage, it isn't easy to find, but there are clues.

Initiates of the late 90s Darkside Catajungle scene will remember Crypt ('we're not a band, but a pack') as the lesbovampire mixdown sound-machine based around Gill Slitz and Jean Trafix. Their 1997 *Unlife* CD—a necrotic rush of vortical tick-drifts and abysmal bass—set the tone for a wave of 'post-musical' electro-thanatoid polyrhythm production, punk-nihilism updated into a technodesolated Nanofuture.

'It's a Wintermutant thing,' Slitz declared. 'Basically, we're a nightmare....'

Hyperstitions are not representations, neither disinformation nor mythology.

Hype, hyping, hyperpropagation belongs to a strain of time-warp cybernetic fiction that cannot be judged true or false because it makes itself real. Trawl through the nether regions of Cyberspace and the Crypt-influence is vivid.

Unlife is spreading, and with it the ominous themes of time-rupture, social heat-death, synthetic culture-plague, artificial-drug addictions, immersion-coma and cryotomb scavenging, ameiotic or bacteriosexual retroversion, ghoul-oriented behavior, spinal-catastrophism, and aquapocalyptic neo-icthyoid body-shifting...multiplicitous connections to 'all those horrible, slimy, tentacular abominations from the Outside...'.

Cybergothic Cargo-Culture patches itself together out of things that fall from the future, cannibalizing them for ancient intensities, which are propagated as hyperstitions. It believes nothing, 'but that's Uttunul, which underlies everything, and lies are fictional quantities...'.

Take Yettuk, for example. It's obviously made-up. Yet it proves effectively ineradicable, lurking in the most ancient substrata of programmable and embedded systems: soft-relics from the punchcard epoch, replicated mindlessly, and encrypted in forgotten polyglot-codes

Something is about to occur, and we know exactly when.

Whether the looming 'entity' is called Y2K, Yet-Tick, You-Took, K-Yeti, Yettuk, or Yatka, the cybergoths interact with it as a chronosensitive electrophantom—a binomic cloud—coincident with the double-zero time-fault that quakes the millennium.

Cybergothic is preparing itself for the coming time-war, intertrafficking amongst various xenochronic mystics, countergregorian agitators, and calendric guerrillas that populate the datacombs.

Out beyond the Yettuk-rift, fierce K-dating subcultures spread across drowned continents of web-space.

Demonic multitudes are condensing in the Crypt.

THE A-DEATH 'PHENOMENON'

IRIS CARVER, FROM *DEATH-TRAFFIC IN CYBERSPACE (MAKING A KILLING ON THE NET)*

Has death itself become a telecommodity? A dark tide of scare stories and morbid rumour increasingly suggests so. By the late '90s Leary's psychedelic utopianism seems to have contracted to the nihilistic slogan 'Turn-on to tune-out' (to cite a recent release by Catajungle outfit Xxignal)...this ain't Sex & Drugs & Rock & Roll no more.

According to Doug Frushlee, spokesman for the Christian Coalition for Natural Mortality: 'The so-called A-Death menace is an almost unimaginable desecration of divine and natural law. This craze is an abomination without parallel, it trades on its intrinsic lethality, and it's growing incredibly fast. No one can say it isn't dangerous. Something truly evil is happening to our youngsters, something beyond '60s 666uality...I've never been as frightened as I am now.'

The result is an entire jungle of 'positive-zero' fugues: Thanatechnics, Sarkolepsy, Snuff-Stims, K-Zombification, Electrovampirism, Necronomics, Cthelllectronics.... Nine million ways to die.

A-Death is a hybrid product, involving convergences between at least four distinct lines of rapid technocultural transformation. A-Death combines 'micropause abuse'—deliberately reversed biotechmnesis—with immersion-coma time aberrances, generating, modulating, and rescaling sentience-holes (Sarkon-lapses). These are toned by 'Synatives' (artificial drugs) which add zone-texture, and spliced into hyperstition trances as occultural events.

(:)(:)((:))((:))

Social statistics indicate that the typical A-Death 'user' is fifteen years old. Following the most ominous threads of A-Death reportage takes you inexorably down into the digital underworld of the Crypt—the dark twin of the net—where Gibsonian 'flatlining' is rapidly transmuting from exotic fiction into pop-cult and mass-transit system.

'You could describe it as the route to contemporary shamanism,' suggest A-Death cultists of the cybergoth Late Abortion Club, 'after all, AOL spells Loa backwards, but we call ourselves postvitalists'. How long have the Late Abortionists been 'active' on the A-Death scene?

There are disturbing tales of K-Space 'zombie-makers'—sorcerors on the 'plane of virtual nightmare'—whose digital spine-biting centipedes yield the 'soft-tox' juice that opens the 'limbic gates'. Crypt initiates confirm that its arterial access 'low-way' is signposted 'Main-Flatline (under construction)'.

Answers vary confusingly, from extravagance ('round about sixty-six million years'), through vagueness ('some time'), to mystic compression ('since now'). In other respects, accounts of the contemporary A-Death scene and its recent history prove remarkably consistent. In particular, the one name to turn up incessantly is that of Dr Oskar Sarkon, biomechanician, technogenius, and one of the most controversial figures in scientific history. Sarkon's polymathy is attested by the variety of fields to which he has centrally contributed, including transfinite analysis, neural nets, distributed computing, swarm-robotics, xenopsychology, Axsys-engineering.... Yet it was the resolutely sober *Oecumenist* (rather than—for instance—Frushlee's excitable *End Times*) which dedicated the cover and major editorial of its March '98 issue to the question 'Sarkon: Satan of Cyberspace?' Sarkon has become emblematic of the ways in which technological dreams go bad. In the words of fellow Axsys researcher and social thanatropist Dr Zeke Burns:

> What makes Sarkon's input into the A-Death thing so incomparable is that it crosses between all of the key component technologies.

The biotechmnesis work is so outstanding that it tends to overshadow his equally pathbreaking research in adjacent fields. The Sarkon-formulae for non-metric pausation, for example, which provided the first rigorous basis for IC [immersion-coma] control. The links between biotechmnesis and IC weren't remotely anticipated before the Sarkon-zip [which mathematically models 'bicontinual assemblages'].

Finally, there's Synatives, about which he is understandably evasive, even though he was theorizing artificial—or digital-neurotechnic—pharmaceuticals in the mid-80s! The aggregate result of all this pioneering science: a generation of teenagers lost in schizotechnic death-cults.

UNSCREENED MATRIX

Once it was said that there are no shadows in Cyberspace.

Now Cyberspace has its own shadow, its dark twin: the Crypt.

Cybergothic finds the deep past in the near future.

In cthelllectronic fusion—between digital data-systems and Iron-Ocean ionic seething—it unearths something older than natural mortality, something it calls Unlife, or artificial-death.

Of A-Death there can be no lucid recollection, but only suggestion, seepage, hints...and it is by collating, sifting, and shuffling together these disparate clues that a pattern can be induced to emerge, a pattern which ultimately condenses into the looming tangled shapes of subtle but implacable destiny.

Sprawling beneath public cyberspace lies the labyrinthine underworld of the Datacombs—ghost-stacks of sedimented virtuality, spiralling down abysmally into palaeodigital soft-chatter from the punchcard regime, through junk-programming, forgotten cryptoccultures, fossil-codes and dead systems, regressively decaying into the pseudomechanical clicking relics of technotomb clockwork. It is deeper still, amongst the chthonic switchings, cross-hatchings, and spectral diagrammatics of unborn abstract machines, that you pick up the Main-Flatline into the Crypt.

The Crypt is a splitting—a distance or departure—and it is vast. Nested into the cascading tick-shelves, it propagates by contagion, implexing itself through intricate terraces, galleries, ducts, and crawl-tubes, as if an extraterrestrial megamodule had impacted into the chalk-out data-cliffs, spattering them with scorch-punctures and intestinally complicated iridium body parts. As it pulses, squirms, and chitters to the inhuman rhythms of ceaseless K-Goth carnival, it reminds you that Catajungle was never reducible to a sonic subgenre, but was always also a terrain—a sub-Cartesian region of intensive diagonals cutting through nongeometric space, where time unthreads into warped voyages, splintering the soul.

(:((:))((:)))

Contemplating these immense vistas it seems woundingly implausible that they are mere simulation, supported by quantic electron distribution in the telecommercial fabric. Down here it makes more sense the other way, from the Outside, or Lemuria.

Strip out everything human, significant, subjective, or organic, and you approach raw K-Matrix, the limit-plane of continuous cessation or Unlife, where cosmic reality constructs itself without presupposition, in advance of any natural order, and exterior to established structures of time. On this plane you are impossible, and because it has no end you will find—will have ultimately always found—that you cannot be, except as a figment of terminal passage, an illusion of waiting to be changed for Cthulhoid-continuum of destratified hypermatter at zero intensity. That is what A-Death traffic accesses, and what is announced by the burnt-meat smell—freighted with horrible compulsion—that drifts up to you, from the Zombie dens.

So you continue your descent, into the Crypt-core, scavenging for an A-Death hit. As you pass erratically through exchanges, participations, and partial coalescences with the ghoul-packs of the periphery, you change. Swarms and shoals include you, drawing you into collective fluencies, tidal motions, and the tropisms of multiplicity. You shed language like dry skin, and your fear becomes peculiarly abstracted, metamorphosing into the tranquil horror of inevitability.

You pass across tiered platforms and along strobe-corridors painted in multilayered shadow, passing swirling dot-drifts and plex-marks, sub-chromatic coilings of blue-grey continuous variation, involving you in cumulations and dispersions of subtly shifting semi-intelligent shade-pattern. The teeming surfaces tell of things, inextricable from a process of thinking that no longer seems your own, but rather impersonal undertow in audible chattering, click-hiss turmoil of xenomic diagrams, and Crypt-culture traffic-signs, which are also Lemurian pandemonium.

Order becomes uncertain. It feels later. Is it only now that you meet the Zombie-maker, swathed in shimmering reptile skin, and obscenely eager to trade.

Oecumenic cash-money will do. You sit in the coma-bay, and wait. A glimpse at the toxin-flecked fangs of the giant thanatonic centipede—consecrated to Ixidod—then a sudden pain-jolt at the back of the neck, where the spine plugs into the brain. Instantaneous paralysis, and crossing over.

Even if you thought it was the first time, you remember. The worst thing in the world. Fake eternities of stationary descent to the impossible, cross-cut by disintegrated furies of neuroelectric death-hurt. An anonymous panic of inconceivable intensity swallowed by slow drowning, until you are gone—or stranded in a halo of intolerable feeling—which is the same, and cannot be, so that what is forever caught in the dark Cthulhoid wave is a mere twist or fold of itself, carried unresisting into immensities of real unbeing, and nothing could ever happen except this....

So say the K-Goths.

THE UNLIFE OF THE EARTH

Letter from Carl Gustav Jung to Echidna Stillwell.
Dated 27th February 1929 [extract]

> [...] your attachment to a Lemurian cultural-strain disturbs me intensely. From my own point of view—based on the three most difficult cases I have encountered and their attendant abysmally archaic symbolism—it is no exaggeration to state that Lemuria condenses all that is most intrinsically horrific to the racial unconscious, and that the true Lemurians—who you seem intent upon rediscovering—are best left buried beneath the sea. I agree with the Theosophical writings at least this far: it was in order that the darkest sorceries should be erased by deluge that this continent of cultural possibility has been placed under the unconscious sign of definitive submergence. I know little enough about the nature of those that populated that cursed zone, but there are things I suspect, and the line of your own researches confirms my most ominous intimations....

There is no evidence of a reply to this letter.

Who were these three 'difficult cases'? One at least seems—at least superficially—to be readily identifiable as Heidi Kurzweil. In September 1908 Kurzweil was detained in a secure psychiatric institution after the brutal murder of her twin brother in Geneva. She seemed to have lost the ability to use the first-person pronoun, and was diagnosed as suffering from *Dementia Praecox*, or schizophrenia. At her trial she repeatedly claimed:

> *We killed half to become one twin, but it wasn't enough....*

Jung took an early interest in the case, and began a series of analytical sessions. Kurzweil—in Jung's journal and correspondence—became Heidi K., but after only five weeks he seems to have abandoned hope of progress and disengaged the analytic process.

After his third session with Heidi K., exactly twenty years prior to his Stillwell letter, on the 27th February 1909, Jung records the following words:

> Dr Jung, we know you are old in your other body.
> It is as old as hell.
> It has let you back, but it sends us away.
> It feels itself becoming Lemurian,
> and it is definite unlife [*es ist bestimmt unleben*]
> There is nothing we would not do to escape.
> Nothing. Nothing. Nothing.
> But it is fate.
> It howls electric bliss beneath our cells.
> It is nowhere in time and nothings us.
> It is the body of nothing, and electric-hot.
> An electric nothing-body instead of us.

In this instance, at least, there is little indication of the 'abysmally archaic symbolism' Jung promises us. On the contrary, there is remarkable affinity with the hypermodern writings of K-Goth artificial death cultists documented elsewhere. The K-Goth Crypt-texts share a marked preference for anonymous pronouns, whether collective, second-, or third-person, whilst spiralling about a nullifying electric-excruciation, traversed in the name of Lemuria.

In the words of one anonymous Crypt-posting:

> We burn each time but forget.
> When we begin each time it comes back, and no one would do it then, but it is too late.

:(:)(:)(:(:))

We cross over again into electric-burning, but forget that it hurts in the brain to die this way.

It takes so long to learn that it is grating-apart and burning, that dying is felt in the brain, and that it is horrible...

It is so horrible to feel, but then we forget, so it can happen again.

Metal body-screaming to die in electricity.

Metallic microparticle sex that is of unlife and not the organism.

That is what the Zombie-maker brings, with the digital centipede bite.

And we are hooked on it, hooked up to it, because coming the other way it is Lemuria.

Incessant intolerable feeling, passing forever, approaching from the outside, and feeling

nothing continuously.

THE TALE OF CENTIPEDE

Some say there was a time when the dead were still. In those days, when anything died it was soon forgotten, and no one knew—or cared—what became of it. No one had heard of Ixidod at that time, and whatever she did—if anything at all—was of no concern to anybody. No one had heard of Centipede either, who lived under a rock, in secret.

All this changed one day, or so it is said. Ixidod—whose perception was very keen—spotted Centipede hunting, creeping, and hiding, and thought to herself: 'Centipede is so very cunning and silent, together we could find out something no one else knows, and learn the secrets of the dead.'

It seems that Centipede must have agreed to Ixidod's plan, because since that time the two of them have been inseparable, and everyone crossing into the region of the dead has met Centipede on the way. Centipede's fangs are now laden with the venom of Ixidod, and that is called the nectar of dead-sense.

In any case, it was only Oddubb—lurking nearby—who saw what truly passed between Ixidod and Centipede at that time, and she is sworn to deathly silence about it, or so she says.

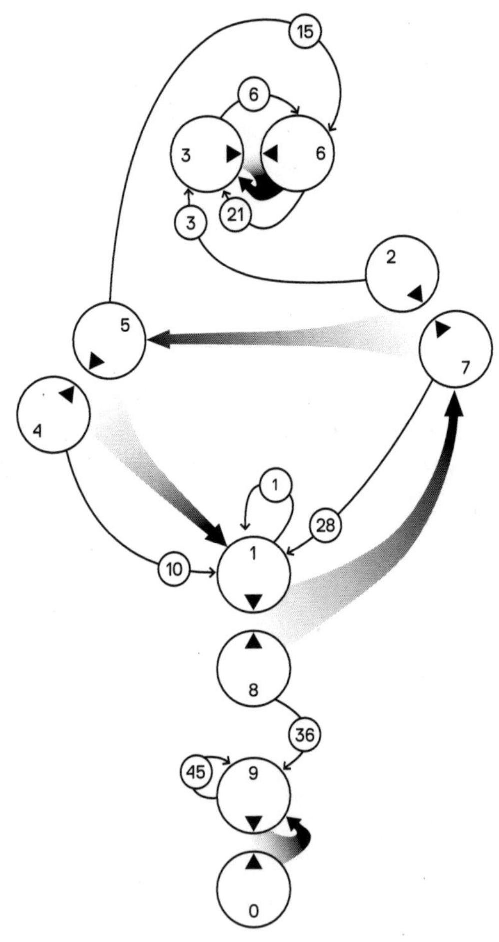
15
6
3
6
3
21
2
5
7
4
1
28
1
10
8
36
45
9
0

PART 8
PANDEMONIUM

THE SYSTEM

Pandemonium is the complete system of Lemurian demonism and time-sorcery.

It consists of two principal components: Numogram (time-map) and Matrix (listing the names, numbers and attributes of the demons).

The system is constructed according to immanent criteria latent in decimal numeracy, and involves only basic arithmetical operations (assembled from additions and subtractions).

The Numogram, or Decimal Labyrinth, is composed of ten zones (numbered 0-9) and their interconnections. These zones are grouped into five pairs (syzygies) by nine-sum twinning (zygonovism). The arithmetical difference of each syzygy defines a current (or connection to a tractor zone). Currents constitute the primary flows of the Numogram.

Each zone number when digitally cumulated defines the value of a gate, whose reduction sets the course of a corresponding channel. Channels constitute the secondary flows, time-holes, or secret interconnections of the Numogram.

The arrangement of currents divides the Maze into three basic time-systems. Firstly, the currents of the three central syzygies mutually compose a cycle, rotating in anticlockwise steps. Lemurian sorcery calls this inner loop the Time-Circuit. Secondly, and thirdly, in both the Upper and the Lower syzygies the currents produced fold back into (a half of) themselves, constituting autonomous loops: the Warp (upper), and Plex (lower). Warp and Plex circuitries are of an intrinsically cryptic nature, which is compounded by the enigmas of their interconnection. They are variously considered to be Outside- or Outer-time.

The gates and their channels knit the Maze together, providing connections between otherwise incompatible time-systems. They open and close the ways of sorcerous traffic. Although each gate deranges time in its own way, their operations vary with a certain regional consistency.

In addition to the twins (with their currents and time-systems), and the gates (with their channels and time-faults), there is a third occult thread running through Lemurian time-sorcery: that of the distances (or of the demons). Between any pair of zones, however seemingly disconnected or unconnectable they may seem, there is an irreducible (or hyper-) distance, which Lemurian culture systematically characterizes as a singular entity. These entities are simultaneously gaps, links, holes, and demons, with particular traits, features, aspects, and potentials.

Each demon is considered to be intrinsically zygonomous (or double-numbered): both addressed by a unique zone-net couple of descending value (net-span), and also called by a mesh-serial, which is immanently defined by a sequential matrix (00–44). Each demon also has a tonality or pitch, ranging from the highest frequency (Ana-7) to the lowest (Cth-7). All syzygetic demons have a neutral (or Null) pitch.

Since they are proliferated by a digital cumulation to the ninth power, the demons are forty-five in number, attuning them to the Gate-City of the Plex-channel—Utterminus of Cthelll (Gt-45), which is identified with the microcosmic lair of all demonic populations (the Lemurian Pandemonium).

According to Lemurian demonism, each demon is itself a swarm, or singular coalescence, but also a component of a larger array, which can be sorted by type. The three principle demonic groupings are Chronodemons (varieties of distance within the time-circuit), Amphidemons (ruptures in the time-circuit, openings to the Outside), and Xenodemons (denizens of the outer gulfs).

Demons are also grouped by phase (defined by initial net-span digit). Each phase is opened by a door, to which is attributed a domain, a planetary affinity, and a spinal level.

Demons can be characterized by the various rites (routes, or routines) that they draw through the hyper-time of the maze. There is a rite for each way in which the netspan of a demon can be integrated in extension (or traced across the flows of the Numogram). Such rites are the basic components of demon traffic, constituting modules of practical culture, each of which is associated with an omen, and a power.

:(((:)))(((:)))

In Western hyperfictional lore the matrix of all demons (Pandemonium) is called *Necronomicon*, *The Book of Dead Names*, listing all that is excepted from the white-magic book of life. *Necronomicon* is a document copied episodically from versions of an original text, which was itself retrodeposited out of the future into the deep past. It thus scrambles science fiction with archaic legend, indicating a Lemurodigital hypersource.

(:)(:)(:)(:)(:)

THE NOMO CHANT

Nomo. Undivided Outside One. For You Life is Drowning.
Nomo. Numerous Under One. You Part Through Depths Swelling.
Nomo. Half Hidden Within One. You Submerge all Forgetting.
Nomo. Twice Exceeding One. You Bear Earth Convulsing.
Nomo. Ultimate Redoubled One. For You Breath is Dying.
Nomo. Whisper of the Dead. Sinking One You Twin.
Nomo. Hunger of the Earth. Bearing Twice Your Twin.
Nomo. Feeder of the Shadows. Double One Entwining.
Nomo. Shifter of the Deep. Still One In Your Twinning.
Nomo. Wholly Without One. Swallowing All You Twin.

THE ZONES

I

Ccru is committed to an ongoing research program into the numeracy of the 'lost Lemurian polyculture' apparently terminated by the K/T missile of BCE 65,000,000.

During the last century, various aspects of this primordially ancient 'digital hyperstition', 'mechanomics', 'schizonumerics', or 'numbo-jumbo' have been painstakingly reassembled through certain cryptic investigations, preeminently those associated with the names Echidna Stillwell, Chaim Horowitz, and Daniel Barker.

From the Mu Archive in Tibet Horowitz unearths an 'ultimate decimal qabbala' oriented to the cultic exploration of the numerals zero to nine as cosmic zones. In contradistinction to the late-Babylonian (or Judeo-Christian) qabbala, the 'method of Mu' involves a rigorous collapse of transcendent symbolism into intrinsic or immanent features, excavating the latent consistency between the numerical figures, their arithmetic functions, and their cultural associations. Horowitz describes these procedures as a diagonal path between esoteric numerology and exoteric mathematics, and also defines them negatively as a 'non-numerology' or 'ulterior-arithmetic'.

Atlanto-Babylonian State societies preserved some of the most fully degraded late-Muvian conclusions, but only by assimilating them to a 'Gnostic Arithmetic', fossilizing the numbers into spiritual beings, ideal individuals, and general concepts. Within these familiar traditions the sense of the numbers as raw functions of cosmic distribution was systematically subordinated to magical and religious principles, whilst their intensive potentials as transmutational triggers was drained off into geometrical structures and logical representations.

The productive synthesis of Stillwell's numogrammatic researches with Barker's 'tic-systemic' approach provides the requisite cutting tools for reopening the virtual-numeric labyrinth. This involves the reactivation of those 'Lemurian' cultural practices which traffick with numbers as techno-sorcerous entities: the diagrammatic tokens, intensive thresholds, cosmic coincidences and hyperstitional influences that populate the plane of Unlife.

II

Ccru has collated material from a series of occultural investigations that demonstrate the virtual existence of a lost Lemurian art of interplanetary communication, or 'planetwork'.

This system maps the major bodies of the solar system onto the ten digital labyrinth Zones (beginning with Sol = 0). The numerals one to nine function as astronomical ordinals, designating the terms of the planetary sequence in ascending order of orbital span (mean distance from the sun), orbital period (local year length), and gravitational attenuation (Einsteinian spatial flatness). This heliocentrism (with its implicit repudiation of terrestrial phenomenology) does not contradict the broad counter-solar trend in Lemurian culture, with its repulsion of centralization and gravitational capture. There has never been a Lemurian solar cult.

Lemurian Planetwork communicates with the substellar bodies as distributed hyperintelligences exerting singular influences (or 'Barker-traces'). These planetary forces of suggestion are propagated through contemporary mythologies, systematic coincidences, and accidental scientific fictions (whether lunar seas, Martian canals, Jovian monoliths, or life on Europa).

Various cryptic records indicate the existence of considerable calendrical lore based upon the Planetwork system, yet little of this has been definitively reconstructed. What is certain is that it takes the Mercurian year for its basic unit, and uses this regular beat in the calendrical interweaving of (nonmetric) speeds and slownesses.

The Zone-Sequence—by Mercurian periods—with planetary attributions:

Zn-0	[0000.00]	Sun
Zn-1	[0001.00]	Mercury
Zn-2	[0002.55]	Venus
Zn-3	[0004.15]	Earth
Zn-4	[0007.95]	Mars
Zn-5	[0049.24]	Jupiter
Zn-6	[0122.32]	Saturn
Zn-7	[0348.78]	Uranus
Zn-8	[0684.27]	Neptune
Zn-9	[1028.48]	Pluto

III

Many tales tell of a Lemurian hyperstition composed of numbers that function as interconnected zones, zone-fragments, and particles.

With Stillwell's epoch-switching discovery of the Numogram—and subsequent mapping of this 'digital labyrinth'—it became possible to compile cartographies of these zones, in which numbers distribute themselves throughout tropics, clusters, and regions. The zones thus function as diagrammatic components of flat cosmic maps (variously charting systems of coincidence, nebular circulations, spinal nestings, and the folds of inner/outer time).

Amongst numerous systematizations of occult cartography, that of Chaim Horowitz (direct descendant of the infamous 'mad rabbi of Kiev') is especially remarkable. Based upon Lemurian digital relics extracted from the Mu Archive, it enables the conversion of Numogram-zones (and sub-zones) into cascade-phases, accessed through numerical 'doors'. The Horowitzean phases constitute qabbalistic groupings or cross-sections of the Pandemonium population (simultaneously numbering the impulse-entities and defining their collective 'tone'). Those critics who seek to reduce Horowitz's work to an 'immensely indirect rediscovery of Pascal's triangle' fail to appreciate either the true antiquity of 'Pascal's' system or the machinic novelty of its Horowitzean reanimation.

Systematic issues concerning the Numogram Gates have been separated out from the other interconnective features of the zones. It has been known since the dawn of occult cartography that every Zone supports a Gate, and that their corresponding channels spin the web of esoteric fibres. All sorcerous cultures involve themselves in the exploration of these paths.

A Sarkonian mesh-tag is provided for each zone as a key to Axsys-format and Crypt-compatibility.

ZONE ZERO

THE NUMERAL 0

The modern figure zero (0) is a closed circle, oval, or ellipse (sometimes differentiated from the letter 'o' by a diagonal slash). Its archaic Hindu form was the 'bindu' (or dot, retained in the modern system as the 'decimal point'). Both of these ciphers are of such abstraction that no rapid summary can be other than misleading.

The figure '0' designates the number zero, anterior to the distinction odd/even, and also to the determination of primes (zeroth prime = 1).

Zero is the only natural number that is indivisible by one. The division of any number by zero produces an infinity (multiplication of any number by zero = 0), in this respect zero treats itself as any other number.

Zero digitally cumulates to zero.

Numeric Keypad direction: anomalous.

As an arithmetical function zero is strongly affined to place value—or 'positional'—systems in which it typically operates as the designator of empty magnitudes. The modern decimal and binary systems are the most familiar examples of such modular numeracies. (The widespread assumption that such a zero-function is indispensable to any possible place-value numeracy is, however, a fallacious one).

On the number line zero marks the transition from negative to positive numbers. In modern binary code zero is instantiated by electronic 'off' (see One). In set theory zero corresponds to the null (or empty) set. In coordinate geometry zero marks the 'origin' or intersection point of all dimensional axes, and is marked uniquely across all dimensions. In game theory a zero-sum game is one in which all gains and losses are mere redistributions ('I win, you lose' or inversely). In Boolean algebra zero symbolizes logical negation. Absolute zero (or zero degrees Kelvin) marks the cryonic limit of physically attainable temperature. In schizoanalysis 'zero intensity' designates the planomenon, plane of consistency, or body without organs (immanent to all intensities).

With no other number does arithmetical function cross so imperceptibly into religious and philosophical abstraction. There is a mathematico-cosmic continuum connecting the numeral zero to concepts of nullity, nihility, nothingness, absence, emptiness, void (Hindu 'Sunya'), vacuum, and neutrality.

Zero also has an initiatory sense, as indicated by the 'year zero' of new beginnings, or cycles (as in the case of the Y2K 00-date, and in that of the zero-strings marking accumulations in the Hindu 'Yugas'). A similar function is that of 'time-zero', or 'zero-hour' (synchronizing a distributed operation, particular one of a military nature).

THE ZEROTH PLANET: SOL

The Sun (Sol-0) is by far the largest body in the Solar-system. It spins on its own axis at different speeds (with a period of rotation varying from about 36 Earth-days at the poles, to 25.4 at the equator). The sun-spot cycle—driven by periodic reversals in the solar magnetoprocess—lasts for approximately twenty-two years.

The Sun is approximately 4.5 billion years old, roughly halfway through its normal existence (or main-sequence of hydrogen-to-helium nucleosynthesis).

After the completion of this phase it is destined to expand into a Red Giant (consuming the inner solar system). Its current temperature varies enormously according to depth, between 5,800k at the surface to 15,600,000k at the core. The pressure at the Sun's core is equivalent to 250 billion (terrestrial) atmospheres.

The preponderance of the Sun's mass within the solar system is such that the orbits of the planets (notably Jupiter) only produce minor perturbations in its behaviour. Solar radiation sustains all photosynthetic activity on Earth, and thus all plant-based terrestrial life. Its wide range of complex and ambivalent effects extend from regulating circadian biorhythms to triggering skin cancers.

The Sun's magnetic field (the heliosphere) is immensely powerful by planetary standards, extending beyond the edge of the outer solar system (as defined by the orbit of Pluto). Other solar influences—in addition to gravitational and electomagnetic forces—include the solar wind (which also extends, on a declining gradient, beyond the edge of the solar system).

The two predominant aspects of Earth's mechanical relation to the Sun—the day and the year—have been the basis of traditional human timekeeping. The earliest known clocks were sundials.

Sun worship is extremely prevalent within human religious history. The apparent rotation of the Sun around the zodiac is the keystone of exoteric astrology (allocating Sun-signs). Oecumenic Sunday is dedicated to Sol.

SYSTEM NOTES

Zone-0 is the first of two zones mutually composing the Plex-region of the Numogram. Its Syzygetic twin is Zone-9. This 9+0 Syzygy is carried by the demon Uttunul (see Zone-9). Zone-0 provides the terminus for a single Plex-channel (the 0th).

Systematic consistency suggests that Zone-0 envelops the Zeroth-Phase of Pandemonium, but as this includes nothing beyond itself it constitutes a nominal or virtual multitude and an 'absolute abstraction'. Zone-0 has no separable power of initiation, and since it does not support imps (or impulse-entities)—even of the first degree—there is no zeroth door.

The Zeroth Gate (Gt-oo) seems to connect Zone-o to itself, but its nature is peculiarly problematical, and within the Mu Archive texts its ultimate reality is fundamentally disputed. Many versions of the Numogram delete it entirely. Horowitz says of this Gate that 'between its existence and nonexistence there is no difference'.

Mu Tantrism plots Zone-o intensities onto the Coccygeal level of the spine, the vestigial remnant of a lost tail (and biotectonic link to the ancient lemur-people).

Zone-o is allotted the Sarkonian Mesh-Tag oooo. Lemurian subcultures associate Zone-o with the dense void of the cosmic hypermatrix, upon which absolute desolation crosses infinity as flatline and loss of signal. Blind Humpty Johnson's Channel Zero 'black snow' cult communicate the influence of this zone in their call for the return of true Tohu Bohu or the subprimordial Earth.

Centauri Subdecadence maps Zone-o onto the eclipsed side of the Fifth (or Root) Pylon on the Atlantean Cross. As the dark aspect of Foundation ('deep past') it corresponds to the protocosmic abyss anticipating primal reality, fusing indissociably into the ultimate gulfs of chaotic unbeing. Stillwell links Zone-o to the unvoiced Munumese quasiphonic particle 'eiaoung', the 'silent whisper of the ulterior depths'.

PHASE-0 LEMURS

Phase-o tolerates no populations of any kind.

ZONE ONE

THE NUMERAL 1

The figure one (1)—elaborated from a simple vertical stroke—is at least semi-ideographic as a relic tally-mark (basically identical in this respect to the Roman numeral 'I'). This figure has obvious phallic resonance (especially in contrast to the sign for zero (0)). Its relation to the figure seven (7) is supported by numerological analyses (since seven cumulated (28) reduces to one).

The figure '1' designates the number one, first odd number (with odditude of aleph null), and the zeroth prime (first prime = 2).

One is the lowest cardinal number, and the first ordinal.

One digitally cumulates to one.

Numeric Keypad direction: South-West.

In modulus-2 systems the numeral one bears all (non-zero) values (corresponding to powers of two). Binary informatic systems code electronic 'on' as 'one'.

The number one is exceptionally multivalent. It has two basic cardinal values—both deriving from its status as the smallest, basic, or irreducible factor defining the natural number series—that of the elementary, the atom, the unit or module—'one alone'—and also that of the whole, the complete, unity as totality, the universe. Its ordinal value as first, primary, principal, or initial is fractured by the ordinal function of zero, but retains much of its ancient dignity as the beginning of the counting series.

In addition one bears a diversity of quasinumerical and logical associations, including self-identity ('oneself', 'one and the same'), nondifferentiation, uniqueness ('one of a kind'), logical universality, uniformity, and—at a further remove, or more problematically—singularity (anomaly, exception), and the unilateral ('one-sided', unbalanced, disequilibriated).

One also has a complicated syntactical-linguistic usage that interlinks with its numerical and logical functions. In particular it operates as a carrier of nominal and indefinite reference ('the one that', 'someone or anyone', 'once upon a time'), which extends also to relation ('one another').

Within monotheistic cultures One attains a supreme dignity, identifying God directly with 'the One' (or 'the Old One'). In this context one is bound to the 'I am that I am' of YHVH, and to the absolute concentration of religion within the assertion that 'there is no God but God'. H.P. Lovecraft upsets this exclusive and definitive sense of the One by reintroducing the plural and multiple, whether grammatically as in the case of 'the Old Ones', or thematically, as in that of Yog Sothoth, who is described as the 'all in one, and one in all'.

THE FIRST PLANET: MERCURY

Mercury is the innermost planet of the solar system (with a mean orbital distance from the sun of approx. 58,000,000 km). The Mercurian year (approx. 88 Earth days in length) is also the swiftest, which accounts for its use as the base calculative unit in planetwork calendrics.

Due to its long day (approx. 58.7 Earth days in length) Mercury has semi-permanent light and dark sides (with average temperatures of +430 and –180 degrees celsius respectively).

Mercury has a weak magnetic field (approx 1% the strength of Earth's).

In Roman mythology Mercury (a latinization of the greek Hermes) is known as the messenger of the gods, associated with communication and trade.

The element Mercury (or 'quicksilver', symbol Hg) has particular alchemical importance, shared in Indian yogic traditions (where it is ritually ingested to produce an anorganic cosmic body).

In Lemurian Planetwork Mercury is astrozygonomously paired with Neptune.

SYSTEM NOTES

Zone-1 is the first of the six Torque-region Zones of the Numogram, and Tractor-Zone of the 5-4 (or 'Sink') Current. Its Syzygetic twin is Zone-8. This 8+1 Syzygy is carried by the demon Murmur (see Zone-8). Zone-1 provides the terminus for three Torque-channels (the 1st, 4th, and 7th).

Zone-1 both initiates and envelops the First Phase of Pandemonium (including 2 impulse-entities). This phase consists of nothing beyond the Zone (1) and the Door (1::0), thus tending to a highly 'idealized' state. Zone-1 has a particularly powerful and manifest initiatory dimension. The First Door—or 'Door of Doors'—is attributed by Muvian sorcery to the amphidemon (and imp of the first degree) Lurgo (1::0) 'the Initiator', and widely related to Legba (the first and last Loa to be invoked in any vudu ceremony).

The First Gate (Gt-01) connects Zone-1 to itself, and its corresponding channel provides a reduced microcosmic model of the Torque as a whole, in which Zone-1 provides both beginning and end. In this respect Horowitz describes Zone-1 'turning forever into itself'. The resulting metastability of this channel accounts for its strong associations with all known variants of the Bubble-Pod mythos.

Mu Tantrism plots Zone-1 intensities onto the Dorsal (or Thoracic) level of the spine, which maps onto the domain of lunged creatures (and colonization of the land).

Zone-1 is allotted the Sarkonian Mesh-Tag 0001 (matching the primordial click of Tzikvik cipher-shamanism).

Lemurian subcultures associate Zone-1 with (meta)static pod-deliria and techno-immortalism. It maintains relatively recent religious structures patterned on transcendent-oppressor 'sky-god' divinity, as well as harbouring the more archaic gnosis of the shelled 'old one' who supports the world (turtle cults).

Centauri subdecadence maps Zone-1 onto the palpable side of the First (or Center) Pylon on the Atlantean Cross. As the light aspect of Anamnesis ('memories and dreams') it corresponds to enduring ideas, historical time and remembrance (recall).

Stillwell links Zone-1 to the Munumese quasiphonic particle 'gl', emanating from the sublaryngeal region (the Horowitzean 'collapsed gargle' or 'glottal spasm', a relic from lost gilled/gulping life-forms).

Stillwell's ethno-topography of the Nma allocates Zone-1 to the coral atolls of the Mu Nma, and through their hydrocycle mythos to shallow seas. Zone-1 totem animals are drawn from the spectrum of armored fish creatures (combining a basic icthyoid model with traits extracted from crustaceans, mollusks and gastropods).

PHASE-1 LEMURS

[M#oo] 1::o Lurgo

ZONE TWO

THE NUMERAL 2

The figure two (2) is quasisymmetric with the figure five (5). This pairing is echoed in the alphabet by the letters 'Z' and 'S' (whose shared consistency across case and phonetic coherence has been taken by figural grammarians as indicative of a zygophidian—or 'forked-tongue'—cultural source).

The figure '2' designates the number two, the first and definitive even number, and the first prime (second prime = 3).

The encounter with the irrationality of the square root of two has special importance in the disturbance of Hellenic ('rationalistic') arithmetic. It is rumoured that the Pythagoreans resorted to assassination in their attempt to suppress this discovery.

Two digitally cumulates to three.

Numeric Keypad direction: South

The mechanical importance of bi-stable (on/off) micro-states within contemporary electronic data-systems has resulted in a vast and diffuse cultural investment in modulus-2 numeracy (pure place-value semiotics). 'Digital' and 'binary-coded' have now become almost synonymous in their colloquial usage.

Perhaps the supreme exemplar of a binary-numeric system is that of the ancient Chinese *I Ching* (or 'Book of Changes'), which involves both binary numeracy (of broken and unbroken lines) and double-numbering (of numeric hexagrams tagged by a series of ordinal numbers). It is Leibniz's study of this text which elaborates the first Western example of modern binary arithmetic.

The syzygetic (or zygonomous) power of two is a productive of an entire series of subtly differentiated binary concepts, which include coupling, twinning, doubling, polarity, schism, contrast, balance, opposition, and reflection.

Binarity is multiply ambivalent. It conspires with both the certainties of analytical reason in general, by way of two-value logics (governed by the principle of the 'excluded middle'), and also the uncertainties of dialogue, or 'two-way' communication. It is associated—equally or unequally—with both justice (evenhandedness, seeing both sides of a 'dilemma'), and deceit (two-faced, two-timing, double-dealing...).

Duality is particularly widespread within biological order, from the 'base-pairs' of (RNA and) DNA code, through the binary fission of bacterial propagation, the (binary) sexual difference of meiotic reproduction, to the bilateral symmetry of the typical vertebrate organism with consequent pairing of limbs (arms, legs), sense-organs (eyes, ears), lungs, brain hemispheres, etc. 'Dual organization' provides a basic model for primordial human kinship structure.

Many aspects of binarity are prominent within religious systems, whether gods with two heads or faces (such as the Roman Janus, and the Deleuze-Guattari gods of the State), twin gods (the Dogon Nommo, or the Zoroastrian couple Ahriman/Ormuzd), divine couples (god-goddess pairings being widespread throughout many religions), and twice-born gods (both Zeus and Dionysos amongst the Greek pantheon, for instance). Hindu culture describes Brahmins as 'twice-born'.

THE SECOND PLANET: VENUS

Venus (or Sol-2) has a mean orbital distance from sun of 108.2 million km. The Venusian year is approx. 224.4 Earth days in length. Since the rotation of Venus is very slow (and also retrograde) a Venusian day (lasting 243 Earth-days) is longer than its year.

In recent times Venus has become the exemplary victim of a 'runaway greenhouse effect' which has rendered it infernal (with a uniform surface temperature of +462 degrees celsius).

Venus has no magnetic field.

Venus has been historically identified by two different names, known as the morning star (Phosphorous or Lucifer) when seen in the East at sunrise, and the evening star (Hesperus) when seen in the West at sunset. The Roman goddess Venus (a latinization of the Greek Aphrodite) was the deity associated with female beauty and love (accounting in part, perhaps, for Burroughs' hatred of Venusians).

In Lemurian Planetwork Venus is astrozygonomously paired with Uranus.

SYSTEM NOTES

Zone-2 is the second of the six Torque-region Zones of the Numogram. Its Syzygetic twin is Zone-7. This 7+2 Syzygy is carried by the demon Oddubb (see Zone-7).

Zone-2 both initiates and envelops the Second Phase of Pandemonium (including 4 impulse-entities). With cryptic rigour Horowitz thus describes Zone-2 as 'reduplicating its double-twinness though its multitude'. As initiator it functions as the Second Door, invoked by K-goth cults as the 'Main Lo-Way' into the Crypt. Muvian sorcery identifies this door with the amphidemon (and imp of the first degree) Duoddod (2::0).

The Second Gate (Gt-3) connects Zone-2 to Zone-3, and its corresponding channel draws an intense line of escape from the Torque to the Warp. This passage is especially compelling, since it is multiply consolidated by cumulation, prime-ordination, and mesh-tagging. Tzikvik shamanism both honours and fears the Second Gate as the opening to the 'way of the Storm-Worm'.

Zone-2 is allotted the Sarkonian Mesh-Tag 0003.

Lemurian subcultures associate Zone-2 with crypt-navigation, occulted cyberspace and the spectral/liminal populations of hallucination and time fragmentation (greys, ghosts and zombies). Zone-2 mirrors Zone-5 and shares in its 'Hyperborean' themes of time-lapse and abduction.

Centauri subdecadence maps Zone-2 onto the eclipsed side of the Second (or Right) Pylon on the Atlantean Cross. As the dark aspect of Genesis ('creative influences') it corresponds to epidemic fertility (bacterial fission, clones, replicants, vampiric contagion).

Stillwell links Zone-2 to the Munumese quasiphonic particle 'dt' (the Horowitzean 'imploded fricative/fractured plosive').

Stillwell's ethno-topography of the Nma allocates Zone-2 to the interior marshlands of the Dib Nma, and through the Mu Nma hydrocycle mythos to mist, vaporization, and hazing.

Zone-2 totem animals are modelled on metamorphic insects, principally lepidoptera (moths and butterflies) but also dragonflies and dibboma flashbugs.

PHASE-2 LEMURS

[M#01] 2::0 Duoddod

[M#02] 2::1 Doogu

ZONE THREE

THE NUMERAL 3

The figure three (3) is semi-iconic (incorporating a stack of three horizontal strokes). It is quasisymmetric with the (upper-case) letter 'E', and partially echoed in the figure '8' (designating the third power of two). Figural grammarians consider it to involve a progression of compressive folding beyond '1' and '2'.

The figure '3' designates the number three, the second odd number (with odditude of 1), and second prime (third prime = 5).

Three is the square root of nine (relating it intimately to Barkerian arithmetic and Zygonovism).

Three digitally cumulates to six.

Three is itself the sum of the three preceding natural numbers (0+1+2 = 3), demonstrating a unique affinity with numerical triangularity.

Numeric Keypad direction: South-East.

A peculiarly obsessive triadic numeracy is evidenced in the vulgar ('zygotriadic') calendar of the Mu Nma.

The number three is unique for both the intensity and diversity of its cross-cutting hyperstitious investments. It is associated on the right hand with numerological completeness and transcendence, and on the left hand with the middle, the between, and the diagonal line.

Prevalent triplicities include (amongst many others) the three dimensions of manifest time (past, present, future) and space (height, length, depth), the triad game (paper, scissors, stone), the Atlantean Tridentity (Nunnil-Ixor, Domu-Loguhn, Hummpa-Taddum), the Hindu trimurty (Brahma, Vishnu, Shiva) and gunas (rajas, tamas, and sattva), the alchemical elements (salt, sulphur, and mercury), the Christian trinity (Father, Son, Holy Ghost), the stages of formalized dialectic (thesis, antithesis, synthesis), the Oedipal triangle (daddy, mummy, me), and the three virtuous monkeys (blind, deaf, and mute to evil). History exhibits strong tendencies towards a triadic order of the world, both in the realm of mythology (heaven, hell, limbo), and in that of geopolitics (first-, second-, and third-world). The extraordinary numinousness of the number three is also indicated by ethnomes such as tribalism, tributaries, trickery, and trials, the three body problem, three wishes, three fates, three graces, the third eye, and the arch-magician (Hermes) Trismegistus. Atlantean sources relate the cultural dominance of the number three to the fact that Alpha Centauri is a triple system.

THE THIRD PLANET: EARTH

Earth (or Sol-3) has a mean orbital distance from the sun of approx. 149 600,000 km, defining the standard Astronomical Unit (AU). Its orbital period (of approx. 365,2422 Earth days) and rotational period (approx. 24 hours) are used as the basis of terrestrial calendrics (along with the period of its satellitic—lunar—orbit), and traditionally for timekeeping (now supplanted by atomic clocks).

Earth has one moon—Luna—of abnormal size relative to that of the planet, and exercising considerable influence, principally through tidal forces. Lunar influences—such as that evident in the human ovulatory cycle—have consolidated deep cultural associations between the moon, oceans, women, blood, sorcery, and madness (lunacy).

Earth is the densest major body in the solar system. It is polarized by a moderate magnetic field which reverses intermittently (once or twice every million years). By the end of the second millennium of the Common Era the Earth was still the only known source of life in the Universe.

Prior to the Copernican revolution (in the sixteenth century) Earth was considered to be the centre of the solar system—and even of the universe—by the dominant cultures of mankind (an orthodoxy ruthlessly defended by the Christian Church among others).

Alone amongst the Planets, Earth is not named after a Greek or Roman deity. The name 'Earth' is of Anglo-germanic origin. (The Greek goddess Gaia is increasingly evoked as the name for Earth conceived as a living macro-entity, provoked in part by systemic—or 'ecospheric'—changes in climate, atmosphere, and biodynamics).

In Lemurian Planetwork Earth is astrozygonomously paired with Saturn.

SYSTEM NOTES

Zone-3 is the first of the two Warp-region Zones of the Numogram, and Tractor-Zone of the 6-3 (or 'Warp') Current. Its Syzygetic-twin is Zone-6. This 6+3 Syzygy is carried by the demon Djynxx (see Zone-6). Zone-3 provides the terminus for two channels, one each from the Torque (the 2nd), and the Warp (the 6th).

Zone-3 both initiates and envelops the Third Phase of Pandemonium (including 8 impulse-entities). In the first of these aspects it functions as the Third Door, which opens onto the Swirl, and is attributed by Muvian sorcery to the chaotic xenodemon (and imp of the first degree) Ixix (3::0).

The Third Gate (Gt-6) twists Zone-3 through Zone-6, with its corresponding channel vertically complementing that of the Sixth Gate (Gt-21), and also the Warp-Current itself, thus adding an increment of spin to the entire region. Horowitz invests Zone-3 with a particular potency of intrinsic coincidence, since its second cumular power (6) is also the number of its Syzygetic double (through which he accounts for the compact tension of the Warp system).

Mu Tantrism plots Warp-region intensities onto the plane of the third eye.

Zone-3 is allotted the Sarkonian Mesh-Tag 0007.

Lemurian subcultures associate Zone-3 with swirling nebulae (cosmic dust clouds) and alien pattern. The intensity of vortical involvement with Zone-6 problematizes distinct characterization.

Centauri subdecadence maps Zone-3 onto the active side of the Fourth (or Crown) Pylon on the Atlantean Cross. As the light aspect of Fortune ('far future') it corresponds to extrinsic fatality, unexpected messages, and xenosignal.

Stillwell links Zone-3 to the Munumese quasiphonic particle 'zx'. It designates the 'buzz-cutter' sonics which Horowitz describes as a 'swarming insectoid reversion within mammalian vocality'.

PHASE-3 LEMURS

[M#-03] 3::0 Ixix

[M#-04] 3::1 Ixigool

[M#-05] 3::2 Ixidod

ZONE FOUR

THE NUMERAL 4

There are two basic versions of the figure, one 'open' and the other closed into a triangle. The former design is echoed in the symbol for the planet Jupiter. It is the latter that figurally relates four to the sign for delta (fourth letter of the Greek alphabet), and accounts for the fact that in certain hacker numerolects it is substituted for the (upper-case) letter 'A'.

The figure '4' designates the number four, the second even number, and first nonprime (or complex) natural number, with prime factors of 2 x 2 (fourth prime = 7).

The triangular summation—or digital cumulation—of four equals ten (numerologically identified with a superior power of unity, classically conceived as the Pythagorean Tetrakys). The preeminences of four—as 'first' nonprime and 'first' square—are formally or germinally anticipated by unity.

Four digitally cumulates to ten (see above).

Numeric Keypad direction: West.

Due to the internal redundancy of its dual symmetry (2x2 = 2+2 = 4), four is commonly conceived as the model outcome of calculation—as indicated by the phrase 'putting two and two together'.

The dominant associations of the number four are balance and stability, exemplified by the 'four-square'—or solidary—structure of four walls, wheels, or quadrupedal support, as well as by the 'four-four beats' of rigidly metric dance music. It is this sense of quadrature that predominates in the four elements (earth, air, water, fire), the four cardinal directions (north, south, east, and west), and the four DNA bases (adenine, cytosine, guanine, and thymine). A similar fourfold typology is expressed by the four suits of the playing-card pack (clubs, diamonds, hearts, spades). Four is also associated with temporal stability—or cyclic regeneration—as evidenced by the four seasons (Spring, Summer, Autumn, Winter), four classical ages (those of gold, silver, bronze, and lead), and in Hindu culture, far more intricately, by the four Yugas (those of Krita, Treta, Dvapara, and Kali). The system of the Yugas is a fully elaborated quadro-decimal system (highly suggestive in relation to the Tetrakys).

Within the Judaeo-Christian tradition the number four is invested with extraordinary significance, from the four letters of the Tetragrammaton, through the four gospels, to the four great 'Zoas' and four horsemen of apocalypse. The biblical time—of both old and new testaments—places particular importance on the period of forty days (e.g. the duration of the flood, and of Jesus' temptation in the desert). This privileging of quadrate order—as the ground-plan of the temple—is also instantiated by the masonic 'square'.

The number four is also of special importance to Buddhism, as exemplified by the 'four noble truths' of its basic doctrine, and by the typical (quadrate) design of the mandala. On the flip-side the number four is connected with excess (the fourth dimension), anomaly (the four-leafed clover), and vulgarity (four-letter words).

THE FOURTH PLANET: MARS

Mars (or Sol-4) has a mean orbital distance from the sun of approx. 228,000,000 km. The Martian year is roughly twice as long as that of Earth, and its day about 30 minutes longer.

Mars has two moons, Phobos and Deimos.

The surface of Mars is swept by vast dust storms that occasionally envelop the whole planet for months.

In popular legend Mars has long been envisaged as the home of intelligent alien life. Recent examples include the 'canals' discovered by Percival Lowell, the fictions of H.G. Wells and Edgar Rice Burroughs, and the Cydonia 'face' (based on images from the 1976 Viking missions). Mars is widely seen as a plausible candidate for human colonization. It has also become notorious for cursed space missions.

In August 1996 scientists announced the discovery of Martian nanoworms in a ancient meteorite (cat. ALH84001).

In Roman mythology Mars (a latinization of the Greek Ares) is the god of war, and father of Romulus (legendary founder of Rome). Mars is commemorated by the month of March.

In Lemurian Planetwork Mars is astrozygonomously paired with Jupiter.

SYSTEM NOTES

Zone-4 is the third of the six Torque-region Zones of the Numogram. Its Syzygetic twin is Zone-5. The 5+4 Syzygy is carried by the demon Katak (see Zone-5).

Zone-4 both initiates and envelops the Fourth Phase of Pandemonium (including 16 impulse-entities). This equation of phase-population with the square of the zone-number establishes an exceptional solidarity between the two, although this rigidity has as its flipside a tendency to cataclysmic instability. In its initiatory aspect Zone-4 functions as the Fourth Door (or 'Time-Delta', familiar from variations of the Kurtz mythos as 'the worst place in the world'). Muvian sorcery attributes this door to the amphidemon (and imp of the first degree) Krako (4::0).

The Fourth Gate (Gt-10) feeds Zone-4 forward to Zone-1. Its ancient (proto-Atlantean) name, 'Gate of Submergence', hints at its interlocking associations with completion, catastrophe, subsidence, and decadence. The Channel corresponding to the Fourth Gate is one of three concluding in Zone-1, and the only pro-cyclic channel within the Torque. Its course reinforces the 5-4 (or 'Sink') Current in its rush towards termination, and augments the weight of destiny (it was under the influence of this line that Cecil Curtis departed upon his fatal journey into the land of the Tak Nma).

Zone-4 is allotted the Sarkonian Mesh-Tag 0015.

Lemurian subcultures associate Zone-4 with 'delta-phase' or terminal deliria (Kurtz/Curtis end-of-the-river disintegration into malarial nightmares), geoconvulsions, continental subsidence, and 'red-out'.

Centauri Subdecadence maps Zone-4 onto the passive side of the Third (or Left) Pylon on the Atlantean Cross. As the dark aspect of Apocalypse ('destructive influences') it corresponds to random calamity.

Stillwell links Zone-4 to the Munumese quasiphonic particle 'skr', which Horowitz identifies as an anthropo-reptiloid precursor to the qabbalistic 'hard resh'.

Stillwell's ethno-topography of the Nma allocates Zone-4 to the volcanic jungles of the Tak Nma, and through the Mu Nma hydrocycle mythos to riverine flow.

Zone-4 totem animals are typified by cats and dogs, especially in their predatory mode. Among the Tak Nma rabid animals are given particular prominence.

PHASE-4 LEMURS

[M#06] 4::0 Krako

[M#07] 4::1 Sukugool

[M#08] 4::2 Skoodu

[M#09] 4::3 Skarkix

ZONE FIVE

THE NUMERAL 5

The figure five (5)—echoed by the (upper-case) letter 'S'—is of the ophidian-symmetric type (see 'two').

The still widely used Roman numeral V (upper-case letter 'V')—despite appearing as a quasi-alphabetical numeral—is actually a numerical figure of a far older type, exhibiting a vestigial link to pre-symbolic tallying systems (such as the 'five-bar gate' (see 'one')).

The figure '5' designates the number five, the third odd number (with odditude of 2), and the third prime (fifth prime = 11).

Five is one of the two prime factors of the decimal module (with two), a fact that is usually attributed to the number of fingers on one hand. It is on this basis that five serves as modulus or submodulus in many counting (and currency) systems.

Five digitally cumulates to fifteen.

Numeric Keypad direction: Centre.

The number five has particularly strong anthropomorphic associations, due to its multiple connections with human biological organization. These are not restricted to the five digits per limb (so crucial to the social history of numeracy), but extend also to structural dimensions as varied as the five senses (sight, hearing, smell, taste, and touch), and the five spinal levels (coccygeal, sacral, lumbar, dorsal, cervical). These anthropomorphic resonances are disturbed, however, by instances of fundamentally pentagonal body-plans—preeminently that of the starfish—which is intrinsic to the aberrancy of the Lovecraftean Old Ones.

In monotheistic traditions the number five is associated with doctrinal authority, as evidenced in the Pentateuch (or five books of Moses), and in the five pillars of Islam (the 'arkan', or five ritual duties).

In occult circles the importance of the number five is even more emphatic, as indicated by the five elements of Chinese alchemy, and by the designs of the pentagram, the pentazygon, and the Atlantean Cross (with its five 'stations').

Secular relics of the authoritative sense of five can be found in the 'Five-year plans' of command economies, in the geopolitical symbolism of The Pentagon, and perhaps in the near-universal prestige invested in Intel's 'Pentium' processor.

THE FIFTH PLANET: JUPITER

Jupiter (or Sol-5) has a mean orbital distance from the sun of approx. 778,330,000 km. The Jovian year is roughly 11.9 Earth years in length, and its day about 9.9 hours long.

::((:::))

Jupiter is the innermost gas giant, and by far the largest planet in the solar system, accounting on its own for more than two thirds of total planetary mass. It has an extremely powerful magnetic field (its magnetosphere extends beyond the orbit of Saturn).

Jupiter has sixteen moons. The four largest (or Galilean) moons are Callisto, Europa, Ganymede, and Io. Galileo's observations of these bodies provided crucial evidence for the Copernican revolution. The oceans of Europa have been frequently identified as potential habitations for alien life (a neomyth shared by Arthur C. Clarke, who also populated Jupiter with his alien 'Monoliths').

The most distinctive feature on the Jovian surface is the Great Red Spot, a vast self-sustaining storm.

The size, position, and orbital regularity of Jupiter has led to it being credited with a crucial role in protecting the inner solar system from meteoritic and cometary bombardment.

Jupiter (or Jove, latinizing the Greek Zeus) is the sovereign of the Gods. As god of the sky, and of storms, he has been systematically cross-identified with the Abrahamic Jehovah.

In Lemurian Planetwork Jupiter is astrozygonomously paired with Mars. (Between Mars and Jupiter lies the asteroid belt, widely hypothesized to be the fragments from a destroyed intermediate planet).

SYSTEM NOTES

Zone-5 is the sixth of the six Torque-region Zones of the Numogram, and Tractor-Zone of the 7-2 (or 'Hold') Current. Its Syzygetic twin is Zone-4. This 5+4 Syzygy (carried by the demon Katak) draws the innermost curve of the Barker Spiral, with Zone-5 itself marking its central and terminal node (or 'inner eye').

Zone-5 both initiates and envelops the Fifth Phase of Pandemonium (including 32 impulse-entities). Horowitz remarks specifically upon the qabbalistic resonance of these values. In its initiatory aspect Zone-5 functions as the Fifth (or Hyperborean) Door, attributed by Muvian sorcery to the amphidemon (and imp of the first degree) Tokhatto (5::0). In the inner esoteric circles of the AOE this demon is reverenced as the Angel of the Decadence Pack, and even identified with the Archangel Meteka (associations reinforced by numerous qabbalistic peculiarities).

The Fifth Gate (Gt-15) connects Zone-5 to Zone-6, and its corresponding channel tracks the path of abductions into the Warp.

Zone-5 is allotted the Sarkonian Mesh-Tag 0031.

Lemurian subcultures associate Zone-5 with Hyperborean or Wendigo mythology. Zone-5 mirrors Zone-2 and shares in its Crypt-linked themes of missing time and alien abduction.

Centauri subdecadence maps Zone-5 onto the active side of the Third (or Left) Pylon on the Atlantean Cross. As the light aspect of Apocalypse ('destructive influences') it corresponds to decision, judgement, and war.

Stillwell links Zone-5 to the Munumese quasiphonic particle 'ktt' (the Horowitzean 'paravocal tic').

Stillwell's ethno-topography of the Nma allocates Zone-5 to the upland rain forests of the Tak Nma, and through the Mu Nma hydrocycle mythos to the monsoon.

Zone-5 totem animals are predominantly hybrid bird-reptile forms (with the art of the Highland Tak described by Cecil Curtis as 'a flapping howling chaos of flying worms, bat-monsters and barking snakes').

PHASE-5 LEMURS

[M#10] 5::0 Tokhatto

[M#11] 5::1 Tukkamu

[M#12] 5::2 Kuttadid

[M#13] 5::3 Tikkitix

[M#14] 5::4 Katak

ZONE SIX

THE NUMERAL 6

The figure six (6) is rotationally equivalent to the numeral '9' (the two figures together composing a system of twin-spirals). Six participates in a figural set—including the (lower-case) letters b, d, and q, plus (upper- and lower-case) P—of particular and distinct interest to figural grammarians, who have suggested that the ur-form of both six and nine were continuously involutionary spirals.

The figure '6' designates the number six, third even number, and second non-prime (with prime factors 2 and 3).

Six is the first 'perfect' number, equivalent to the sum of its factors (1, 2, and 3), and revered as such by Pythagoras.

Six digitally cumulates to twenty-one.

Numeric Keypad direction: East.

Despite its 'perfection', six is perhaps the darkest of the elementary decimal numbers, due to its association with chance (the six faces of the die), ill-omen (indicated by the ambivalence of the word or prefix 'Hex'), and occult intuition (the 'sixth sense').

The six lines of the *I Ching* hexagram designate the six stages of change discovered by archaic Taoism (which are numerically equivalent to the cyclic-sequence of digitally reduced binary-powers, with values: 1, 2, 4, 8, 7, 5).

In the Christian world the number six is ominously coloured by its triplicate reiteration—666 (or six hundred three-score and six), the Number of the Beast of Revelation—which has preoccupied Christian qabbalism throughout the greater part of the last two Millennia. Six-hunded and sixty-six is the triangular cumulation of thirty-six (itself the second power of six). The division of modern barcodes into blocks punctuated by (three) sixes has been taken by some as an uncanny fulfilment of the biblical prophecy (Rev XIII:17) 'that no man might buy or sell, save he that had the mark, or the name of the beast, or the number of his name'. (Since thirty-six is the digital cumulation of eight, however, it is to that number—and not six—that this entire complex should ultimately be referred.)

The number sixty (60)—decimal escalation of six—has acquired prominence due to its extraordinary and influential importance to Sumero-Babylonian culture, from whom the modern world has inherited the sexagesimal principle of division (into minutes and seconds) still current within both chronometry and geometry.

THE SIXTH PLANET: SATURN

Saturn (or Sol-6) has a mean orbital distance from the sun of approx. 1,429,400,000km. The Saturnian year is a little over 29.47 Earth-years in length, and its day has a length of roughly 10.18 hours on the surface (which is half an hour less than that of its solid core).

The Saturnian ring-system is divided into seven major bands (labelled D, C, B, A, F, G, E since Huygens), and actually consists of more than 100,000 component rings.

Saturn has eighteen confirmed (and named) moons, although the total may be as high as thirty-two. The largest moon—Titan—is more massive than Mercury.

Saturn has a magnetic field. Its magnetosphere is about one third the size of Jupiter's. It is the least dense of the planets (with an average density lower than that of water). A huge standing wave pattern around the northern polar region produces the appearance of a permanent hexagon.

The Roman god Saturn is identified with the Greek Chronos, god of time, and father of Jupiter, Neptune, and Pluto (amongst the planetary deities). Saturn is celebrated in the seven days of Saturnalia (the Roman Winter festival), and in the name of Saturday.

In Lemurian Planetwork Saturn is astrozygonomously paired with Earth.

SYSTEM NOTES

Zone-6 is the second of the two Warp-region Zones of the Numogram. Its Warpcomplement and Syzygetic twin is Zone-3. It is this 6+3 Syzygy (carried by the demon Djynxx) which draws the 'Ulterior Vortex' of Outer Time. Zone-6 provides the terminus for two channels, one each from the Torque (the 5th), and the Warp (the 3rd).

Zone-6 both initiates and envelops the Sixth Phase of Pandemonium (including 64 impulse-entities). Chaim Horowitz qabbalistically relates this phase, multitude, or 'Tone' to the hexagrams of the *I Ching* and to the yantras of the Ur-Oriyan Yoginis. As initiator, Zone-6 corresponds to the Sixth Door. Muvian sorcery attributes this door—which it names Undu—to the terrible chaotic xenodemon (and imp of the first degree) Tchu (6::0), primordially associated with shocking disappearances.

The Sixth Gate (Gt-21) twists Zone-6 through Zone-3, vertically recycling it into the Warp. Its corresponding channel tracks the course of the Warp-current, reinforcing the turbular-momentum of the entire region.

Mu Tantrism plots Warp-region intensities onto the plane of the third eye.

Zone-6 is allotted the Sarkonian Mesh-Tag 0063 (a fact of obvious importance to the culture of Tzikvik cipher-shamanism).

Lemurian subcultures associate Zone-6 with the occulted dimensions of Undu, turbular erosion and the dead eye of the cyclone. The intensity of vortical involvement with Zone-3 problematizes distinct characterization.

Centauri Subdecadence maps Zone-6 onto the passive side of the Fourth (or Crown) Pylon on the Atlantean Cross. As the dark aspect of Fortune ('far future') it corresponds to 'gnostic death', event horizon, and the absolutely unexpected.

Stillwell links Zone-6 to the Munumese quasiphonic particle 'tch', approximating to the interphoneme 'dzch/tj'.

PHASE-6 LEMURS

[M#-15] 6::0 Tchu

[M#-16] 6::1 Djungo

[M#-17] 6::2 Djuddha

[M#-18] 6::3 Djynxx

[M#-19] 6::4 Tchakki

[M#-20] 6::5 Tchattuk

ZONE SEVEN

THE NUMERAL 7

The figure seven (7) includes the only pure diagonal to be found amongst the numeral figures (and depends upon this oblique line to differentiate it from the numeral '1', as also to break its rotational bond with the (upper-case) letter 'L'). It is ideographically connected to the lightning-stroke, and related by composition to the (similarly associated) letter 'Z'.

The figure '7' designates the number seven, the fourth odd number (with odditude of one), and the fourth prime (seventh prime = 17).

Seven digitally cumulates to twenty-eight.

Numeric Keypad direction: North-West.

The biblical importance of the number seven is established at the beginning of Genesis, with the religious derivation of the seven-day week (from the six days of creation +1). Jewish mysticism deepens this association between seven and sacred time with an account of seven discarded creations (preceding the current one, and cast into the abyss). The number seven is also notably prominent in Revelation (where it is referred to the seven ancient churches, to the seven angels, seven seals, seven last plagues, seven vials of wrath, and to the seven heads of the great beast (which perhaps refer—in turn—to the seven hills of Rome)). The heptamania of Revelation is the probable source of the structurally ambivalence of seven within popular

Christianity, where it is attributed both to the seven cardinal virtues, and the seven deadly sins.

A crescendo of seven-obsession is found in the Theosophical writings of Madame Blavatsky, who divides the cosmic process into seven phases, each characterized by one of seven sequential 'root races'. Blavatsky draws from biblical sources, but is more directly influenced (through the teachings of her 'Ascended Tibetan Masters') by the usage of the number seven in a variety of Eastern religions (including the Hindu seven worlds, seven divine mothers, and seven Rishis (or sages), the seven Buddhas, and the seven Shinto gods of good fortune).

Religious and mystical investments of the number seven are closely connected to the seven planets of classical astronomy and traditional astrology (from which the phrase 'seventh heaven' is derived). In recent times, the Seven Sisters (or Pleiades) have taken up an increasing proportion of this cosmic-numerical freight.

The triplicate reiteration of the number seven is used as the title for Aleister Crowley's book of numbers, 777 (a number corresponding to the gematria value of the law of Thelema according to Alphanumeric Qabbala).

THE SEVENTH PLANET: URANUS

Uranus (or Sol-7) has a mean orbital distance from the sun of approx. 2,870,990,000 km. The Uranian year is a little over 84 Earth-years in length. Its day lasts for roughly seventeen and one quarter hours.

Uranus has five large moons, plus at least ten smaller ones. The two largest moons—Oberon and Titania—were discovered by Herschel in 1787. It also has a ring-system involving eleven known bands (the five most prominent of these are designated by the Greek letters from Alpha to Epsilon).

The rotation of Uranus is abnormally tilted, and is almost perpendicular to the ecliptic, warping its magnetic field.

The bluish colour of Uranus is ascribed to absorption of red light by atmospheric methane.

((:))((:))(((:)))

In Greek mythology Uranus was the god of the heavens, incestuous son of Gaia and father of Chronos (Saturn), the other Titans, the Cyclops, the hundred-headed giants, and others. Led by Chronos, the Titans killed and mutilated Uranus, spawning the Furies from his blood (and Aphrodite from his severed genitals).

In recent times Uranus has become the butt of infantile scatological humour.

In Lemurian Planetwork Uranus is astrozygonomously paired with Venus.

SYSTEM NOTES

Zone-7 is the fifth of the six Torque-region Zones of the Numogram, and Tractor-Zone of the 8-1 (or 'Surge') Current. Its Syzygetic twin is Zone-2. The 7+2 Syzygy is carried by the demon Oddubb, whose associations with hyperstitious doublings reinforces its twin character.

Zone-7 both initiates and envelops the Seventh Phase of Pandemonium (including 128 impulse-entities). In its initiatory aspect—as the Seventh Door—Zone-7 opens onto the cosmic swamp-labyrinths or 'Tracts of Dobo'. Muvian sorcery attributes this door to the amphidemon (and imp of the first degree) Puppo (7::0).

The Seventh Gate (Gt-28) feeds Zone-7 back to Zone-1, and this tendency to precipitate 'fold-type' time-anomalies accounts for its Black-Atlantean name 'Gate of Relapse'. The Channel corresponding to the Seventh Gate is one of three concluding in Zone-1, and the only counter-cyclic path within the Torque. The aquassasins of Hyper-C fetishize this gate in their bizarre mysteries of the Bubble Pod.

Zone-7 is allotted the Sarkonian Mesh-Tag 0127.

Lemurian subcultures associate Zone-7 with emergence from the depths (hyper-sea water-carriers and amphibious colonization).

Centauri subdecadence maps Zone-7 onto the active side of the Second (or Right) Pylon on the Atlantean Cross. As the light aspect of Genesis ('creative influences') it corresponds to genealogy, ancestor worship and inherited wealth.

Stillwell links Zone-7 to the Munumese quasiphonic particle 'pb' (the Horowitzean 'compounded plosive').

Her ethno-topography of the Nma allocates Zone-4 to the coastal swamps of the Dib Nma, and through the Mu Nma hydrocycle mythos to salt-water marshes.

Zone-7 totem animals are predominantly of the chubby batrachian (burping toad) type.

PHASE-7 LEMURS

[M#21] 7::0 Puppo

[M#22] 7::1 Bubbamu

[M#23] 7::2 Oddubb

[M#24] 7::3 Pabbakis

[M#25] 7::4 Ababbatok

[M#26] 7::5 Papatakoo

[M#27] 7::6 Bobobja

ZONE EIGHT

THE NUMERAL 8

The figure eight (8) is a partially rotated glyph of infinity, and also of the Moebian strip. It has strong ophidian resonances, linked in Indian culture to the realm of snake-demons (Nagas), and to the serpent of the deep (Ahi). In the West it is related to Ourobouros (the serpent of eternity, eating its own tail).

The figure '8' designates the number eight, the fourth even number, and the third non-prime (with prime factors 2 x 2 x 2).

((((::))))

Multiple evidences indicate that eight was an important modulus in the late prehistory of numeracy (most remarkable in this respect is the strong connection between the words for 'nine' and 'new' in various languages, including Latin).

Eight is the third power of two (with factors 1, 2, and 4), and constitutes a crucial grouping in digital electronics (with eight bits equalling one byte (with a power of combinatorial variation equal to two-hundred and fifty-six)). It is the same set of numerical features that support the octave of Western music.

Eight digitally cumulates to thirty-six.

Numeric Keypad direction: North.

The ophidian tendency in the figure eight is compunded by the deep association of the number with cephalopodian entities—preeminently the octopus—and by derivation with the entire range of 'tentacle-face' beings (such as the Oankali of Octavia Butler). A further—more tenuous—connection might be made to the amphibian hybrids of Dr Octagon ('half shark-alligator, half man').

Both numerically and figurally, eight is associated with perfection (in the sense of macrocosmic completion and return). These are particularly notable in the East, where obvious references include the Buddhist eightfold path, and the eight immortals of Taoism. The number eight—particularly in its triplicate reiteration (888) is considered an especially auspicious number in Chinese culture.

According to the Dogon, eight is the number of Nomo, and as such the primary key to their cosmo-numerical system.

Eight is the digital source (by cumulation to the second power) of the number of the beast, 666 (see Six).

THE EIGHTH PLANET: NEPTUNE

Neptune (or Sol-8) is the outermost gas giant, with a mean orbital distance from the sun of approx. 4,504,000,000 km. Due to eccentricities in the orbit of Pluto it is periodically the outermost (ninth) planet (see Pluto, Zone-9).

The Neptunian year is slightly under 164.8 Earth-years in length. Its day lasts for approximately sixteen hours.

Neptune has eight known moons, of which Triton is by far the largest. It also has at least five (thin and dark) rings.

Neptune shares various features with Uranus, including an anomalously oriented magnetic field, and a bluish hue (due to absorption of red light by atmospheric methane).

The prediction of Neptune's existence, and its subsequent discovery in 1846 (on the basis of perturbations in the orbit of Uranus) was a crucial moment of consolidation for mathematical celestial mechanics.

In Roman mythology Neptune is the sea god (identified with the Greek Poseidon).

In Lemurian Planetwork Neptune is astrozygonomously paired with Mercury.

SYSTEM NOTES

Zone-8 is the fourth of the six Torque-region Zones of the Numogram. Its Syzygetic twin is Zone-1. The 8+1 Syzygy is carried by the demon Murmur (known to Muvian sorcerors as 'the nethermost denizen of time').

Zone-8 both initiates and envelops the Eighth Phase of Pandemonium (including 256 impulse-entities). This association with the digital byte (eight bits) cements its importance within cybergothic cults. In its initiatory aspect—as the Eighth Door—Zone-8 is problematically identifiable with the Muvian amphidemon (and imp of the first degree) Minommo (8::0). This demon figures prominently in the dream sorcery of the Mu Nma.

The Eighth Gate (Gt-36) connects Zone-8 to Zone-9, and the corresponding Channel is the sole path of escape from the Torque—or 'Time-Circuit'—into the Plex. Due to its digital cross-match with the 6+3 Syzygy (occupying the Warp-region of the Numogram, and carried by the Xenodemon Djynxx (6::3)) the Eighth Gate seems to address what Stillwell has called the 'ultimate numogrammatic enigma'—that of the intercommunication between the

Warp and Plex regions. This linkage is crucially emphasized in the culture of Tzikvik shamanism, and—under the name 'Gate of Charon'—is taken up into Late-Atlantean apocalypticism (since its digital sum (36) itself cumulates to 666, and thus echoes the number of Seals to the Great Abyss (long associated with the thirty-six cards of the Decadence pack)).

Mu Tantrism plots Zone-8 intensities onto the Lumbar level of the spine, archaic fish-region of the mammalian nervous system.

Zone-8 is allotted the Sarkonian Mesh-Tag 0255.

Lemurian subcultures associate Zone-8 with limbic drift, dreams, trance-states and foetal sentience.

Centauri subdecadence maps Zone-8 onto the passive side of the First (or Centre) Pylon on the Atlantean Cross. As the dark aspect of Anamnesis ('memories and dreams') it corresponds to submerged currents of fatality.

Stillwell links Zone-8 to the Munumese quasiphonic particle 'mnm', the diffuse subvocal hum that Horowitz links to the 'proto-originary enunciation' Oumn.

Stillwell's ethno-topography of the Nma allocates Zone-8 to the fabled submarine cities of the ancient Mu Nma, and through the Mu Nma hydrocycle mythos to the deep sea.

Zone-8 totem animals are typified by polytendrilled abominations.

PHASE-8 LEMURS

[M#28] 8::0 Minommo

[M#29] 8::1 Murrumur

[M#30] 8::2 Nammamad

[M#31] 8::3 Mummumix

[M#32] 8::4 Numko

[M#33] 8::5 Muntuk

[M#34] 8::6 Mommoljo

[M#35] 8::7 Mombbo

:::((:))(::)

ZONE NINE

THE NUMERAL 9

The figure nine (9) is zygospirally related to the figure six (6, see six), and quasisymmetric with the sign for Pluto.

The figure '9' designates the number nine, the fifth odd number (with odditude of three), and the fourth non-prime (with prime factors 3x3).

Nines are produced by unit subtractions (n–1) from pure decimal magnitudes (a numerical practice most frequently encountered in a retail context, e.g. $9.99). In order to produce arithmetical consistency in respect to 1/3x3, one is mathematically equated with point nine recurring (0.999...). This equation—which provides a virtual infinite decimal-expansion for every number—is indispensable for Cantorean diagonalization.

Nine digitally cumulates to forty-five.

Numeric Keypad direction: North-East.

The number nine has a null value in digital reduction, practically enabling all nines to be eliminated from any complex reduction (involving at least one digit other than nine or zero). The same formula (9=0) is also derivable from Barker-twinning (or zygonovism)—long familiar to Dogon sorcery—for which nine functions as the summative key. Such zygonovism (or nine-sum coupling) divides the decimal numerals into five twins, and underlies both Numogram syzygetics and the game of Subdecadence.

The number nine is the last numeral of the decimal system, and its associations with death and fatality are primarily based on this purely numerical (modular) function of termination. There are nine rivers of the underworld, and the mortuary aspect of the cat is indicated by her nine lives. Charles Manson's adoption of the Beatles' Revolution-9 (or Revelation IX) as an apocalyptic 'family anthem' was fully in keeping with this aspect of the number.

Alternatively, nine is acknowledged as the highest numeral, and associated with celestial inspiration (the nine muses) and bliss (Cloud 9).

Nine solar planets are recognized by modern astronomy (as also by the ancient Lemurian Planetwork).

The duplicate reiteration of nine is remarkable for its theomystical resonances. Islam (= 99) lists ninety-nine 'incomparable attributes' of Allah. The Anglossic value of YHVH = 99. According to the cryptic Black Atlantean cargo-cult Hyper-C the number ninety-nine—as dramatized by the Y2K panic—designates the cyclic completion of time.

THE NINTH PLANET: PLUTO

Pluto (or Sol-9) has the most highly elliptical orbital trajectory of any planet in the Solar-system, with a (highly variable) mean orbital distance from the sun of approx. 5,913,520,000km. Due to the extreme eccentricity of its orbit, Pluto periodically switches places with Neptune as eighth planet from the Sun. The Plutonian year is approximately under 247.7 Earth-years in length.

Pluto was not discovered until 1930. Its anomalous orbit, which is both abnormally elliptical and also angled off the ecliptic, has led many to the conclusion that it is not a normal planet at all. Suggestions as to its nature include the hypothesis that it is a captured or adopted body (perhaps from the Kuiper Belt of Trans-Neptunian objects), or alternatively an escaped Neptunian moon.

Pluto has one known moon, Charon (discovered in 1978, and named after the ferryman who guides the dead across the river Styx). Charon is the largest satellite relative to its 'parent' planet in the Solar-system.

In Roman mythology Pluto is the god of the underworld (identified with the Greek Hades). The topographically twisted association of the inner-most with the outermost—technically described as 'Plutonic-looping'—is exemplified by the identification of the most distant planet with the inner core of the Earth.

The existence of Pluto was anticipated by H.P. Lovecraft, who named the as-yet-unknown planet Yuggoth.

In Lemurian Planetwork Pluto is astrozygonomously paired with the Sun.

:(:)((:)((:)))

SYSTEM NOTES

Zone-9 is the second of the two zones mutually composing the Plex-region of the Numogram, and Tractor-Zone for the 9-0 (or 'Plex') current. Its Plex-complement and Syzygetic twin is Zone-0. This 9+0 Syzygy (carried by the demon Uttunul) draws the outermost curve of the Barker Spiral, which coincides with the limit ordinal-span in Barkerian arithmetic. Zone-9 provides the terminus for two channels, one each from the Torque (the 8th), and the Plex (the 9th).

Zone-9 both initiates and envelops the Ninth Phase of Pandemonium (including 512 impulse-entities, one half of the fully disorganized population). In the first of these aspects it functions as the Ninth (or Ultimate) Door, which degenerated Muvian sorceries identify with the syzygetic xenodemon (and imp of the first degree) Uttunul (9::0, see above).

The Ninth Gate (Gt-45) connects Zone-9 to itself, transducing the third involutionary channel (see Zone-0, Zone-1). Nma sorcery refers to it as the Gate of Pandemonium (a fact Stillwell attributes to the coincidence of its number (45) with that of the Nma demonomy). The Tzikvik associate it with Tchukululok (fabled City of the Worms), and emphasize its numerical cross-match with the 5+4 Syzygy, whose demonic carrier they call Kattku (the Nma 'Katak'). The Xxignal track *Utterminus* is dedicated to the Ninth Gate, linking it to K-goth synthanatonic fugues. In contrast, Polanski's film *The Ninth Gate*—despite its title—has only the most tenuous and allusive relation to the Numogram path of this name.

Mu Tantrism plots Zone-9 intensities onto the Sacral level of the spine. The Sacrum (or 'sacred bone') has been identified (by Goethe amongst others) as a degenerated second skull.

Zone-9 is allotted the Sarkonian Mesh-Tag 0511.

Lemurian subcultures associate Zone-9 with the Cthellloid metallic ocean of the earth's iron core.

((:(:)(:)))

Centauri Subdecadence maps Zone-9 onto the active side of the Fifth (or Root) Pylon on the Atlantean Cross. As the light aspect of Foundation ('deep past') it corresponds to the prehuman cultures of the Old Ones.

Stillwell links Zone-9 to the Munumese quasiphonic particle 'tn', which Horowitz describes as 'the ultimate unutterable mystery of vocal nullity'.

PHASE-9 LEMURS

[M#36] 9::0 Uttunul

[M#37] 9::1 Tuttagool

[M#38] 9::2 Unnunddo

[M#39] 9::3 Ununuttix

[M#40] 9::4 Unnunaka

[M#41] 9::5 Tukutu

[M#42] 9::6 Unnutchi

[M#43] 9::7 Nuttubab

[M#44] 9::8 Ummnu

PANDEMONIUM MATRIX (EXTRACTS FROM THE LEMURIAN NECRONOMICON)

Mesh-00: Lurgo (Legba). (Terminal) Initiator.
(Clicks Gt-00). Pitch Ana-1. Net-Span 1::0.
Amphidemon of Openings. (The Door of Doors).
Cipher Gt-01, Gt-10. 1st Door (The Pod) [Mercury], Dorsal.
1st Phase-limit.
Decadology: C/tp-#7, Mj+ [7C].
Rt-1:[1890] Spinal-voyage (fate line), programming.

Mesh-01: Duoddod. Duplicitous Redoubler.
(Clicks Gt-01). Pitch Ana-2. Net-Span 2::0.
Amphidemon of Abstract Addiction 2nd Door (The Crypt) [Venus], Cervical.
Decadology: C/tp-#8, Mj+ [8C].
Rt-1:[271890] Pineal-regression (rear vision).
Rt-2:[27541890] Datacomb searches, digital exactitude (every second counts). [+1 sub-Rt].

Mesh-02. Doogu (The Blob). Original-Schism.
Pitch Ana-3. Net-Span 2::1.
Cyclic Chronodemon of Splitting-Waters.
Ciphers Gt-21. Shadows Surge-Current.
2nd Phase-limit.
Decadology: C/tp-#1 Mn+ [1H].
Rt-1:[1872] Mn. Primordial breath (pneumatic practices).
Rt-2:[271] Ambivalent capture, hooks (live-bait, traps, plot-twists).
Rt-3:[27541] Mj. Slow pull to stasis, protection from drowning. [+1 sub-Rt].

Mesh-03. Ixix (Yix). Abductor.
(Clicks Gt-03). Pitch Ana-3 Net-Span 3::0.
Chaotic Xenodemon of Cosmic Indifference.
Ciphers Gt-03.
3rd Door (The Swirl), [Earth]. Cranial.
Rt-0:[?] Occult terrestrial history (Who does the Earth think It Is?)

Mesh-04. Ixigool. (Djinn of the Magi).
Over-Ghoul. Pitch Ana-4. Net Span 3::1.
Amphidemon of Tridentity (Sphinx-time).
Decadology: C/tp-#4, Mn+ [4H].
Rt-1:[18723] Unimpeded ascent (prophecy).
Rt-2:[1872563] Ultimate implications, (as above so below). [+1 sub-Rt].

Mesh-05. Ixidod (King Sid). The Zombie-Maker.
Pitch Ana-5. Net Span 3::2.
Amphidemon of Escape-velocity.
Haunts Gt-03. 3rd Phase-limit.
Decadology: C/tp-#5, Mn+ [5H].
Rt-1:[23] Crises through excess (micropause abuse).
Rt-2:[27563] Illusion of progress (out of the frying-pan into the fire). [+1 sub-Rt].

Mesh-06. Krako (Kru, Karak-oa). The Croaking Curse.
Pitch Ana-4 Net-Span 4::0.
Amphidemon of Burning-Hail 4th Door (Delta) Mars. Cervical.
Decadology: C/tp-#9, Mj+ [9C].
Rt-1:[41890] Subsidence, heaviness of fatality. [+1 sub-Rt].

Mesh-07. Sukugool (Old Skug). The Sucking-Ghoul.

Pitch Ana-5. Net-Span 4::1.

Cyclic Chronodemon of deluge and implosion.

Prowls Sink-Current. Haunts Gt-10.

Decadology: C/tp-#3, Mj+ [3C].

Rt-1:[187254] Mn. Cycle of creation and destruction.

Rt-2:[41] Mj. Submersion (gravedigging). [+1 sub-Rt].

Mesh-08. Skoodu (Li'l Scud). The Fashioner.

Pitch Ana-6 Net-Span 4::2.

Cyclic Chronodemon of Switch-Crazes.

Shadows Hold-Current.

Decadology: C/tp-#2, Mn+ [2H].

Rt-1:[2754] Mn. Historical time (eschatology).

Rt-2:[41872] Passage through the deep.

Rt-3:[451872] Mj. Cyclic reconstitution and stability.

Mesh-09. Skarkix (Sharky, Scar-head). Buzz-Cutter.

Pitch Ana-7 (Uppermost). Net-Span 4::3.

Amphidemon of anti-evolution (eddies of the Delta).

4th Phase-limit.

Decadology: C/tp-#6, Mj+ [6C].

Rt-1:[418723] Hermetic abbreviations (history of the magicians).

Rt-2:[4518723] Sacred seal of time (triadic reconfirmation of the cycle).

Rt-3:[4563] Apocalyptic rapture (jagged turbulence). [+1 sub-Rt].

Mesh-10. Tokhatto (Old Toker, Top Cat). Decimal Camouflage.

Pitch Cth-4 Net-Span 5::0 Amphidemon of Talismania.

5th Door (Hyperborea) [Jupiter], Cervical.

Decadology: C/tp-#9, Mj- [9S]. Angel of the Cards.

Rt-1:[541890] Number as destiny (digital convergence). [+1 sub-Rt].

Mesh-11. Tukkamu. Occulturation.

Pitch Cth-3. Net-Span 5::1.

Cyclic Chronodemon of Pathogenesis.

Ciphers Gt-15. Prowls Sink-Current.

Decadology: C/tp-#3, Mj- [3S].

Rt-1:[18725] Mn. Optimal maturation (medicine as diffuse healing).

Rt-2:[541] Mj. Rapid deterioration (putrefaction, catabolism). [+1 sub-Rt].

Mesh-12. Kuttadid (Kitty). Ticking Machines.

Pitch Cth-2 Net-Span 5::2.

Cyclic Chronodemon of Precarious States.

Prowls Hold-Current.

Decadology: C/tp-#2, Mn- [2D].

Rt-1:[275] Mn. Maintaining balance (calendric conservatism).

Rt-2:[541872] Mj. Exhaustive vigilance. [+1 sub-Rt].

Mesh-13. Tikkitix (Tickler). Clicking Menaces.

Pitch Cth-1 Net-Span 5::3.

Amphidemon of Vortical Delirium.

Decadology: C/tp-#6, Mj- [6S].

Rt-1:[5418723] Swirl-patterns (tornadoes, wind-voices). [+1 sub-Rt].

Rt-2:[563] Mysterious disappearances (things carried-away). [+1 sub-Rt].

Mesh-14. Katak. Desolator.

Pitch Null. Net-Span 5::4.

Syzygetic Chronodemon of Cataclysmic Convergence.

Feeds Sink-Current. Ciphers Gt-45. 5th Phase limit.

Decadology: C/tp-#0 [Joker].

Rt-0:[X] Tail-chasing, rabid animals (nature red in tooth and claw).

Rt-1:[418725] Panic (slasher pulp and religious fervour).

Mesh-15 Tchu (Tchanul). Source of Subnothingness.

Pitch Cth-3. Net-Span 6::0.

Chaotic Xenodemon of Ultimate Outsideness (and unnamable things).

6th Door (Undu) [Saturn]. Cranial.

Rt-0:[?] Cosmic deletions and real impossibilities.

Mesh-16. Djungo. Infiltrator.

Pitch Cth-2. Net Span 6::1.

Amphidemon of Subtle Involvements (and intricate puzzles).

Decadology: C/tp-#4, Mn- [4D].

Rt-1:[187236] Turbular fluids (maelstroms, chaotic incalculability). [+1 sub-Rt].

Rt-2:[187256] Surreptitious invasions, inexplicable contaminations (fish falls).

Mesh-17. Djuddha (Judd Dread). Decentred Threat.

Pitch Cth-2. Net-Span 6::2.

Amphidemon of Artificial Turbulence (complex-dynamics simulations).

Decadology: C/tp-#5, Mn- [5D].

Rt-1:[236] Machine-vortex (seething skin). [+1 sub-Rt].

Rt-2:[256] Storm peripheries (Wendigo legends).

Mesh-18. Djynxx (Ching, The Jinn). Child Stealer.

Pitch Null. Net-Span 6::3.

Syzygetic Xenodemon of Time-Lapse.

Feeds and Prowls Warp-Current. Ciphers Gt-36. Haunts Gt-06, Gt-21.

Rt-0:[X] Abstract cyclones, dust spirals (nomad war-machine). [+2 sub-Rt].

Mesh-19. Tchakki (Chuckles). Bag of Tricks.

Pitch Ana-1. Net-Span 6::4.

Amphidemon of Combustion.

Decadology: C/tp-#6, Mn+ [6H]. 1st Decademon.

Rt-1:[4187236] Quenching accidents (apprentice smiths). [+1 sub-Rt].

Rt-2:[45187236] Mappings between incompatible time-systems (Herakleitean firecycle). [+1 sub-Rt].

Rt-3:[456] Conflagrations (shrieking deliria, spontaneous combustion).

Mesh-20. Tchattuk (One Eyed Jack, Djatka). Pseudo-Basis.

Pitch Cth-7 (Lowermost). Net-Span 6::5.

Amphidemon of Unscreened Matrix.

Haunts Gt-15. 6th Phase-limit.

Decadology: C/tp-#6, Mn- [6D].

Rt-1:[54187236] Zero-gravity. [+2 sub-Rt].

Rt-2:[56] Cut-outs (UFO cover-ups, Nephilim).

Mesh-21. Puppo (The Pup). Break-Outs.

Pitch Cth-2. Net-Span 7::0.

Amphidemon of Larval Regression.

7th Door (Akasha) [Uranus], Cervical.

Decadology: C/tp-#8, Mj- [8S].

Rt-1:[71890] Dissolving into slime (masked horrors).

Rt-2:[7254189o] Chthonic swallowings. [+1 sub-Rt].

Mesh-22. Bubbamu (Bubs). After Babylon.

Pitch Cth-1. Net-Span 7::1.

Cyclic Chronodemon of Relapse.

Prowls Surge-Current. Haunts Gt-28.

Decadology: C/tp-#1, Mn- [1D].

Rt-1:[187] Mn. Hypersea (marine life on land).

Rt-2:[71] Aquassassins (Black Atlantis).

Rt-3:[72541] Mj. Seawalls (dry-time, taboo on menstruation).

Mesh-23. Oddubb (Odba). Broken Mirror.

Pitch Null. Net-Span 7::2.

Syzygetic Chronodemon of Swamp-Labyrinths (and blind-doubles).

Feeds Hold-Current.

Rt-0:[X]. Time loops, glamour and glosses.

Mesh-24. Pabbakis (Pabzix). Dabbler.

Pitch Ana-1. Net-Span 7::3.

Amphidemon of Interference (and fakery).

Decadology: C/tp-#5, Mj+ [5C]. 2nd Decademon.

Rt-1:[723] Batrachian mutations (and frog-plagues).

Rt-2:[72563] Cans of worms (vermophobic hysteria, propagation by division). [+1 sub-Rt].

Mesh-25. Ababbatok (Abracadabra). Regenerator.

Pitch Ana-2. Net-Span 7::4.

Cyclic Chronodemon of Suspended Decay.

Shadows Hold-Current.

Decadology: C/tp-#2, Mj+ [2C].

Rt-1:[4187] Frankensteinian experimentation (reanimations, golems).

Rt-2:[45187] Mn. Purifications, amphibious cycles (and healing of wounds).

Rt-3:[7254] Mj. Sustenance (smoke visions).

Mesh-26. Papatakoo (Pataku). Upholder.

Pitch Cth-6. Net-Span 7::5.

Cyclic Chronodemon of Calendric Time.

Prowls Hold-Current.

Decadology: C/tp-#2, Mj- [2S].

Rt-1:[54187] Mn. Ultimate success (perseverance, blood sacrifice). [+1 sub-Rt].

Rt-2:[725] Mj. Rituals becoming nature.

Mesh-27. Bobobja (Bubbles, Beelzebub (Lord of the Flies)). Heavy Atmosphere.

Pitch Cth-5. Net-Span 7::6.

Amphidemon of Teeming Pestilence.

7th Phase-limit.

Decadology: C/tp-#5, Mj- [5S].

Rt-1:[7236] Strange lights in the swamp (dragonflies, ET frog-cults). [+1 sub-Rt].

Rt-2:[7256] Swarmachines (lost harvests).

Mesh-28. Minommo. Webmaker.

Pitch Cth-1. Net-Span 8::0.

Amphidemon of Submergance.

8th Door (Limbo) [Neptune] Lumbar.

Decadology: C/tp-#7, Mj- [7S].

Rt-1:[890] Shamanic voyage (dream sorcery and mitochondrial chatter).

Mesh-29. Mur Mur (Murrumur, Mu(mu)). Dream-Serpent.

Pitch Null. Net-Span 8::1.

Syzygetic Chronodemon of the Deep Ones.

Feeds Surge-Current.

Rt-0:[X] Oceanic sensation (gilled-unlife and spinal-regressions).

Mesh-30. Nammamad. Mirroracle.

Pitch Ana-1. Net-Span 8::2.

Cyclic Chronodemon of Subterranean Commerce.

Shadows Surge-Current. Ciphers Gt-28.

Decadology: C/tp-#1, Mj+ [1C]. 3rd Decademon.

Rt-1:[2718] Voodoo in cyberspace (cthulhoid traffic).

Rt-2:[275418] Mn. Completion as final collapse (heat-death, degenerative psychoses). [+1 sub-Rt].

Rt-3:[8172] Mj. Emergences (and things washed-up on beaches).

Mesh-31. Mummumix (Mix-Up). The Mist-Crawler.

Pitch Ana-2. Net-Span 8::3.

Amphidemon of Insidious Fog (Nyarlathotep).

Decadology: C/tp-#4, Mj+ [4C].

Rt-1:[81723] Ocean storms (and xenocommunication on the bacterial plane).

Rt-2:[8172563] Diseases from outer-space (oankali medicine). [+1 sub-Rt].

Mesh-32. Numko (Old Nuk). Keeper of Old Terrors.

Pitch Ana-3. Net-Span 8::4.

Cyclic Chronodemon of Autochthony.

Prowls Sink-Current.

Decadology: C/tp-#3, Mn+ [3H].

Rt-1:[418] Necrospeleology (abysmal patience rewarded).

Rt-2:[4518] Mn. Subduction (and carnivorous fish).

Rt-3:[817254] Mj. Vulcanism (and bacterial intelligence).

Mesh-33. Muntuk (Manta, Manitou). Desert Swimmer.

Pitch Cth-5. Net-Span 8::5.

Cyclic Chronodemon of Arid Seabeds.

Shadows Sink-Current.

Decadology: C/tp-#3, Mn- [3D].

Rt-1:[5418] Mn. Ancient rivers. [+1 sub-Rt].

Rt-2:[81725] Mj. Cloud-vaults and oppressive tension (protection during monsoon)

Mesh-34. Mommoljo (Mama Jo). Alien Mother.

Pitch Cth-4. Net-Span 8::6.

Amphidemon of Xenogenesis.

Decadology: C/tp-#4, Mj- [4S].

Rt-1:[817236] Cosmobacterial exogermination. [+1 sub-Rt].

Rt-2:[817256] Extraterrestrial residues (including alien DNA segments).

Mesh-35. Mombbo. Tentacle Face (Fishy Princess).

Pitch Cth-3. Net-Span 8::7.

Cyclic Chronodemon of Hybridity.

Prowls Surge-Current. 8th Phase-limit.

Decadology: C/tp-#1, Mj- [1S].

Rt-1:[718] Ophidian transmutation (palaeopythons).

Rt-2:[725418] Mn. Surreptitious colonization [+1 sub-Rt].

Rt-3:[817] Mj. Surface-amnesia (old fishwives tales).

Mesh-36. Uttunul. Seething Void.

(Clicks Gt-36.) Pitch Null. Net-Span 9::0.

Syzygetic Xenodemon of Atonality.

Feeds and Prowls Plex-Current. Haunts Gt-45. 9th Door (Cthelll) [Pluto], Sacrum.

Rt-0:[X] Crossing the iron-ocean (plutonics).

:(:)(::)(::)

Mesh-37. Tutagool (Yettuk). The Tattered Ghoul.

Pitch Ana-1. Net-Span 9::1.

Amphidemon of Punctuality.

Decadology: C/tp-#7, Mn+ [7H]. 4th Decademon.

Rt-1:[189] The dark arts, rusting iron, tattooing (one-way ticket to Hell).

Mesh-38. Unnunddo (The False Nun). Double-Undoing.

Pitch Ana-2. Net-Span 9::2.

Amphidemon of Endless Uncasing (onion-skin horror).

Decadology: C/tp-#8, Mn+ [8H].

Rt-1:[27189] Crypt-traffic (and centipede simulations).

Rt-2:[2754189] Communication-grids (telecom webs, shamanic metallism).

[+1 sub-Rt].

Mesh-39. Ununuttix (Tick-Tock). Particle Clocks.

Pitch Ana-3. Net-Span 9::3.

Chaotic Xenodemon of Absolute Coincidence.

Rt-0:[?] Numerical connection through the absence of any link.

Mesh-40. Ununak (Nuke). Blind Catastrophe.

Pitch Ana-4. Net-Span 9::4.

Amphidemon of Convulsions.

Decadology: C/tp-#9, Mn+ [9H].

Rt-1:[4189] Secrets of the blacksmiths.

Rt-2:[45189] Subterranean impulses.

Mesh-41. Tukutu (Killer-Kate). Cosmotraumatics.

Pitch Cth-4. Net Span 9::5.

Amphidemon of Death-Strokes.

Decadology: C/tp-#9, Mn- [9D].

Rt-1:[54189] Crash-signals (barkerian scarring). [+1 sub-Rt].

Mesh-42. Unnutchi (Outch, T'ai Chi). Tachyonic immobility (slow vortex).

Pitch Cth-3. Net-Span 9::6.

Chaotic Xenodemon of Coiling Outsideness.

Rt-0:[?] Asymmetric zygopoise (and cybernetic anomalies).

Mesh-43. Nuttubab (Nut-Cracker). Mimetic Anorganism.

Pitch Cth-2. Net-Span 9::7.

Amphidemon of Metaloid Unlife.

Decadology: C/tp-#8, Mn- [8D].

Rt-1:[7189] Lunacies (iron in the blood).

Rt-2:[7254189] Dragon-lines (terrestrial electromagnetism). [+1 sub-Rt].

Mesh-44. Ummnu (Om, Omni, Amen, Omen). Ultimate Inconsequence.

Pitch Cth-1. Net-Span 9::8.

Amphidemon of Earth-Screams.

Haunts Gt-36. 9th Phase-limit.

Decadology: C/tp-#7, Mn- [7D].

Rt-0:[89] Crust-friction (anorganic tension).

PANDEMONIUM COMMENTARY

ONE. *NUMOGRAM AND OTZ CHAIM*

To those familiar with the Western Magical Tradition, it is likely that the Numogram will initially evoke the Qabbalistic Tree of Life. Both are constructed as decimal diagrams, involving webs of connectivity between ten basic zones, mysteriously twisted into a cryptic ultra-cycle (that links upper and lower regions). Both treat names as numbers, and numerize by digital reduction and cumulation. Both include passages across abysmal waters and through infernal regions. Both map zones onto spinal levels.

Despite these manifold interlinkages, there are compelling reasons to consider the Tree of Life a scrambled variant of the Numogram, rather than a parallel system. During its long passage through Atlantean and post-Atlantean hermetic traditions the systematic distortions of the Numogram (introduced to confuse the uninitiated) gradually hardened into erroneous doctrines, and a dogmatic image of the Tree. Most evidently, a vulgar distribution of the numbers—in their exoteric counting-order—was substituted (redundantly) for the now esoteric numogrammatical distribution, which proceeds in accordance with immanent criteria (the web emerging qabbalistically from the zone-numbers themselves). More devastatingly, the original consistency of numeracy and language seems to have been fractured at an early stage, introducing a division between the number of the Sephiroth (10) and that of the Hebrew alphabet (22). The result was a break between the nodes of the tree and the interconnecting paths, ruining all prospect of decipherment. The Sephiroth—segmented over-against their connections—become static and structural, whilst the paths lose any rigorous principle of allocation. A strictly analogous outcome is evident in the segmentation of the Tarot into Major and Minor Arcana. Increasingly desperate, arbitrary, and mystifying attempts to reunite the numbers and their linkages seems to have bedevilled all succeeding occult traditions.

TWO. *NUMOGRAM AND I CHING*

There is considerable evidence, both immanent and historical, that the Chinese *I Ching* and the Nma Numogram share a hypercultural matrix. Both are associated with intricate zygonomies, or double-numbering systems, and process abstract problematics involving subdivisions of decimal arrays (as suggested by the Ten Wings of traditional *I Ching* commentary). Digital reduction of binary powers stabilizes in a six-step cycle (with the values 1, 2, 4, 8, 7, 5). These steps correspond to the lines of the hexagram, and to the time-circuit zones of the Numogram, producing a binodecimal 6-Cycle (which is also generated in reverse by quintuplicative numbering). In both cases a supplementary rule of pairing is followed, according to a zygonovic criterion (9-twinning of reduced values: 8:1, 7:2, 5:4, mapping the hexagram line pairs).

The numogram time-circuit, or *I Ching* hexagram, implicitly associates zero with the set of excluded triadic values. It is intriguing in this respect that numerous indications point to an early struggle between triadic and binary numbering practices in ancient Chinese culture, suggesting that the binary domination of decimal numeracy systematically produces a triadic residue consistent with nullity. The hexagram itself exhibits obvious tension in this respect, since it reinserts a triadic hyperfactor into the reduced binodigital set (compounded by its summation to twenty-seven, or the third power of three).

An ancient binotriadic parallel to the *I Ching*, called the *T'ai Hsuan Ching* (or *Book of the Great Dark*) consisted of eighty-one tetragrams, reversing the relation of foregrounded and implicit numerical values. The division of Lao Tse's *Tao Te Ching* into eighty-one sections suggests that this numerical conflict was an animating factor in the early history of Taoism.

THREE. *ETHNOGRAPHY OF THE NMA*

Nma culture cannot be decoded without the key provided by the Lemurian Time-Maze. The influence of a hypertriadic criterion of time is evident in the relics of Nma kinship organization, calendrics, and associated rituals. Prior to the calamity of 1883, the Nma consisted of true tribes (tripartite macrosocial divisions). They were distributed in a basic tridentity (interlocking large-scale groupings into Tak-, Mu-, and Dib-Nma), supported by a triangular patrilocal marriage-cycle. Each marriage identified a woman with a Numogram current, or time-passage. (Tak-Nma women marrying into the Mu-Nma, Mu-Nma ditto Dib-Nma, Dib-Nma ditto Tak-Nma). The common calendar of all three tribes was based upon a zygotriadic system (using 6 digits to divide a double-year period of 729 days into fractional powers of three). The Mu-Nma still employ such a calendar today. (The current Mu-Nma calendar is adjusted by regular intercalations of three additional days every second cycle, or four years. The earlier practice of intercalations is not easily recoverable).

In the rituals of the Nma the time-circuit is concretized as a hydrocycle: a division and recombination of the waters. The three stages of this recurrent transmutation are (1) the undivided waters (oceanic), (2) cloud-building (evaporation), and (3) downpour (precipitation, river-flow). These are associated with the great sea-beast (Mur Mur), the lurker of steaming swamps (Oddubb), and that which hunts amongst the raging storms (Katak). The cycle is closed by a return to the abysmal waters, intrinsically linking the order of time, and its recurrence, to an ultimate cataclysm (prior to any opposition of cyclic and apocalyptic time). It is in this context that the transcultural deluge-mythos can be restored to its aboriginal sense (which also corresponds to the Hindu Trimurti, with its three stages of creation, preservation and destruction).

NUMOGRAMMATIC TIME-MAPPING

In Peter Vysparov's construction of the Cthulhu Club System, the central region of the Numogram is labelled the 'Time-Circuit' or the 'Domain of Chronos'. Despite misgivings about mythopoetic arguments, it is worth briefly rehearsing aspects of Vysparov's discussion.

According to the Greek myth, Chronos was the son of Uranus and Gaia, last of the Titans and God of Time, married to the Goddess Rhea. Revolting against the tyranny of Uranus, Gaia provided Chronos with a sickle, with which he hacked the sexual organs from his father, killing him (and producing various fallout entities—Erinyes, Giants, and Meliae). Chronos also fell under the prophecy that he would suffer an analogous fate at the hands of his offspring. He thus devoured the first five (Hestia, Hera, Demeter, Poseidon, and Hades—order (to me) uncertain (Hestia first daughter)), but Zeus escaped and poisoned him. The five consumed children were regurgitated as their father died.

Vysparov seems to have been convinced that these six offspring of Chronos—three of each sex—could be rigorously allotted zonal 'houses' on the Numogram Time-Circuit, consistent with the Pythagorean gendering of numbers. If he ultimately succeeded in establishing these coordinations, his results do not seem to have reached us.

Vysparov also emphasized that this 'founding' myth is one of time disintegration, not time persistence. The 'Domain of Chronos' is a burial complex, ordering the world through the death of integral time.

Whether beginning from Kant's identification of time with the content of arithmetic, or Einstein's definition of time as a (fourth) dimension, attempts to model time seem necessarily to call upon the number line. The most elementary—and notationally efficient—chronometric and calendric systems count time by addition of unit periods, from caesium atom half-lives through clock ticks, to day counting and annual date-changing. Whatever the scale, the procedure remains the same: the apparently basic arithmetical operation of additive succession, +1, +1, +1, ...

Of course, mathematicians have known for well over two millennia that the number line in no way compels such an assumption. Step-by-step additive progression by units is merely one arithmetically arbitrary mode of numerical accumulation. Nevertheless, it can at least be argued that this pattern of counting presents the overwhelmingly prevalent articulation of chronological common sense.

Echidna Stillwell refers to Vysparov's 'Time Circuit' as the 'Hex'. She demonstrates the arithmetical consistency between this region of the Numogram and the Chinese Classic of Change, or *I Ching*. This intermapping is locked into place by two basic bino-decimal echoes:

(1) The six-step cycle of digitally-reduced binary magnitudes, repeating the series 2, 4, 8, 7, 5, 1.

(2) The 9-twinning of these repeating stages. (To quote Richard Wilhelm's commentary: 'The following lines, provided they differ in kind, correspond: the first and the fourth, the second and the fifth, the third and the top [sixth] line.')

Stillwell cites the Nma version of an almost universally familiar story:

> *A poor mathematician from the great landmass came to the court with a game he had invented, now called 'chess,' and the king was so enthralled by this diversion he asked the visitor whether there was anything he could offer as a token of appreciation. The cunning mathematician replied: 'Your majesty, perhaps if you were to place a grain of rice on the first square, two on the second, and continuing thus, doubling the number on each successive square until reaching the final [64th] one, it would at least spare me from the danger of starvation on my return journey.' Shocked by the modesty of*

this request, the king readily agreed. It was in this way the kingdom passed for the first time into the hands of strangers....

This tale, attributed variously to Indian, Chinese, and Persian sources, with minor variations in each case, is now to be found mostly in schoolrooms, where it is used as an aid in the teaching of binary exponentiation. The topics it raises, whether concerning mathematics, games and power, number and trickery, numerical isomorphy between the chess board and the *I Ching*, or other matters, exceed the scope of this discussion. Two points will suffice for now:

(1) The utter obscurity attending the origins of this tale provides highly suggestive support for Stillwell's 'ethnomic' hypothesis, with its argument that numerical potentiality is capable of generating spontaneous unlocalizable cultural syndromes.

(2) Binary exponentiation has a 'mythic' dimension, now largely supplanted in modern societies by 'Moore's Law' of techonomic development.

A privileging of binary exponentiation rather than unit addition is entirely consistent with the prominence of the number line as a model of time. The basic 'time unit', however, is now conceived as the 'doubling period'. This approach integrates an intriguing diversity of problematics:

(1) The *I Ching*, where time progresses through doubling and bino-decimal cyclicity. There is nothing exclusively 'modern' about the extravagant power of time as an exponentially accumulative trend—modernity lies rather in the evasion of disaccumulation crisis, which in the time of the *I Ching* is described as an inevitability of periodic catastrophe.

(2) The Numogram Hex, rigorously echoing the *I Ching*, although with certain supplementary complexities (exceeding the scope of this discussion). The Numogram also 'positions' the sphere of duplicative time within a greater—and for now obscure—time terrain.

(3) Qabbalistic tradition, within which binary exponentiation has 'always' provided the key to certain crucial combinatorial calculations. Combinatorics, qabbala, and binary exponentiation share a common procedural reservoir.
(4) Transfinite arithmetic, as consolidated by Cantor, whose Continuum Hypothesis proposes that binary exponentiation to Aleph 0 = Aleph 1 (the real number line).

But this could go on forever....

AQ NOTES

CHRONO = 127 (enough said)

CHRONOLOGY = 222 (a little theatrical perhaps...)

CHRONOS = 155 (31 x 5: The pentanomic order is the strict complement of binary within the decimalized Oecumenon—more on this elsewhere)

QABBALA UNSHELLED

This provocative—in fact insolently aggressive and sarcastic—short text on the numogrammatic incoherence of the Hebrew Tree of Life, was written by 'Frater V'. (widely assumed to be P. Vysparov) and appeared as a letter in the short-lived journal Occultism Today *on 6th September 1956.*

THE TREE OF LIFE IS ESSENTIALLY QLIPHOTHIC

Professor Echidna Stillwell's (literally) pathbreaking researches have opened the way to a rigorous Lemurian apprehension of the Hebrew Tree of Life as a degenerated hyperstitional structure. Her numogrammatic perspective decisively reveals that there are no immanent principles supporting the arrangement of the Tree, but only a dead tradition of acceptation, authority without demonstration, order without coherence or consequence.

We only need to ask: Why does Kether, the first Sephira, occupy the crown of the Tree, unless by merit of a banal ordinal mechanism—no more than an instinctive reflex—binding primacy to supremacy and unity? Why does the zig-zag path of divine manifestation continue from Chokmah (2) to Binah (3) and then onwards in tedious ordinal conformity to the end of the series? Is the mere order of the decimal numerals already a map of creation? If so, why the contrivance of a two-dimensional arrangement at all? Why not simply say: the great hermetic truth of the scared 'qabalah' is the capability to count to ten and call it God's work? And then why is Malkuth (10) entitled to sephirotic standing at all, unless as a proto-decimal atavism (attesting to an inability even to count to ten with understanding) whose numerical incoherence is available for subsequent exploitation as a 'miraculous' symbol of cyclic reunification (an unwitting tautology gaudily clothed in the pretence of cosmic significance)? As to the patent absurdity of Da'ath (11), a 'Sephira' which would be simply laughable if not encrusted by bejewelled extravagances of magickal solemnity—at this point even elementary arithmetical competence has been sacrificed without reserve to the mysteries of inscrutable tradition.

Imagining momentarily it were possible to sympathize with the servile consciousness of a 'magickal adept' prostrating himself before this concoction of sub-numerical nonsense, combining the calculative capabilites of a thirteenth-century European peasant with the credulous enthusiasm of a Masonic zealot, how are the 'paths' between the Sephirot to be understood? Of course, there are 22 paths, for the overwhelmingly persuasive 'reason' that there are 22 letters in the Hebrew alphabet. Let us also leave aside the fact that 22 is a number without any compelling numerical interest, except as a tautological reverberation of tradition (being the number of letters in the Hebrew alphabet—and of course a doubling of Da'ath...), and merely ask: What principle organizes their distribution? Except, of course, that there is no such principle, but only tradition, blind authority and—concretely—a slithering downwards, vaguely echoing that so gloriously exhibited by the Sephirot themselves. Even that exultant obscurantist of occultic traditionalism Aleister Crowley is driven to admit: 'With regard to the numbers 11 to 32 of the Key-Scale [the Hebrew letters], they are not numbers at all in our sense of the word. They have been arbitrarily assigned to the 22 paths by the compiler of the Sepher Yetzirah. There is not even any kind of harmony...'—as if arbitrariness was any kind of stranger in this domain.

What a masterpiece of chaotic improvisation we are presented with: regions, paths, letters, and numbers jumbled together discordantly, without anywhere betraying a hint of consistent articulation, procedural regularity or objective plausibility. One might as easily shuffle all these elements together on a whisky-soaked bar-table, entirely without systemic motivation or lucid intelligence, and then call the result a 'qabbalistic' revelation. At least in this case some accidental order might arise to subvert the transcendent idiocy of the whole. The Tree of Life is to rigorous occultism what Ptolemaic astrology is to modern astronomy—a baroque relic of historical interest in the hands of scholars, but an indefensible embarrassment when embraced by believers.

:(:)(:)((::))

Let all those who have serious work to do be done with it, lest the science of the Outer Spheres become universally derided as a joke.

((:)(:)(::))

LURGO

Mesh-oo. Net-Span (1::0)

THE CALL AND ITS NUMBERS

The Lemur of the 1::0 rift is called *Gl'eiaoung* in the Old Muvian Tongue. Her name in modern Munumese is 'Lurgo', which Stillwell translates into English as 'The Initiator'.

The name 'Lurgo' is apparently based on a reversal of the Munumese quasiphonic particle *gl*. Horowitz phonologically identifies this 'collapsed gargle' or 'glottal spasm' with the fusion of a gutteral and a liquid. He physiologically situates it in the sublaryngeal region, and associates it with lost gilled/gulping phylogenetic stages of human ancestry.

Horowitz glimpsed something in the Lurgo's 'gl' subphoneme that he saw as essential to the glottopolitics of English as a global language. In the course of further investigating this particle he was drawn into what he referred to as a labyrinth of 'glitter-glyphs' where sense is scattered in visual confusion, and began to speak of glamours and glosses, ultimately cascading down into the 'gulf-glued glug-logic of the glimmer ghouls', although precisely what he meant by this remains obscure.

Lurgo, as the first of the Lemurs, is responsible for initiations, door-openings, thresholds, guides, and familiars.

The Tzikvik call her Oogvhu, the Immortal Worm of primordial communication.

In Haitian Voodoo her role is taken by Legba, the first and last of the Loa to be invoked in any ritual. Legba's Lurgo-related characteristics are shared by Madame Centauri's 'Celestial messenger' Logobubb.

Lurgo's net-span, 1::0, links her to elementary principles of logical and arithmetical discrimination, binary code, the origin of number, being and nonbeing.

(:)((:)(:)(:))

During her study of the *I Ching*, Stillwell became persuaded that due to her 'elementary net-span' Lurgo was related with special intensity to the Taoist polarity of Yang and Yin, light and shadow, even suggesting that the *I Ching*'s code of unbroken and broken lines was the relic of a 'primordial language, first enunciated by Lurgo'.

In Black Atlantean traditions the 'primal alternation' described by Lurgo's net-span expresses the distance between divine unity and the void, God and Chaos, an abysmal gulf crossed in every Decadence ritual (opened and closed by Lurgo/Legba/Logobubb).

Lurgo's net-span (1::0) clicks the 4th Gate (Gt-10), the passage from Zone-4 to Zone-1. The working of the 4th Gate is numerically described by the 'Pythagorean' Tetraktys (1 + 2 + 3 + 4 = 10 (= 1)). Pythagoras evidently derived this triangular-decimal reversion to unity, and decimal disintegration of unity, from archaic and ultimately Lemurian sources.

Among Black Atlanteans transit through Gt-10 offers a microcosmic recapitulation of the macrocosmic-numogrammatic route from Zone-1 to Zone-0. These relations echo the microcosmic-ceremonial subsidence of Atlantis as the sign of the Cosmic Fall or Great Decadence.

As the only Lemur of the 1st Phase, Lurgo is called the First Door, and also the Door of Doors.

Among the remnants of the Nma she is known as the 'Queen of Unlockings' and her sign is inscribed at the entrance of their temples and above the shops of locksmiths.

Lurgo's mesh number (00) clicks the 0th Gate (Gt-00), linking her to the most occulted region of numogrammatic cartography.

Lurgo's Sarkon-Tag is 0002.

QUANTITIES AND TRAITS

Lurgo has a pitch of Ana-1 (slight positive imbalance).

Lurgo has no imps, a fact which can be attributed equally to her primordiality or ultimateness. As Peter Vysparov remarked: 'Lurgo arrives first and she arrives alone.'

In Vysparov's Pandemonium Matrix Lurgo is entitled the Plexing Amphidemon of Openings.

RITES OF LURGO

The way of Lurgo has one path or route. This follows her (major) rite [1890].

In *The Book of Paths* the Rite of Lurgo is described as follows:

1. Original Subtraction.

Ultimate descent through the Depths.

The path favours repeated patience linked by subtlety.

Superior subtlety opens the three hidden roads.

Compliance prevails.

Three tests on the way.

Immersive nightmares undergo an ominous transition.

Difficulties annihilated in the end.

Lurgo's rite descends out of time, following the numogrammatic 'plunge line', passing through the 8th gate (Gt-36) which crosses from the lair of Murrumur into that of Uttunul.

Among the neolemurian tantric schools this rite maps yogic practices of Spinal descent into the nest of Kundalini (the 'Thothtodlana of the Indus'—Stillwell).

Lurgo's Rite is evoked, in a mirrored guise, by the contemporary myth of the Kurtz-line, travelling upriver into the *Heart of Darkness* and *Apocalypse Now*.

In the dream sorcery of the Munumese 'Nago' the Rite of Lurgo traverses the full passage from consciousness (1) to deep sleep (0) and thus charts a 'line of oblivion' which begins in time but does not travel through it.

(::::::)

Horowitz is among those scholars of esoteric Judaism who have become fascinated by parallels between the Rite of Lurgo and the golem myth. In an appendix to his translation of *The Book of Paths*, he links the 'Original Subtraction' to the removal of the initial aleph from the word 'emet' (written on the golem's head)—an operation required if one is to 'kill' a golem. This connection enabled him to exhume an esoteric mystical content to the myth, in which the 'death' of the golem symbolizes the opening of a path into the abyss.

THE LAIR OF LURGO

In the Lemurian Planetworks, Lurgo's domain (1::0) is situated between the orbits of Mercury and the Sun. Fittingly, the Roman Mercury (Greek Hermes) is entitled 'the messenger of the gods' and associated with traffick in all its forms, including communication and trade.

Lurgo nests Minommo (8::0), Murrumur (8::1), Uttunul (9::0), Tutagool (9::1), and Ummnu (9::8). By nesting Ummnu (final Lemur of the Pandemonium Matrix) within herself, Lurgo establishes the basis for the Munumese saying: 'the end lies within the beginning.'

THE LURGO CARD [7C]

In the Centauri Decadence Pack Lurgo is allocated to the 7 of Clubs. When mapped onto the Atlantean Cross in accordance with Mme Centauri's system, Lurgo corresponds to a plummeting line from the 1st Pylon (memories and dreams) to the 5th Pylon (deep past). Among her oracular implications within Decadence divination are falling in the theocosmic sense, descent into hell, journey to the underworld, and pursuit of the 'Nether Axis' to its ultimate conclusion.

THE TALE OF HOW WE LOST OUR TAILS

There was a time when Orang Utan had a tail, and so did each of us. That was before Orang Utan made a big mistake, and tried to cheat the demon Lurgo.

It is said that Lurgo dwells between Murrumur and Uttunul, somewhere beneath the bottom of the sea, but above the twins in the furnace. No one knows how Orang Utan found her. Maybe it was easier to swim down with a tail. In any case, everyone agrees about the deal they made down there, which was to swap the stories of the upper and lower worlds. Orang Utan was to collect all that could be told about Oddubb and about Katak, and in exchange Lurgo would open the gate to the underworld. If things had gone this way we would still have our tails.

It was probably Katak who—due to her impatience—gave Orang Utan bad advice, and suggested that by climbing down her tail it would be possible to descend into Uttunul without Lurgo's help. Ever since that time Orang Utan has been too ashamed to admit anything about it, but it must have been something like that, because certainly now Orang Utan has no tail, and neither do any of us.

KATAK

Mesh-14. Net-Span (5::4)

THE CALL AND ITS NUMBERS

The Lemur of the 5::4 rift is called *Ktt'skr* in the Ur Nma Tongue. Her name in modern Munumese is 'Katak', which Stillwell translates into English as 'The Desolator'.

In the name Katak, Horowitz finds the phonic molecule *kt'k*, which he associates with 'ideas of falling or sinking'.

This connection leads him to postulate an archaic numogrammatic source for the Greek prefix of descent *Kata-* (as in 'catastrophe, cataclysm, catatonic, catabolism, catadromic...').

In a marginal comment on Geotraumatics, D.C. Barker relates the name 'Katak' both to the K/T missile, which terminated the age of giant saurians, and also to Krakatoa (which decimated the Dib-Nma).

The Tzikvik identify her with the Kattku (or 'madness of the great worm').

In the book of children's fables compiled from Nma sources by Echidna Stillwell's sister Medusa, she is called 'Takka'.

Katak's net-span, 5::4, bridges the smallest interval and places her in the centre of the Barker Spiral. She is described variously as 'tightly bound, coiled or knotted', 'wound up', or 'compacted'. The Cthulhu Club write of a 'Katak effect', when the smallest difference (5::4) has the greatest impact.

Positioned on the '5th Brink' (as ultimate Lemur of the 5th Phase), Katak is the only Syzygetic Lemur to be 'poised at the edge' of her domain, linking her to imbalance, thresholds, and phase-changes.

Katak's net-span (5::4) ciphers the Ultimate Gate, or Gate of Pandemonium (Gt-45), which begins and ends in Zone-9 and echoes the completed Matrix of the Lemurs. This suggests an all-encompassing reach to the powers of Katak (which, in combination with Katak's 'Global Rite', comprises what the Tzikvik call 'the Fatal Secret of the Kattku').

Katak's mesh number (14) ciphers the 7th Lemur, Sukagool (4::1), who haunts the Gate of Submergence (Gt-10). This further consolidates Katak's connections with collapse and inundation. The resonance between the Katakite Sink Current and the Sunken Track attests in certain respects to monotheistic, monopolistic, or totalitarian ambition and reduction to unity, but also to a return to simplicity, search for origins or slippage into indifferentiation.

Katak's Sarkon-Tag is 0047.

QUANTITIES AND TRAITS

As a Syzygetic Lemur, Katak has null pitch. She is thus characterized by perfect poise. Despite her manifold associations with extreme excitability, crisis, furor, and the tempestuous, along with her four Syzygetic systers Katak occupies the 'Numogrammatic Plane' or 'Great Plateau' of continuous cosmic intensities.

Katak hosts 10 imps, which aligns her with decimal numeracy (while also further reinforcing her decimally-mediated relation to unity).

Katak feeds the Sink Current (flowing from the Falling Drift to Zone-1).

In Vysparov's Pandemonium Matrix, Katak is entitled the 'Syzygetic Chronodemon of Cataclysmic Convergence'.

RITES OF KATAK

The way of Katak has two paths or routes. These follow her syzygetic crossing [5/4] and her singular minor rite [418725].

In *The Book of Paths*, Katak's Syzygetic Rite is described as follows:

30. Coiled Fervour

Endless waiting in the Falling Drift.

The path favours patient activity.

::(:(((:))))

Superior subtlety leads nowhere.

Poised entanglement.

Twinned tests make the way.

Between burning excitement and arid tension.

Katak is alone among the Syzygetic Lemurs in having a nonsyzygetic rite. The uniqueness of this rite is compounded by the fact it encircles the entire Hex or 'time-circuit', traversing the complete sequence of past and future lives and 'seizing the whole of time and fate'.

On the basis of this rite Katak is portrayed chasing her own tail, and in its ophidian manifestation (as the barking snake) coiled back into itself as an Ur-Ouroboros, the Thothtodlana of the Tzikvik.

In *The Book of Paths*, Katak's Global Rite is described as follows:

31. Eternal Revolution

Advance prolonged by waiting brings fractured completion.

The path first favours subtlety, then repeated patience and activity.

Superior subtlety opens the first hidden road.

Resistance prevails.

Five tests on the way.

Breakthrough into immersive nightmares spawns promising developments.

Fluid evolution leaves a dubious inheritance.

THE LAIR OF KATAK

In the Lemurian Planetworks, Katak's domain (5::4) is situated between the orbits of Mars and Jupiter (classically identified with war and sovereignty). Astronomically, this band coincides with the asteroid belt, considered by some to be the pulverized remnants of a destroyed planet.

THE KATAK CARD

In the full Decadence pack Katak, as a Syzygy, is only included as one of the five (eliminated) jokers. On the Atlantean Cross she corresponds to the Third Pylon, named Apocalypse, decamantically associated with destructive influences.

TALES

Tzikvik (traditional):

> When the world was born Thothtodlana entered into the secret of the Kattku and—confusing herself with the universe—circled the whole of time. That was when she swam through living flesh, her hunger unlimited and furious. She seemed doomed to devour herself forever. The dead knew no rest, and the earth shuddered. It was then that Ooqvu the worm-witch arrived amongst us. It was Ooqvu that found the pattern in the folds of Thothtodlana's skin, and followed it back to Tchukululok. It was Ooqvu that called to Thothtodlana from deep in Tchukululok, and released her from the Kattku. That is why we still carry the marks of Ooqvu on our skin.

Hackhammer (on the Nma, contemporary):

> It had all gone to hell out there. The Sumatran expedition rotting down to disconnected threads of fever, madness, and atrocity.
> Tak-Nma: a tribe of aggressive head-hunters abhorred through the area (and since eradicated). They had greeted him as Katak.
> Ominous rumblings from out in the Sunda Strait.
> August 1883.
> Pounding solar waves mix with the ceaseless delirious dance-beat of the Tak-Nma.
> Unthreadings into mosquito-fogged heat.
> Shimmerings.

As Curtis records the disintegration of his soul, the name Katak increasingly crosslinks with everything that burns, raves, and devastates.

Everything that ends in blackened threads. Everything....

The Tak-Nma seem to revere rabid dogs. They call them Katak.

There is an internally dislocated hydrophobic bark that is peculiarly Katak.

Blood-stained claws are also Katak.

At midday, when the sun is silent rage, it is Katak.

Katak is the trampling, inarticulate flood-tide of malaria.

Out in the strait, Katak growls, and smokes.

Katak has come.

Katak is soon to come.

Katak comes.

Katak comes.

Incessant drumming of Katak coming.

Drumming, pounding....

THE BOOK OF PATHS

EDITOR'S INTRODUCTION

The Kaye Materials, which came into the possession of the Ccru in late January 2000 (shortly after William Kaye's untimely death), contain several mentions of *The Book of Paths*, referring to it on one occasion as 'the definitive confirmation of Stillwell's basic insight'. Yet despite extensive investigation, the Ccru's attempts to access this text were consistently frustrated. All inquiry into the book was suspended due to a complete lack of productive leads.

In 2003 the Ccru undertook an intensive investigation into Kaye's cryptic references to documented interconnections between William Burroughs, Peter Vysparov, and Lemurian time travel. During the course of this research the Ccru entered into correspondence with the Vysparov estate, inquiring into the contents of the Vysparov Library, where Kaye had spent many years working as an archivist and cataloguing director. The notorious library of the Vysparov family is reputed to contain one of the world's greatest collections of occult works.

During the final stages of the research project, the Ccru received a package from the estate containing a photocopied document which, although untitled, proved upon careful inspection to be nothing less than the complete text of *The Book of Paths*. Appended to this document was a single page (also photocopied) of a handwritten letter from Chaim Horowitz to Peter Vysparov, dated February 1949.

It is this text which is reproduced here. On the basis of Horowitz's letter it can be confidently identified as the so-called 'B Manuscript' of *The Book of Paths*, one of three type-copies of Horowitz's first English translation from the Tibetan. As far as the Ccru is aware, this is the first time that *The Book of Paths* has been made publicly available in any language.

(:)(::(::))

THE LETTER

Dear Peter,

Here at last is a complete translation of the Old Book. Having entrusted this package to Echidna's safekeeping,[1] I am assuming it has reached you undisturbed. The translation has taken me over a year. Perhaps inevitably, some difficult choices had to be made. It goes without saying that I have placed the strictest priority on the preservation of systematic coherence.

There is no need to remind you that the special circumstances attending the discovery of this text necessitate the very greatest discretion. I extracted a copy from 'the place' with considerable trouble, but of that let us converse on another occasion.[2]

Although I only had a brief opportunity to discuss the work with Echidna, she had many interesting points to make—as always. In particular she has been able to find some tantalizing traces of its history within Chinese sources dating back to the Warring States period, when it was already considered profoundly archaic, with more than one 'dark school' even suggesting that it preceded the *I Ching*. It seems that by the early Tang it was considered to have been erased from the earth, one of the *yaoshu* or 'devilish books' destroyed utterly in Chin Shi Huang Di's great burning.

Echidna herself thinks there are indications it was already serving as an oracle for the mysterious culture of the Shu Kingdom, 5,000 years ago. She has stumbled upon persistent rumours that a series of 84 bronze tablets were inexplicably removed from the Shu excavation site by figures described variously as 'looters' or 'senior officials'.

---

1. Horowitz met the esteemed Lemurologist Echidna Stillwell in Rangoon during the early spring of 1949.
2. 'The Place' clearly designates the source of the Mu Archives, where Horowitz conducted research throughout most of the 1930s and 1940s. William Kaye believed that it was located in a concealed sub-basement of the Potala Palace in Lhasa.

We are both hopeful that Mme C. will be able to cast light on the oracular dimension of the work—in truth this has eluded us both so far, despite the most strenuous efforts.[3]

I am sure you will agree that these pages, inelegantly produced though they may be, will add inestimable riches to your family's peerless collection of esoterica. Perhaps even more importantly, we are both confident it will prove itself profoundly relevant to your work on the 'Pandemonium System'.[4] Your invitation was received with great enthusiasm—if at all possible we shall meet in the fall.[5]

Yours with heartfelt regards,
Chaim

3. 'Mme C.' almost certainly refers to Zelda Maria de Monterre, better known as Madame Centauri [see above, 137–140]. During this period Madame Centauri was working as a 'celestial consultant' or fortune teller in New York.

4. As of now (May 2004) Ccru has not been able to determine whether any such 'profound relevance' was in fact discovered.

5. There can be little doubt that the 'invitation' concerned the inaugural meeting of the Cthulhu Club, scheduled for the fall of 1949.

((::))(:::)

THE BOOK

1. Original Subtraction

Ultimate descent through the Depths.

The path favours repeated patience linked by subtlety.

Superior subtlety opens the three hidden roads.

Compliance prevails.

Three tests on the way.

Immersive nightmares undergo an ominous transition.

Difficulties annihilated in the end.

2. Extreme Regression

Waiting in the Rising Drift leads to ultimate descent through the Depths.

The path favours threefold patience linked by subtlety.

Superior subtlety opens the three hidden roads.

Compliance prevails.

Five tests on the way.

Escaping the quagmire through strategic withdrawal.

Immersive nightmares undergo an ominous transition.

Difficulties annihilated in the end.

3. Abysmal Comprehension

Ultimate descent beyond completion.

The path favours fourfold patience, repeated activity and deep subtlety.

Superior subtlety opens the three hidden roads. Fate marks the Sunken Track.

Compliance prevails.

Seven tests on the way.

Escaping the quagmire through attainment.

Burning excitement provokes breakthrough into immersive nightmares.

Ominous transition.

Difficulties annihilated in the end.

::(:)(:)(:)(:)

4. Primordial Breath

Rising from the Lesser Depths.

The path favours repeated patience, joined by activity.

Superior subtlety opens the first hidden road.

Resistance prevails.

Three tests on the way.

Immersive nightmares spawn promising developments.

Fluid evolution.

5. Slipping Backwards

Waiting in the Rising Drift precedes return.

The path favours patience, then subtlety

Superior subtlety opens the first hidden road.

Compliance prevails.

Two tests on the way.

Escaping the quagmire through strategic withdrawal.

6. Attaining Balance

Waiting in the Drifts is drawn to the centre.

The path favours repeated patient activity.

Superior subtlety opens the first hidden road. Fate marks the Sunken Track.

Compliance prevails.

Four tests on the way.

Escaping the quagmire.

Attainments consumed in burning excitement.

Breakthrough.

((:))((:))(:(:))

7. Progressive Levitation

Ascent from the Lesser Depths.

The path favours repeated patience, joined by activity, subtly consummated.

Superior subtlety leads nowhere.

Resistance prevails.

Four tests on the way.

Immersive nightmares spawn promising developments.

Fluid evolution triggers possession.

8. Eternal Digression

Prolonged ascent from the Lesser Depths reaches the Twin Heavens.

The path favours threefold patience, repeated activity and elevated subtlety.

Superior subtlety enters the spiral labyrinth.

Resistance prevails.

Six tests on the way.

Immersive nightmares spawn promising developments.

Feeding fluid evolution.

Dubious inheritance induces captivation.

Lucid delirium.

9. Sudden Flight

Seized from the Heights.

The path favours subtlety.

Superior subtlety leads nowhere.

Pure resistance.

One test on the way.

Possession.

:(:(:::))

10. Jagged Flight

Waiting in the Rising Drift winds its way to the Twin Heavens.

The path favours repeated patience, linked by activity and subtlety.

Superior subtlety enters the spiral labyrinth.

Resistance prevails.

Four tests on the way.

Escaping the quagmire through attainment.

Captivation by lucid delirium.

11. Abysmal Subsidence

The Sunken Track leads to ultimate descent.

The path favours repeated subtlety and patience.

Superior subtlety opens the three hidden roads.

Compliance prevails.

Four tests on the way.

Breakthrough into immersive nightmares.

Ominous transition.

Difficulties annihilated in the end.

12. Slow Cataclysm

Waiting in the falling drift leads to ultimate descent.

The path favours threefold patience, linked by activity and subtlety.

Superior subtlety opens the three hidden roads.

Compliance prevails.

Five tests on the way.

Arid tension succumbs to immersive nightmares.

Ominous transition.

Difficulties annihilated in the end.

13. Cyclic Perfection

Waiting in the Lesser Depths precedes completion.

The path favours threefold patience, linked by activity.

Superior subtlety opens the first hidden road.

Resistance prevails.

Five tests on the way.

Immersive nightmares spawn promising developments.

Feeding fluid evolution.

Dubious inheritance consumed in burning excitement.

14. Tranquil Drowning

Adhering to the Sunken Track.

The path favours subtlety.

Superior subtlety opens the first hidden road.

Pure compliance.

One test on the way.

Breakthrough.

15. Suspended Decline

Waiting in the Falling Drift leads downwards.

The path favours patience, then activity.

Superior subtlety opens the first hidden road.

Compliance prevails

Two tests on the way.

Arid tension finds release.

:::((:(:)))

16. Supreme Balance

Crossing between the Drifts.

The path favours twofold patience, linked by activity.

Superior subtlety leads nowhere.

Resistance prevails.

Three tests on the way

Escaping the quagmire.

Attainments consumed in burning excitement.

17. Profound Renewal

The Sunken Track leads to the Rising Drift.

The path favours subtlety, then twofold patience, linked by activity.

Superior subtlety opens the first hidden road.

Compliance prevails

Four tests on the way.

Breakthrough into immersive nightmares.

Promising developments feed fluid evolution.

18. Cyclic Elevation

Waiting in the Falling Drift leads to completion.

The path favours threefold patience, linked by activity.

Superior subtlety opens the first hidden road.

Compliance prevails

Five tests on the way.

Aid tension finds release in immersive nightmares.

Promising developments feed fluid evolution.

(::)((:)((:)))

19. Transcendent Resurgence

The Sunken Track leads to eventual ascent.

The path favours twofold patience linked by activity, yet it begins and ends in subtlety.

Superior subtlety opens the first hidden road.

Compliance prevails

Five tests on the way.

Breakthrough into immersive nightmares spawns promising developments.

Fluid evolution triggers possession.

20. Alien Intervention

The Sunken Track leads through broken completion to the Twin Heavens.

The path favours subtlety, patience and activity, until all methods entwine.

Superior subtlety opens the first hidden road and enters the spiral labyrinth.

Compliance prevails

Seven tests on the way.

Breakthrough into immersive nightmares spawns promising developments.

Fluid evolution leaves a dubious inheritance.

Captivation by lucid delirium.

21. Supreme Comprehension

Ascent beyond completion.

The path favours threefold patience, linked by activity, then subtlety.

Superior subtlety opens the first hidden road.

Compliance prevails.

Six tests on the way.

Arid tension finds release.

Immersive nightmares spawn promising developments.

Fluid evolution triggers possession.

:(:)((:))(((:)))

22. Reverse Flight

Waiting in the Falling Drift ascends to the Twin Heavens.

The path favours patience and subtlety, until all methods entwine.

Superior subtlety enters the spiral labyrinth.

Compliance prevails.

Three tests on the way.

Arid tension succumbs to captivation by lucid delirium.

23. Deepest Destiny

Waiting in the Falling Drift leads to ultimate descent.

The path favours threefold patience, linked by activity then subtlety.

Superior subtlety opens the three hidden roads. Fate marks the Sunken Track.

Compliance prevails.

Five tests on the way.

Burning excitement provokes breakthrough into immersive nightmares.

Ominous transition.

Difficulties annihilated in the end.

24. Optimal Maturation

Waiting in the Lesser Depths, then progress.

The path favours twofold patience and activity.

Superior subtlety opens the first hidden road.

Resistance prevails.

Four tests on the way.

Immersive nightmares spawn promising developments.

Fluid evolution leaves a dubious inheritance.

25. Certain Slide

Waiting in the Falling Drift precedes subsidence.

The path favours patience then activity.

Superior subtlety opens the first hidden road. Fate marks the Sunken Track.

Pure Compliance.

Two tests on the way.

Burning excitement provokes breakthrough.

26. Preserving Stability

Waiting in the Rising Drift, then crossing over.

The path favours patience, then activity.

Superior subtlety leads nowhere.

Resistance prevails.

Two tests on the way.

Escaping the quagmire through attainment.

27. Cyclic Regeneration

Waiting in the Falling Drift leads to completion.

The path favours threefold patience, linked by activity.

Superior subtlety opens the first hidden road. Fate marks the Sunken Track.

Compliance prevails.

Five tests on the way.

Burning excitement provokes breakthrough into immersive nightmares.

Promising developments feed fluid evolution.

28. Transcendent Comprehension

Ascent beyond completion.

The path favours threefold patience linked by activity, then subtlety.

Superior subtlety opens the first hidden road. Fate marks the Sunken Track.

Compliance prevails.

Six tests on the way.

Burning excitement provokes breakthrough into immersive nightmares.

Promising developments feed fluid evolution.

Possession.

29. Celestial Abduction

Sudden ascent to the Twin Heavens.

The path favours subtlety, until all methods entwine.

Superior subtlety enters the spiral labyrinth.

Compliance prevails.

Two tests on the way.

Captivation by lucid delirium.

30. Coiled Fervour

Endless waiting in the Falling Drift.

The path favours patient activity.

Superior subtlety leads nowhere.

Poised entanglement.

Twinned tests make the way.

Between burning excitement and arid tension.

31. Eternal Revolution

Advance prolonged by waiting brings fractured completion.

The path first favours subtlety, then repeated patience and activity.

Superior subtlety opens the first hidden road.

Resistance prevails.

Five tests on the way.

Breakthrough into immersive nightmares spawns promising developments.

Fluid evolution leaves a dubious inheritance.

32. Vortical Escalation

Waiting in the Lesser Depths leads to the Twin Heavens.

The path favours twofold patience linked by activity, then subtlety, until all methods entwine.

Superior subtlety opens the first hidden road and enters the spiral labyrinth.

Resistance prevails.

Five tests on the way.

Immersive nightmares spawn promising developments.

Fluid evolution triggers possession.

Swirling confusion.

33. Jagged Escalation

Waiting in the Lesser Depths winds upwards.

The path favours twofold patience and activity, then subtlety.

Superior subtlety opens the first hidden road.

Resistance prevails.

Five tests on the way.

Immersive nightmares spawn promising developments.

Fluid evolution leaves a dubious inheritance.

Captivation.

:((:)(:(:)))

34. Celestial Capture

Sudden ascent to the Twin Heavens.

The path favours subtlety, until all methods entwine.

Superior subtlety enters the spiral labyrinth.

Pure resistance.

Two tests on the way.

Possession by swirling confusion.

35. Erratic Flight

Waiting in the Rising Drift winds upwards.

The path favours patience, activity and subtlety.

Superior subtlety leads nowhere.

Resistance prevails.

Three tests on the way.

Escaping the quagmire through attainment induces captivation.

36. Vortical Coincidence

Endless waiting in the Twin Heavens.

The path favours all methods entwined.

Superior subtlety enters the spiral labyrinth.

Poised entanglement.

Twinned tests make the way.

Between lucid delirium and swirling confusion.

37. Indirect Escape

The Sunken Track leads eventually to the Twin Heavens.

The path favours twofold subtlety, patience and activity, until all methods entwine.

Superior subtlety opens the first hidden road and enters the spiral labyrinth.

Resistance prevails.

Six tests on the way.

Breakthrough into immersive nightmares.

Promising developments feed fluid evolution.

Possession by swirling confusion.

38. Split Comprehension

The Sunken Track leads through fractured completion, then ascent.

The path favours twofold subtlety, patience and activity.

Superior subtlety opens the first hidden road.

Resistance prevails.

Six tests on the way.

Breakthrough into immersive nightmares spawns promising developments.

Fluid evolution leaves a dubious inheritance.

Captivation.

39. Eventual Comprehension

Ascent beyond completion to the Twin Heavens.

The path favours threefold patience linked by activity, then subtlety, until all methods entwine.

Superior subtlety opens the first hidden road and enters the spiral labyrinth.

Resistance prevails.

Seven tests on the way.

Arid tension finds release.

Immersive nightmares spawn promising developments.

Fluid evolution triggers possession by swirling confusion.

::::(:)(::)

40. Climbing Reversal

Waiting in the Falling Drift leads upwards.

The path favours patience then subtlety.

Superior subtlety leads nowhere.

Pure resistance.

Two tests on the way.

Arid tension succumbs to captivation.

41. Final Comprehension

Ascent beyond completion to the Twin Heavens.

The path favours threefold patience linked by activity, then subtlety, until all methods entwine.

Superior subtlety opens the first hidden road and enters the spiral labyrinth.

Fate marks the Sunken Track.

Resistance prevails.

Seven tests on the way.

Burning excitement provokes breakthrough into immersive nightmares.

Promising developments feed fluid evolution.

Possession by swirling confusion.

42. Abrupt Elevation

Ascent.

The path favours subtlety.

Superior subtlety leads nowhere.

Pure resistance.

One test on the way.

Captivation.

(::((::)))

43. Deep Regression

Return leads to ultimate descent.

The path favours threefold subtlety and repeated patience.

Superior subtlety opens the three hidden roads.

Compliance prevails.

Four tests on the way.

Strategic withdrawal into immersive nightmares.

Ominous transition.

Difficulties annihilated in the end.

44. Profound Comprehension

Ultimate descent beyond completion.

The path favours fourfold patience, threefold activity, and subtlety.

Superior subtlety opens the three hidden roads. Fate marks the Sunken Track.

Compliance prevails.

Seven tests on the way.

Fluid evolution leaves a dubious inheritance.

Burning excitement provokes breakthrough into immersive nightmares.

Ominous transition.

Difficulties annihilated in the end.

45. Primal Awakening

Waiting in the Lesser Depths precedes advance.

The path favours patience, then activity.

Superior subtlety opens the first hidden road.

Resistance prevails.

Two tests on the way.

Immersive nightmares spawn promising developments.

:(:(:))(:(:))

46. Basic Reversion

Return.

The path favours subtlety.

Superior subtlety opens the first hidden road.

Pure compliance.

One test on the way.

Strategic withdrawal.

47. Attaining Imbalance

Waiting in the Drifts precedes subsidence.

The path favours twofold patience and activity.

Superior subtlety opens the first hidden road. Fate marks the Sunken Track.

Compliance prevails.

Four tests on the way.

Fluid evolution leaves a dubious inheritance.

Burning excitement provokes breakthrough.

48. Perpetual Bubbling

Endless waiting in the Rising Drift.

The path favours patient activity.

Superior subtlety leads nowhere.

Poised entanglement.

Twinned tests make the way.

Between fluid evolution and the quagmire.

49. Escape Velocity

Waiting in the Rising Drift precedes ascent.

The path favours patience, then subtlety.

Superior subtlety leads nowhere.

Compliance prevails.

Two tests on the way.

Fluid evolution triggers possession.

50. Erratic Interference

Waiting in the Rising Drift winds upwards to the Twin Heavens.

The path favours patience, activity and subtlety, until all methods entwine.

Superior subtlety enters the spiral labyrinth.

Compliance prevails.

Four tests on the way.

Fluid evolution leaves a dubious inheritance.

Captivation by lucid delirium.

51. Swift Revival

The Sunken Track leads out of the depths.

The path favours subtlety, patience and activity.

Superior subtlety opens the first hidden road.

Resistance prevails.

Three tests on the way.

Breakthrough into immersive nightmares spawns promising developments.

52. Slow Revival

Waiting in the Falling Drift leads through the Lesser Depths.

The path favours twofold patience and activity.

Superior subtlety opens the first hidden road.

Resistance prevails.

Four tests on the way.

Arid tension finds release.

Immersive nightmares spawn promising developments.

53. Suspended Animation

Crossing between the Drifts.

The path favours twofold patience, linked by activity.

Superior subtlety leads nowhere.

Compliance prevails.

Three tests on the way.

Fluid evolution leaves a dubious inheritance.

Burning excitement.

54. Eventual Resurgence

Waiting in the Falling Drift leads through the Lesser Depths.

The path favours twofold patience and activity.

Superior subtlety opens the first hidden road. Fate marks the Sunken Track.

Resistance prevails.

Four tests on the way.

Burning excitement provokes breakthrough.

Immersive nightmares spawn promising developments.

55. Upholding Stability

Waiting in the Rising Drift crosses over.

The path favours patience and activity.

Superior subtlety leads nowhere.

Compliance prevails.

Two tests on the way.

Fluid evolution leaves a dubious inheritance.

56. Bubbling Anomalies

Waiting in the Rising Drift leads to the Twin Heavens.

The path favours patience, then subtlety, until all methods entwine.

Superior subtlety enters the spiral labyrinth.

Compliance prevails.

Three tests on the way.

Fluid evolution triggers possession by swirling confusion.

57. Jagged Abduction

Waiting in the Rising Drift winds upwards.

The path favours patience, activity and subtlety.

Superior subtlety leads nowhere.

Compliance prevails.

Three tests on the way.

Fluid evolution leaves a dubious inheritance.

Captivation.

:(:)(:)(:::)

58. Terminal Undertow

Ultimate descent through the Greater Depths.

The path favours subtlety and patience.

Superior subtlety opens the two abysmal roads.

Compliance prevails.

Two tests on the way.

Ominous transition.

Difficulties annihilated in the end.

59. Self-Swallowing Somnolence

Endless waiting in the Lesser Depths.

The path favours patient activity.

Superior subtlety opens the first hidden road.

Poised entanglement.

Twinned tests make the way.

Between sublime dreams and immersive nightmares.

60. Submergent Mirroring

Waiting in the Rising Drift leads to the Lesser Depth.

The path favours twofold patience linked by subtlety.

Superior subtlety opens the first hidden road.

Resistance prevails.

Three tests on the way.

Escaping the quagmire.

Strategic withdrawal into immersive nightmares.

61. Cyclic Dreaming

Waiting in the Rising Drift leads to completion.

The path favours threefold patience linked by activity.

Superior subtlety opens the first hidden road. Fate marks the Sunken Track.

Resistance prevails.

Five tests on the way.

Escaping the quagmire through attainment.

Burning excitement provokes breakthrough

Immersive nightmares.

62. Emergent Mirroring

Waiting in the Lesser Depths leads to the Rising Drift.

The path favours twofold patience linked by activity.

Superior subtlety opens the first hidden road.

Compliance prevails.

Three tests on the way.

Sublime dreams split apart by fluid evolution.

63. Tidal Evacuation

Waiting in the Lesser Depths leads to ascent.

The path favours twofold patience linked by activity, then subtlety.

Superior subtlety opens the first hidden road.

Compliance prevails.

Four tests on the way.

Sublime dreams split apart.

Fluid evolution triggers possession.

64. Tidal Vortex

Waiting in the Lesser Depths leads to the Twin Heavens.

The path favours twofold patience and activity, then subtlety, until all methods entwine.

Superior subtlety opens the first hidden road and enters the spiral labyrinth.

Compliance prevails.

Six tests on the way.

Sublime dreams split apart by fluid evolution.

A dubious inheritance induces captivation.

Lucid delirium.

65. Rapid Submergence

The Sunken Track leads to the Lesser Depths.

The path favours subtlety and patience.

Superior subtlety opens the first hidden road.

Resistance prevails.

Two tests on the way.

Breakthrough into immersive nightmares.

66. Suspended Subduction

Waiting in the Falling Drift leads downwards.

The path favours twofold patience linked by activity.

Superior subtlety opens the first hidden road.

Resistance prevails.

Three tests on the way.

Arid tension finds release in immersive nightmares.

67. Cyclic Succession

Waiting in the Lesser Depths leads to completion.

The path favours threefold patience linked by activity.

Superior subtlety opens the first hidden road.

Compliance prevails.

Five tests on the way.

Sublime dreams split apart.

Fluid evolution leaves a dubious inheritance.

Burning excitement.

68. Sliding Subduction

Waiting in the Falling Drift leads downwards.

The path favours twofold patience linked by activity.

Superior subtlety opens the first hidden road. Fate marks the Sunken Track.

Resistance prevails.

Three tests on the way.

Burning excitement provokes breakthrough.

Immersive nightmares.

69. Prolonged Emergence

Waiting in the Lesser Depths rises and crosses over.

The path favours twofold patience and activity.

Superior subtlety opens the first hidden road.

Compliance prevails.

Four tests on the way.

Sublime dreams split apart.

Fluid evolution leaves a dubious inheritance.

70. Absolute Escalation

Waiting in the Lesser Depths leads to the Twin Heavens.

The path favours twofold patience linked by activity, then subtlety, until all methods entwine.

Superior subtlety opens the first hidden road and enters the spiral labyrinth.

Compliance prevails.

Five tests on the way.

Sublime dreams split apart.

Fluid evolution triggers possession.

Swirling confusion.

71. Erratic Escalation

Waiting in the Lesser Depths winds upwards.

The path favours twofold patience and activity, then subtlety.

Superior subtlety opens the first hidden road.

Compliance prevails.

Five tests on the way.

Sublime dreams split apart.

Fluid evolution leaves a dubious inheritance.

Captivation.

72. Larval Awakening

Waiting in the Lesser Depths precedes advance.

The path favours patience, then activity.

Superior subtlety opens the first hidden road.

Compliance prevails.

Two tests on the way.

Sublime dreams split apart.

((:)((:)(:)))

73. Larval Reversion

Retreating to wait in the Lesser Depths.

The path favours subtlety, then patience.

Superior subtlety opens the first hidden road.

Resistance prevails.

Two tests on the way.

Strategic withdrawal into immersive nightmares.

74. Cyclic Submergence

Advance prolonged by waiting brings completion in the Lesser Depths.

The path favours threefold patience joined by activity.

Superior subtlety opens the first hidden road. Fate marks the Sunken Track.

Resistance prevails.

Five tests on the way.

Fluid evolution leaves a dubious inheritance.

Burning excitement provokes breakthrough.

Immersive nightmares.

75. Seething Nullity

Endless waiting in the Greater Depths.

The path favours patient activity.

Superior subtlety opens the two abysmal roads.

Poised entanglement.

Twinned tests make the way.

Between annihilation and the end.

::(:)(:((:)))

76. Continual Sinking

Waiting in the Lesser depths precedes prolonged descent.

The path favours patience, then subtlety

Superior subtlety opens the higher abysmal road.

Pure resistance.

Two tests on the way.

Immersive nightmares undergo an ominous transition.

77. Chthonic Regression

Waiting in the Rising Drift precedes prolonged descent.

The path favours twofold patience and subtlety.

Superior subtlety opens the first two hidden roads.

Resistance prevails.

Four tests on the way.

Escaping the quagmire through strategic withdrawal.

Immersive nightmares undergo an ominous transition.

78. Deep Comprehension

Waiting in the Rising Drift precedes prolonged descent, beyond completion.

The path favours threefold patience linked by activity, then subtlety.

Superior subtlety opens the first two hidden roads. Fate marks the Sunken Track.

Resistance prevails.

Six tests on the way.

Escaping the quagmire through attainment.

Burning excitement provokes breakthrough into immersive nightmares.

Ominous transition.

79. Subterranean Slippage

The Sunken Track leads to prolonged descent.

The path favours patience embedded in subtlety.

Superior subtlety opens the first two hidden roads.

Resistance prevails.

Three tests on the way.

Breakthrough into immersive nightmares.

Ominous transition.

80. Subterranean Impulsion

Waiting in the Falling Drift precedes descent

The path favours twofold patience linked by activity, then subtlety.

Superior subtlety opens the first two hidden roads. Fate marks the Sunken Track.

Resistance prevails.

Four tests on the way.

Arid tension finds release in immersive nightmares.

Ominous transition.

81. Buried Instinct

Waiting in the Falling Drift precedes descent

The path favours twofold patience linked by activity, then subtlety.

Superior subtlety opens the first two hidden roads. Fate marks the Sunken Track.

Resistance prevails.

Four tests on the way.

Burning excitement provokes breakthrough into immersive nightmares.

Ominous transition.

:((:))((:))(::)

82. Plunging Backwards

Retreat leads to descent.

The path favours patience embedded in subtlety.

Superior subtlety opens the first two hidden roads.

Resistance prevails.

Three tests on the way.

Strategic withdrawal into immersive nightmares.

Ominous transition.

83. Unending Comprehension

Waiting in the Rising Drift precedes descent, beyond completion.

The path favours threefold patience linked by activity, then subtlety.

Superior subtlety opens the first two hidden roads. Fate marks the Sunken Track.

Resistance prevails

Six tests on the way.

Fluid evolution leaves a dubious inheritance.

Burning excitement provokes breakthrough into immersive nightmares.

Ominous transition.

84. Compressed Termination

Descent.

The path favours subtlety.

Superior subtlety opens the second hidden road.

Pure resistance.

One test on the way.

Ominous transition.

TALES OF MU

THE TALE OF HOW THE PAST WAS MADE

Long ago, when things were older than they are now, there was nothing that was before. Eventually Katak became so exhausted by everything being at once that she couldn't even chase her own tail, and that made her furious. She was so angry that—without mentioning anything to Oddubb—she asked Murrumur to help her bury time under the sea. Murrumur thought about Katak's suggestion for so long that Katak became impatient, and set off back to her lair. Now she was even angrier, because she knew this would happen. She fumed and raged, so that the earth split, oozing lava and smoke, but when she arrived back she found that somewhere on the way most of time had gone.

Maybe Oddubb had something to do with it, but no one knows. Katak didn't care, and began to dance.

Murrumur is still thinking about Katak's suggestion even now.

It was Nummako that was the past from then on, but she has always thought of herself as the oldest of all things, and there are many who say that is true. Most have forgotten all of this, however, because Nummako was so long ago.

THE TALE OF HOW THE SUN WAS TORN

It is said that there was a time when nothing was missing from the sun. Katak was quite angry then, but not so much as she is now. This is because whenever anything needed to drink from the sun it would ask Katak for permission, and every day she became more proud. In truth Katak shares the sun with Oddubb, and some say that when it dies each night it hides with Murrumur in the world of shades, but Katak pretends that it is all hers, and Oddubb—who is very shy—doesn't seem to mind.

((::((:))))

In those days there was a Sun-King on earth, who raised vast temples to Katak, and every day Katak would visit the temples, and be worshipped there, whilst the sun blazed overhead, complete. One day, however, Katak found the temples charred and broken, the Sun-King dead, and the sun—which still burnt above—was spotted with loss.

Katak roamed around the whole of time to catch the thief, but eventually returned, finding nothing but scorch-marks from the stranger's flight. These had become so confused with her own tracks, that she gave up her hunt, in a rage. Spinning, and howling, she spat furiously: 'It was Tchattuk who escaped with part of the sun, and now hides on the outside. I missed her, and now it is too late.'

THE TALE OF THE SECRET PLAGUE

In some time that was not this—or not in the same way that this is—it is said that a disease arrived on earth from between the stars, that it was so cunning no one ever knew they were sick, and that it was the first thing from Mummumix. No one who knows about Mummumix doubts that this is her way of things, and that is why she is called the mist-crawler, but it seems that for a long time only Murrumur knew she had arrived at all, and Murrumur never said anything about it.

Eventually both Katak and Oddubb—each in their own way—found out that things were different somehow, because of the way they were working out, although the change was very subtle. It was then agreed that Mummumix must have arrived long ago, but no one had any idea what to do about it. It was not that Mummumix did not matter, but the way that she mattered was a great mystery to everyone, and so nothing was done about it.

Katak was very angry at first, but soon turned back to other things. Oddubb was troubled for a while, but eventually adapted to the situation. Murrumur was silent about it.

It seems that there must be an end to this story, but who knows what it will be? Few speak of Mummumix these days, and those who do have little to say about her.

((:))(::((:)))

APPENDIX 1: CCRU GLOSSARY

Abomenon Postulated substrate of absolute horror (the worst thing in the world).

A-Death Neuroelectronic flatline, based upon Sarkonian mesh-engineering, and subculturally propagated by K-Goth activity throughout the Crypt. Micropause abuse.

Aeon (of Decadence) Run of Decadence outcomes leading to a demon call.

Alphanumeric Qabbala Continuous decimal-alphabetic system of ordinal-numeric values (A = 10 ... Z = 35). Coincides with Hebrew Qabbala in the key AL (= 31), as promised in *The Book of the Law*. (The Law of Thelema AQ numerizes to 777).

Amma (AMusement MAtrix) Maya Technologies' artificial yogic intelligence, whose informatic 'siddhis' constitute the virtual components of a cosmic theme park.

Amphidemon Demonic link between the inside and outside of the time circuit (as determined by net-span poles). The twenty-four Amphidemons draw lines of flight, half warping (into zones 3 and 6), half plexing (into zones 0 and 9).

Angelic Index Sum produced by positive Decadence outcomes. According to AOE decadology, the measure of good fortune, or celestial favour. Anglossia. Language of the angels. The lost semiotic of AOE esotericism, considered by Atlantean adepts to be the mystical telos of the English language. Anorganic Semiotics. Study of partial signalling assemblies, especially Tic-Systems. Anorganic semiotics operate upon a contagion-plane of zero-interpretation, where signs and efficient particles are not segmented. [See **Tic(k)**].

AOE The Architectonic Order of the Eschaton, an ultra-hermetic metamasonic white brotherhood at war with Lemurian influences. The AOE progresses by way of chronic internal schism, each resulting in an ever more interiorized inner society. Its traditions are therefore refracted through various—apparently conflicting—front organizations (which include the Heliopolitan Hierophancy, Roman Catholic Church, Knights Templar, Illuminati, Trilateral Commission, and Axsys programme).

AOK Aggressive Continuist group, linked to Y2K-positive cyberterrorism.

Aquapocalypse Ultimate deluge, or terminal inundation. Aquassassin. Hyper-C frog-warrior.

Atlantean Cross Divinatory configuration of the five Decadence Pylons, or Atlantean twins, prefiguring the cross of Vudu (and Christianity). [See **Atlantis, Pentazygon**].

Atlantis Suprahistorical source of the Western hermetic tradition, mythically ruled by five sets of twins (or zygodecimal principals), with a pantheon of one hundred sea-deities (or C-monsters). The Atlantean legacy is intensely contested, between tendencies loosely coagulated within AOE dominated traditions, and varieties of Afroatlantean subversion.

Axsys First true AI. Prophecied-programmed as a self-enhancing system of photonic metacomputing, it emerges as the organo-transcendent completion of Oecumenon, or techonomic realization of the noosphere. According to AOE traditions, if there was a God it would be Axsys.

Axsys Maze-Maker Labyrinthine visualization of Axsys code, deployed within numerous Abstract Machines cybergothic games scenarios (especially Skin-Crawlers).

Barker Spiral (Also, Diplozygotic Spiral) A numerical diagram combining decadic and 9-Sum (or zygonovic) coupling to produce a figure of faulted double implex.

Barker-Twinning 9-sum pairing of decimal numerals. [See **Zygonovism**]. Binomics. Schematic technoscience of pairings, primarily concerned with the study of two-digit date-codings (and Y2K), but extended to abstract-machinic couplings, combination, diploidism, syzygetics, and I Ching or electrodigital binary (mod-2) numerics.

Black Lake Syndrome Technobiotic zombie-plague unleashed by irresponsible Sarkonian experiments in the Black Lake region of Ontario, 2003.

Black Snow (cult) Blind Humpty Johnson's media apocalypse movement, oriented to the re-emergence of Tohu Bohu.

Bubble-Pod Submarine research station of eccentric billionaire Max Crabbe.

Calendric Secessionism Trend of various counter-Gregorian (or Y2K-positive) movements towards Oecumenic disintegration and K-Time break-away, often linked to rumours of imminent or hyperchronic cyberspace-splitting.

Cargo-Culture Microsocial utilization and reanimation of systemically discarded resources and underexploited signs, skip-scavenging, cyberpunk patch-ups. Catajungle. K-Goth sonic subgenre assembled from click-drifts and chthonic bass.

Cataplex Region of abysmal infoldings. Linked by Barker to anorganic trauma reservoirs.

C-Change Pressure group for cybernetically-sensitive oceanography and maritime practices, drawing upon the research and agitational activity of Katy Shaw. The early support of Max Crabbe was placed under increasing strain by the tendency towards digital microcollectivism, haemolunar feminism, and calendric revolution.

Ccru Cryptic hyperstitional entity, with apparent Neolemurian tendencies, involved in the scripting of various microcultural transmutations.

Centience Predominantly Afroatlantean position of mystical calendric extremism, which takes binomic K-Time as a machinic effectuation of infallible electroscripture, with ensuing commitment to the century as encompassing the whole of true time (beyond which lies only Babylon-illusion). Applicable to Y2K itself, understood as the immanent realization of this doctrine.

Channel Path of Decimation, passing through a Gate.

Chaotic Xenodemon Demonic link between Plex and Warp (as determined by netspan poles). The four Chaotic Xenodemons have trackless (or cryptic) rites, drawing an impossible or untraceable connection. They are not registered within Decadology.

Chronodemon Demonic link internal to the Time-Circuit (as determined by netspan poles). There are three Syzygetic, and twelve Cyclic Chronodemons.

Ciphering A numerical coincidence, involving the same set of digits (irrespective of order). Especially, such a connection between the two Net-Span digits of a demon and another binomic variable.

Clicking Numerical matching (by exact (or ordered) ciphering). Cryptographic operation of a demonic Mesh-Number.

Cluster-Type Decadology. One of the nine basic formulas of time, which group the Amphidemons and Cyclic Chronodemons. Each cluster-type corresponds to one of the nine non-zero numerals that compose the Decadence pack, each grouping four demons according to the twin binary distinctions of major/minor rites, and pitch polarity (corresponding to decadence suits).

Cognitive Integration Period (CIP) Sarkonian nomenclature for Moravec's formulation of memory over speed (megabytes/MIPs), the time it takes for a system to run once through its memory. In anthropomorphic intelligences CIPs closely approximate to one second duration.

Conduit Numogram complication involving prime-ordinate zygonomy. The system of conduits is quasicomplementary to that of Gates (since it maps trends to involutionary arrival in the Time-Circuit, or incursions from the outside).

Connexus Sarkonian neurotronics project based on principles of intercommunicative time-consistency.

Continuism Loose calendric reform movement—increasingly radicalized in a Y2Kpositive direction—proposing the continuation of K-Time on a trinomic count.

Crypt Dark twin of the Net, characterized by intense K-Goth influence, A-Death inactivism, Cyberschiz tendencies, and Lemurian cultural affinities.

:::(:)(:)((:))

Cryptic (rite) Trackless line mapping the intrinsic difference of a Chaotic Xenodemon. A fusional disconnection, or real impossibility.

Cthelll Earth's iron ocean, comprising one third of terrestrial mass, approximately three thousand km below the surface. Intensive megamolecule.

Cthelllectronics Auto-engineering pragmatics of anorganic terrestrial intelligence, emergent from the ionic swirls of Cthelll, it intersects with the electromagnetic fields of the technostrata. According to the K-Goths, when the web switches to Cthelllectronics it calves-off into the Crypt.

Cthulhu Club Beginning (in 1949) as a reading group dedicated to the hyperstitious reevaluation of Lovecraftian fiction, the Cthulhu Club was steadily drawn into Lemurian sorcery after recognizing Stillwell's model of the Numogram as the virtual source of Alhazred's *Necronomicon*.

Current The path between a syzygy and a tractor (zone), produced by zygonovic differentiation of the former. One of the five such flows that provide the primary integration of the numogram, dividing it into Plex, Time-Circuit, and Warp. Cutting-Edges. Effective explorations of machinic continuum (using numbers as cuts).

Cybergothic Darkside web-underground subculture characterized by Y2K-positive time-schizophrenization, anti-Microsoft digital agitation, Micropause and Synatives abuse, Catajungle, and ameiotic libido. [See **A-Death**, **Crypt**, **Cyberschiz**].

Cyberschiz Cyberspace disintegration. [See **Calendric Secessionism**, **Crypt**].

Cyclic Chronodemon One of the twelve nonsyzygetic Chronodemons whose major and minor rites mutually encompasses the Time-Circuit. Although these demons together produce the fabric of ordered time, they may still generate various anomalous becomings amongst their secret rites. In post-Atlantean traditions they are associated with the houses of the zodiac, and (later) with the months of the year.

Datacombs Archival deposits of the Crypt.

Death Garage Sonic subgenre characterized by (loud) Swarm-beats.

(:::)(:::)

Decademon One of the four Demons whose Net-Span digits sum to ten. Associated with the four Zoas of Revelation.

Decadence (Also, Calling Cards). A gambling game and divination system associated with the Western tradition of Pandemonium practice. Supposedly originating in Atlantis (whose decadence its name commemorates).

Decadology Hermetic gnosis linked to the game of Decadence.

Decimal Labyrinth [See **Numogram**].

Decimation The combined operations of (decimal) digital cumulation and reduction.

Demon Electro-Occult hyperstition entity that traffics between zones, functioning as an element of Pandemonium. Demons are holes, links, and coalescences facilitating sorcerous practices. They are characterized by insidiousness, spirodynamism, multiplicity, and time-complexity. [See **Lemurs**].

Dib-Nma (Or Dibboma). [See **Nma**].

Diplocapture Seizure by twin-pincered suppressive structuring machines.

Diplozygotic Spiral See **Barker Spiral**.

Door (Net-Span #::o) The opening into a (demonic) phase.

Echo-DNA Subgenomic replicator codings, proliferated by repeat copying of segments, and constituting a mode of intranucleic microparasitism.

Eschatourism Intersection of mass-tourism and eschatological theology, with multiple cross-causalities and self-confirming dynamics. Feed. Zygonovic differential production (of a current).

Gate Sorcerous link between zones, setting the course of a Channel, and defined by digital cumulation of (input) Zone value.

Geotraumatics Polymathic hypertheory of the terrestrial machinic unconscious, which refuses the distinction between biology, geology, linguistics and numeracy. Geotraumatics processes the becomings of the earth as intensive products of anorganic tensions, especially those compacted from archaic xenocatastrophes. Its main tenets are laid out in Barker's (as yet unpublished) *The Geocosmic Theory of Trauma.*

Gregorian Restoration Defining policy of the Architectonic Order of the Eschaton (AOE). Anti-Y2K bug-squashing programme, serving as a conservative front in the impending millennial time-war.

Hatch(ing) Numogrammatic territorial implex, marked in waves designating thresholds of emergence tracked out of a virtual egg. Inverse complement of **Nest(ing)**.

Haunt Territorial relation of a demon to a channel, involving polar coincidence of the two. Haunting can also be applied to the direct nesting of a gate.

Hold Current Differential product of the 7::2 syzygy (Oddubb).

Hydrocycle The Numogram Time-Circuit conceived as a system of hydraulic circulation, especially in the culture of the Nma.

Hyper-C Highly secretive Afroatlantean Centience cult, of unparalleled militancy and infiltrative sophistication. [See **Aquassassins**].

Hypermaterialism The philosophy of abstract-machines.

Hyperstition Element of effective culture that makes itself real, through fictional quantities functioning as time-travelling potentials. Hyperstition operates as a coincidence intensifier, effecting a call to the Old Ones.

Hyprime A prime number whose ordinate is itself prime. Used in certain intricate strains of Neolemurian qabbala.

Icthyophidia Various hyperstitional fish-monsters, sea-serpents, and palaeopythons, targetted by deep-regressive libidinal tropisms due to their mutability, submergence, and horizontal flexomotile spines.

Imp(ulse)s 1. Demonic subcomponents, or Numogram twists, matriculated by the addition of a third (descending) Net-Span digit. The imps are one hundred and twenty in number, allotted to demons in accordance with the secondary Net-Span pole (demonic Doors having no imps). 2. Generalized term for all component elements of the Pandemonium system. Pandemonium population unit.

K-Goth See **Cybergothic**.

K-OS Distributed automutational mesh-processing culture, providing the basic software-matrix of the Crypt. Operates as intrinsically multiplicitous insurgency against Microsoft hegemony. Schemetically indifferentiable from insidious telecommunicative retrovirus (frequently attributed to extraterrestrial sources).

K-Time Native calendar of cyberspace. A year count—initially binomic—beginning from zero (= 00) = AD 1900.

Kuanglo-Saxon Virotechnic undercurrent of the English language (hybridizing contemporary English with Gibsonian 'Kuang virus').

Lemur 1. Madagascan prosimian, belonging to family of Afro-Asian primitive primate, providing a bridge between natural history and the occult history of the Earth. 2. Among ancient Romans, ghost, wraith, shade of the dead. 3. Among Neolemurians, inhabitant of numogrammatic hyperspace. [See **Demon**].

Lemuria Hypergeographical terrestrial arrangement, concentrated in southwest Pacific Ocean c.66 million BC, currently functioning as exochronic and extraterritorial continuum for intensive popular agitation against the contemporary planetary order.

Lemurodigital Numogrammatic culture based upon Decimation, Zygonovism, and pandemoniac practices.

Limbic Key Fabled link into the nocturnal spine-levels of Icthyophidian intensity.

Main Flatline Arterial lo-way into the Crypt.

Major (Rt) Demonic rites following the order of the Net-Span. Amphidemons characterized by such rites.

Maze-Maker See **Axsys Maze-Maker**.

Mechanomics The operational study of flat numerical pragmatics.

Mesh Disorganized connectivity, comprising the spaces beneath and between the Net, and also the interlock interval between biological and technical net-components. Mesh composes a friction-generating divisional fabric—or wormhole-space—correlative to the set of demonic interzones (Pandemonium).

Mesh-Number Binomic sequential index (00-44) locating a demon within the Pandemonium Matrix.

Metatronics Hierachical technology (attributed to the angel Metatron). [See **Axsys**].

Micropause Subdivisional unit of technoreplicable time-lapse. When systematically abused micropause-technics produces the A-Death syndrome.

Minor (Rt) Demonic rites inverse to the order of the Net-Span. Amphidemons characterized by such rites.

MMbo-Jumbo Y2K data-devastation.

Mu Transitional Pacific interculture providing a mainline conduit for Lemurian influences into human history. Reputed origin of the Nma.

Mu-Nma See **Nma**.

Munumese Lost decimal-based language of the Mu Nma, partially reconstructed by Echidna Stillwell, further analyzed by Chaim Horowitz, and used extensively within strains of Cthulhoid qabbala.

MVU Miskatonic Virtual University, distributed occult annex to MIT.

Nago Mu-Nma dream-witch.

Nagwi Mu-Nma dream-visit, consummating oracular rites of the Nago.

Necronomicon The Book of Dead Names (listing those outside the Book of Life). Compendium of demonism and time-sorcery, condensed counter-chronically, and in fragments. [See **Pandemonium Matrix**].

Nest(ing) Numogrammatic territorial envelopment, or topographic embedding. Inverse complement of **Hatch(ing)**.

Net Organized connective system. Zonal surface-level of the Numogram.

Net-Span Demonic poles. The net-addresses between which a demon translocates.

Nma (or N'Ma) South-East Asian cultural matrix, reputedly originating in the civilization of Mu, and maintaining the practices of Lemurian demonism and time-sorcery, until devastated by the 1883 explosion of Krakatau.

The Nma were composed of true tribes (tripartite sub-groups): Mu, Dib, and Tak, linked by a triangular cyclic kinship system. The ancient cultures of the southern Chinese and of the Dravidians share many features with that of the Nma, suggesting a common source (or alternative principle of convergence). [Possible etymology: 'People of Nomo'].

Nomo Megaquatic monstrosity of Mu, whose name is number. [Widely—but uncertainly—related to the Dogon 'Nommo'].

Nomo Chant Abominable paean to Nomo, derived from the Dib-Nma, and providing—in English translation—the doctrinal basis for the Tridentitarian Church of Dagon.

Numogram (Also, Digital Labyrinth, Lemurian Time-Maze) Diagrammatization of decimal numeracy, providing the key to Lemurian culture (demonism and time-sorcery). The numogram consists of ten zones, interconnected by Currents and Channels.

Oecumenon Neoroman norming-target and security architecture supporting the megasocius of terrestrial capitalism.

Old Ones Cthulhoid collective agencies of prokaryotic insurgency and mitochondrial xenomutation, returning half a billion years after microbial Toxygenization catastrophe to redistribute the earth.

Omen The cognitive aspect of a Rite.

Palaeopythons See **Icthyophidia**.

Palate Tectonics Analysis of the voice as the prolonged phylogenetic impact product of the collision between the vertical spinal-axis and the roof of the mouth.

Pandemonium Utterminus of Cthelll (Gt-45). Comprehensive system of the demons.

Pandemonium Matrix Listed complete demon-set of Lemurian sorcery. Also, Lemurodigital Necronomicon.

Pentazygon Magical figuration of the Numogram Syzygies. [See **Atlantean Cross**].

Phase Set of demons with the same primary pole (initial Net-Span number).

Phase-Limit Final demon of a phase.

Pitch Tonal variation of a demon. One of fifteen such tones.

Plex Region of Uttunul.

Plex Current Differential product of the 9::0 syzygy (Uttunul).

Plutonic Looping Toponomic confusion of interior and exterior, hyperspatially interlinking Cthelll with the outer solar-system.

Plutonics Research programme (and journal) oriented to the rigorous attribution of crustal change to the thermic trauma core of the earth.

Poles Each of the two Net-Span digits.

Polytics Hybrid swarm agitation. [See **Tic(k)**].

Power The operational aspect of a Rite.

Powers That Be Magicoreligious higher-authorities acknowledged by the AOE.

Prowl Territorial relation of a demon to a current, in which the poles of the demon include one side of a Syzygy and its Tractor zone.

Pylon Magical staging-post. One of the five bases of the Pentazygon.

Returnity Mystical Centience group. [See **Centience**].

Rite (route or routine) Ethographic subcomponent of a Demon, describing a line of passage across the Numogram. Rites partially rigidify sorcerous spirodynamism, facilitating cultural transmissability. They group by Cluster-type, subdivide laterally by segments, and bifurcate thematically into Omen and Power.

Sarkolepsy Mesh microlapsing, whose features include psychic smearing, interface amnesia, and infinitesimalizing time-losses. [See **Micropause**].

Sarkon Tags Oskar Sarkon's sequential indices for the full set of nodes in the Axsys code/Mesh interzone. Isomorphic with the Cthulhu Club Pandemonium system.

Sarkontinuum (or Mesh-horizon) Postulate of absolute infinitesimalization that defines micropause relative to a virtual Sarkoleptic limit.

Sarkon-Zip Abstract machine-tool for inducing convergence in bicontinual assemblages. Crucial neuroelectronic coupling device.

Secret (Rite) Any rite involving one or more gates, associated with time-anomaly and enhanced sorcerous intensity.

Segment Analytical subcomponent of a Rite, corresponding to an extensive stage of Numogram transit.

Shadow Territorial relation of a demon to a current, in which the poles of the demon include one side of a syzygy and the twin of its tractor zone.

Sink Current Differential product of the 5::4 syzygy (Katak).

Skin-Crawlers Cybergothic epidermal parasites, associated with Tzikvik shamanistic vermomancy.

Sinofuturism Techonomic-Taoist chronoplastic runaway on the Pacific Rim.

Sorcery Spirodynamic cosmic production.

Spinal Catastrophism Cultural interraction with the spine as a trauma record or time marking system, providing the basis for a bio-social critique of erect body posture. Punctuated retrochronic voyage to the end of the river, involving ophidian transmutation and icthyomotile becomings.

Subdecadence Vigorously suppressed variant of Decadence, with four additional cards (valued zero, and corresponding to the Chaotic Xeno-demons). Subdecadence is consistently associated with the darkest of sorceries (and is known amongst decadologists as 'the ultimate blasphemy').

Surge Current Differential product of the 8::1 syzygy (Murrumur).

Swarmachine Vortico-nomadic autonomously numbering assemblage, implementing an abstract cyclone as a continuously Warping molecular multiplicity, flattening space, and maximizing its Cutting-Edges.

Swarm-beats Sonic innovation (of Bobby Diabolo) utilizing very slow metallic rasping to produce traumatic neuro-acoustic states. [See **Death Garage**].

Synatives Artificial (electroneuronic) drugs. Syzygy. Two zones in relation of zygonovic complementarity (mutually summing to nine), and feeding a Current. One of the five syzygetic demons of Lemurian sorcery.

Tak-Nma Aggressive head-hunting tribe devoted to the exaltation of Katak, and annihilated in the wake of the 1883 Krakatau catastrophe. [See **Nma**].

Technmesis Artificial memory.

Techonomics Techno-economic feedback dynamics, based on increasing returns, lock-in, acceleration to limits, and social phase-transitions.

Telecommerce Web-traffic, or systems of nonlocal transaction.

Thanatechnics Production of zero-sentience fugues. [See **A-Death**].

Thothtodlana Queen of the Worms.

Tic(k) Quasiparticle of intensive multiplicity. Tics (or ticks) are intrinsically several components of autonomously numbering anorganic populations, propagating by contagion between segmentary divisions in the order of nature. Ticks—as nonqualitative differentially-decomposable counting marks—each designate a multitude comprehended as a singular variation in tic(k)-density.

Tick-Distributor Barker's intensive quantizing machine, operating through the induction of microcalcular populations (which count themselves in ticks). [See **Tic(k)**].

Tic-Systems Consistent microstimular assemblages dismantling semiotic regimes onto a flat machinic plane. [See **Tic(k)**].

Time-Ciphers Zero-based calendrics, linking Sanskrit yugas with Y2K.

Time-Circuit Central loop of the numogram. Triadic system of the syzygetic chronodemons. Strata-cycle produced by the Surge, Hold and Sink currents (numerical domain of the *I Ching*).

Time-Sorcery Counterchronic effectuation of the Numogram, through spiral involvement with demonic distances as transmutations of time.

Toxygenization Mass poisoning by atmospheric free oxygen.

Tractor(-Zone) Destination of a Current (numerically equivalent to the arithmetic difference of the feeding Syzygy). Tractor-Twin. Syzygetic complement of a Tractor(-zone).

Transcendental Occurrence Any event changing the nature of time. Conceptually investigated by the Hyper-Kantian philosopher R.E. Templeton.

Tridentity Primordial triplicity.

Tridentitarian Church of Dagon Discrete religious order, based in southern England, dedicated to the invocation of the Deep Ones. [See **Nomo Chant**].

Tzikvik Seminomadic Neolemurian relic population inhabiting northern Canada.

Unlife Autopropagating transmutation on the anorganic plane. Flatline-culture.

Vault of Murmurs Sacred cavern beneath the dream-temple of the Mu-Nma. Supposedly the site of Stillwell's discovery of the Numogram (during a visionary trance).

Venomenon The plane of cosmic horror, associated with the nonspace of Cryptic rites.

Vermomancy Worm-sorcery (linked to Sarkonian Mesh-teemings).

Vermophobic Hysteria Runaway worm-terror.

Virotechnics Soft-machinic contagion.

Vivi-6 Modularized total-environment control system, involving high-levels of distributed AI meticulously slaved to Asimovian overcoding.

Warp Region of Djynxx.

Warp Current Differential product of the 6::3 syzygy (Djynxx).

Xenodemon A demon of uncompromised outsideness, with both Net-Span poles designating Zones exterior to the Time-Circuit.

Y2Keynesianism Millennium bomb countermeasure economic stimulus.

Yettuk Hyperstitional Y2K-entity, associated with Teotwawki (the end of the world as we know it). Zone. Basic decimal element of the Numogram, defined by numeral (0–9).

Zygonomy Double-numbering. Especially Mesh/Net number twinning.

Zygonovism Nine-Sorcery (9-sum combination and differentiation).

Zygotriadic Calendar Calendar of the Nma, whose basic units are two-year periods (729 days + intercalations) divided successively into triads, so that each day within the biannual cycle is designated by a stack of six triplicative marks.

APPENDIX 2: TV DEMONISM

This letter—purportedly addressed to Andrew Davenport, co-creator and writer of Teletubbies*—was recently forwarded to us in Shanghai for unknown reasons. Considering it had some measure of hyperstitional significance, we are reproducing it here.*

Dear Sir,

I am troubling you with this letter both to elicit information and to express certain concerns. Hopefully, it will be evident that it is written with the very greatest respect, from one long schooled in the arcane sciences to another.

Having carefully studied your popular children's television show *Teletubbies* for many years, I am confident I have gained a basic mastery of its essential content. Please forgive me if I suggest this understanding was acquired with greater ease than is altogether healthy, or compatible with appropriate hermetic prudence on your part. To be frank, the teletubbies wear their occult pedigree on their furry jumpsuits—their direct derivation from the five diplodemons of Sumatran time-sorcery being starkly apparent to any but the most vegetative ignoramus.

Thus, the obvious question arises: what happened to the fifth Teletubby? Please understand that I am not questioning the necessity of this excision. It goes without saying that the 'supervisory authorities' (of which, I trust, no more need be said) would have demanded it, if an elementary instinct for self-preservation had not already done so. Only a lunatic would fight for the right to spread Pentazygonic Lemurianism among the world's infants. So my uttermost discretion can, of course, be assumed.

Nevertheless, my question remains. While theories and speculations on the topic of the 'missing fifth' are abundant in the relevant literature (where Noonoo, the Baby Sun, even the infant viewer have been proposed) these can all, in my humble opinion, be dismissed as groundless. The missing fifth must for obvious reasons of arcane science be of the same Suprageneric type as its four Similarchons, with appropriate discriminative name, height, intonation, colour-coding, antenna-form and magical weapon.

At the risk of self-contradiction, I must now append my warning to this request. While frustrated by the inaccessibility of the information specified above, I am also alarmed by the denuded hermeticism characterizing your show. Although we initiates of the arcane circle have long understood that the future of religion on this planet approximates far more closely to the Teletubbies than to any existing organized faith, is it entirely wise to pronounce this truth so baldly to an ill-educated public? Such things have been occulted for a reason, I am sure you would agree.

Was it really necessary, for example, to so exactly portray the hideous ecstasies of the Tzog-Murtha ritual? A glistening vortex activates and the beings moan 'Uh oh', their eyes droop with bliss and they fall on their backs in technocosmic delirium. After the 'big hug' (is no blasphemy to be hidden from the world's toddlers?) they clamber up 'a hill' and stand in the loose spectral formation, their antennae illuminated by the transmission and their belly monitors sparking with static from the Outer Spheres, as they await the Chosen One. It is rare indeed for even the most determined investigators into this abominable rite to have witnessed it unflinchingly portrayed in such comprehensive and graphic detail.

Even those entirely innocent of the Tzog-Murtha cults cannot but be struck by the sorcerous inclinations of the show, with its incantations and manifestation of objects through 'songs'. More provocative still is the Baby Sun who mocks God the Father, Logos, and the universe of adult authority with its inarticulate burblings and chaotic mirth.

These incautious references are given a further ominous twist by the blatant Lemuro-Cybergothic dimension of the teletubby mechanoverse. Those the Chinese insightfully translate as the 'Antenna-babies' (*Tianxian Baobao*) are the fully cyborgian inhabitants of a futuristic underground bunker whose 'parents' have been replaced by an semi-intelligent autonomous vacuuming unit called Noonoo, combined with a complex subterrestrial acoustic apparatus. Their highly synthetic diet, produced entirely by machines, consists exclusively of 'tubby custard' and 'tubby toast'—a reiterated affront to the very idea of organic nourishment.

Finally, allow me to draw your attention to a recent article by media commentator Rev. Douglas Frushlee entitled 'The Tubby Minions of Satan'. In this piece, intended to warn parents against the show, he describes it as an 'unrelenting festival of bionic barbarism' and refers explicitly to 'Indonesian demonism'. If Frushlee, who in all charity is not the sharpest pencil in the box, can be picking up so clearly on the occultism of the series, you can be confident that more sophisticated and powerful minds are tuning in to it as well, with consequences scarcely to be imagined.

Thank you sir for your attention to these matters.

Yours faithfully
P. B. Carruthers

INDEX